the
Ribbon
Leaf

Lori Weber

Red Deer Press

Published in Canada by Red Deer Press,
209 Wicksteed Avenue, Unit 51, Toronto, ON M4G 0B1

Published in the United States by Red Deer Press,
311 Washington Street, Brighton, MA 02135

Red Deer Press acknowledges with thanks the Canada Council for the Arts and the Ontario Arts
Council for their support of our publishing program. We acknowledge the financial support of the
Government of Canada through the Canada Book Fund (CBF) for our publishing activities.

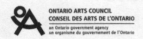 

Library and Archives Canada Cataloguing in Publication
Title: The ribbon leaf / Lori Weber.
Names: Weber, Lori, 1959- author.
Identifiers: Canadiana 20210395079 | ISBN 9780889956636 (softcover)
Subjects: LCGFT: Novels.
Classification: LCC PS8645.E24 R53 2022 | DDC jC813/.6—dc23

Publisher Cataloging-in-Publication Data (U.S.)
Names: Weber, Lori, 1959-,author.
Title: Ribbon Leaf / Lori Weber.
Description: Markham, Ontario : Red Deer Press, 2022. | Summary: "When
Edie escapes to Canada, each girl comes of age on opposite sides of the ocean.
Without knowing how the other is doing, they keep hope that their bond of
friendship remains." -- Provided by publisher.
Identifiers: ISBN 978-0-88995-663-6 (paperback)
Subjects: LCSH: World War, 1939-945 – Jews -- Juvenile fiction. | Holocaust,
Jewish (1939-1945) -- Juvenile fiction. | Friendship in youth -- Juvenile fiction. |
BISAC: YOUNG ADULT FICTION / Historical / Holocaust.
Classification: LCC PZ7.W434Ri | DDC 8i3.6 – dc23

Edited for the Press by Beverley Brenna
Text and cover design by Tanya Montini
Printed in Canada by AIIM - Avant Imaging and Integrated Media

www.reddeerpress.com

This book is dedicated to children everywhere
who grew up under the shadow of war
and to my dad, Wolfgang, who was one of them.
—L.W.

"All wars, whether just or unjust, disastrous or victorious, are waged against the child."

— Eglantyne Jebb (British social activist who founded Save the Children and drafted the document that became the Declaration of the Rights of the Child)

1938

SABINE

I.

If anyone asks what my father does, I tell them he saves lives. That's because he designs medical instruments that doctors use to cut people open and make them well again—razors, scalpels, lancets, trocars, saws. Many nights, after dinner, he pulls his new creations out of a roll of felt that has been sitting in his pants pocket all day, gathering the heat of his body, so that the blades are warm. When he passes the model instruments around the table, Hans and I must only touch the felt, but sometimes he lets us run our fingers over the special handles that are ebony or tortoise shell, materials that will be changed to stainless steel later on.

When I ask Papa how he inserts the blades into the

handles without bolts, he says, "It is my secret, Sabine. You know I would never reveal my secrets." Then he smiles broadly under his bushy moustache.

Papa's factory is the red brick building behind the train station, down near the river. I know it well because I bring him his lunch, hot soup and a roll, each day at noon. When I walk beside the river, I think how hard it is to believe it's the same one that Johann Strauss made famous in "The Blue Danube" waltz. Here, the river slinks through my hometown, dark as mud, and I wonder if it's so dirty because it's where the factory dumps its waste.

Papa is always waiting for me by the tall black iron gates, holding up the shiny penny he'll slip into my hand in exchange for the pail.

"Kiss on the cheek, Sabine," he says, tapping the hollow spot under his cheekbone. "Never forget to kiss your papa goodbye."

"I won't," I reply, waving as he disappears.

My best friend, Edie, sometimes comes with me, but she waits at the foot of the hill on the edge of town. Later, we lie in the grass and stare up at the castle that sits on top, its turret chipped all around, like broken teeth.

Edie tells me wonderful stories about the castles she saw when she visited her aunt and uncle in Munich last summer. One has tall white turrets that twist toward the clouds like vanilla ice cream. Another has a high canopy bed where Napoleon actually slept, along with a fancy commode that Josephine used to do her business. Edie, who wants to be an actress, hoists up a pretend long dress, then squats in the field, mimicking Napoleon's queen, and we laugh so hard we also have to pee.

"You should come with me next time," Edie says. "Please!"

"I'll try again," I say, even though I know my parents will say no. When I was little, they said I could go on holidays with the Pinkers when I was older, but I'm twelve now and they still won't let me. They just look at each other and shake their heads whenever I ask, but neither of them ever tells me why.

I don't understand adults. They seem to think everything should suddenly be forbidden. Mama's been bringing our clothes to Edie's father to alter or mend forever—she says his stitches are works of art—but now Papa says she shouldn't—it's *verboten*. Herr Pinker refused to register, which means his shop is illegal.

Last weekend, people were marching up and down outside the greengrocers at the end of Schinkelstrasse, holding up signs that said *Raus Juden* and *Kauft nicht bei Juden*. Mama grabbed my hand and pulled me away. Behind us, the yelling got louder and there was a big bang. Mama wouldn't answer me when I asked her why Jews had to get out and why we weren't supposed to buy anything from them.

There's so much I can't figure out, like last week, when Edie and I were reading *Heidi* together, under the big oak tree by the Danube. The pictures of Heidi's old grandfather remind us of her papa, with his white hair and long white beard, the apple cheeks when he smiles. We started yodeling really loud and two old women stopped to give us dirty looks. One even shook her finger at us and said it should be *verboten*, the two of us together like that, reading from the same book. They wouldn't leave until we moved on.

It makes me sad, but I know Papa would agree with the old cranks. I am not allowed to go to Edie's house anymore and I miss playing movie stars with her. We'd go through the box of clothes in her father's storage room in the basement of their apartment building and find all kinds of treasures. Edie once found a feather boa and wrapped it around her neck like Lola Lola, the nightclub singer in the movie *Blue Angel*. She sang into a microphone-shoe, crooning out "Falling in Love Again" in a deep smoky voice, and I opened the tiny window to let her voice float out past the bushes, onto the street. Another time she wrapped a long silk scarf around her neck and transformed into Camille, pretend-smoking a long pencil. She died of tuberculosis too, writhing around on the basement floor in a way that was so real, I felt pain in my chest.

"Let's pinky swear, no ... Pinker swear, that one day we'll both be big stars and we'll always wear glittery clothes," Edie said, flipping her dark curls away from her face. "You'll be a special guest at my movie premieres and I'll be special guest at yours."

"No, Edie," I replied. "You're going to be the star, not me. One day, you'll be on stage at one of those grand theatres in Berlin or Paris and the photographers' flashbulbs will be sparkling around you. I'll just be there to watch."

But now, I'm not so sure.

2.

On Wednesdays, Hans runs off to his Hitler Youth meetings, wearing his special uniform: black shorts and khaki shirt, a leather tie around his neck, and a red armband with a black swastika around his upper arm. The first time she saw it, Mama gasped, but Hans just shot out his arm and said, "Heil Hitler." Papa laughed and said, "I'm proud of you, son. You look ready for battle." I thought he looked stupid, especially when he clicked his heels together and stuck up his fists, like he was in the boxing ring at school.

Tonight, Hans brings home a picture of the Führer, exactly like the one that hangs everywhere at our school. Hitler's blue eyes are stern but soft at the same time, and his little moustache looks like a food smudge on his upper lip. Hans cradles the picture, then walks over to Papa's Iron Cross and lifts it off the nail. Papa's smile falls as Hans hangs Hitler in its place. I don't know why Papa doesn't yell. His Iron Cross is very special to him. It's black with silver trim, a "W" in the centre. The imperial crown sits on top and on the bottom is the date, 1914. It dangles from the striped ribbon that once held it onto the breast of his uniform when he fought in the

German Imperial Army. Papa makes Mama polish it at least once a week.

Mama's face turns to stone, but she keeps making *spätzle* for dinner, cutting the noodle dough off the edge of a wooden board with the special chopping blade Papa made her.

We all have to dress up because Opa is coming for dinner. Mama says he shouldn't be living alone, not since Oma died, but he's too stubborn to come live with us. He'd have to sleep in the pantry off our kitchen, where we keep our flour and potatoes and carrots. Mama said she could move those things somewhere else, but Opa says he'd feel like a big sack of food lying on the cot, waiting for someone to come in and eat him.

When Opa comes for dinner we have to wait until he's sitting before we sit, and we mustn't take a bite of our food until Opa starts eating. Papa says that it's because Opa grew up in the old Germany and he was always strict, even when Papa was a boy. We have to accept that even though the times are changing, not everyone is changing with the times.

Papa and Opa like to talk about the old Germany, when everyone was cold and hungry. Papa remembers his mother burning worthless money for heat when he came back from the war.

"Standing in lineups for hours every day to buy bread is what killed your Oma. It sucked the life out of her legs," says Papa.

"But all that changed when Adolph Hitler came to power and stood up to the bullies that were pushing Germany around. Now," Opa says, scratching his scraggly white beard, "we have food and work and good schools, and Herr Hitler will even pay to send you out to the big city to the theatre or concert hall."

Papa agrees that Herr Hitler truly is our Führer, our leader.

"Mama, give Sabine and Hans some beer so we can all clink our glasses together and say a toast to Herr Hitler," Opa orders.

The beer is bitter in my throat and makes me squint.

Then Opa starts singing "The Flag on High" song that our teacher makes us sing at school. Hans joins in, his voice strong.

Millions are looking upon the swastika full of hope,
The day of freedom and of bread dawns!

Millions are looking upon the swastika full of hope,
The day of freedom and of bread dawns!

Opa's hands shake and his shoulders droop, like it's taking all of his energy to keep up with Hans, who is singing like he's on an opera stage. When they sing about bread, Papa grabs the big black loaf and tears it up, throwing us each a big piece as he laughs and twirls around the table.

3.

One Monday morning our teacher, Frau Farber, tells us we need to find our new seats. She has written our names on little pieces of paper, and drawn a colourful picture on each one, a flower or bee or bird. Mine is at the front near the window beside a tall girl with long blonde braids, but I have always sat beside Edie, ever since Grade 1. Mama even took a picture of me and Edie on our first day, holding our shiny *Zuckertüten*, the huge cones filled with candy, chocolate and pencils. We were wearing the matching white dresses that Edie's papa made for us, with the yellow trim. Now, Edie is way in the back, sitting with Rosa and Johanna and Hedda.

None of them are her friends. Poor Edie looks miserable and doesn't wave back when I wave at her.

The day is long and dull. At the end I take my name card and run to show Edie the colourful butterfly beside my name. She holds up hers—a bright yellow star with six points. I tell her it's nice but she just shrugs. Everyone in her row has the same star and I wouldn't like it either if everyone around me had the same picture. Maybe that's why Edie doesn't talk the whole way home.

I think of asking her if she wants to stop in the park, where we sometimes sit to watch the birds, but then we see the signs. Neither of us moves or even breathes as we read them: *Nicht für Juden*. And on the bench across the pathway: *Nur für Juden*—one bench for Jews and one not for Jews—one for Edie and one for me. Silently, we move on.

When we get to Edie's house, a tall apartment building a block before my house, she doesn't ask me to come up. She just whispers goodbye, like her voice has been swallowed.

4.

Hans brings a pile of pamphlets home from his Hitler Youth meeting and spreads them around the table. "Look at them," he orders me. He's practically holding the back of my head and forcing me to face them. I read the titles: *Eat Jewish Food and You'll Die; The Jews Are Our Misfortune;* and *Never Patronize the Jews.*

"Pick them up and open them," he snaps.

"You can't tell me what to do, Hans. You're not my boss," I snap back.

Hans laughs. "You won't be able to refuse my orders for much longer."

I'm about to argue with him when Papa calls us both into the living room to listen to his new radio, a black one with a big round speaker. "It's a *Volksempfänger VE 30*," he said when he brought it home on the weekend. "Only thirty marks. Thanks to Hitler, everyone can afford one." He turns the dials and Hitler's voice, crackling slightly, sails into our parlour. I listen while I sit knitting at Mama's feet. I'm unraveling the yarn from an old sweater that has grown too small, and re-stitching it into a pretty scarf that will keep my neck warm, now that winter is almost here.

When Hitler finally stops talking, Papa turns off the radio and asks Hans to show him the knife he has now added to his uniform. Papa holds it and turns it around slowly, his nose close to the blade.

"Well," says Hans. "Do you like it?"

I stop knitting and lean over Papa to peek. The knife is short and stubby with a black handle, probably Bakelite, decorated with an enamel diamond, red squares and a swastika. Papa nods his head and Hans beams.

"Did you read the motto?" he asks. "*Blut und Ehre.*"

I wonder what a boys club has to with blood and honour. Judging by Mama's face, she is wondering the same.

5.

Loud noises wake me from a sound sleep. At first, I think I'm dreaming, but Mama and Papa must hear it too. I can hear them talking on the other side of the wall. Then Hans runs out of his room, already dressed in his uniform. At the front door Mama tries to hold him back, but Papa says, "Hans has to do what he thinks is right, Gisela. He is a young man now." But why does Hans have to run out in the middle of the night just because the sound of smashing glass is all around us, like the entire town is exploding. Then Papa leaves too, and it's just me and Mama. Without a sound, she crawls into my bed and holds me, putting her hands over my ears—but it doesn't stop the noise.

When I wake up the sun is shining and, for a minute, it's like nothing bad has happened. My arm is dead asleep under Mama's shoulder and I have to use my other hand to pull it out. It tingles as the blood rushes back in. I put on my dress and grab my coat from the hook in the hall. Mama wouldn't want me going out but I have to know what happened last night. Papa and Hans are not even home yet.

The streets are eerily quiet. There's only a faint noise in the distance, so I turn to follow it to the centre of town. Something crunches under my feet and suddenly I'm sliding, as if I'm walking on ice. Broken glass is everywhere, filling the streets like a million icicles. Broken windows sit in many of the storefronts, big holes rimmed by jagged glass. I stop at Edie's father's shop. Where it used to say "Tailor Pinker" is now a gaping hole.

Up ahead, young men are hunched over in a circle, their arms pumping. I recognize a voice, laughing loudly above the others. It's Hans. I watch him bend down and pull up a handful of dark material. Herr Goldman's head sticks up, swollen and bloody. Why would anyone want to hurt the shoe seller? Hans turns him around and kicks him, sending him sprawling a few feet away. The guys all laugh and surround him again, like they're playing a game. I remember Herr Goldman measuring our feet, first my brother's and then mine, inside the steel mould, sliding the tabs until they fit snuggly against my socks. He told Mama we should leave half an inch for growth at the top, then he tugged my pigtail. "Such pretty hair," he said. "I was sure it couldn't be real." When we left he gave each of us a lollipop. Mine was cherry. The flavour burst in my mouth when I licked it.

6.

School is closed for two days, even though no windows there were smashed. When I return to class, the yellow star row at the back is empty. Frau Farber tells us school is now *nicht für Juden*. "We are rebuilding our nation," she says, "making it over, getting rid of the garbage. Heil Hitler." Because she said it, we all have to jump up and say it too, pointing our arms toward our Führer's face.

On my way home, I stand across from Edie's building, looking up, hoping she'll come to the window, but there is no sign of life. I want to ring her bell, but my brother has forbidden me. When I told him he wasn't my father, Papa jumped in and said he agreed. "It is *verboten*."

7.

Today after school I don't go straight home. Instead, I sneak into town. Many stores now have wooden windows. The sidewalks have been cleared of glass but the stars are still there, painted on the walls, like the sky has fallen.

My feet take me to Tailor Pinker's, one cobblestone at a time. I check the street to make sure no one's watching, then push open the door, its bell tinkling as I enter the dark space. I see a shape in the back and suck in my breath, until I see that it's Edie's father, rolling up a bolt of fabric. He freezes, and his hands hold up the bolt, like a weapon. Our eyes catch in the dim. Glass shards litter the floor. I sweep them with my shoes as I move toward him, the sound echoing in the near-empty shop.

"Sabine," Herr Pinker says. "You shouldn't be here. It's not safe!"

"I need to know how Edie is. Is she okay?" He reaches out and strokes my hair, and I think what Hans would say if he saw. I remember how it used to scare me when I was little, to watch Herr Pinker work, because of the row of pins he held between his lips. I always imagined him swallowing one by mistake.

"She will be fine. She's gone to Munich with her

mother. They will be safe there until all of this *mishegas* is over."

"*Mishegas*?" I ask.

"Madness," he says.

I'm about to speak when we hear heavy footsteps just outside the shop. "Quick, Sabine. In here," says Herr Pinker, pushing me behind his desk. "Wrap yourself up." I sink down into a mess of material, crawling under several layers until I can't see anything at all. But I can hear and that is bad enough. There are at least three different voices, but they're all saying the same thing. "*Raus*, get out, dirty rat. This isn't your store anymore." I wait for Herr Pinker to defend himself and say that it is, but he doesn't. Then the door slams shut and everything goes quiet.

I wait a few minutes, then crawl out of my cave. It feels like there's glass in my throat as I run home.

8.

The pine tree is glowing with candles, a goose is roasting in the oven, and *Christstollen* is cooling on the counter. Mama has filled two plates with gingerbread cookies and candied walnuts. Opa is talking about Austria, where his mother was born, and how happy he is that it's finally

part of Germany, "where it rightfully belongs." Hans is
wearing his boxing mitts, showing off his right-punch-
left-punch-right-punch combination, bouncing around
the table like a kangaroo. "The next Max Schmeling,"
Opa says, putting up his own fists, his hands full of veins
that pop out of his skin like noodles.

"No, better than Schmeling. Hans would never lose
to a schwarz. Right, Hans?" says Papa. Mama and I look
at each other and roll our eyes. When Opa, Papa and
Hans start talking about boxing, they can go on forever.
They are still upset that Schmeling lost his fight to Joe
Louis, a Black fighter, in America. They say Louis fought
dirty and the match was fixed.

After dinner, Mama plays the piano and we gather
to sing "Silent Night." Hans raises his hand and tells us
to listen. He stares out the window as he sings, his eyes
far away:

> *Silent Night, Holy night,*
> *All is calm, all is bright,*
> *Adolph Hitler is Germany's star*
> *Showing us greatness and glory afar*
> *Bringing us Germans the might.*

Opa claps and Papa opens a bottle of schnapps. I unwrap my new hair ribbons and say my own little prayer for Edie, hundreds of kilometres away in Munich. Snow is falling on our streets, the air is still, and if I look up it is impossible to tell that such things as Opa describes are happening in the world. I tell myself that maybe the same snow is falling on Edie's new street, making everything white and bright, even though I know that probably isn't true.

EDIE

I.

I'm sitting on the train to Munich beside Mama. It's just the two of us, since Papa couldn't come, and we're in third class, on terribly hard wooden seats, surrounded by people who look as miserable as we do. I tell Mama I'm hungry and ask if we can go to the dining car, but she says, "No, Edie, not today." When I ask her why not she says we're not allowed. When I ask her why not she just shakes her head and pulls out some bread and cheese from her bag. All around us people lower their eyes as if they know the answer to my question but won't say. Going to the dining car is my favourite part of the trip. I love spreading the white linen napkin over my lap and picking up the heavy silver cutlery. It makes me feel glamorous and important, like my favourite movie star, Marlene Dietrich.

"Stop asking so many questions," Mama tells me. But that's not what Papa says. *Always ask, always question, he says. Otherwise, you are a puppet and not a person.*

Except, a few weeks ago, when I came home and told Papa that Frau Farber made me return the gold medal I won in gymnastics, Papa didn't question it. He just hung his head and there were tears in his eyes, like there were this morning when we said goodbye at the station.

2.

Aunt Naomi and Uncle Max meet us at the station, and they're both crying too. Uncle Max says, "Let's get you both home," and takes my hand. When we drive past the synagogue where Mama and I used to sit in the balcony and stare up at the magnificent arches in the ceiling, I can see that its windows are gone—the roof is collapsed and the stone walls are charred black, like after a fire. Terrible words are painted on the front—Germany should be *Judenfrei*. Jew Free. Would Papa have sent us here, if he could see this?

When we walk into the house, Mama and I both gasp. Aunt Naomi and Uncle Max must have been robbed.

Their living room is almost bare. The rose-patterned sofa and its matching chair look lost without the small wooden tables nearby. The corner where the grand piano used to stand is empty too. Four black holes darken the floor where the piano legs have left their mark, like bruises in the wood. If I close my eyes, I can hear Uncle Max playing something beautiful, like Chopin or Schubert. I hear us all clapping when he finishes, Mama calling encore, encore. The corner cabinet is still there, but the china figurines that used to fill it have disappeared. The diamond shapes in the glass catch the sun and sparkle, but that doesn't help. It's still a sad sight.

The worst shock is the walls. All the paintings are gone, even the Max Liebermann that Papa said was worth a fortune. Now, there are no more gardens or dancers, no more Bengal tigers or Greek goddesses. Just blank walls. You can tell where the paintings once hung because the striped wallpaper is darker there, looking like a patchwork of squares and rectangles.

Papa always told Mama not to be jealous of her older sister's wealth. "We're just as happy, and we go to bed with a full belly every night. And we have our Edie. Children are the biggest blessing, right Hannah?" Then he'd tickle her chin or pinch her cheek, just to make her smile. Now, standing here, I wonder what Mama is thinking. Is she glad her sister's house looks more like ours, or is she just as confused as I am?

3.

Aunt Naomi brings out some bread and cheese and cold cuts, along with pickles on a gold-rimmed pickle plate, a silver fork sticking into one. "Old habits die hard," she says to Mama, who smiles. Every word echoes through the empty house.

Uncle Max has barely looked up since we got here, as if he doesn't want to see how much is missing. After a few bites, he says, "I'm glad we did it, Naomi. It's those who don't who'll be sorry, not us. I wasn't going to let those bastards get hold of my paintings. This way, Herr Weber has them and I trust him. He'll get us the money." His voice is growing louder and he's starting to sound like his old self.

"Right Edie?" he says, throwing his arm over me. "It's all for Edie. She's our future. We may be finished, who knows, but as long as we have Edie we have a future." Then Uncle Max jumps up and lifts me with him, twirling me to the empty corner, where the piano used to be.

"We don't need a piano to make music. It's here, in our heads," he says, letting go of one hand and pointing to his temple. "Don't worry, ladies, your uncle Max has it all under control." Suddenly, I slip from his grasp and fall to the floor. Mama and Aunt Naomi stare at me for a few seconds, then start to laugh. The sound booms and echoes, and before long Uncle Max and I are laughing too. I want us to keep laughing forever because then I don't have to think about why Uncle Max had to get rid of all his belongings so that I could have a future.

4.

Uncle Max leaves home early every morning to try to get us the visas we need to leave Germany. Mama and my aunt have their hearts set on Canada, where they have a cousin named Louisa. They've never met her, but her mother was my Oma's sister.

"Canada's doors are shut to us," Uncle Max explains at night, after another day of trying. "I've stood in line there ten times already. I'm trying my best. The only place we could get to quickly right now is Shanghai. It's the only place on earth that doesn't ask for visas. Thousands are going. We wouldn't be alone."

"You can't be serious, Max," Aunt Naomi says.

"Tell us you're joking," says Mama.

"When I get the money for the paintings, maybe I can try for Canada. But even then, we'd have to pretend we're farmers. Look at these lawyer hands, do they look like a farmer's hands?" Uncle Max collapses onto the sofa and covers his face with his long elegant fingers. Aunt Naomi sits beside him and rubs his back.

"I'll write to Louisa again, to try to make her understand how desperate we are. Once she understands, I'm sure she'll offer to help," she says, but Uncle Max just shrugs.

5.

A week later, Uncle Max comes home and announces, "Canada. Don't ask me how, but we're going. Herr Weber sold the paintings, way below value, but in these times maybe not too bad. The three of us have no value, but the paintings—they speak. The man asked if we had farming experience and I said yes. He looked doubtful and then I showed him the check with the letter from Herr Weber. Suddenly, they could see cracks and corns all over my fingers. Dirt even, under the nails. Not only did I get the visas, I also booked passage. We leave in two weeks." Mama and Aunt Naomi throw their arms around him and kiss his cheeks. "And you, little Edie. You're not going to kiss your Uncle Max?"

I don't know why I'm supposed to be happy. I have a sick feeling in my stomach that only grows as they talk about packing and what to bring. We're each allowed two bags. No one has mentioned Papa. He's the unspoken word among us. It's like we all know he can't come with us, but no one wants to say that out loud.

6.

Every day we fly around filling out forms and standing in long lineups. When we finally get our passports, I want to scream. They've written Sara Edie, which isn't my name. Then I look at Mama's and see that she has become Sara Hannah. Aunt Naomi is now Sara Naomi and Uncle Max is Israel Max. All our passports have a big red "J" stamped in the corner.

On the way home from the passport office, Mama clutches her purse so tightly her fingers are blue. We pass the local café and Uncle Max suggests we pop in to warm up and celebrate. Mama and Aunt Naomi look unsure, but Uncle Max is already opening the door. "Come on, ladies," he says. "They know us here. Surely, they won't begrudge us a coffee."

We take a table in the back corner and Uncle Max orders three coffees and a hot chocolate. When the waitress hands over the tray, she says, "Drink and leave quickly. I don't want any trouble." Those words ruin the taste of the hot chocolate, even though it's piled high with whipped cream and chocolate shavings.

A few minutes later, the front door opens and four men in brown suits step noisily inside. Tight belts are wrapped around their middles and shiny black boots stretch to their knees. Aunt Naomi reaches across the table to grab Uncle Max's arm and upends my hot chocolate, knocking the glass against my plate. The four men turn toward us and we are caught by eight piercing eyes.

Suddenly, they're upon us. Sticks rain down as the men shout, "*Raus raus scheiße Juden.*" I throw up my arms to cover my face, then Mama pulls me out of my chair. We scramble out the door, and Aunt Naomi follows, her hair tumbling out of its bun. But Uncle Max is still inside and the noise is getting louder. The men are laughing, like something's funny, and furniture is crashing. A few seconds later, the door flies open and Uncle Max shoots out of the café, landing on his back, his face dripping with a mixture of coffee and hot chocolate, gobs of whipped cream covering his eyes.

7.

The next day, Uncle Max's arm is so sore he can barely stand the pain and he convinces Aunt Naomi to call Dr. Kohn. "This could ruin everything," he says, his voice cracking. "You heard those men. We have to be in perfect health or they won't let us board."

Dr. Kohn arrives, clutching his black leather bag. He rolls up Uncle Max's sleeve, takes one look and says, "It's not broken, just sprained." When Dr. Kohn asks Uncle Max how this happened, he says that he fell. Dr. Kohn mutters, "It seems many of us have become quite clumsy lately."

"We're leaving for Canada. We have the tickets and everything. It's nearly impossible—we're incredibly fortunate. Can you give me something for the pain?"

"You are lucky," replies Dr. Kohn. "So many are trying. I can give you some strong medication. You will sing your way past the inspection."

Aunt Naomi jumps up and says, "Thank you for

everything, Dr. Kohn, not just this, but for all the years."
They hesitate, standing almost nose to nose, and I think
they might kiss. "I hope you and Mrs. Kohn and your
whole family can follow us sometime."

Dr. Kohn takes her hands and says, "Maybe, we'll see.
A doctor is like the captain of a ship, you know. He cannot
leave first. Now that we can't go to the hospitals, what
would people like your husband do if me and the other
doctors left? Lawyers might be dispensable, but doctors?"

I think Uncle Max might take offense, but he smiles.
It must be an old joke between these two.

8.

We divide the valuables my aunt and uncle managed to
keep, between the suitcases, in case one gets lost. Aunt
Naomi says we'll need these treasures to get set up in the
new world. That's what they keep calling Canada, the
new world. I never realized that we lived in an old world. I
remember the movie theatre in Munich I went to just last
year, with its high balconies and red velvet curtains. Are the
movie theatres in Canada even newer? At least there won't
be a big *Juden unerwünscht* sign on the marquee because
there, in the new world, Uncle Max promised Jews will be

welcome wherever they want to go.

Uncle Max keeps reminding Aunt Naomi that if it's not worth money, we shouldn't bring it, and when she asks him, what about sentimental value, he says, "No room for sentiment when you're fighting for your life." In the end, the only valuables we pack are the silver cutlery, divided between the eight suitcases and wrapped in socks and underwear, and the best of Aunt Naomi's jewelry, the pieces with real gems set into solid gold. She lets me choose my favourite antique brooch, a delicate flower made of pearls with one emerald leaf, and Mama helps me sew it into the hem of my coat.

On the day of the trip, we leave a bit later so that the streetcar won't be too crowded. If it is, Jews are last and don't always get a spot. Uncle Max says not to pay attention to people's comments—to keep our eyes ahead on the voyage. This turns out to be good advice because I overhear some people talk about how glad they are to see more dirty Jews leave the country.

9.

The ride to Paris is long and uncomfortable but none of us complains. I sit beside the window and pretend the outside is a movie flashing past, a long one with no real plot, just loads of scenery. At each station a new cast of characters enters the movie: soldiers and rich-looking people stepping happily into the first-class cars, poorer ones into second, and everyone else into third, near us. It seems no one counted the number of seats available in third class, so we're squashed together, four on a bench that was made for three, kids curled on blankets in the passageway. The air is heavy with the smell of different foods, sauerkraut and beets, apples and plums.

As we near the station closest to home, I imagine Papa jumping on board, looking smart in a newly tailored suit, our treasures jammed into two suitcases. We don't have any silver or jewels, but surely he'd bring one of my porcelain dolls. And Mama's ivory brush set, the one Papa bought her when they first married, with the matching ivory combs to pull back her hair.

But Stuttgart comes and goes. My heart snags, like it's stuck on one of the rails.

We finally reach the Gare Saint-Lazare train station in Paris, where we have an hour to wait for the connecting train to Le Havre. I wish we had time to see the Eiffel Tower, or wander up the Champs Elysées to the Arc de

Triomphe. Sabine would die of envy if I did. We always talked about going to Paris together one day.

Mama has run into one of the many station cafés to buy us sandwiches and coffee. I watch her walking back toward us and notice a change in her step. These last few weeks in Munich her head was always down and she took little steps, but here, her head is up and she's walking like she used to. She's every bit as pretty as the young stylish women who surround us, with their tight-fitting coats, colourful hats and high-heeled shoes.

10.

Our ship looks like one of those big ships in movies, the kind where lovers wave to each other, one on deck, the other on the ground below. I want to run up the gangplank and jump on board, but I'm stuck in another long lineup. Mama holds my hand so tightly I've lost feeling in my fingers.

We enter a big brick building and line up again in front of one of the many tables where men are sitting with piles of paper. A man asks our names, one at a time, and we have to answer for ourselves. Mama pinches me when I say Edie Pinker, because I forgot to add the Sara.

Then I have to step behind a screen, where a doctor asks me to cough and listens to my chest with a stethoscope. He makes me say *ahh* while he looks down my throat. Finally, I have to bend and touch my toes and he walks his fingers along my spine, which almost tickles. He smiles and slips me a candy.

Then we join another lineup, moving our luggage foot by foot until we're finally on the gangplank, the upper deck of the ship only feet away, the grey ocean stretching to the horizon. Once on board, we follow the crowd down narrow metal stairs, through several corridors, and down more stairs to a large room full of wooden bunkbeds. A man in a sailor's cap points us to a corner where four empty bunks await us. For a second, I hold my breath. What if something nasty is written on the wooden boards, like "Jews Stay Away" or "Jews Not Welcome" ...? What will we do?

But there is nothing. This is our home for the next week and nothing here tells us we don't belong.

II.

The trip over the Atlantic Ocean is a blur of sleeping and waking, and feeling sicker than I've ever felt in my life. Mama and Aunt Naomi take turns bringing me bread and water and emptying the buckets I keep filling. The ship rocks constantly, swishing around my insides until I can't hold anything in. I cry for Papa all day and at night I dream of him here beside me, his big hand on my forehead, telling me not to worry. At one point, I throw up on the beautiful new dress he unwraps for me and I claw at my clothes, begging Mama to rinse them in the salty water. Through it all, I hear Mama and Aunt Naomi talking, using words like *delirious* and *fever*. If the ship would just stop moving, I'd be fine. But it whirls and swirls, tossing out my insides.

Then, finally, the ship slows and my stomach slows with it. I am so skinny, my nightgown slides off me, exposing two pokey shoulder bones. My hair is string beans hanging down my face and I smell so bad I can't imagine they'll want me in the new world. Mama brings a bucket of water and some soap and tries to wash me as best she can, but the smell of sick remains. Mama hugs me, getting suds on her shirt. Then she is crying and I know she's thinking of Papa. "He'll join us too, Edie. We left him enough things to sell. You'll see; he'll be here soon. Now, let's be strong, okay?" She pours the rest of the water over my hair, pats it dry, then combs it back into a braid.

12.

My legs are weak as we follow a long line of people to the top deck of the ship. I keep wanting to sit but can't, because every few seconds we move a couple of inches. A fat white seagull circles and lands on the railing ahead and I keep my eyes on it as Mama gently pushes me forward. Beyond the ship stands a row of low stone buildings, and a white one with a big silver dome on top. Just past it a church steeple sticks up, topped by a giant copper angel. She's leaning forward with open arms, big green wings spread behind her. I keep my eyes on her, imagining her lifting me up and helping me move.

Finally, we trudge down the gangplank and into a red brick building. Rows and rows of benches are already full of people and we find room in the back. Once again, we wait for our names to be called, then speak to a man at a table who checks our papers and gives us new documents. On a table in the corner sit plates of oranges that are all cut up. I haven't tasted an orange in so long, I want to grab them all, but Mama says I mustn't take more than one. I'm suddenly so hungry, my stomach is making loud grumbling sounds. Everyone hears it and laughs. "So, your stomach has finally woken up, little Edie," says Uncle Max.

We pile into a black taxi and wind through the strange snow-filled streets of Montreal to Louisa's house, a tall brick building with a staircase on the outside. Children are playing out front, throwing snowballs and chasing each other under the streetlights. Some are using long wooden sticks to knock a ball of some kind into a garbage can lying on its side.

We climb the winding stairs and Aunt Naomi rings the bell. A few seconds later, a tall woman with short brown hair opens the door. She has the same dimple on her chin that both Aunt Naomi and Mama have. Aunt Naomi puts her hand out to shake, but Louisa grabs her and pulls her close. She kisses her quickly, once on each cheek. Then she does the same to the rest of us. I don't think I've ever seen so many kisses.

"Come on in, out of the cold," she says. "And pardon my bad German. I haven't used it since my mother died twenty years ago. My goodness, I knew you were coming but now that you're here I can't believe it."

Louisa leads us down a long hallway, past two closed

doors, to a small room behind the kitchen. There are two beds, one on each side of the room. The walls are unfinished, with thick beams running floor to ceiling every few metres. The back wall has a thick grey blanket hanging on it. "That's to keep the cold out, because of the back door. It's not a palace," says Louisa, "but it's the best we can do." Mama and Aunt Naomi look at each other and try to smile. "And it's not forever," Louisa adds.

"No," says Uncle Max. "Not forever." He looks at the bare rough walls and I wonder if he's thinking of his beautiful paintings that are gone forever.

13.

Mid-week we hang one of Louisa's old sheets down the middle of the room to give us some privacy, me and Mama on one side, Aunt Naomi and Uncle Max on the other. The room gets so cold at night I have to snuggle right up against Mama to keep warm. She sleeps with her coat on because she's next to the wall. Louisa said to keep the door open so some of the coal heat enters our room, but once we heard Brian, Louisa's husband, complain about wasted money so now Uncle Max insists we keep it closed. Brian leaves for work at the shipyards early in the morning, before the sun comes up, so we don't see him much. In the evening he takes his dinner plate into the parlour and eats off a tray, listening to the radio and shouting out news that only Aunt Naomi can understand. When it's about Germany she translates for us. People are saying that another war in Europe is right around the corner.

Louisa wears pajamas around the house and only gets dressed if she's going out. She smokes constantly so the little kitchen is always hazy. In the morning, she makes something called toast but forgets to turn over the bread and burns it half the time, which she seems to find funny. There's a crucifix over the kitchen sink because Brian is Catholic. Louisa became Catholic when she married him, so the two of them go to mass Sunday morning, which is the first time we're alone in the house. We sit in the parlour, beside the coal heater, and feel warmer than we have since we arrived.

In the afternoon, we bundle up as best we can and take our first walk along Wellington Street, looking at all the goods for sale in the shop windows. Many are decorated for Christmas, with strings of lights, twisting garlands of red and green, and cardboard images of Sankt Nikolaus, who Aunt Naomi says is called Santa

Claus here. Mama sees a red coat with fur trim that she likes and I think how easily Papa could make it for her, if only he could see it. The "Five and Dime" has rows and rows of colourful candy in glass jars and Mama promises we can come back when the store is open. There is a German delicatessen called Wetzler's, where huge slabs of salami and trays of knockwurst sit in the window. A string of pretzels makes our mouths water, and a small sign on the door says "Help Wanted." Aunt Naomi says she should apply, but Uncle Max isn't sure. "Will they see us as German or Jewish?" he asks. I don't understand. I thought that wouldn't matter in the new world.

14.

Louisa says we can put a menorah in the window for Chanukah, but to be careful because these back rooms can go up in flames like a tinder box. For eight nights we recite the prayers, each time ending with a prayer for Papa. I think about him a lot, especially at night when I'm lying in bed beside Mama, listening to the sounds of the city outside the window. The traffic here never seems to stop and when the streetcar runs past the corner, our walls shake. I want to tell Papa everything, even about the funny man who delivers Brian's beer in the basket of a bicycle. Mama says I can put it all in a letter and we'll send it to him, but the way she says it makes me think she doesn't believe he'll ever receive it.

The last night of Chanukah is also Christmas Eve, and Louisa puts up a Christmas tree in the parlour and invites us to join them. The smell of pine fills the tiny room, and red lights flash on and off the branches. On the radio, someone named Bing Crosby is singing about a white Christmas and then the Andrews Sisters sing a song with German words. We all sing along with the chorus, "Bei Mir Bist Du Schön." The words roll comfortably off my tongue and I wonder if English will ever do the same.

Brian pulls Louisa up and they dance around, trying not to step on our toes. Then Uncle Max rises too and offers his hand to Aunt Naomi. Mama pushes the coffee table to the side to make room for the two twirling couples. Then she looks at me and winks and we join them. After this song, we all switch partners and I find myself dancing with Brian, who is so tall I barely reach his chest. He spins me round and I can't help laughing. Then Mama and Brian hook up, while Louisa and Uncle

Max dance. Poor Mama! I know she wishes it were Papa instead of Brian, dipping her so far back her head is almost hitting the ground.

In the middle of our dancing, a girl in a bright red dress twirls into the room. Her shoulder length hair bounces and her lips are covered in bright red lipstick that matches her dress. "Merry Christmas," she calls out.

"This is Annette, our upstairs neighbour," says Louisa. She says *Annette* in a way that sounds disapproving.

"Hey, everyone," Annette says, flashing us a wide smile. "Welcome. I hope you like Montreal so far. These are from me. It's just not Christmas without candy canes." She holds up a plate filled with red and green candy.

"Here, have one," she says, standing so close I can see the gold flecks in her eyes. I don't know what to say. She is the most beautiful girl I've ever seen in my life.

"They won't hurt you," she adds, laughing. "See?" She unwraps one and sticks it in her mouth, between her red lips. "Yummy."

She puts the plate on the coffee table and spins around. "Well, I've gotta run. It's our busiest night at the club. Have a good one, everyone." She waves and I think living here might not be so bad after all.

1939

SABINE

I.

There are blossoms on the trees and birds singing in the branches. Everything in my hometown is new—including me. Mama says I've grown two inches since last spring, so she has to let down all my hems. She does her best, but the old hem line still shows. If Herr Pinker's shop was still there, we could bring my skirts to him. He'd sew a ribbon over the lines and make them look stylish. But, even if he were still there, doing business with him would be *verboten*. I can just hear Hans reminding me of that in his stern voice.

I do have one new skirt, a dark blue one that I have to wear with a stiff white blouse and black handkerchief knotted tightly around my neck—the official uniform of

the *Bund Deutscher Mädel*, the League of German Girls.
I have to wear my long brown hair in braids, flat shoes
and no jewelry. Maria, our group leader, says the Führer
likes his girls to look natural and healthy. I wonder if
Maria has ever seen Marlene Dietrich. She's beautiful
and she wears eye pencil and lipstick. But Mama told
me not to ask any questions when I'm at my meetings,
which is exactly what the motto I had to memorize
says: *Don't talk, don't debate, live a National Socialist life in
discipline, composure and comradery.*

So I keep my questions locked up inside my head,
shut tight like the old box of clothes in Edie's basement.

2.

On Saturday, our group spends the night in a barn
outside of town. We sleep on the hay and watch the
moon through the cracks in the high ceiling. Outside,
our campfire is still shooting up sparks, each one a little
orange rocket aiming for the sky. Earlier, we roasted
sausages on the end of sticks and sang songs about
Germany. Before that we hiked over the mountains,
weaving in and out of the tall pines to make our legs
stronger. We held hands, two by two, and every ten

minutes Maria made us switch partners, so that we'd get to know each other. Some of the girls are from my school, others aren't, but no hand was Edie's and I tried not to think about that. When Inge was my partner, she lowered her head toward mine and whispered, *Jude Freundin*, lightly, like the whisper of wind through the leaves. Then she squeezed my hand so tightly I wanted to scream, but didn't. Inge is seventeen, so she's allowed to do whatever she wants to a thirteen-year-old like me. I recited the BDM motto over and over, pretending I was Inge's friend and not the friend of a Jew.

3.

Today, Frau Farber is in a wonderful mood. She says we don't have to do any work—no spelling drills, no calculations, no memorization of the rivers and lakes of our country. That's because tomorrow, April 20, is our Führer's fiftieth birthday. All the classrooms and hallways are decorated with red flags, and the teachers hand out little ones on sticks to all the kids. The huge picture of Hitler in the foyer is surrounded by gold leaves, and the smaller one in our classroom with red ribbons. Instead of lessons, we're making a present to send to Hitler: each class is decorating one part of a huge eagle. Our Head Mistress will take the bird to Berlin on the train, and deliver it herself when she attends the grand parade tomorrow. She came to our class and said, "With each shiny button you attach, the Führer will know how much you love him." I throw myself harder into the work, to show everyone that I love my Führer as much as they do, even though I'm not sure that's true.

4.

Hans has been promoted to group leader for the Jungvolk. Now he'll get to tell the younger boys what to do and how to do it. "That little crybaby Werner won't be able to snivel for too much longer," he says. As if Hans needed any more reason to be bossy. The other day I put on some lipstick from the tube Edie and I used to use when we played movie stars. Hans pulled me by the hair to the washroom and made me wash it off. "All that American stuff is not appropriate for German girls. You're a disgrace to the Führer," he spat. "You should sit and mend my socks instead of dressing up like a whore." The worst part was that Mama was right there watching and she just let him do it. Afterward, she pulled out a pile of mending and threaded a needle and showed me how to go in and out, tightening up the holes in my brother's socks.

5.

Mama and I listen to the radio as we knit or sew. I love it when Lale Andersen sings "Lili Marlene" or when Zarah Leander sings "I Know a Miracle will Happen." Mama's favourite shows are *A German Almanac*, where ordinary families from around the country talk about their lives in Bavaria, Saxony, or Franconia, and the *Wünschkonzert* for the Winter Charity Drive. It plays special requests for Beethoven, Wagner, and folk songs about love. Mama used to love Mozart operas, but now those have been banned. When I ask Mama why, she says, "Sabine, you ask too many questions, but if you must know, his librettos were written by Jews." Mama blushes when she says it.

Tonight, the news comes on and the announcer talks about a ship, the St. Louis, carrying a thousand Jewish *flüchtlingen*. The refugees were turned away in Cuba and America and the ship is now returning to Europe. The man says he's not surprised. "Why would other countries want to take in Europe's unwanted Jews?" he says. "Why would they import the problems we're getting rid of?"

Maybe Edie was on that ship. Does this mean she'll move back into her third floor flat where the windows are always dark and there is no sign of life? Maybe, from time to time, we could still hang out together, when Hans isn't looking and the rest of the town has gone to sleep. Or, maybe I'm just a fool, like Hans always says I am.

6.

Opa has moved into the pantry off the kitchen. He couldn't live alone any longer. He had stopped eating and is so thin we can see his ribs when he washes. He says he can't get the smell of onions and potatoes out of his nose, and he hangs a poster on his door showing poor and hungry people—underneath, it says *Hitler, Our Last Hope*. Inside, above his tiny bed, he has written Hitler's slogan himself, in his old-fashioned curly script, on a piece of paper: "Give me four years and you will not recognize Germany." When I bring him his hot milk at night, I wonder what that slogan is really promising. Wouldn't it be strange not to recognize my own country?

7.

Hans comes home with a bundle of black fur in his arms

and asks Mama for a small cardboard box.

"What for, Hans? What is that?" asks Mama. We both run over to see. It's a black puppy, with a pink button nose, but it's not moving.

"Where did you find it?" I ask.

"Me and my group found six puppies in the woods, nestled against their mother's belly. It was perfect," says Hans. "One for each boy, a test, to show their allegiance to the Führer, to show their obedience to the future."

Mama's hand shoots up to her mouth and she gasps. I wait for her other hand to slap my brother, but it doesn't. She just stares at him like he's someone she doesn't know, someone who has just walked in off the street. Then she goes off to find the box Hans asked for.

Opa's slogan has already come true—I don't recognize my country, or my brother.

8.

In the long summer break, I go to BDM meetings every day. Maria organizes us into groups and sends us out to collect old toys to give to kids who have none. Other days, we climb the hills and gather herbs to use for medicine: horsetail, yarrow, plantain, willow leaves and the pretty linden tree blossoms. We belt out the "Horst Wessel Song," the words echoing through the forests, as we find nettles for soup, dandelion and sorrel leaves for salad, and wild mushrooms. Back at our clubhouse, we make *eintopf* in a huge pot and bring bowls of soup to the older widows in our town.

Other days, we learn the folk dances of our ancestors. We watch movies that show us what the Jews did to our country, how they stole our money and made Germany so poor we almost starved. When we march past Tailor Pinker's shop, which is now Tailor Fritz's, Gabi says she's glad people finally got the message: *Kauft nicht bei Juden.* But how can people buy from Jews when there are no Jewish shops left in town? Then I march faster so people won't suspect that I'm thinking about Herr Pinker and wondering where he is. If he's in his apartment, I wonder how he's managing to eat when no shops will sell to Jews. I wish I could bring him a bowl of soup.

9.

Opa lays out a pile of pennies on the table and moves them so fast they are just a copper blur. Suddenly, one is behind my ear and his old bony hand is pulling it out of my hair, or from under my chin. How does Opa do that? Then I remember: Edie's father used to do the same trick with buttons, plucking them out of Edie's dark curls. "Opa, I'm thirteen now, too old for childish tricks," I tell him. Mama says that was mean but I don't care. Opa wanders over to the radio to listen to news about the changes he is so happy to see. When he likes what he hears he tugs on his long white beard, as if he's trying to pull it off and make himself younger.

10.

"September 3, 1939. A day all Germans will remember forever," the radio announcer says. "Germany is at war." Hans runs around shooting imaginary guns in the air, as if he's a cowboy chasing Indians, like the ones in the Karl May books he and his friends like to read. When they were younger, they'd play cowboys and Indians and they always made the cowboys win, which seems unfair to me. The Indians were there first, living peacefully in their teepees. Hans said if the cowboys didn't kill them, the Indians would scalp them. The whole game looked dumb to me.

"I hope the war lasts three years," Hans says. "Then I

can participate." To be mean, I stick out my tongue and remind him that the Nazi slogan is *Total War, Shortest War*. Too bad for Hans.

II.

Within days there are changes: we're not allowed to keep houselights on after dark, except where we have heavy curtains. Men paint phosphorescent stripes on the streets in town; people shield their bicycle lights with red cloth and pin shining badges on their coats. The newspapers and radio are not allowed to announce the weather, but Opa says it's "*Führerwetter*" on nice days and "*Jüdischewetter*" on bad ones.

We get our ration cards that are filled with stamps: blue for meat, yellow for cheese and milk, white for sweet stuff, green for eggs, orange for bread, pink for flour, tea and coffee, and purple for fruit and nuts. I can spend sixty Deutschmarks for clothes in the next eighteen months. That means more ugly hemlines and hand-me-downs from my mother. I think of that box of clothes in the basement of Edie's building and wonder if Edie would think badly of me if I tried to find it.

12.

Frau Schilling becomes our block warden. She runs around at night in a black suit and a helmet that looks like an overturned bowl, checking for any shaft of light. Mama doesn't like the way she's allowed to creep up our front stairs and press her ear against our door, listening, snooping, looking for ways to turn us in to the local National Socialist Party office. Mama says Frau Schilling's shoes scrape the stone walkway like rat's claws, and that we should turn on some Mozart, to give her a heart attack. Then Mama throws her head back and laughs in a way I haven't heard her do for such a long time, it almost scares me. I imagine Frau Schilling, her ear against our window, scribbling away in her little book, taking note of Mama's joy.

13.

Papa eats dinner so quietly, we're all afraid to speak. Only Opa talks, going on about Poland, "our first real conquest." He says Germany had no choice. "They were massacring our German brothers stuck on their side of the border." Hans has already set up a map of the world on the kitchen wall and he stuck a little red pin into the heart of Warsaw, to match the ones in Austria and the Sudetenland.

After dinner, Papa says he has something to tell us: "I'm being sent to Berlin, to lead a factory there, but I can't tell you where or why. It's top secret. I leave right after New Year's. It's a very big honour to be asked to do this. Of course, I had to agree to join the party first, but that seems a small price to pay." Mama slumps over her plate when Papa speaks, her face as white as the potatoes.

"Did you hear about that girl, not much older than you, Sabine, who was caught hiding her Jewish boyfriend inside her wardrobe? The Gestapo took both of them away in their pajamas, crying like babies," says Hans, like he didn't hear Papa's news. "The officials are cleaning up, sweeping people into a giant dust bin."

Mama cries into her napkin and Papa pats her shoulder. I don't know if she's crying for the couple or because Papa is going away. Or what one has to do with the other. I only know that somehow they are all part of the same thing: the war. I think of Papa's beautiful knives, the ones that save lives, slicing out tumors with their precision and craftsmanship. It's no surprise the army wants him.

14.

The stairwell is dark, which would make Frau Schilling happy. I tiptoe, trying to avoid the creaks, and knock lightly on Edie's door. My heart is pounding under my coat. I wait, but there's no answer. Then I hear the lightest step on the other side, as though a bird has landed on the wood. The door opens and Herr Pinker, looking much thinner, opens up.

"Sabine," he whispers, his eyes wide. "What are you doing here?"

"I came to see if you're okay," I answer. He pulls me inside, gently. When I see Edie's dolls on her bed through the open door, something catches in my throat. I can't believe she'd leave them behind.

"Don't worry about me," says Herr Pinker. "I'm fine. I'm staying to guard our things, until all this is over, *Schatz*. But you mustn't come back here." Behind him, braced against the window, sits his Iron Cross. The glass case is cracked, but the medal is still shiny. He sees me look at it and shakes his head. Then he reaches out his hand and runs it over my hair, like he did in his shop. "Go now, *Kind*," he says, pushing me toward the door. I turn and throw my arms around his middle, burying my face in his chest.

15.

Our Christmas meal is skimpier than last year's. Mama used all her yellow, green and pink stamps to bake a cake, and the plate of nuts is small. But there is enough for all of us to have something.

"Everyone has to give things up during wartime and we have more than most," says Papa. Opa is served his plate in bed because he can't get up anymore. The circulation in his legs is bad. We gather at the end of the pantry to sing some songs. We light a few candles and make sure the blackout curtains are drawn. In a few days, Papa will be gone. I never thought Christmas could be so sad.

EDIE

I.

A few days into the new year, Mama holds my hand as we walk to my new Canadian school two blocks from home. My heart beats so loudly I think it will burst through my chest and leap out of my new navy tunic. Papa would be so glad to see me going back to school. His dream was for me to go to university. "That way," he said, "there will never be closed doors." The doors to this school are grey, with stone owls perched on either side. Across the top, etched into the stone, is the school's name: *Verdun High School*. I know Mama can't come in with me, so we say goodbye, squeezing our gloved hands. Groups of kids dot the yard, but I don't dare try to join one. When a bell rings, everyone runs to form lines in front of two doors, one for the girls and one for the boys. I'm swept up by the crowd and follow along until I see the classroom I was told to go to, on the paper we received—room number six.

The teacher, Miss Madison, tells the class my name and then places me at a desk near the front. She tells me to ask her if I don't understand something. Several times during the day, while the other kids are working, she comes and sits beside me and talks to me more slowly. The math is super easy and I'm glad that numbers are numbers in any language. For reading, she gives me a different book and tells me to make a list of all the words I don't know in a special scribbler that has a page for each letter of the alphabet. My homework will be to make a sentence with each new word. At something called recess I lean against a brick wall and eat my apple. A lot of kids look at me, but no one comes over. If only one of the faces were Sabine's. By now, we'd be deep in a game of hopscotch.

2.

Aunt Naomi brings home knockwurst and peppered salami from Wetzler's Deli, where she is now working. Brian smothers his sausage with sauerkraut, spooning it out of the huge glass jar Aunt Naomi brought home yesterday. "This is where the Krauts belong. Pickled in a big jar," he says. Something inside me prickles when he says that, because we're German too. Or at least we used to be. Then I think of those brownshirts who beat up Uncle Max and decide Brian's right—I'd love to bottle them up and watch them drown in stinky water. Because of them, Papa's on the other side of the ocean, eating alone.

At night I do my homework in the parlour, sitting on the floor, beside the coal heater. Sometimes, Annette will knock on the window and wave at me on her way out. I jump onto the sofa and wave back. I love the way she almost dances down the stairs. I want to call out and ask her to take me with her. If Louisa sees her, she says, "That girl's headed for trouble," but I don't know why.

3.

In the second week of school, a blonde girl runs up behind me and asks where I'm from. I say Germany and she says, "Oh wow! My grandfather came from there too." When the bell rings she stands beside me and takes my hand. I think of the animals going onto Noah's Ark, two by two. When our teacher calls for volunteers to wash the boards,

my new friend, Dorothy, says, "We'll do it," and makes
me follow her to the washroom where we wet some rags.
She starts at one end of the blackboard and I start at the
other. When we meet in the middle she smiles at me and
everything about the day suddenly seems okay.

Dorothy, who says to call her Dot, lets me hang
around with her and her friend Betty at recess. They talk
about their favourite movie stars, like Cary Grant and
Errol Flynn. They've seen *The Adventures of Robin Hood*
and can't believe I've never even heard of it. Betty says,
"Don't they have movies in Germany?" I want to list all
the movies I've seen, but they're old now. If I tell them
Jews weren't allowed in movie theatres and still aren't,
they'll want to know why not and I don't know if I could
explain it. Maybe they'll think something's wrong with
me, like I smell bad or have head lice.

"I was too busy getting ready to move across the
ocean to go to movies," I say.

"Ooo, all the best romantic scenes take place on
ships," says Dot.

"Did you have any romance on the ship?" asks Betty
and I shake my head, remembering how sick I'd been.

"You're so lucky. I've never been anywhere," adds

Dot and I smile. They link their arms through mine as we walk back into class, as if I'm something special now.

4.

Mama has found a job teaching at the Jewish Endeavor Sewing School for a few dollars a week. Uncle Max said the owner took one look at the way Mama handled a needle and hired her. She'll be teaching a group of twelve young women to cut patterns and sew and alter. Mama is so happy, she's practically twirling around the kitchen, helping Louisa make dinner. She's an excellent seamstress. That's how she and Papa met, when she did her apprenticeship in the store where Papa worked. He was twenty years older than her, but it didn't matter. Mama said after one week, she knew, like her heart had been sewn up with white lace and would never open for anyone else. He taught her everything he knew about stitching, his big hands guiding hers over the fabric, his head bent close to hers in a way that must have been romantic. They were married within the month. Then Papa opened his own shop and Mama helped out, mostly doing the fine work, like stitching on lace or embroidering decorations. She'd sew on the trim, like the yellow ribbon around the hem of the matching dresses Papa made me and Sabine.

My mind drifts back to us in our dresses, running through puddles or in and out of the market stalls. Our mothers looked for us under all the tables, but we stayed still as stone, entwining fingers so tightly they were blue by the time they found us. The farm lady always laughed and gave us each a big red apple to eat. Now, she'd probably only give one to Sabine. She'd spit on mine first, or slip a piece of glass inside the flesh, like the wicked queen in "Snow White."

Uncle Max is excited too. He didn't find work, but seeing all the stores when he accompanied Mama to The Main, what everybody calls Saint-Laurent Boulevard, made him feel at home. They saw Feldman's, Reitman's, Brownstein's, Reichstein's and Steinberg's. And there were restaurants named Schwartz's and Wilensky's and Kravitz's. They stopped at Schwartz's Hebrew Deli and shared a smoked meat sandwich and coffee and listened to people talk about what was happening in our old country. It seems like everyone knew someone who was trying to get out but couldn't. "Mackenzie King's got the doors locked tighter than a nun's knees," one man said and everyone laughed.

"It made me so nervous to hear people badmouth the Prime Minister. Imagine if we'd said something like that about you know who," Mama told me afterward, her eyes twinkling.

5.

Annette has movie posters on her walls and doesn't seem embarrassed that nylon stockings are draped over the coal heater to dry. When I ask her where her parents sleep, she laughs. "My parents are back in the boonies, honey," she says. Then she explains that "boonies" means country or small town. "Lachute, to be exact," she says. "Population twelve. Excitement level, nil. Chance I'd ever return, minus a thousand."

I've never met a young woman who lives alone. I didn't think such a thing was even possible. Then I remember that Greta Garbo was twenty when she moved from Sweden to California and she still lives alone. So why shouldn't Annette? She has a poster of *Camille* on the wall, showing Robert Taylor grabbing Greta's shoulders. "Have you seen it?" Annette asks.

"Yes, in Munich," I say.

"Didn't you love the part where she's dying and

Armand finds her again? That reunion on the sickbed is just so heavenly." Annette plunges backward onto her bed and throws her arm over her forehead like she's Camille. Watching her takes me back to Papa's storage room in the basement of our building, dressing up with Sabine. It's hard to believe that was me, playacting so freely, writhing in pain with tuberculosis when I imitated Camille. Annette wouldn't believe me if I told her.

"Hey kid, do you know the jitterbug?" she asks, and I'm glad for the distraction. Thinking of Sabine always makes me sad.

"The what?" I ask.

Annette laughs. "It's a dance. I'm learning it so I can stop peddling cigarettes and get into one of the cabarets, like the Crystal Palace or the Cabaret Frolics. Want me to teach you?"

Before I can answer, fast-paced music is blaring from the record player and Annette is swinging her hips across the room to where I'm sitting. She pulls me up and starts spinning me this way and that, then she crouches down and tells me to jump over her back. When we both go crashing to the floor I think Annette will be mad, but she's doubled over laughing.

"I'll get us some Cokes," she says. She hands me a bottle of dark liquid and tells me to drink up. It's like my throat is being attacked by fizzing bubbles that sting as they go down, but it's delicious. "To us, kid," Annette says, clinking her bottle against mine.

"To us," I reply. It's the most perfect hour I've had all year.

6.

Dot invites me and Betty over after school to listen to *The Aldrich Family* on the radio. It's their favourite show and when the opening comes on, they join Henry's mother in shouting, "Henreeeeeeeeeeeeeeee! Henree Al-drich!" The story's about a boy who goes on a blind date that turns disastrous, from what I can tell. I don't catch all of it because the characters talk so fast. We drink Coke, sitting cross-legged on the braided rug and at the end of the show, when fast music comes on, Dot and Betty try to jitterbug. They're nowhere near as good as Annette. Betty calls, "What's the matter? Don't people like to have fun in Germany?" Suddenly, it feels like there's an ocean between me and these girls, wider than the one we sailed across to get here.

7.

Two envelopes sit on the kitchen table, "Return to Sender" stamped in red across our old address in Germany. Our letters to Papa. Aunt Naomi brings home bratwurst and beet salad but nobody eats a bite. It's like the letters are casting a spell on us, making us unable to lift our forks. Finally, Uncle Max says, "We don't know for sure what it means. We can't make assumptions."

Mama thanks Aunt Naomi for the food but says she isn't hungry. I know that can't be true. I wonder if it's because the food came from a German deli. But Herr and Frau Wetzler are so nice. When I go to the shop, they give me salted pretzels for free.

"Well, I'm hungry enough to eat a horse," Brian says. All we hear are the sounds of his utensils scraping the plate. "Waste not, want not," he says.

Even Louisa shoots him a dirty look.

8.

One Saturday, Annette knocks on the door and asks if I can come downtown with her for lunch. I haven't been downtown yet and I am practically bouncing up and down when Mama says yes.

"Great! I have a sister your age and she's the only thing I miss from home," says Annette. "Come on up and we'll get ready."

I sit on the couch and watch her shake out her curls and paint her toenails.

"Your clothes, kid. No offense, but is that all you have?"

I nod, looking down at my navy skirt and white blouse that seem so out of style next to Annette's mint-green dress, with its tight sash at the waist and its bow under the collar.

"Here, try these on," she says, handing me a pair of boots with laces all the way up the side. "And what about this top?" She tosses me a red sweater with shiny buttons down the front, along with a red hat and scarf. I feel completely new as we head to the streetcar in the lightly falling snow. Annette waves at the iceman, who is making his deliveries today from a sled pulled by two horses, and he waves back. We walk in his tracks, where the snow isn't as deep.

On Sainte-Catherine Street we sidestep the slushy puddles, then stand in front of the decorated windows at Simpson's and Eaton's and Morgan's, looking at all the wonderful things. Each window is done up like a movie set, telling its own story. I love the fox fur scarves wrapped around the mannequins' necks. I wish I could buy one for Mama, to help her keep warm. Annette points across the street to the Top Hat Café and tells me that's where she works. The sign is in the shape of a giant top hat, like the one Fred Astaire wore when he danced with Ginger Rogers.

"I saw that movie in Berlin," I say.

"You've sure been around, kid. Look up there. My first job was as a hostess at the Normandie Roof." She points to the top of the Mount Royal Hotel. "It was a great job, but the maître-d' had wandering hands, if you know what I mean." I don't tell her I don't.

We step into Woolworth's and sit at a round counter. Annette orders us each a hot dog and fries. I dip the fries in red sauce called ketchup, just like Annette. For dessert we each have a parfait that comes in a tall glass with a long spoon that we use to dig through the layers of whipped cream and chocolate ice cream to scoop up the cherries on the bottom.

The cherries are the colour of Annette's lips. On the streetcar home, she loops her arm through mine and I think Uncle Max was right. This new world is wonderful.

9.

After every test, Dot and Betty compare their marks. When we get our math tests back, I hide mine and don't show them that I got 100. Betty, who got 75, wants to know my score, but I just shrug. "My parents said girls don't need arithmetic anyways. Girls never do as good as boys," she says. But Mama is great with numbers and so am I. Mama did all of Papa's accounts for him and she's started doing some at the sewing school too. But I still don't say anything. I don't want to stand out in any way.

10.

By April the snow has stopped falling and tiny buds appear on some of the branches. Mama and I walk around Woodland Park and listen to baby birds chirping. We throw bits of stale bread to the mother robins, who fly them up to the nests. "Mama," I say, watching the red-breasted robins hunt for more crumbs, "tell me the truth. Where do you think Papa is now?" At school, we listen to the news on the radio and every time something comes on about Germany my heart stops, especially when they talk about crackdowns and riots. One announcer said, "Shame on Canada for not doing more to help rescue the

Jews who are being persecuted."

"You're getting older now Edie, so I can't hide things from you anymore. The truth is, I don't know. Without mail I can't get news. But things are bad there now. We can only pray that something will happen to get rid of Hitler and the Nazis before things get worse. One thing I know is your papa would be so happy to see us safe. We're like those birds up in the nest—even though Louisa's back room isn't the coziest. And," she points, "Papa would be like that bird there, fighting off the others to get us food. If we were there, it would be worse for him."

A ship's horn blasts across the river, its sound like a long lonely cry and I imagine it's Papa, agreeing with Mama.

II.

We paint Easter eggs in class, and I make sure mine are as pretty as the rest. At the end of the day, when all the kids are saying goodbye and talking about what they're doing for the long Easter weekend, I just shrug and say I don't know. I'm not trying to hide the fact that I'm Jewish at school, but I'm not *not* hiding it either. What would Papa say to that?

For Passover, Uncle Max brings home a pack of Matzah from a deli on The Main. We don't eat with Louisa and Brian and instead say a prayer over the flat bread in our room, our blankets wrapped around our backs for warmth. We look like a tribe in the desert, huddled under tents. Uncle Max tells the story of Passover, where Moses freed the Hebrew slaves from Egypt and led them to safety across the waters that parted in half to let them through.

I pray that wherever Papa is, rough waters are parting so that he can join us.

12.

The King and Queen of England are visiting Montreal, so Miss Madison tells us we don't have to come to class as long we promise to attend the parade. The crowds on Sainte-Catherine Street are so thick, Uncle Max and I can barely see the road. We push our way to Morgan's department store, where a big balcony has been added to the front of the building, its roof in the shape of a crown. On it stands a life-sized statue of King George and Queen Elizabeth. Chants of "God save the King" fill the air as everyone waves little Union Jacks.

Uncle Max pulls me in front of him so I can actually

see the row of black cars heading toward us. "They must be in that one," he shouts, pointing to the biggest one in the middle. Sure enough, a minute later, the King and Queen of England roll past, waving from the back seat. The Queen's face is warm and friendly. When she turns in my direction, I feel like she's smiling right at me.

Uncle Max bends down and shouts in my ear, "These are the people who might save your papa, Edie." I wave my flag even faster, to encourage them.

13.

On the last day of school, Miss Madison wishes us all a wonderful summer and says she'll see us in September. Everyone hangs around saying goodbye, making promises to stay in touch. Dot says she and Betty will see me, for sure. The city is building a new pool, the Natatorium, down by the river and maybe we can all go swimming together, or to Belmont Park which is full of amazing rides. She makes it sound like so much fun. She makes it sound like all the stuff we're hearing on the radio isn't real, the world is still the same and Papa's life isn't in danger. If I do all those fun things with her, will it mean I've stopped caring about him?

14.

Annette has a new boyfriend, Vincent, who looks like Cary Grant. "He doesn't like me working," Annette tells me one day when I'm at her place, watching her get ready for a date. "He says I don't have to anymore, but I'm not sure. If I let him pay my rent and everything, you know what that will make me, don't you?"

"No, what?"

"A kept woman, and I'm not sure I'm ready for that. I've got to be careful. I'm pretty much on my own here, you know?"

"But you have me and Mama," I say. "And Louisa." But it's true we couldn't help her with money. Mama is paying rent to Louisa and Brian now, for our room. Plus she's saving so we can get our own place. She doesn't want us to spend another winter in that cold back room. Uncle Max says his bones are still sore.

"That's sweet, kid. A girl's gotta grab her chances, though," says Annette. "Always remember that kid. Opportunity doesn't knock twice. Vincent's a gentleman and there's not many of them around, at least not in this city."

I want to tell her that Papa is a gentleman. I never once heard Papa speak meanly to Mama, not even when she broke his best sewing machine, but I never talk about Papa to Annette.

Later, I watch Vincent run around the car to open the door for Annette. When he gets in he reaches across the steering wheel and kisses her cheek. She waves up at me and I wonder how she knew I was watching.

15.

Mama is letting me go to Belmont Park with Dot and Betty. She even gives me a quarter, and so do Uncle Max and Aunt Naomi. Louisa contributes too, taking a quarter out of the tin on top of the ice box. Brian pulls another one out of his pocket and hands it over. "Make it an even buck," he says.

"Every kid in this city remembers their first trip to Belmont Park," says Louisa. "It's a special thing. Have cotton candy for me—it's delicious." I look around the table and blink, trying not to cry. Everyone is being so generous.

The number 17 streetcar rolls through busy streets, then past fields and farms. We loop arms and sing the "Beer Barrel Polka" over and over, belting out the chorus about having a "barrel of fun." When we get to the part about how "the gang's all here," I force myself to keep

singing and not to think of Papa. The gang is all here—
me and Dot and Betty—who can be sort of nice, in spite
of her stupid questions. Everyone is watching us, but Dot
and Betty don't seem to care. Even the ticket-taker laughs
when he punches our tickets, so it must be all right.

We enter the park under an arch where the words
"Belmont Park" are lit up. The sound of laughter and
screaming fills the air. We buy our tickets and walk past
The Whip and the Tumble Bug to get to The Cyclone.
Betty says it's the only place to start. The roller coaster
looms above us, looking like a wooden railroad that got
twisted in a storm. We stand in line for the five-cent ride,
watching people shoot guns at moving ducks or pitch
balls into baskets.

The three of us share a car, with me in the middle.
My knuckles are white on the bar as we whip around
a corner and stop at the top of a long drop. I gasp, then
close my eyes and feel my stomach rise into my mouth
as the car flies down. Dot and Betty are screaming beside
me, their hands in the air. Then, without thinking, I
am too. It's like I'm falling into another time and place.
There's no time to think or remember. There's just the
feeling of flying—free as a swooping sea bird.

16.

For lunch we buy hot dogs from a chip wagon and swirling sticks of cotton candy. Thick grains of sugar stick to my teeth, but it's delicious, like Louisa said. In the middle of the grounds a huge mechanical fat lady with red lips keeps shaking and laughing. The sign at her feet says "*La grosse femme*, Laffing Sal."

Beyond her stands a building that says "Freak Show." A huge placard announces the attractions—a bearded lady, a midget, a man with seven fingers on each hand, and "many other phenomes."

"Oh, I love these," says Dot. "Let's go in!"

The dark hallway is lined with cages, a bare lightbulb hanging from the ceiling in each, lighting up the person inside. In one, a midget is sitting on top of a trunk reading a newspaper that almost hides his body. In another, an enormous woman, almost the size of Laffing Sal, lies on a bed, looking like a huge puffed-up eiderdown. The man with seven fingers is sitting with his back to us, writing a letter at a desk. "Oh, I can see them," Dot says, "if you look over his shoulder." Betty is on her tiptoes, trying to see better.

"What if he hears us? Won't he feel terrible?" I ask.

"We're supposed to look. That's why we're here," says Betty.

At the end of the hall, a sign says, "The Hirsute Hebrew."

"What does hirsute mean?" asks Betty, as she runs ahead. I couldn't answer, even if I knew. But I do know what the word *Hebrew* means. Up ahead, Dot and Betty have covered their mouths with their hands.

"You have to see this," they both call out.

"He's like an orangutan," Dot exclaims as I shuffle toward them.

"Worse, like a gorilla," adds Betty. I take a deep breath and lift my head.

The man is sitting on a plain wooden chair facing us. He's wearing short pants and his chest is bare, exposing the piles of hair growing out of it. The same mat of hair covers his arms, his neck, and even his face. His eyes stare out from the hair, looking right past us, like we're not even here. The only other thing on him is a thick silver chain. At the end of it hangs a Star of David. When I see it my whole body turns numb and I too cover my mouth. The food in my stomach starts to bubble up, like a volcano. I run outside, and vomit on a patch of grass. My entire lunch comes out of me, including the cotton candy, faster than if I were spinning upside down on the Roll-O-Plane.

Dot and Betty are standing over me.

"What happened?" asks Dot.

"She ate too much cotton candy," says Betty. "She's not used to it, like us."

I raise myself from the grass and nod. I don't bother trying to correct them.

17.

Uncle Max and Aunt Naomi are moving closer to The Main. They say we can go with them, but their new place is small, smaller than here. Uncle Max says they could get a pull-out sofa for the living room, if that's what we really want. Sometimes, at night, we hear Brian ask Louisa how much longer we'll be here. I know they're hoping we'll say yes to Uncle Max's offer. If only Papa were here, the three of us would get our own place.

"Edie and I can look after ourselves, so don't worry about us," Mama says. "We always expected to make our own way one day, didn't we Edie?"

"Yes, Mama." I guess it's true, if she says so.

18.

Mama and I walk along the river, past the new Natatorium. I wonder if Dot and Betty are in there, twirling around in the water like dolphins or suntanning on the cement side. I haven't heard from them since Belmont Park and, in a way, that's okay. The picnic tables here are full of people eating and drinking and laughing, but Mama and I walk silently, watching the choppy water. Finally, Mama turns to me and says, "I don't want you to worry, Edie. I'm making good money and I'm saving for us. Even if Papa never makes it here, we'll be okay. Max and Naomi will always be here for us. They're not abandoning us. They're just trying to get established."

We walk along further, watching kids play volleyball and badminton. I wonder what it's like to be them.

19.

Annette takes me downtown to see *The Wizard of Oz*. When the wicked witch unleashes the evil monkeys and Dorothy has to run for her life, we grab each other's hands and scrunch down in our seats. But the worst part is when Toto pulls back the curtain to reveal that the wizard is fake. I can feel Dorothy's hope draining through me and leaking out onto the cinema floor.

"If you could click your heels and go anywhere, where would you go?" Annette asks later, when we're sitting at the shiny Woolworth's counter eating ice cream sundaes. "I'd go to Paris, to see the real Folies Bergère."

"I'd click my heels and make my papa float across the ocean in a balloon."

"Oh Edie. You never talk about your father. Why doesn't he just come on his own?" Annette asks.

"It's not that easy," I answer. "You can't just get out ... if you're Jewish." I hold my breath and feel my heart pounding. I have never told Annette, or anyone else here, that I'm Jewish. She may already know, from Louisa. I pray it won't make a difference. I don't mind losing Dot and Betty, but I can't lose Annette. When we link arms on the streetcar, I'm sure people think she's my big sister.

"Well," says Annette. "If Dorothy could find a way out of Oz, your father will find a way out of Germany. Here, have my cherries." She scoops out the purplish berries from the bottom of her dish and plops them into mine.

"I hope so," I say. In my mind, I skip down a yellow brick road toward Papa.

20.

Uncle Max is going to be helping his new friend, Mr. Brownstein, open Montreal's newest department store on The Main. "It will be four floors high and full of wonderful stuff. Hannah, when it's all set up, you'll be head of alterations. And when Jacob joins us, well, he'll be our head tailor, of course." There is a light in Uncle Max's eyes, like he used to have.

Later, as he and Aunt Naomi are packing their few possessions, I overhear Uncle Max try to talk Mama into moving with them. "It will be better for Edie, Hannah. She can go to Baron Byng High School. And you already work down there. Please think about it. It's more important than ever that our people stick together."

"We'll be fine, Max. Please don't worry. And didn't we leave Germany because we wanted to be where we could just be people? Edie's doing well at school here. It doesn't matter if she's Jewish. A school where everyone is Jewish or a neighbourhood where everyone is Jewish. Is that what we came to the new world for? It sounds like what we left. Isn't that what you keep talking about, how they are rounding us up and creating ghettos?"

Uncle Max looks angry and Aunt Naomi crosses the

room to Mama and puts her arms around her. "Let's not fight. We're not going far. You can visit anytime and we'll see a lot of each other. Max, Hannah just wants to stay put. I can understand that. Max is right—we do have to stick together. But we don't have to live two feet away to do that."

Uncle Max turns to me and says, "And this one, such a beauty! In a few years you'll be our top model, showing off all the Paris styles for the wealthy women of Montreal." I feel myself blush.

21.

Brian knocks on our door and tells us to come quick. We follow him to the parlour where he turns up the volume on the radio and tells everyone to be quiet. A man is announcing that Germany has invaded Poland, *going boldly against the treaty and launching a surprise attack before dawn this morning. Although initial reports show that the Poles are fighting back bravely, it can only be a matter of time before the world will be at war.*

Nobody says a word for a long time. Then, finally, Brian stands up and says, "Well, that's it folks. Hang on to your hats. It's only a matter of time until Canada is dragged into Europe—again."

Why does Brian fix his eyes on me and Mama as he says this, like it's our fault?

22.

On Sunday, when Louisa and Brian come home from church, we gather around the radio to listen to the same man announce that Great Britain and France have declared war on Germany. *Mark this day in your calendars,* the man says, *September 3, 1939. A date history will no doubt remember for a long time to come.*

"What did I tell you," says Brian. "Canada will be next. We can't leave the Brits hanging."

Back in our room, Mama and I sit on our beds and pray for Papa. If he didn't get out before now, he'll be stuck. We each have our own bed, now that Uncle Max and Aunt Naomi are gone. Mama sewed some pretty curtains and bedspreads from material at work. The room is brighter than ever, but it doesn't help.

23.

I don't want to go back to school, but Mama says I have to. "Now, more than ever," she says. But I don't get that, not with so much going on in the world. The mood in the classroom is different. Our new homeroom teacher, Mrs. Bouchard, says that we'll follow the war daily and make it part of our Grade 9 history and geography lessons.

"It may seem far away, but it's not," she says. "In time, you may all know someone who is right in the middle of it. Information is power." I don't know why she'd say such a stupid thing. Sometimes you can know everything and still have no power.

24.

Mrs. Bouchard turns on the radio at 1 PM for the war report and we find out that a passenger ship called the SS *Athenia* was torpedoed by a German submarine off the coast of Ireland. The announcer says: *"On board were 1100 passengers, including 500 Jewish refugees desperate to flee Europe before the war escalates. Also on board were 469 Canadians, including many crew members. Rescue operations ran through the night, with at least six nearby vessels pitching in."*

As the bold voice goes on I'm barely listening. All I can think about is the ship, lying in pieces at the bottom of the Atlantic Ocean, along with 500 Jewish refugees.

Later that evening, Annette comes downstairs in tears. She's just found out that her friend, Hannah Baker, was one of those crew members. The two of them used to waitress together at the Top Hat. Mama rubs her back and tells her she's sorry, but her eyes are far away, and I wonder if she too is thinking of Papa. What if he was one of those Jewish refugees?

25.

Today, there's a special announcement by Prime Minister Mackenzie King. Mrs. Bouchard cranks up the volume and we hear him say: *"There is no home in Canada, no family and no individual whose fortunes and freedom are not bound up in the present struggle. I appeal to my fellow Canadians to unite in a national effort to save from destruction all that makes life itself worth living and to preserve for future generations those liberties and institutions which others have bequeathed to us."*

When he's done, Mrs. Bouchard puts her hand over her heart and motions for everyone to stand. She makes us sing "God Save the King" and salute the Union Jack that hangs in the corner of our classroom.

"You can have free time for the rest of the day. It's not every day that a Canadian prime minister announces that we're at war," says Mrs. Bouchard, taking her seat.

Dot and Betty are bouncing with excitement in the corner. "My sister says they'll probably open a base in Verdun, because of the river. Imagine all the handsome sailors," says Dot.

"Wait. Aren't you our enemy now?" asks Betty, pointing at me. "I mean, you're from Germany, aren't you?" Other kids stare at me and I can feel myself grow hot.

"We came here to get away from Germany. We're on your side," I say.

"But how?" asks a guy named Gary. "How can you be against your own country? That doesn't make sense."

I remember the day Frau Farber made me move to the back of the class with the other Jewish kids. And how she stopped asking us questions or calling on us to read or do math at the board. And how we weren't allowed at assemblies and how I had to return my gold medal. Somehow, I know that the way I answer will decide how I'm treated in this school for the rest of the year. "I was born in Germany but my family is Jewish, for your information. And, for us, the war didn't just start today. It started many years ago. Why else do you think I'd leave my best friend and my papa so far behind? The Germans have already tried to kill me."

Gary's eyes grow wide and there is complete silence in the room. I sit down with my head held high and take out my history book. If anyone tells me to move, I'll refuse. When the bell rings and I'm packing up, a paper flower falls onto my desk, intricate as a rose, with dozens of paper petals. Gary turns and smiles at me from the door.

26.

Brian has joined the Royal Canadian Navy. "I've spent almost every waking hour of my adult life down at the docks, I might as well make the leap into the water," he says. After dinner, he shows off his navy blue uniform, which has an anchor on the sleeve, and a hat that looks like a white dinner plate. Louisa says she's proud of him, but she looks scared too. "We're going to get those U-Boats, one by one. No more Canadians are going to be killed by those Krauts." He turns his arm into a machine gun and fires a round of invisible shells around the kitchen. He stops at Mama. "Sorry, Hannah. Didn't mean to scare you."

Mama holds up her arms, like she's surrendering. "Don't apologize," she says. "It's about time the world tries to stop the Nazis." I wonder if she also didn't like the word

"Krauts." Sauerkraut is our favourite food and Mama picks up a jar sometimes on her way home from work.

27.

Annette quit her job at the Top Hat Café. Vincent gave her something called an ultimatum: work there or be his girl. Now, when she gets ready to go out, she talks about what he wants her to wear and how he wants her to fix her hair. "He doesn't like me to wear too much makeup," she says. "Just enough but not so much that I've crossed the line." When he honks, she kisses my cheek, leaving a light brush of red, and says, "See ya, kid," before running down the stairs. I feel like she's crossing a line whenever she leaves me.

28.

On the weekend, Mama and I head to the German deli to buy some bread. We gasp when we see it. The front windows are smashed and someone has painted the words "Germans go home" on the door. There is no sign of the Wetzlers anywhere. "Poor people," Mama says. "We know how they feel, don't we Edie?" On a jagged piece of glass, someone has painted a Swastika. It's in the exact spot where the Star of David was painted onto Papa's shop window.

29.

The day that Brian leaves for training in Halifax, Mama and I stay in our room, to give him and Louisa some privacy. We can hear Louisa crying. A few minutes later, Brian taps on our door and opens it up. "Goodbye ladies," he says. "Please look out for Louisa when I'm gone. She's not as strong as she pretends to be." Then he salutes, like he's already on board the ship. Mama runs to the street corner and calls her boss at the sewing school and tells him she'll be late. She spends the morning in Louisa's room, hugging her and bringing breakfast on a tray.

30.

We spend the last night of Chanukah in Uncle Max and Aunt Naomi's new apartment. It's on a corner, above a sandwich shop. Uncle Max was right—it *is* tiny, but they already have pretty pictures cut from magazines on the walls. Red and green lights from a store across the street flash on and off, filling the room with a colourful pulse, and fat snow is falling, turning the little window into a lacy curtain. We say a special prayer for Papa, hoping he's safe, wherever he is and that, somehow, he's eating good food on this special night.

1940

SABINE

I.

We all walk Papa to the train station. Hans carries his big suitcase, which holds all of Papa's medical instruments. It's so heavy Hans keeps scraping it along the cobblestones and I imagine the leather scratching underneath. I want to tease him about how all that boxing hasn't made him as strong as he thinks, but nobody is speaking and I don't want to break the heavy silence. It drags and scrapes as much as Papa's luggage.

The station platform is packed with people. Some are pacing back and forth under the wooden awning, others are clustered in groups, like us. Papa will take two trains, a shorter one to Stuttgart, then a longer one to Berlin. In his leather handbag, which he carries strapped across his chest, are important designs that he says he must never lose. I wonder if they look like all the other designs Papa has shown us over the years—sheets of onionskin paper covered in a mess of arrows and numbers, the outline of instruments emerging like a magic trick.

Papa holds Mama against his chest when the train appears. He kisses the top of my head and says, "When I see you next you'll be a young woman. Mama, don't let the boys get too close." He laughs but Mama doesn't laugh back. She holds her embroidered handkerchief under her eyes, catching the drip in a cluster of roses.

"Promise you'll send a telegram when you arrive, Hermann," Mama says.

"Of course, of course, I will. Don't worry. Hans, look after Sabine and Mama." He shakes my brother's hand and adds, "Make me proud, son."

"I will, Papa. Heil Hitler," Hans replies, throwing up his arm. Papa does it back, then heads to the train. His coat balloons around him as he climbs the stairs, right above a puff of steam.

2.

Maria announces that party officials are looking for BDM

girls to help out in a new *Kinderlandverschickung* camp that's opening outside our town, one of hundreds around the country. "The homes are not for evacuations," Maria explains. "They're an opportunity for kids from big cities to have fun and adventure in the fresh air of the countryside."

After the meeting, Maria calls me over and says, "I think you would be perfect for this job, Sabine. You're quiet and you won't be the type of girl to run her mouth off. Should I forward your name?"

I know it will look bad if I say no, and besides, most girls stop going to school at fourteen and I'll have nothing else to do with my time. "Thank you, Maria. Yes, please," I say.

"Heil Hitler," says Maria and I lift my arm and say it back.

Mama is pleased. She says it will be a chance for me to meet kids from big cities, kids who've been to department stores and ridden on subways. That could be fun. Opa hears her from his pantry and calls out that there's nothing wrong with small towns. "They are the heart and soul of Germany, with their good decent folk. In the city, everyone is corrupted by American music and movies."

Mama just shakes her head and drifts away from the table.

3.

Hans has become obsessed with the study of heads. He uses a tape and compass to measure skulls, then consults the charts and diagrams in his Hitler Youth handbook. He even hangs a poster of different head types on the wall in the kitchen, as if he needs to keep reminding himself which is his.

He practices on Opa and determines that Opa is a Nordic type—strong and pure. "Of course," says Opa, "What else would I be?" I think he looks anything but strong. The doctor says his kidneys are failing and that's why he's getting thinner each day.

When Gabi and Inge come over to plan our next BDM collection date, they ask Hans to measure their skulls. He takes his time wrapping the tape around their foreheads, touching their hair on purpose.

"Well, I'm happy to announce that your new friends are all Nordic girls, not like *that friend* you used to bring home, Sabine."

He means Edie. Has he really forgotten her name?

4.

Our next-door neighbour has another baby, her fourth. Some officials from the Nazi party come by to award her the *Mutterkreuz*, the Mother Cross. She shows off the bright blue cross with the Swastika in the middle by hanging it from her baby's carriage. When she walks past our house, she holds her head high and doesn't speak to Mama, as though she can't be bothered saying hello to someone who only gave two children to the Fatherland.

"You should have more children, Mama," says Hans. "It's your duty."

"What happens between a woman and her husband is nobody else's business, Hans," Mama replies.

"That's not true, Mama. Everything we do is now the Führer's business. Everything we do is for him. Maybe when Papa comes home," he says. But Mama shoots him the meanest look I've ever seen her give and it silences even Hans, who never seems to run out of opinions.

5.

Mama and I go into town with our ration stamps. We buy three bars of Unity Soap that has to last us four months. It's a disgusting greyish green, and full of grit that hurts

my skin. It seems like years ago that we had soft pink soap
that smelled like flowers. This soap doesn't even lather and
it leaves the tub full of scum that Mama has to scrub away.
It's probably a good thing that we're only allowed to take
baths on the weekends now, to save water. We also pick up
toilet rolls that are rough and brown, like wrapping paper.
When we buy a tin of herring, the shopkeeper pulls open
the corner and Mama gasps. The man explains it's a new
order, to prevent hoarding. "People should just buy what
they need for the moment. We are all in this together," he
says, as if Mama was trying to do something wrong.

Around the corner, away from the main square, a
small woman in a dark coat is standing under a sign that
says *Jüdische Winterhilfe*. I didn't know there was also
a Jewish Winter Relief. At her feet is a box with some
food and clothing in it. Mama tells me to wait here while
she runs across and slips the opened tin into the box.
Suddenly, some brownshirts come marching down the
street, their tall boots loud on the stone. Mama runs back
to me and I turn to see what the woman will do, but the
sign, the woman and the box are already gone, vanished
in a flash, like some trick by the famous Houdini.

I hope the tin of herring's on its way to Herr Pinker.

6.

BDM teams go door to door, selling homemade goods we made at our meetings—crocheted coasters to put under coffee cups and little packages of ginger-spice cookies wrapped in red ribbons. All the money will go to the Winter Relief Fund. At each house, we ask for donations of warm clothing: underpants, undershirts, socks, suspenders, warmers, hats, earmuffs, scarves, gloves or furs of any kind. Sometimes, we have to pull them from the women's fingers, like a mini tug-of-war, and I know the items belong to sons and husbands who are away fighting.

Suddenly, we're on Edie's street, moving closer and closer to her building. I don't want to go inside, but I can't say that to Gabi and Inge. We do the first two floors and collect more money and goods. When Gabi starts up the stairs, I want to tell her not to bother, but how can I do that without saying why? So, we all go up, my heart pounding louder than last time. But we stop halfway. Painted on the Pinkers' door is a yellow Jewish star.

"No point in going any further," says Inge. "They should find a way of telling us below, so we don't waste our energy. So inconsiderate."

We wind back down, our arms piled with goods which we deposit in a wagon.

"Oh no," I say. "I must have dropped my mitts. I'll have to run back up."

"Do it fast," orders Gabi.

I take the stairs two at a time and toss a warm hat and two packets of cookies on the top step, near Herr Pinker's door. I feel bad doing it that way, as if I'm tossing a bone to a stray dog, but I have no choice. The other girls are not happy waiting and their feet are cold. We haul our load to the meeting hall, where Maria is very impressed with our work. I hope she won't add up the money and calculate how many packets of cookies we sold. If she does, I'll say I got hungry and ate some myself. How much trouble could I get in for that?

7.

In the spring, Hans's head gets even bigger when he wins a fight in Ulm. He was representing our province, Baden-Württemberg, in the 16-17-year-old division. Our local branch of the *Völkischer Beobachter* publishes an article with a big picture of him in the ring, his fists raised, a gold medallion hanging around his neck. Opa tapes a copy of the article above his bed and Mama sends a copy to Papa. Nobody bothers to mention that we usually use that newspaper for toilet paper because it's softer than the rolls we get with our ration stamps.

That same night, Hans and Opa are excited because the Führer himself is on the radio, announcing that everyone has to fly a flag from their window for eight days to salute our soldiers for their successes and to get them in the mood for conquering France. Hans runs to our window and unfurls his long Nazi flag.

"Good timing," says Opa in his raspy voice. "They'll think this display is for you, for your victory."

I want to rip it away but I'm afraid of what Hans will do to me with his prize-winning fists.

8.

On the radio, Hitler says, "Dunkirk has fallen ... with it has ended the greatest battle of world history. Soldiers! My confidence in you knew no bounds. You have not disappointed me." Hans and Opa cheer. A few weeks later, Hans moves his map from the kitchen to above Opa's bed, so that Opa can watch as he sticks a pin in Paris. I can only imagine the smiles on their faces.

9.

Summer comes and Gabi and Inge, now eighteen, leave for their *Pflichtjahr*. For their duty year, they're going all the way to Poland, to help teach the people who live there how to clean and cook like proper Germans. They had special training where they learned important things about hygiene and setting a table the German way, with flowers in the middle.

The whole group goes with them to the train station and waves at the dirty windows, like we did with Papa. Then I go home to help Mama feed Opa his broth and give him his sponge bath with our dwindling supply of soap. In the evening, Mama moves the radio as close to the pantry as she can so that he can follow the Führer's successes without getting up. If we turn the dial away from the state station, a jamming noise squeals through the speaker and hurts our ears.

Hans has added red pins to Denmark, Norway, Luxembourg, the Netherlands, Norway and France. The map looks like it has a rash. Hans is impatient to stick a pin in the one place that he's most anxious to conquer, but Great Britain's air force is strong. Opa says, "Don't worry, ours is stronger, and it's only a matter of time."

Hans is sitting on the end of Opa's bed, a red pin in his hand like a blister.

10.

The KLV is finally set up in an old guesthouse outside of town, at the foot of a trail through the mountains. It's a long white building with dark wood trim crisscrossing the walls. Mama and Papa and Hans and I used to go there for dinner, after we'd hiked through the woods on Saturday afternoons, when Mama would collect edible mushrooms in a burlap bag. Sometimes, Papa would play old songs on the piano. Other people in the room would sing along with him and Hans and I would dance like they taught us to at school, with our arms around each other.

Soon after the KLV is established, twenty girls arrive by train. I'm up at the guesthouse, waiting to greet them in my BDM uniform. I watch them come down the road, walking two-by-two, their little bags strapped over their shoulders. They're so young, I wonder if they've ever spent a night away from home.

Their beds are waiting for them, four in each room, and I try to smile as much as I can as I help them settle in. Frau Prinz, the *Hausmutter*, told me not to be too kind. She said that would just make them homesick right away. She told me not to touch them, so I don't, even though I'd like to give them a hug or stroke their hair— they look like they could use the affection. One girl peed on the walk and it has dribbled into her socks. I bring up a cloth and water and help her wash and change. "Don't worry," I tell her, "I've done that too. Everyone has, at one time." Her eyes go wide like she doesn't know whether to believe me, but a small smile curls on her lips.

I'm glad Frau Prinz isn't watching.

II.

Mid-week an older girl named Emma shows up at the camp. She's on her own duty year. Now, I have help in the kitchen when I'm peeling potatoes and carrots for the midday meal or washing dishes in the deep stone sink. Emma has her own little room in the attic, and she doesn't say much, but by the end of the week she starts talking to me.

"I can't believe the most exciting thing that's happened to me all week was watching some owls crack open their eggs and get born," she says.

"I love owls," I respond. We're washing sheets on the stove, boiling them in a big pot. We each have a long wooden spoon that we use to swish around the material.

"Let's pretend we're witches, getting this pot ready for Frau Prinz," Emma says. I freeze. If Frau Prinz heard that, we'll both be in trouble. But it's also really funny, so I hide my mouth behind my hand and laugh in a way that I haven't done since Edie left.

12.

Maria orders everyone at our BDM meeting to watch a new movie called *Jud Süß*. It's about a Jewish man who tricks the Duke of Württemberg into lifting a ban on Jews in the city of Stuttgart. Then the Jew rapes a sweet German girl and attacks her papa and fiancé.

Emma whispers in my ear that she's from Stuttgart. "It's a beautiful city," she says.

"Do you think this movie is true?" I ask her.

"I've never heard of anything like that happening. It's probably what Papa would call *propaganda*."

"What's that?"

"Lies, basically."

Emma goes on to tell me that her papa was taken

away by the Nazis last year for speaking against them and just two months ago her mother was taken too, to a place called Ravensbrück. Emma lived with her aunt and uncle until coming here.

"It's movies like this that are getting Jews killed," she whispers.

Maria shushes us from the back of the room. We're supposed to fully concentrate, as if we might run into this *Süß* guy on the streets of our town and have to be able to recognize him. If not, he'll throw his cloak over us and scare us with his long pointed nose and crooked teeth.

I want to ask Emma what she meant about Jews being killed.

13.

The doctor says it's a miracle that Opa is still hanging on. "Perhaps he's just waiting for the big victory, right Hermann?" jokes the doctor. Opa smiles weakly. The doctor leaves a bottle of medicine for Opa's pain. Mama waits until after the nightly war report to give it to him on a soup spoon, otherwise he can't concentrate. The medicine makes him dopey and if he tries to speak his words slur. Mama's hands are worn raw from washing Opa's sheets and we're low on laundry powder, so they never really come clean. I can smell his pee all over the house.

I wonder how someone as frail as Opa can keep clinging to life. He is constantly asking for news about papa. We share the postcards and telegrams that he sends, but they don't reveal much. Papa can't tell us exactly what he's doing but it has something to do with designing things that are needed for the war. I imagine beautiful guns, with mother-of-pearl handles, like his knives. But I don't like to think about what the guns are used for. So many thoughts swirl in my head at night when I go to bed. Maybe it would be easier to be like Hans. Hans is so sure about everything, like who our enemy is. Everyone says it's the Jews but how can they be so threatening, especially now, when we rarely see them.

My only enemy is Hans. Since his boxing victory, he's been unbearable. The other day he held his fist up to Mama and told her she needed to make better food, even with the rationing. I'm sure Papa wouldn't approve, but I'm not allowed to write to him.

14.

Hans is working feverishly on his *Ahnenpaß*. He spends

hours in the church basement going through records, writing down the names and dates of our ancestors, or wandering through the old cemetery, looking for stones of dead people we may be related to. If he wants to join Hitler's elite police force, the *Schutzstaffel*, he needs to be able to prove that he has Aryan blood all the way back to 1800 and to be a senior officer he needs to make it to 1750. He's pretty close to 1800 now, which isn't that hard since Opa was born in 1857, and when he's not drugged or sleeping, he can give Hans details on his parents. But word of mouth is not enough for the Nazi officials. You have to be able to prove your ancestry with official records. I wonder what Hans would do if he uncovered something he didn't want to know.

15.

At our BDM meeting, Maria is lecturing about "foreign elements." She has put up an even bigger map than the one Hans has at home, and she has different coloured pins: red for victory, yellow for getting close, and green for enroute—like traffic lights.

"Our town is now free of racially impure elements," she says and a huge lump travels up my throat. If I say something, she'll tell the officials and they'll visit our house and threaten Mama, so I swallow it. It scrapes like a million pins, reminding me of Herr Pinker. Then Maria distributes class readers, the type we used in school.

"We're doing some work for the schools today," she says. "Turn to page 132. Now, grab and rip with all your might, to get rid of that filth."

It's the poem "Lorelei," which tells the story of a siren who sits on a famous rock in the Rhine and lures sailors to their deaths. We read it over and over in class and even sang it at a concert for our parents. But now it is *verboten*, like so many other things.

"The author was a Jew," says Maria, as if that changes the poem.

16.

Emma rolls her eyes when Frau Prinz says something ridiculous, like how we should never run. "Girls don't run," Frau Prinz repeats. "They walk quickly but elegantly." Sometimes, between chores, Emma and I go out back into the large field and practice walking quickly and elegantly, but we always end up breaking into a run. We make daisy chains and wear them like crowns, pretending we're queens of the hilltop. Emma tells me about a thing called a concentration camp and I don't know whether to believe her. I thought concentration was when you paid close attention to the teacher at school.

"But it also means when you put a lot of things together in one place. In this case, it's people who the government says are hurting Germany. Like my parents," she says. "They're practically Communists." She tells me that Ravensbrück, where her mother is, is also a concentration camp. I thought it was just a town. Emma knows so much and I wonder if living in a big city, with more newspapers and a university, makes that happen. If so, that's where I'd like to live one day, when the war is over. In this town, nobody seems to know much about anything.

17.

I always look up at Edie's window when I'm walking home, hoping to see a sign of life. It's been six months since I last visited Herr Pinker. I'm dying to talk to Emma about Edie and her family, to get her opinion. Maybe she'd tell me I'm wasting my time, that there's no hope anyone is still living there. But little things tell me there is hope. The curtains, which are always pulled tight, sometimes seem to shake. And the line where they meet in the middle isn't always in the same spot. Sometimes it's a bit to the right, other times to the left. Maybe Herr Pinker is getting help from that woman on the street who was collecting money. Not all the Jews in our town are gone. From time to time, I see someone who I know is Jewish walking quickly, pressed against the walls or fences, never meandering. Sometimes, I see someone who could be Herr Pinker even, from a distance, but he never looks up.

One day, a dim light is shining in the basement window of Edie's building, where the Pinkers' storeroom was. But the light is so faint, I can't be sure, and the bushes in front of the window obscure the view even more. In my mind, I see Edie down there, rummaging through the box of old clothes, transforming herself into someone new. And me, standing beside her, eager to join the show.

I can't imagine I ever once played so freely with a Jew.

18.

Hans has been chosen to go north and work as a flak helper. His group leader said it's because Hans is strong and diligent, plus he has a positive attitude. He'll be living his dream, helping real soldiers fire bullets at enemy planes. He'll have a whole new uniform and everything.

"A seventeen-year-old shouldn't be asked to do such work," says Mama.

"But that's ridiculous," says Hans. "I'm practically a man, Mama. We all need to pitch in. You and Sabine can finish working on the *Ahnenpaß*. I'll be fine, you'll see. To try to stop me is to go against Hitler." Mama doesn't say any more.

We're only allowed to walk with Hans to the station, where he's meeting up with two other Hitler Youth who have also been chosen, but he tells us we can't hang around waiting for the train. It would be too embarrassing.

"We'll say goodbye here, Mama," he says, holding out his hand, his jaw clenched tight. He turns to me and his blue eyes betray a hint of water. "Be good, Sabine," he says.

Mama is holding her arms tight at her sides, and I know she wants to throw them around my brother's broad shoulders. He is wearing a dark green jacket that looks new. "You'll write often?" she asks.

Hans nods. "I'll be fine, Mama." Then his friends are calling him and the sound of the train chugging closer drowns out our final goodbyes. A larger group of Hitler Youth, there to wave Hans and the others goodbye, starts singing "The Flag on High":

> *Our banner flutters before us*
> *Our banner represents the new era*
> *Our banner leads us to eternity*
> *Yes, our banner means more to us than death.*

Poor Mama! When they sing the last line, she sucks in her breath and I have to tug on her to make her let it out.

19.

Saturday afternoons all the girls at the KLV are given rhythmic gymnastics lessons in the field. Emma and I are allowed to join in. We prance around swirling ribbons above our heads, trampling the tall grass underneath. We throw balls to our partners, then see how many times we can twirl before catching them. Our instructor, Isabella, is tall and elegant. She can roll a ball down the entire length of her leg, then flick it up so that it arches over her head like a rainbow. Then she spins, and catches it dead centre in front of her chest.

"I performed for Hitler, in Berlin and Nuremberg, with a group of forty girls," Isabella says. "If you're good enough, I might be able to get you a spot, but you have to train hard, at least four hours every day. The last time I performed, Hitler singled me out and shook my hand. I almost melted there on the spot. When that man stares into your eyes it's like an electric charge." She stares off dreamily, like she's reliving the moment.

Emma doesn't do what Isabella says. Instead, she places the ball at her feet and kicks it in and out of an imaginary obstacle course. When she reaches the trees, she kicks it hard. "Score!" she shouts, throwing her arms in the air. Frau Prinz, who is watching from the sidelines, calls her over and tells her she either has to fall in line or go to her room. Emma twirls over to me and picks up one of the large hoops we are now working with. "Old witch," she mutters, laughing. When she's sure Frau Prinz isn't looking, she slips the hoop around her neck and sticks out her tongue, as if it's a noose.

Something inside me flips and flutters with joy.

20.

Emma and I partner up for the next collection drive

through town. We ask people for tinfoil, empty toothpaste tubes, old razor blades and any other small metal objects they may not be using. We invite people to slip money into an old tin, for the Winter Relief. Emma says we should ask the women for their wedding bands, just to see their faces. Then she says we should ask for sweets, for the orphans, but eat them ourselves. "After all, I'm almost an orphan," she says.

Yesterday, Frau Prinz said she's been ordered to read out the names of any dead parents after the flag ceremony, but so far none of the girls' parents have been on the list. Emma reached over and took my hand right before Frau Prinz opened her mouth and it shocked me. I hadn't felt a friend's hand in mine since Edie left.

We turn onto Edie's block. This time, I know what's waiting for us at the top of the stairs. I've never told Emma about Edie, but I've wanted to, a million times. I don't know why it's so hard. We do the first two floors. The tin and metal clink together in our box. Maybe they'll end up in Papa's factory, where they'll be melted and moulded into one of his designs. When we start up the stairs, I let Emma go first. When she sees the star she stops, turns to me and says, "Oh."

I swallow, then say, "I used to be best friends with the girl who lived here." It bothers me that I said "used to." But it seems funny to say "am." Edie's been gone for two years and I don't even know where she is. "Her father's still here," I add. "At least he was a few months ago."

Without saying a word, Emma reaches into the money tin and pulls out a handful of coins. She lines them up outside Herr Pinker's door. "These might help," she says. Then we wind back down, silent as mice.

21.

Mama doesn't bake anything for Christmas. Mama doesn't do much of anything anymore. She sits on the sofa and stares at nothing. There isn't much for her to mend, with Papa and Hans gone, and we have so few things to wear, now that our clothes are rationed. I ask her if she wants to come with me to the KLV for Christmas. She can help me and Emma in the kitchen and sing with us later, but she says no, so I go without her. On my way there, I think of Papa and what he might be doing for Christmas. Emma said Berlin has already been bombed many times, but I know Papa's all right because he still writes to us, even though each letter sounds exactly the same and doesn't tell us much. We've only had one letter from Hans so far. He's somewhere near Frankfurt on the Rhine. I know Mama has been hoping for another one. That would have been the best Christmas present for her. The best for me would be some word from Edie. Emma said thousands and thousands of Jews have left Germany. Maybe Edie was one of them, like Herr Pinker hoped. Maybe one day a postcard from far away will pop through the mail slot in our door and she'll tell me she's safe and sound in another country.

EDIE

I.

Everything in the house is different with Brian gone. Mama and I spend more time in the parlour, listening to the radio with Louisa. She and Mama are teaching me how to knit. They hold their needles different ways, but Louisa convinces Mama that I should learn the Canadian way, with the yarn looped in my right hand. We make piles of socks, scarves, hats and balaclavas that Louisa takes down to St. Willibrord's Church, where the Red Cross collects them for the men in service. As we work, Louisa tells us stories of when she first came to Canada as a young girl.

"I remember all the trees, miles and miles of them from the train window. Halifax to Montreal, twenty-four hours of trees! My papa teased me and told me we were going to live in a tree house with the monkeys and I believed him."

She tells us how she met Brian, waitressing at a downtown deli. "He'd sit sipping his coffee for hours, gulping long after there was nothing in the cup, all because he was too scared to ask me out." She stops knitting and stares at the coal stove. "I didn't tell him I was Jewish until we were engaged, when he had to meet my parents. He wasn't too happy about it. I mean, he'd never met a Jew before and his family is very Catholic. I had to convert or he wouldn't have married me."

Mama nods as though she understands, but I don't. I thought everything was different here.

"Sometimes, I think that's why I lost the baby, you know, because I deceived him. Or because of the mixed blood."

Mama stops knitting. "That is complete nonsense, Louisa. There's no biological reason that Jewish and Christian blood can't mix. Don't talk like that. You sound like Hitler."

Louisa and I look at each other, shocked. We've never heard Mama say that name out loud. Suddenly, we all burst out laughing, as if Mama has cracked the funniest joke. We laugh so hard tears run down our hands, wet the yarn, and make our needles squeak.

2.

Annette often joins us because Vincent is busier than ever with his company, shipping millions of cigarettes overseas for soldiers.

"You need to get married and have a family," Mama tells her.

Annette laughs. "I'm not ready for that, Mrs. Pinker. I'm way too young. I want to see the world first."

"We've seen the world and it's not so great. Better you stay here and make babies," says Mama. I can't believe she would say something so embarrassing.

"Let's let the old ladies knit," Annette says suddenly, as if she can read my mind. "We can go upstairs and cut up the rug." It makes me laugh to think that a year ago I would have pictured me and Annette on our knees with scissors, chopping up her rug. Now I know it means to dance. English is such a funny language.

"Can I, Mama?" Mama shrugs and I can tell she doesn't want me to, but I go anyway.

3.

One day in class, Mrs. Bouchard makes me and Eva and John stand up. "Their parents came from Germany," she announces, "but Edie and Eva and John are Canadians now. Nothing that's happening over there is their fault. Is that understood?" I wonder if my face is as red as Eva's. When we listen to the war news after lunch, everyone stares at us, as if we're responsible for Germany's victory in Norway. I feel like I have a target on my forehead, bright as that yellow star.

"My uncle says Germans use a lot of ordinary people to do their dirty work and that you can't trust any of them," Betty says in a loud voice when the broadcast is over. "Not you, of course, Edie. I mean, you're not really German."

I'm expecting Dot to agree, but she reminds Betty that her grandparents were born in Germany. "Do you want me to get locked up too?"

I watch them go off after school to smoke cigarettes beside the aqueduct. They're probably trying to impress the new civil defence patrolmen who are guarding the treatment plant, guns strapped across their chest, ready to defend our drinking water.

At school we heard that the navy is stringing nets across the entrance to the harbors, to capture German submarines. It's like everything we left behind is sneaking closer and closer. Everything except Papa.

4.

Mama's school is taking in more students than ever thanks to all the sewing that's needed to supply the army, navy and air force. Her boss tells her to forget about teaching the girls fancy stitches and focus on basic straight-line sewing. "Anyone could teach them now. They don't need what I have to offer," Mama says, sounding sad. The school is on the top floor of the factory and Mama says each sewing machine is like a fire, adding more heat to the room. Every day a girl passes out and has to be carried into the fresh air. Mama herself comes home soaked in sweat and her eyes have become wrinkled from all the close-up staring she has to do. What would Papa say if he knew?

Uncle Max and Aunt Naomi beg us to move closer every time we visit them. Mama could walk to her school if we did, but I'd be so far from Annette, I couldn't stand it. She's the only person who knows how to make me laugh.

5.

Mrs. Bouchard turns each news broadcast into a geography lesson, calling on kids to come up and pin cards to the map to show what's happening. The Germans take Denmark and Norway, then Holland and Belgium too. I can't believe they're moving so fast. They've captured almost all of Europe. I thought the Canadians were going over to help, but it doesn't seem to be working.

In May we listen in class to Winston Churchill's speech from London:

You ask, what is our policy? I will say: It is to wage war, by sea, land and air, with all our might and with all the strength that God can give us; to wage war against a monstrous tyranny, never surpassed in the dark, lamentable catalogue of human crime. That is our policy. You ask, what is our aim? I can answer in one word: Victory—victory at all costs, victory in spite of all terror; victory however long and hard the road may be; for without victory there is no survival.

My skin is covered in goose bumps by the time he stops talking.

The cadets in our class spend the rest of the period showing off their crisp beige uniforms. Their pants are so stiff you can hear them crinkle when they sit and our principal makes an exception to the no-hat rule, just for them.

6.

The Nazis march into Paris on the exact day that Grade 9 ends. Mrs. Bouchard, who has family there, gives up pretending to be optimistic. The voice of the announcer is sadder than I've ever heard it, like he's been defeated too. When he says there'll be a swastika flying from the Eiffel Tower, Mrs. Bouchard grabs the base of her neck and massages it, as though it's sore.

"Remember to do what you can for the war effort," she says as we file out. "Join whatever group you can—collections, donations. Every little bit counts." I wonder what she'd say about the group protesting the war down on Wellington, carrying signs telling men not to register. Mama and I have watched the police trying to push them away from the recruitment tables. They shoo them across the street, but before long they cross again, and it all gets loud. Once, a few men started fighting and a crowd gathered to watch. Mama doesn't want us to stay when that's happening and neither do I.

7.

With school finished, I hang out at Annette's most afternoons. She puts blood-red lipstick on my lips and lets me paint her nails and set her hair in rollers. As I work, she tells me about the places Vincent has taken her to. "We saw Nan Blakstone at the Esquire and then we danced to Buddy Clayton at the 400 Cocktail Lounge. Vincent knows the owners so we got a front table and Buddy winked at me when Vincent's back was turned. My mom would kill me if she knew that we went to a striptease at the Tic Toc. But it was all very tasteful, believe me. Vincent wouldn't have taken me if it were sleazy." When she puts on "Boogie Woogie Bugle Boy," we jitterbug around the room and I wish I were old enough to see some of the exciting shows she tells me about.

8.

Louisa has joined the Women's Red Cross and, most evenings, she heads out to promote the Verdun mayor's

Cigarette Fund around town. She wants Annette to join too, but Annette says she spends enough of her time peddling cigarettes at the clubs. When Mama drops a quarter in Louisa's tin, Louisa pins a red sticker to her collar.

When Louisa is out one night, I find a letter from Brian on the kitchen table. Mama says we shouldn't touch it, but she doesn't stop me when I read it out loud:

Men are shipping out every day. Of course, I can't wait to have my turn. All of us are chomping at the bit to destroy those U-boats. Halifax is crawling with navy but the rest of the city is pretty humdrum. Thank goodness we have our daily portion of "grog"—don't worry, Louisa. I know my limits. I guess we're no worse off here than the boys overseas who are just sitting around doing nothing in Great Britain. They must be even more eager than we are. So far, much of our training's been on dry land. They built a frame that looks like the prow of a ship and we stand in it for an hour while they shake it from side to side, to get us used to the movement. My stomach's like a rock, thanks to your cooking. Just kidding! I miss your cooking and I miss you. Will write soon, Brian.

Mama looks sad when I stop reading and I know she would love to receive a letter like this from Papa, saying how much he misses her.

9.

Annette is one of twenty girls auditioning to join the TNT Revue. They're all standing in line on the stage of a gymnasium in the YMCA. A woman in a grey suit and chunky black shoes is walking up and down inspecting them. "Okay, let's see you move. Johnny," she calls to a man sitting at a piano in the corner. He starts to play some fast music and the girls start to dance. Annette outshines them all. Her face never stops smiling and she kicks her legs so high her knees hit her nose. Next, one by one, the girls sing "Happy Birthday to You" into a microphone. Annette sings it right on key and the woman scribbles notes beside her name.

"Okay, you'll be hearing from us soon," the woman says. "Thanks for coming out, girls."

"You're in for sure," I tell Annette. "You were the best."

"You're sweet, kid. I hope you're right. It's a great opportunity."

On the way home, we stop at a movie theatre on Sainte-Catherine. There's a special on all of July where you can see a movie for free if you buy a fifty-cent War Savings Stamp. Before *Rebecca*, Annette and I watch a war reel that shows hundreds of soldiers being rescued from a place called Dunkirk, in France. The men on the beach can barely stand and have to be carried to the rescue ships. Then another war reel shows the white cliffs of Dover in England, with German planes flying in and British and Canadian ones flying out to meet them. Then there's lots of fire as planes nosedive onto the beach and explode into a thousand pieces. It's all part of the Battle of Britain. When a German plane explodes, the crowd in the cinema cheers.

Outside, a group of men are marching in a circle, carrying placards that say, *Non à la guerre! Jamais à la conscription!*

"Why would people be against the war? Do they want the Nazis to win?" I ask.

Annette squeezes my hand and says, "Vincent is hoping conscription comes in. The more soldiers, the more smokers—the more smokers, the more his export business profits."

Another reason to dislike Vincent, I think.

Last weekend he took Annette to the Mayor's Ball. He and the mayor are good friends now because of the Mayor's Cigarette Fund. Annette's gown was gold, with a silver bow wrapped around her waist. She looked so elegant, like Katharine Hepburn—even with the same twist of hair falling over her eye. The radio was playing big band hits and Annette practiced twirling and making the long skirt whip like a tornado around her ankles as I sat and watched.

"The last time I was at an event like this, I had a cigarette tray hanging over my shoulders. This is progress, kid," she said, tossing me her lipstick.

10.

My new Grade 10 teacher, Mr. Grass, is even more obsessed with the war. He keeps the radio on during class and we listen to the announcer go on and on about the Blitz in London. We do word problems to the sound of bombs exploding and the frantic announcer describing more and more destruction. Mr. Grass barely pays attention to our answers. He tells us if we were in London we'd be doing drills and jumping under our desks. We'd have gas masks in little boxes strapped around our necks. "You're all so lucky to be here," he says. "Never take it for granted."

Why do I feel like he's talking to me when he says that?

II.

Mama and Louisa are reading the pamphlets they brought home from the Red Cross Knitting Circle at St. Willibrord's. Louisa had been trying to get Mama to join her for weeks and finally, last Saturday, she did. I could just picture Mama clicking away faster than anyone and the other women wondering if they should try holding their yarn the way Mama does. The pamphlets are all about food and nutrition. Some of them make me laugh, like the one that says *Serve apples daily and you serve your country too.* How can apples help Canada win the war? Or the one that encourages housewives to save the fat and bones from the meat they serve: *Be a munitions maker right in your own kitchen.*

Annette raps on the window and waves as she runs across the gallery, her costume in a special bag folded over her arm.

"That girl's headed for trouble!" Louisa says. Mama nods and agrees.

But why should Annette just sit home worrying about the war when she can be out dancing with the TNT Revue. She let me try on her cancan costume, with all the red and black layers of lace. She taught me all the moves too and I'm getting pretty good at kicking my legs high. If the Revue is still around in a few years, maybe I can join it too.

12.

Brian sends a letter saying that he's finally shipping out. He includes a photograph of himself on the deck of the HMCS *St. Croix*, smiling as he holds onto a rope. He's not allowed to say anything about where the ship's heading or what the mission is. It's all top secret and it reminds me of the poster I saw in the post office: *Loose lips sink ships.* I studied it while Mama mailed more letters to Papa. I don't know why she bothers. They all come back, like a boomerang.

13.

"Oh, Edie," Annette says. "I thought Vincent was the one, but I was so wrong. Vincent is old. Benny took me to Rockhead's Paradise. It was amazing. I've never been anywhere like it. My parents would've died to see coloured people and white people jiving on the dance floor together. The music was like nothing I've ever heard. The musicians were all from a place called Harlem. Oh Edie, if you were older I'd take you with me just to show you. Here, listen to this. Benny bought it for me." Wild music fills the small apartment, full of trumpets and crazy piano playing. You can't sit still listening to music like that and before long we're swaying around the room.

"It's the Count Basie Orchestra," Annette calls over the music. "Do you like it?"

"I love it," I say. I wonder if Mama and Louisa can hear us thumping from below. I can hear Mama's cough through the floorboards.

The next time Benny comes to pick up Louisa, I hide inside the curtain and study his face at her door. I guess he's what girls would call handsome, but he's nowhere near handsome enough for Annette. And the way he grins when the door pops open bothers me. I think of the short movie we saw at the theatre, where they showed the Germans laying tripwire on the beaches to set off explosions and keep the Allies away. I picture myself setting something up at the bottom of the stairs for Benny, to keep him away from Annette.

14.

Bugle notes introduce the brief reports we listen to throughout the day. The boys in class stand and play pretend instruments with their fingers, while the cadets salute the Union Jack. There's a report about a ship called the *Empress of Britain* that was torpedoed and sunk by U-Boats. *"The biggest and most beautiful luxury liner mankind has ever known,"* says the announcer. It was being used to transport troops when it went down. I spend the rest of the day imagining all those chandeliers, the crystal teardrops coming loose and floating like glass fish, sitting at the bottom of the ocean. Luckily, not many people were killed. Most were rescued in their lifeboats by other ships. Louisa will like that fact. Every time news about the navy comes on, she takes a deep breath and Mama grabs her hand. It's like Brian's absence has become bigger to Mama than Papa's, or at least that's the way it seems. She's always talking to Louisa about him and how she shouldn't worry, but Louisa never asks Mama about Papa.

Mr. Grass keeps the news on for two whole days in the middle of November when the Germans bomb the city of Coventry. The announcer calls the city a *sea of fire*. He says, *"Seven thousand civilians died in the first three weeks of the Blitz alone. Will Coventry meet the same fate?"*

We just sit and listen. There's no point in even trying to do any schoolwork.

15.

I never want to see the newsreel for what happened today—December 29, the worst day of bombing yet in London. The radio announcer says the whole city is in flames and thousands of buildings have been destroyed. People are hiding deep down in the subway tunnels while British and Canadian fighters are *"writing fire in the sky."* This war just keeps getting worse and worse, and so does Mama's cough. Aunt Naomi was shocked when she heard Mama last visit. She begged Mama to take time off work, but she says she can't, not if she and I hope to have our own place to live one day.

Mama coughs so hard some nights it's hard to sleep. In the morning, she's tired from not sleeping but she still has to go to work. When she gets home, she barely eats and goes straight to bed. The back room is already cold. We found some extra blankets at the Salvation Army charity sale and I heap them on top of her, to help her stop shivering. I'm so glad Papa isn't seeing her like this. It would break his heart. Mama was never sick before.

Even lighting the menorah for Chanukah doesn't cheer Mama up. Louisa keeps it right on the coffee table in the parlour, now that Brian's gone. We all say it looks so pretty, but it's like Mama doesn't see it at all.

16.

On New Year's Eve, Mama's cough is so bad that Louisa says we better take her to the hospital. She runs to the corner and calls a taxi while I try to help Mama get dressed, holding her as her whole body shakes. The city streets are alive with people yelling and partying and setting off firecrackers that make us jump as we wind up the mountain to the Royal Victoria Hospital. Louisa holds my hand while Mama is having her lungs X-rayed. "Don't worry, Edie. She'll be fine, probably just a bad cold," Louisa says. "Lots of people here get them, our flats are so drafty."

But I know that's not true. There was blood on Mama's pillow.

When the doctor comes out, he tells us that Mama can't come home. She has something called tuberculosis. "We'll need to transport her to Sainte-Agathe," he says, "to the Mount Sinai Sanatorium. She'll get the help she needs there, plus plenty of fresh mountain air. It's especially for people like her, you know.

"You mean sick people?" I ask.

"Jews," the doctor says, looking a little embarrassed. "It is a wonderful place, I guarantee."

Who knew that here, in the new world, Jewish people would have their own place to be sick?

1941

SABINE

I.

Some boys from the Hitler Youth have come to the KLV to dig a row of latrines in the newly thawed earth. Frau Prinz has been complaining for months that this many people cannot possibly be expected to make use of two toilets. Emma rolls up the waistband of her skirt so that her hem sits above her knees, then insists we practice our poise and grace as close as possible to where the boys, shirtless in the sun, are working. We pitch the golden ball back and forth to the younger girls in a slow, well-formed arc, like Isabella showed us. Emma rises gracefully on her tiptoes when she releases the ball, making her skirt lift even higher. More than once, the boys stop to watch, leaning on their shovels.

My old skirt, on the other hand, is nothing but embarrassing. It was Mama's. She took it in around the waist by giving it an ugly pleat in the front, and the pattern is faded flowers that all look grey. I don't dare try to show it off, but the boys are watching me too. My breasts have grown, and I can feel them pushing against the buttons of my too-small shirt.

"Don't do up all the buttons—keep the top ones loose. That's what I'd do if I had what you have," says Emma. I remember Papa's final joke to Mama about keeping the boys away and how ridiculous that seemed to me, just two years ago.

One of the boys is Werner, the kid Hans used to complain about in his Hitler Youth group, saying he wasn't obedient enough, or enthusiastic enough, or strong enough. Wasn't he also the one who wet himself on one of the campouts? Now, he is tall and sturdy and when he looks at me, he smiles in a crooked way that makes my hands turn to stone and my knees go soft as pudding.

2.

Emma and I are handing out coffee and sandwiches to servicemen at the train station. We have to smile and make them feel welcome and cared for. "Make them feel like princes who are about to inherit a realm," Maria said at our BDM meeting.

"Should we kiss them too, if they ask?" said Emma, but Maria just sighed. I imagine Werner in an army suit and I know I'd kiss him if he asked. But he's only my age, fifteen, so that's not going to happen.

On the far end of the platform, some soldiers are corralling a small group of people into a car at the back of the train. I can see yellow stars pinned to their coats, and their faces are gaunt and confused, like they don't know how they got here. Little kids look up at their parents with big eyes, their arms wrapped around legs or waists. I scan the faces quickly and recognize some of them, like Herr Goldman, the shoe seller. His daughter, Rosa, who is holding his hand, used to be in my class. But I don't see Herr Pinker. Maybe they're all leaving, like Emma said, but why would they need soldiers to help them? For the first time, I'm glad Edie isn't here. It would be terrible to watch her get yelled at, or pushed with the butt end of a rifle. I wouldn't be able to do a thing to help. I'd just have to stand here and watch, like I'm doing now, in a way that's making my stomach queasy.

3.

This week, the BDM girls are allowed to watch the *Wünschkonzert* movie at the little makeshift cinema in our meeting hall. It's about two lovers who are reunited through the radio show. They meet and fall in love in Berlin, at the Olympics, but then Herbert goes off to fight in the Spanish Civil War. He gets injured and Inge moves and the two lose touch with each other. Three years later he's fighting in Poland when he sends a song request, the Olympic fanfare, to the radio show. Inge knows it must be from Herbert. She'd assumed he was dead, but she'd never lost hope. They plan to be reunited in Hamburg, but Herbert's plane is shot down by a British plane. He's rescued in a U-boat and brought back alive. Carl Raddatz and Ilse Werner are great and when they kiss at the end I feel it all the way down in my toes. I close my eyes in the dark and imagine it's me and Werner.

I wonder if Mama lies awake at night thinking about her reunion with Papa. If Hans had had a girlfriend, she might be lying awake thinking about him too. He sent us a picture of himself standing at duty in his uniform, a short grey jacket with an eagle patch on his sleeve and a dark, hard hat. He looked way older than his age, but

I guess I keep forgetting that Hans is almost eighteen now. Still, Hans could never be Carl Raddatz. Not in a million years or after a million battles.

4.

I'm biking home from the shops, our bread for the day in my basket, along with three eggs. Mama used to love to go shopping and stopping to chat with all her friends. Now, she rarely leaves the house. I do most of the shopping around four o'clock on my way home from the KLV. Sometimes, I stay later to give lessons to the girls, helping them with their math and spelling. That way, I see more of Werner. Frau Prinz decided she needed a handyman around and I was thrilled when she picked him. She said she'd been watching the young men closely and he was the best worker. Emma pinched me and said it was fate, just like the U-boat being in the water right where Herbert's plane went down.

I bike slowly because I'm in no hurry to get home. I'm lucky to still have a bike. Most people in town had to give theirs up, for the metal and rubber. But I need mine to perform my duty, so I get to keep it. As usual, when I pass Edie's I go even slower. Emma told me that Germany has now officially decided to deport all the Jews. That's what that group at the station was—a deportation. But Emma's not sure where they're being deported to. She said her aunt told her that, in a carefully hidden way, in her last letter.

I look up, but there's no action behind the curtain. I look down at the basement window, which is partially hidden by a leafy bush, but I don't see any light coming from their storage room either. Then my eye catches something on one of the branches, out of place amongst the green. I get down off my bike to take a closer look. It's a strip of yellow ribbon tied in a bow around a twig. I untie it and hold it close, running my fingers along the satin. Then I gasp. Of course—it's the ribbon Edie's mama sewed around the hems of the matching white dresses Herr Pinker made for me and Edie when we were little. I'd know it anywhere.

But what is it doing here?

5.

Sitting through Frau Prinz's lecture at the KLV the next day is hard. She's teaching us how to make noodles out of almost nothing. In between, she explains how Aryan people are superior to Slavs. Basically, we are more industrious and care more about beauty. That leads us into a lecture about hygiene. Then we gather to listen to the daily war report. Apparently, our troops are proceeding marvelously into Russia and defeating the British Air Force. I picture Hans at the base of the flak gun, handing over ammunition, then ducking for cover. I think of the nursery rhymes Edie and I used to love to listen to on the radio, about witches pushing kids into ovens and wolves threatening to eat them. They were scary, but in a fun way. I wonder what these little girls make of all this talk of bombs and death.

I try to pay attention, but I can't wait until I'm alone with Emma. I've decided I'm going to tell her about the ribbon. After all, she shared with me what her aunt told her. That means she trusts me, and I have to trust her. The more I think about it, the more I'm convinced that the yellow ribbon was a signal. Herr Pinker must have put it there on purpose. And he could only have done that for one person—me.

6.

Emma runs the piece of ribbon through her fingers, her eyes gleaming. "This," she says, "is the type of problem my mother would have sunk her teeth into. We have to do something."

I tell Frau Prinz my mother would like to meet Emma and ask if she can come home with me to spend the night. Frau Prinz says it's against protocol but that spending the night in a proper German home, one that thinks the right way, might be good for Emma. I don't tell her that our block warden, Frau Schilling, doesn't think we're proper. She fined Mama ten pfennigs and reported her for not drawing the curtains all the way last night. Frau Schilling said we're lucky we live in a small town where no one is dropping bombs. If this was a big city that little sliver of light could have spelled the end for us, and for every family around us. Mama said, "I'm not sure I want to live in a world where a little bit of light is such a dangerous thing." Frau Schilling sucked in her breath and stood taller. I thought of Ravensbrück, where Emma's mom now lives, and stepped in.

"Mama's tired," I said. "Opa's been so sick, Mama hasn't slept. Please don't take anything she says right now too seriously." So she gave us a fine and a report, but nothing more.

What would Frau Prinz say to that?

7.

Emma comes up with a plan so fast it makes my head spin. "I grew up listening to my parents and their friends make plans for action, so it comes naturally," she says. We are wearing our BDM uniforms, the scarves perfectly knotted and our shoes polished. "We have to look professional and smile politely at anyone we meet," Emma adds. We take our basket, the one we normally use for collections and tell Mama we have work to do. She's sitting on the couch, staring into space, an old dress in her hands for mending.

"Mama?" I wave in front of her face.

"Okay, goodbye girls," she says to the wall.

It's not hard for us to just walk into Edie's building. We wait a few seconds, to make sure none of the tenants from the first two floors are in the stairwell. Then, instead of going up, we go down. I'd know the way to the Pinkers' storage room blindfolded, I spent so many hours down here playing with Edie. "Let's tiptoe," I say to Emma. "If Herr Pinker is here, he'll have a heart attack hearing loud footsteps." *If* he's here. It suddenly seems almost ridiculous to have made so many assumptions based on a little scrap of ribbon.

Of course, the door is locked, but I brought along the key—a picture of me and Edie wearing our matching yellow-ribbon dresses on the first day of school. I slip it under the crack and we press back against the wall to wait. It isn't long before we hear a soft shuffle. Then Herr Pinker, looking even thinner than last time, opens up.

"Sabine," he whispers. "You found my message." He opens the door wider and waves me inside. But his hand stops flapping when he sees Emma and a flash of fear crosses his face.

"Emma is my friend," I say. "And if Edie were here, they'd be the best of friends too, believe me." When I say "Edie," Herr Pinker hangs his head, like I've hit him.

"I am a terrible old man, for bringing a young girl, and now two, into this. But I didn't know what else to do. I need food." Without waiting another second, Emma pulls out the bread and cheese we hid in the bottom of the basket. Herr Pinker practically grabs them out of her hand and starts to gobble them down. I wonder how long it has been since he last ate. I look around at the small space, no bigger than our pantry at home. Herr Pinker has made a bed out of the bundle of old clothes and built a kind of tent-wall out of bolts of material. If anyone looked in through the window, or even quickly from the door, they wouldn't see him. But he'd be found in a flash if anyone investigated further.

"You can't stay here," I say.

"I have no choice," he answers. "Nowhere else to go. Only onto the trains with the others. And to where? No one knows. I should have gone with Edie and her mother when I had the chance. I thought I could stay and defend our home. Stupid. I was so stupid." Emma and I just look at each other.

"Not stupid," says Emma, finally. "Brave. Very brave."

I don't know if I should ask this, but I really need to know. "Is Edie okay in Munich? Have you heard from her?"

Herr Pinker's face breaks into a huge smile so unexpectedly, it's like sunlight has filtered through the tiny window and brightened up the room. "She's out, Schatz. Out. She and Hannah took a boat to Canada, to Hannah's cousin in Montreal. At least, that was their plan. I don't know if they made it. Even if I don't have food, I have that possibility. I thought it would be enough to sustain me, but ... " He points to his stomach. "The body has its own needs."

8.

Werner carries a stack of wood into the kitchen and I help him unload it beside the stove. With each log I lift, I uncover more and more of him. Now, we're standing so close, I don't know where to look.

"You shouldn't have to do so much work at your age," he says to me.

"And neither should you," I answer.

"Oh yeah, what should we be doing?" Werner smiles. I know he's teasing me, and I can feel my cheeks burning. Then he takes my hand and pulls me out the back door and into the woods. We can hear Frau Prinz talking to the girls as they hang their clothes on the line. She's explaining why missing their parents isn't as important as doing what the Führer has asked them to do. "He wants you to come to the country and get strong, to help build the new Germany after the final victory." My stomach roils. Everywhere we turn, someone is explaining to us why what we're feeling is wrong or how they know better than us what we should be feeling. I want Werner to pull me far enough into the woods so that I can scream without being heard, but nowhere would be far enough for that. I bet even the birds have been trained to listen.

We stop under a massive pine tree and Werner pulls me against him. My head lands on his shoulder and he strokes the back of my head so gently, I feel a waterfall rise in my eyes. It reminds me of the way Mama used to stroke my hair at night, after reading me a story, back when the monsters and ogres were only pictures in my books. Part of me feels silly for crying, but there is no one here to tell me that crying is wrong and I know that Werner understands. I feel it in his hands and in the way he holds his body so still, like he knows I need to just lean.

9.

Emma says I have to draw up a chart in my mind—never on paper—that would tell me exactly where Frau Schilling is when she makes her rounds. That way, I'll have time to sneak out with food, leave it outside the basement window for Herr Pinker and come back safely. "Block wardens are like clocks with legs," she says. I wish I could ask Werner to come with me, just in case, but I'm not sure enough about him yet. I think I could tell him, but I have to get to know him better to be absolutely sure. It won't be hard to sneak out. Mama is glued to her spot on the sofa. By the time Papa comes home from his assignment, she'll be sunk into it, like a fox.

That night, I wait until I hear Frau Schilling's tapping footsteps, exactly ten to reach our front door. Then a few seconds' pause while she puts her ear to the wood, listening for sounds that could get us all killed. Then tap-tap-tap back down the stairs and along the walkway. Our gate makes a tiny screech in the night, like an angry bird.

I pull a dark hat over my head and throw on a dark fall coat. The air is cool as I follow Frau Schilling up the street, staying well back as she checks each house, then goes around the corner onto Edie's street. I check my watch—that took fifteen minutes. I picture Herr Pinker in his fabric hideaway, also listening to her tapping boots, holding his breath, not daring to breathe. It takes her ten minutes to clear his block and turn onto the next one. That means if I wait twenty-five minutes I can run over, leave the food, and make it home before she comes back onto my block and starts all over again. Stupid me! I should have brought something tonight, but then if she'd seen me I would have had to explain why I had food on me. So, it's better this way. If I'm going to do this, I need to think through every move carefully. Emma said her mother handed an anti-war flyer to the wrong person at a meeting and that was it for her. Off to Ravensbrück.

10.

Frau Prinz calls everyone into the dining hall today. We have to sit quietly because the Führer is delivering an important speech about Russia. She turns the volume way up as Hitler starts to speak, his voice so high-pitched he causes static on the *Volksempfänger*. My attention drifts in and out as he goes on and on about history, all the way back to 1914, listing all the ways the world has mistreated our country and all the ways that he and his party have tried to fight for justice. He reminds me of Opa when he says, *"The revival of our people from poverty, misery, and shameful contempt was a sign of a pure internal rebirth."* If Opa is listening, he's probably nodding his frail head in agreement.

The girls are trying their best to concentrate, but they are starting to wiggle in their seats. I'm sure none of this makes much sense to them.

"During the last two decades, however, the Jewish Bolshevik rulers in Moscow have attempted to set not only

Germany, but all of Europe, aflame. Germany has never attempted to spread its National Socialist worldview to Russia. Rather, the Jewish Bolshevik rulers in Moscow have constantly attempted to subject us and the other European peoples to their rule. They have attempted this not only intellectually, but above all through military means. The results of their efforts, in every nation, were only chaos, misery, and starvation ..."

Two or three of the girls are starting to yawn, their heads bowing toward the table. I wish Frau Prinz would let me take them outside to run around.

"The results of our policies are unique in all the world. Our economic and social reorganization has led to the systematic elimination of social and class barriers, with the goal of a true people's community. It was, therefore, difficult for me in August 1939 to send my minister to Moscow to attempt to work against Britain's plans to encircle Germany. I did it only because of my sense of responsibility to the German people, above all in the hope of reaching a lasting understanding and perhaps avoiding the sacrifice that would otherwise be demanded of us."

Frau Prinz shushes two girls who have begun to whisper. I pull them onto my lap and hold them tight as the speech finally winds down to a close.

"The purpose of this front is no longer the protection of the individual nations, but rather the safety of Europe, and therefore the salvation of everyone. I have therefore decided today once again to put the fate of Germany and the future of the German Reich and our people in the hands of our soldiers. May God help us in this battle!"

What must Emma be thinking, with all this talk of Bolsheviks? When I look over at her, she's holding a pretend gun to her head. She catches my eyes and pulls the trigger. I'm not sure how she means it, until she cracks up. Frau Prinz looks at her like she wishes she had a real gun to shoot her with.

II.

Two of the little girls at the KLV, Kristina and Uli, are being punished for wetting their beds. While all the other girls have gone into the woods with Frau Prinz and Emma to collect mushrooms, they have to stand on kitchen chairs with a big pile of soiled bed linen in their arms. Frau Prinz put me in charge of their punishment. "Make sure they hold them up for exactly an hour, no rests. Then they'll appreciate how much work all this nonsense is giving us."

I'm washing dishes and peeling potatoes while the girls stand behind me. I can hear them sniffling. Their tears are probably soaking the sheets, wetting them even more. I want so badly to let them sit, but if someone comes in and finds them and tells Frau Prinz she'll kill me. She has started separating me and Emma as much as possible. She said we were having too much fun together. "Don't you know, nothing about this war should be fun?" she said. "This is serious business. There will be time for fun later, when we get where we want to be." She made it seem like there was some destination we were all marching toward. Emma said she saw Hitler's plans in the Stuttgart newspaper for a place called Germania. At its heart was a domed building so big practically everyone in Germany could sit inside and listen to him speak. Maybe that's our final destination.

Werner comes into the kitchen, carrying a hammer. He's been working on the roof, plugging up holes so that the rain or snow won't come in. When he sees Kristina and Uli he stops and stares, his eyes growing wide. The girls are barely holding up their loads anymore, but bracing them against their thighs. Their little arms must be so sore. "What the hell is wrong with them?" he asks. I explain about the punishment and watch Werner's face turn redder and redder.

"Right," he says, turning to the girls and pulling the dirty sheets from their hands. Then he grasps their waists and lifts them gently down to the floor. "How long do we have?" he asks.

"Maybe half an hour, at the most."

Werner takes the girls' hands and leads them into the field. I follow and before long the girls are running and squealing as they try to catch Werner, who slows down enough to let them. When he's "it" he runs slowly, tripping and falling over on purpose. The girls land on him in a heap. Then he calls out, "Let's get Sabine," and they chase me until they catch me and topple me into the grass. The girls hold down my arms while Werner tickles my belly. We are all squealing with joy.

I wish this moment could go on forever. I wish the girls would disappear and leave me and Werner alone in the field. But another field, far far from this one. A field away from a place where I have to keep one ear listening for sounds in the forest, like the breaking branches and singing I hear now. We run back inside and Werner swings the girls onto their chairs and puts his finger over his lips, to remind them not to say a word. Finally, he places their punishing loads back in their arms and I return to my peeling. Werner is about to return to his ladder, but first he runs over to the sink and kisses my neck. I can hear the girls giggling behind me.

12.

Papa has received high praise for his work, or at least that's what he says in his latest letter. He doesn't say much else, except that he's well and that he misses us. Maybe he can come home for Christmas, he doesn't know yet. He includes a picture of himself in his uniform, with the scarlet armbands, standing outside a long grey building with tiny windows along the top. On the back it says, "*Papa's new factory.*" Mama braces the picture against a candle on our mantelpiece and carries the letter for days, until it's completely crumpled, like a hanky. She finds a bit of new energy and makes her best pot of *eintopf* since

Papa left, even though it is mostly broth and potatoes with just a few pieces of meat. Mama puts most of the meat into my bowl when we eat and brings Opa a bowl of broth. "You need it more than him, you're growing so fast," she says. While she's in Opa's room, feeding him the stew, I fill a small glass jar that used to hold jam and secure the lid. Opa slurps so loudly the sound fills the house. It usually annoys me, but right now I'm glad because I don't have to guess if Mama's finished or not. I make sure a piece of meat makes it into the jar. What a treat that will be for Herr Pinker. Now, I just need to wait until that exact moment when I can leave.

Mama comes out of Opa's room shaking her head. "He's eating less and less," she says. "If your papa doesn't come home soon, he won't get to say goodbye to his father." Then Mama clears the table and asks if I want to sit with her in the living room. She hasn't done that for a long time. I have to slip out in half an hour, but Mama's face is so bright tonight, like Papa's letter was a light that lit it up, I just can't say no. So, I sit beside her and together we stare across the dim room. I notice, for the first time, just how dusty everything is. A fine layer of greyish powder coats the tabletops. That's not something Mama would ever have let happen before Papa left.

Mama pulls out her mending and passes some to me. We turn on the radio and listen to the *Wünschkonzert* as we work. I imagine how happy Mama would be if she heard Papa's name over the wire, sending her a beautiful piece by Brahms or Schubert. But Papa's probably too busy to think about such things. We mend socks and stockings as I hope for Mama to get sleepy. I'm late for my food run to Herr Pinker. Finally, she leans back her head just as Frau Schilling's footsteps come up the walkway. I wait until I'm pretty sure Mama's asleep, grab the jar of *eintopf* and slip out. I'll have to move fast. Frau Schilling loops back onto our street from the top and I can't risk her seeing me return. I place the jar and some bread outside the window, behind the bushes, and rap lightly. Then I leave. The only way I'll know if he is still okay is if the jar is empty in the morning.

13.

Now, all I care about is seeing Werner. As Emma and I do our work in the kitchen, I listen for sounds of him working too. He's usually somewhere above us, preparing the guesthouse for winter, patching up holes in the bedrooms. He always stands with us for the flag ceremony and we watch each other from across the room as we go through the motions of singing and saluting. Sometimes he makes a funny face on purpose and I have to stop myself from laughing.

Frau Prinz has delivered bad news to two girls in one week—both their fathers have been killed in Russia. One of them is Kristina, the girl who had to stand with a stack of sheets in her arms. "You mustn't cry when you hear this news," Frau Prinz has warned the girls. "You must stand proudly and tell everyone around you that your papa was a hero who died for the Fatherland. Each death brings us one step closer to victory for the Führer. If no one was out there doing battle, who would win for us?"

Today, when she calls the name of another dead father, a girl named Eva starts to cry. Emma and I watch her crumple to the floor. Frau Schilling is not impressed. She asks me to take Eva up to her room and put her back to bed for the day. I know she means to punish her, but I grab a piece of bread on the way up and slip it to Eva in bed. I stroke her forehead, the way Mama used to stroke mine when I was upset.

"I'm sorry about your father, Eva. You'll feel better tomorrow," I tell her. But will she?

Werner is standing at the top of the stairs, waiting for me. "Old cow," he says. "Cows have four stomachs, did you know that? I bet that old cow downstairs has four stomachs and no heart at all." Then he pulls me into one of the rooms. I can see the bucket of flour, water and straw that Werner is using to patch up the holes. I think about how there is a hole in Eva's heart, in many of the girls' hearts, and how I wish I had a mixture to fill it.

"If you kiss me, Sabine, I'll have a much better day up here, working all alone," Werner says. We sit on the edge of the bed. He puts his arm around me and I feel myself go hot. Then he leans over and kisses me on the lips. I kiss him back and circle my arms around him. The KLV disappears, the war disappears, my worry about Herr Pinker disappears. Even the sound of Eva sobbing across the hall disappears. I want to take this moment and stretch it into a million. But then the sound of feet fills the house—the girls and Frau Prinz marching into the big room for lessons. I hear her call my name. Werner loosens his grip, but just a little. I know he doesn't want this to end either.

"Old Cow," I say, and we laugh together, quietly, for a few more delicious seconds.

14.

One morning, Mama walks into my room and says, "Your opa is gone." At first, I think she means that he's run away. I imagine his skinny body running down the middle of the road, trailing his soiled sheet behind him. Then Mama puts her head down on the pillow beside me and cries. She sobs so hard she soaks my pillow, her tears drenching the down feathers. I run my hand through her greying hair that has grown so hard and wiry with no nice shampoo to use. I had no idea Mama would take Opa's death so hard. After all, everything he said seemed to annoy her.

"Oh Sabine," she says after a while. "I'm sorry. I forgot that he's your grandfather. I'm the one who should be comforting you."

"It's okay, Mama. Opa and I weren't that close."

I think of Frau Prinz and what she would say about Opa's death. He didn't die for the cause, he died of old age. He lived for the cause though—every day—listening to the war report, praying for that promised final victory,

Heil Hitlering that picture of the Führer over his head ten times a day. Nothing shook his confidence in that man. He was so proud of his son and grandson and their contributions to the war. But what would he have thought of me if he'd known that I was helping to keep the enemy alive? There is no doubt in my mind that Opa thought of Herr Pinker as an enemy, even though Herr Pinker would never have done a thing to hurt him. It's funny, but Edie and I always said they looked alike. They both had that old man white hair and white beard look. And at the end my opa was as skinny as Herr Pinker too.

"We'll have to make arrangements," Mama says. "And we'll have to write a letter to Papa."

"Later, Mama, when I come home," I say. I know Frau Prinz would not find my opa's death a good enough reason to stay away. Not now. Not with death all around us.

15.

I tell Emma about Opa as we're working in the kitchen, making breakfast. There are even more girls now, as another trainload arrived yesterday. Some of the girls are now doubling up in the narrow beds.

"I'm sorry, Sabine," she says.

"It's okay, really. I don't think you would have liked my opa much. It sounds like he was pretty much the opposite of your family."

Emma shrugs. "There are people like him in my family too, believe me. Not everyone was like my parents. I think some of my relatives were happy to see them arrested." I can't imagine that, but she must be right. I mean, it makes sense. If there were more people like Emma's parents, we wouldn't be doing what we're doing. I wouldn't be working here in this old guesthouse; the beds upstairs wouldn't be full of frightened little girls; Werner wouldn't be hanging around waiting for a chance to kiss me; and Herr Pinker wouldn't be growing thinner in a little cupboard in a damp basement. I can't bring him food every night. It's too dangerous. So, some nights he has nothing. At least Opa died in comfort, in a warm bed, with food in his belly.

Something is gnawing at me—a murky idea that's forming in my head but can't take shape. But, as I set the dishes on the long table, it starts to become clearer. Werner comes in carrying a rectangular piece of wood. "I'm going to extend the table," he says. "I'll make it more secure later. This is just for now, until I can find something better."

That's it: something better. The idea becomes so clear I almost drop my whole load of plates. The top ones slide to the ground and shatter. "Sabine, are you okay?" Werner asks. I look from him to Emma, back and forth, several times. I have to tell them. I have to take that chance. I can't carry out this plan on my own.

"I need to talk to both of you," I say. "But no one can hear a thing, so later, when the girls are busy. It's important." Emma is at my feet, picking up the broken pieces and hiding them in a drawer. She knows Frau Prinz will be enraged at my carelessness. There can be no waste right now—everything must go toward the Fatherland. They both say okay at the exact same second and that gives me hope. Maybe this could really work.

16.

The first thing I do when I get home is ask Mama if she's told anyone about Opa yet. "No letters, no one on the street, no neighbours? Not even Papa?" She shakes her head.

"I've just been home all day, cleaning him. I was waiting for you," she says.

I take a deep breath. I must tell Mama—everything depends on her now. Emma was on board right away. Werner was too, once he got over the shock. He didn't know anything at all about Herr Pinker, but he remembers Edie from school. He put his arm around me and squeezed me tightly. "I can't believe you've been doing that," he said. "So brave." But bringing Herr Pinker food is nothing compared to what I'm about to propose to Mama. The food is what Opa would have called "small potatoes," like when Germany annexed Austria with almost no effort at all. Moving Herr Pinker into our pantry, to take Opa's place, will be like taking Great Britain, something Germany has still not managed to do. Hans must be getting more and more frustrated up north, sticking the artillery in the flak guns, trying to down the British planes. On the radio, they keep saying it's just a matter of days until Great Britain is defeated, but that can't be true. They've been saying it for two years. Good! The longer it takes, the longer Hans stays away. We could never do this with him at home.

"Mama, there's something I need to tell you." We sit across from each other at the kitchen table. "First of all, I've been helping Herr Pinker, bringing him food."

Mama's mouth springs opens. "No, no, wait, let me finish, then you can talk. Not every night, but when I can. You look surprised, but he's still alive, and he's still here, in our town. He never left. And today I had an idea. You know you always liked Herr Pinker? I know you did. What would you say if I asked you to help me put him in Opa's place?"

Mama's mouth falls open and a strangled sound comes out.

"Think about it, Mama," I continue. "All Opa did was lie in the pantry. He never went out anymore and hardly anyone around here knew him anyway."

Mama's hand is now covering her mouth. "But Edie, you know we can't do that," she says finally. "How could you ask? Think of Papa and what he would say if he knew. Papa would forbid it. And if we're caught … I can't even say the words." I remember Mama taking clothes to Herr Pinker to mend, or welcoming Edie with a hug when she came over to play. I have to reach that part of her.

"Mama, it would be for Edie. When we were little you said she was like your second daughter."

"But that was before, Sabine. You know that."

"Before what, Mama? There is no before with me

and Edie. I never changed my mind about her and I don't think you did either." Mama bows her head and I can tell she knows I'm right. "I've worked it out. We've worked it out, me and Emma and Werner, and I think it can work, if we're careful." Mama is shaking her head harder now. "Listen Mama. Werner is a master digger. He can dig a hole for Opa in our basement. Then, we bring Herr Pinker here. If anyone comes over, they'll just see a thin old man in the bed. No one will know."

Mama is quiet for a few minutes and I know she's picturing the whole process in her head, like I've been doing all day. "But to put your opa in a hole! It's so wrong," she says finally. "And not to tell Papa that his own father has died. Sabine?"

Part of me knows she's right. That is wrong. But these are not normal times. So many things are wrong right now; isn't that all the more reason to do one right thing in the middle of all the wrong? "But he's dead, Mama, and Herr Pinker is alive. We can help keep him alive for Edie. That's not wrong. Opa won't know. It won't hurt him. But Herr Pinker is cold and hungry. I need to do this for Edie."

"But how, Sabine?"

"We'll have help. Werner and Emma know and they think it's a great idea. They—"

But before I can finish, Mama stands and smacks my face, something she's never done once in my whole life. Two seconds later, she throws her arms around me and pulls me so close I can barely breathe.

"It was dangerous," she says finally, "to tell them. Oh Sabine, I'm scared."

"I know, Mama, me too."

We hold each other in the overly quiet house. No raspy breathing coming from the pantry off the kitchen, no radio. Nothing. Just the two of us, thinking about saving a life.

17.

Werner comes home with me after work the next day, the shovel that he works with at the KLV under his saddle, running the length of the bike. We ride side by side, chatting and whistling, trying to make it seem like we're having the most ordinary day in the world. The streets have become quieter every day—no women chatting on their stoops. No young men, just older ones and, if they're out, they shuffle along looking gloomy.

A few small kids are kicking a ball around but that's all the life we see. Even the shops are getting barer. The windows are stocked so that it seems we aren't running out of food, but inside is a different story. We hardly ever have meat now. I don't know how Werner keeps up his strength. He's going to need it tonight. Mama and I prepared a space in the cellar last night, but the ground is hard. I wish he had someone strong to help him dig.

I hide Werner's bike around back, so the *Warze* won't see it and get suspicious. That's what Werner calls her. The Wart, instead of warden. We eat eggs and cheese with some stale bread for dinner. I give Werner my eggs, for the protein. He doesn't want to take them but I refuse to eat so he finally gives in. Mama seems happy to have Werner here. She washed her hair and put on a clean apron and she asks Werner questions while we eat. I think she's just trying to forget what we're about to do and I know she's still not convinced. We all hold our breath when we hear Frau Schilling walk up to the house. It's not like Werner visiting for supper is breaking any rules, but if she saw him she'd probably warn him about not staying past curfew at nine, and then she'd come back later to check he was gone.

Finally, I show Werner the cellar. "Kiss me," he says, "for encouragement." We hold each other in the dark, and the kiss lasts a long time. I've brought down a candle, but I don't light it until we let go of each other. "It's not going to be easy," he says, looking down.

"No," I reply. "None of this is. What can I do to help? Mama found Papa's old shovel in the shed. I'm glad she never gave it up for metal collections."

"And if the Block Wart comes in for some reason, like she often does, and finds you covered in dirt from head to toe, then what? No way, Sabine, you go upstairs and have a perfectly ordinary evening with your mother. That's the safest way."

I watch as Werner jabs the shovel into the hard dirt, then I leave him and go back up to sit with Mama, who is washing dishes. Neither of us speaks as we listen to the sounds of Werner digging a hole for Opa. I keep a careful eye on the clock. I know exactly when the Old Wart will be back. I'll pop down and tell Werner to take a break. I'll bring him some cold water and let him kiss me again.

18.

Werner finishes digging around eleven. He's covered in dirt and sweat, but smiling when he comes up to tell us. "The earth got softer deeper down, so it was easier at the end," he says. I remember Papa telling us about digging trenches during the last war. He dug and dug for days on end. If Werner had been born back then, he'd have been digging trenches too. All our young men are always digging for death, in one way or another.

"Are we ready, Mama?" I ask. This is going to be the hardest part for her. It's not what a good wife should be doing. I think of that Mother Cross our neighbour is still showing off. Mama would definitely not get a medal for this, but I love her for it. She nods and we follow her into Opa's room. It is so narrow there is barely space for all of us at the same time. Werner takes Opa's top half and Mama and I each take a leg. Opa's lighter than I expected, and smaller too. It's the first time I've actually touched a dead body and I'm surprised by how stiff it already is. If not for the stiffness, he could just be in a very sound sleep. It's not easy to turn around the corner into the steep stairwell, but we do it slowly, with Werner at the bottom, bearing most of the weight. The hole runs the length of the wall so that Opa's body can simply be laid in it. Mama lights a candle and we say the Lord's Prayer together. Then Mama takes a bit of dirt in the shovel and throws it on top of Opa. I do the same.

"I'll do the rest," Werner says. I wait until Mama's gone, then I hug him, pulling him close.

"Thank you so much," I say. "For being here, for doing this. For understanding why. I feel so lucky right now."

19.

Next morning, I leave for the camp extra early. The streets are still dim, with just a hint of light in the sky. I hide my bike around back of Edie's building, grab the bundle of Opa's clothes, and enter, tiptoeing down the stairs as lightly as I possibly can. One bad creak could ruin our entire plan. I rap softly and wait. I've brought back that key, the picture of me and Edie, which I slip under the door. When Herr Pinker opens up, I gasp. The little bit of food I've managed to sneak him has kept him alive, but he's even thinner than last time. And his skin is grey from lack of sun and fresh air. I step inside and we close the door. The smell of waste is so strong, I have to cover my nose. I whisper in his ear, telling him the plan.

It's too dark to read his face, but I can hear the fear in his quick breaths.

"But your father, your brother. When they come home, they'll know," he says.

"That might not happen for a long time. And when it does, we'll figure something out. In the meantime, you'll be safe, possibly for a whole year. Maybe until the war is over. It can't go on forever."

Herr Pinker shakes his head, then we stand still for a few minutes. I look into the cubbyhole where he spends his days. He only comes out to pace around at night, like a cat. Frau Prinz is always saying that Jews are vermin, spreading germs and disease. No doubt she'd change my cat to rat.

"I brought you some of Opa's clothes to change into and Werner and Emma and I will come and get you tonight, around midnight. We'll walk you to our house, then you'll just crawl into bed … and live." Herr Pinker sits back down on his bundle, like his legs don't have the strength to keep standing. I hand him some bread and say, "I'll see you later then, okay? I need to get going. Frau Prinz might be suspicious if I'm late for work. Everything has to be as normal as possible today."

"Okay," he replies softly. And we just leave it at that because there's really nothing else to say.

20.

Emma and Werner come over straight from the camp. Emma has been behaving so well and working so hard, Frau Prinz decided my home must have been a good influence last time, so she is allowed back for a sleepover. We wait until the Wart has passed, then set out to Herr Pinker's. We hug the fences and bushes, the three of us in a row, like cat burglars. It's like we're in a movie, but this isn't a movie, it's real. There will be no applause booming around the theatre at the end of the night.

Herr Pinker is ready, in Opa's old suit. He has put all the material that he used for his bed back into the box and stacked the bolts of cloth on top of it, so no one would suspect someone had been living here. Emma stands at the top of the street and waves to us that it's all clear—no Wart, no people out after curfew, no brownshirts. Werner and I each take an arm and walk him slowly but steadily down the street. At one point, we hear footsteps clopping nearby, echoing off the buildings in the empty street. We pull Herr Pinker into a doorway and stand in front to block him from view. A minute later, a bunch of Hitler Youth appear. They're passing around a bottle and it's clear by the way they're walking that they're already drunk. We hold our breath and try not to make a sound until they pass. Then one of them turns our way and holds up his arm. "Heil Hitler," he slurs. Werner jumps out and says "Heil Hitler" back to him. The whole group starts to move closer. There's no way I can hide Herr Pinker on my own. I can feel him tremble behind me.

"What are you guys doing here?" asks Werner. "Didn't you hear? There's a group of Jewish women begging in the town square. That's where I just came from. You should be there."

"I told you, Dietmar," says one guy. "Nothing ever happens over here."

"To the town square," yells Dietmar, holding up his bottle. He spins and falls and the two others pick him up. They weave in and out, back in the direction of the town square.

"Do a good job," yells Werner. He stands and watches them for a minute, then turns back to us.

"We better hurry. They'll come looking when they find out nothing's there."

We grab Herr Pinker again and finish walking him around the corner to my house. We slip inside, where Mama is waiting. She and Herr Pinker don't say anything to each other, but Mama is smiling and Herr Pinker is saying thank you with his watery eyes. Mama has prepared a hot bath, which means we'll have to go without one this week. An hour later, Herr Pinker is lying in Opa's bed, wearing his pajamas. If we look inside from the doorframe, we don't see any difference to Opa at all. It's just a frail old man with white hair, lying in bed. Something inside me lets go, like even I wasn't sure this could work.

21.

Two weeks later Christmas is here again. Papa can't come home. He's too busy in his new position. He sends us his love and a box of Belgian chocolates. Neither Mama nor I say it out loud, but we're relieved. We had nothing planned for what we'd do if Papa were here.

Just by luck, Christmas almost coincides with Chanukah this year, so Mama brings Herr Pinker a candle that he can light for a few seconds each evening. She invites him to dinner Christmas day and he puts Opa's suit jacket over his pajamas and sits with us. He has joined us a few times at the table, but it makes him nervous. Mama too. She was so jittery she kept spilling bits of soup everywhere. I had to keep reminding her that our curtains couldn't be opened from the outside and that our front door was locked; if anyone came, they'd have to knock first. But it didn't help. So, normally she brings Herr Pinker something to eat in his little room, like she did with Opa. He always closes his eyes and bows his head when she does, but he doesn't say much.

We have a simple Christmas dinner—no goose or *stollen* or gingerbread. But I managed to find a few extra sausages that Mama cut up and added to the stew. Plus, the bread is fresh for a change. I stood in line for hours this morning to buy it. Our meal is simple, but peaceful. I imagine Papa eating a grander dinner, surrounded by lots of important people in army suits, the swastika bands around their arms. And Hans? He's living in a house with other flak helpers, so maybe they're also eating together, comparing stories of danger. What would either of them say if they had a crystal ball to see into our kitchen? Would they be able to tell that the frail old man sitting in Papa's chair was not Opa? Would they pick up the phone and call the local Gestapo office and report us—their own flesh and blood? I remember the words on Hans's knife—blood and honour. Maybe that was more important right now to the country. Doing the right thing for your country, not for your flesh, your family, your blood. Mama and I are doing the right thing. I can feel it in my bones.

EDIE

I.

Mama sits in a wheelchair outside the wide front entrance to the hospital, wrapped in a hospital blanket that swallows her up and makes her look small. Her hand is like a doll's, waving through the opening. The sight of her packed bag sitting on the snowy ground beside her tugs at my heart and a lump rises in my throat.

"Oh, Mama," I cry. I want to throw my arms around her, but the nurse puts up her hand to hold me back.

"I'm so sorry," I cry, standing over her.

"Sorry for what?" she asks.

"I didn't know. I should've seen. I knew you were tired, but I didn't know you were sick."

"Oh Edie," Mama says. Her voice has that whistling

sound that means she's about to cough. The nurse, who has a mask over her face, pulls me back.

"None of us knew," Mama says. "You're not to blame."

"You're going to the best place, Hannah," Uncle Max chimes in. He and Aunt Naomi arrived early this morning, to see Mama off. "I asked around and everyone said so. She'll be back soon, Edie."

"And you can come live with us, if you want, in the meantime," Aunt Naomi adds.

Mama's coughing fills the cold air.

"No, I'll stay with Louisa. Mama promised Brian."

"Okay, it's time," says the nurse. She and a man dressed in white help Mama into the back of the van. I wave until they are down the hill and out of sight.

2.

I sit on my bed in the cold room for the rest of the day. Mama's handiwork is all around me—the bedspreads with their lacy edges and matching curtains. A half-made dress hangs from a hook—she was making it for me, out of leftover pieces from work, but it doesn't look patchy. She had a way of blending the flowers together like a real bouquet. Papa would be so impressed.

Papa!

I fall back on the bed, floppy as a ragdoll.

He'd be crushed if he knew. Mama has to get better, for him as much as me.

3.

Dot and Betty have joined the Junior Red Cross. They set up collection boxes in the foyer where people can drop off unwanted clothes, metal and glass. They hang a sign above the entranceway that says, "Save Lives, Give us Your Knives." Kids who donate something get a gold star sticker on their shirt collars, but I have nothing extra to give—no clothes, no household goods of my own.

Besides, the last thing I want anywhere on my body is a gold star.

4.

Louisa insists that I visit Aunt Naomi and Uncle Max on Saturdays. She says it's important to keep contact with my family, but I think she just wants a day alone. She acts like she's the boss of me now, but I don't need a boss. I'm fifteen, old enough to look after myself.

On the ride uptown, I wonder if my aunt and uncle

will have news about Mama. All communication with the Sanatorium is going through them since they have a phone. But today's just like every other Saturday—no change.

"But she's no worse, either," says Aunt Naomi. "We just need patience."

The weather is warm enough that we can unbutton our coats as we stroll down The Main. Outside the Schubert Bath, people stand in a long lineup, towels rolled under their arms. Men, women and children, all waiting to get clean. It's something I never saw back home—people with no place to bathe. Louisa's flat is cold, but at least we have a bath. And so do Uncle Max and Aunt Naomi—a small tin one that they can barely sit in, but at least it's something. They have to put coins in a boiler box above the bath to heat the water and it takes forever, but it works. I remember our deep porcelain bath with the claw feet back home, how I would sink way under the water and pretend to swim.

Uncle Max says hello to so many people, you'd think he's lived here forever. He stops to talk to two men outside the Balfour Building. After they leave, he points way up to the top windows. "We work with all of them, Edie," he says. "Big bosses in the schmatta business, the

Button Hole Company and the Cute Hat Manufacturing Company. This city is a booming place for clothing. When your papa comes—"

"Max, Max," says Aunt Naomi, cutting him off. "Edie isn't interested in business. Let's go buy some bagels." We pop into a tiny shop where bagels are baking in the fire of a brick oven. The delicious smell of smoked hickory fills the air and I watch the baker expertly catch the row of bagels on a long wooden paddle and pull them out of the oven. I can hardly wait to sink my teeth into the warm dough.

Back at the flat, we listen to the BBC news on the radio and eat the sesame seed bagels covered in creamy cheese. Aunt Naomi also opens a jar of Mrs. Whyte's Pickles.

Uncle Max explodes when he hears that the Germans have entered North Africa. "That's it!" he shouts, pacing on the linoleum that's made to look like a rose-patterned rug. "Like a virus that just keeps spreading. It's not enough they had to take all of Europe. Now they need Africa. What's next, Asia?"

When he says virus I think of Mama, even though I know TB isn't caused by a virus. It's caused by nasty bacteria that are making their home in the tissue of

Mama's lungs. I picture them there, snuggled up like baby mice in a nest, digging in their claws.

When the news is finished, Uncle Max turns to me. "And you, Edie. Do you feel well? No coughing?"

"I'm fine, Uncle Max." Stupid doctor! I wish he'd never told everyone I'm at risk, given that Mama and I shared a room.

"That room's so cold I bet germs freeze the minute they hit the air," I say.

"Oh *Kind*," says Uncle Max, wrapping me in his big arms. I won't tell him that it feels good.

5.

"Picnic time," says Annette, holding up a basket. "Get ready, kid. Benny's between flights and he's taking us out for the day." She points below and there's Benny, sitting behind the steering wheel of a car with no roof, a pair of goggles perched on his forehead. I wonder if it's the same pair he wears when he's ferrying new bomber planes over to Britain.

I run inside and grab a sweater and tell Louisa where I'm going.

"Here, you'll need this," says Annette at the curb,

wrapping a kerchief around my hair and knotting it under my chin.

"Just like in the movies," I say and Annette laughs.

The back seat is tiny and I squeeze in sideways, stretching out my long legs. Benny drives us through the city, past downtown, to the foot of Mount Royal. "Walk or drive up?" he calls back to me.

"Drive," I yell over the wind.

We start the climb, winding around and around the dirt road, until we hit the summit. Benny carries the basket and we find a spot where the sun is warming the grass beside a small lake. For the next hour, we fill up on potato salad and cold chicken and listen to Benny tell us jokes about his huge Irish family. He's the seventh of ten kids and I can't imagine having so many siblings. I can't even image having one. Benny can do magic tricks with coins, like the ones Papa used to do with buttons, pulling them out from behind my ears or Sabine's elbows.

"Time for some kip, girls," Benny says as he stretches out and lays his head in Annette's lap. Before long he's snoring and Annette and I try to hide our giggles behind the pages of our Chatelaine magazines where glamorous women are offering us beauty tips and housewives are revealing the secret to better pie crust—even without butter.

Later, when Benny wakes up, he grabs Annette around the waist and pulls her close. I try not to stare, but it's hard. He's kissing her so hard her head is falling back. Before long they're lying on the picnic blanket, just inches away from me, their eyes closed as they embrace. I bury my face in my magazine and try to imagine what it would be like to be kissed like that. The sun is warming the top of my head, adding to the dreamy feeling that's spreading through my body. I see myself there, stretched out on the blanket. My pulse starts racing and ... I spring to my feet so fast I startle Annette and Benny, who also spring apart.

"What's wrong, kid?" asks Annette.

"Nothing," I say. "A spider, that's all."

"Not you too? What is it with girls and spiders? I've spent half my life killing spiders for my sisters," says Benny, laughing.

On the drive back, Annette squeals when Benny takes the corners too fast, but I'm too busy trying to erase what I was seeing in my mind's eye when I pictured that kiss. Not me and Benny entwined, but me and Annette, our lips touching, our hands around each other's waist.

If they knew, they would've left me stranded on the mountain with the squirrels.

6.

Mama is finally allowed to have visitors, so Uncle Max has borrowed a car and we are making the long drive north to the Mount Sinai Sanatorium. The Laurentian mountains are green and lush, rising and falling way into the distance. In Sainte-Agathe, we turn off the main road and drive toward the town. Aunt Naomi is reading directions that she scribbled on a piece of paper, and Uncle Max is focusing on the road, so neither of them sees it—but I do—a sign, nailed to the side of a tree where the road forked into two, one way for town, the other to the hospital. *Jews Scram. Not wanted in town.* I can't believe my eyes. I want to scream at Uncle Max to turn back so I can read it again, but I also don't want him to know about it. Poor Mama! I'm thankful she was lying in the back of the hospital van and wouldn't have been able to see it.

The Sanatorium is way more impressive than I was expecting—it is a majestic building, with a central tower and three rows of windows leading off either side. A nurse meets us in the cavernous lobby and leads us to a screened porch on the back of the building, overlooking the mountains. At the far end, patients sit in wheelchairs, wrapped in blankets, in spite of the heat. A few are even lying on beds that have been pushed outside. As the nurse wheels Mama closer, tears fill my eyes. I expected her to look stronger, but she's still frail and tiny under her own white blanket. The nurse parks her beside a wicker table and tells us we can't come any closer. "No hugging. No contact, except with your eyes."

"Five months and already you've grown," says Mama. "One day I won't recognize you."

"Oh, Mama, I'm still the same," I say, trying to sound light.

Another nurse brings a tray with a teapot, several cups, and a plate carrying little cakes with pink frosting. One of the forks has a big X on it in white paint. "That one is for you, Mrs. Pinker," she says. "Remember to stir your tea with the handle and keep all your things on this separate table." Mama nods and the nurse leaves.

We talk about Mama's treatments, then about the war, but no one mentions Papa. What can we say? He's suspended somewhere, just like Mama's health.

Mama asks me about school and Louisa and Annette, and I tell her a few things about each. Mama nods and sighs, like she's sorry she's missing out. After an hour the nurse returns and tells us time is up. "We mustn't overdo it on the first visit," she says. "Time for rest." Mama doesn't resist and I can see how tired she looks. I wonder if the nurse will put her back in bed, then wheel her outside after we leave. Mama said she has slept outside several times, even overnight. The crisp mountain air is part of the cure.

On the way back I overhear Aunt Naomi say to Uncle Max, "Well, I didn't see signs on the road, did you?"

"No, but our friends don't lie, Naomi. If they say those signs exist, I believe them."

So they did know! I guess that's why we didn't stop in town for a bite to eat, in spite of our rumbling stomachs.

7.

Every second Monday the air-raid siren wails through the city, but so far we haven't had to take shelter. I don't know where we'd go anyway—this building has no basement. Louisa said the city is building shelters and soon we'll be assigned one. I can't believe the war might actually reach us here in Canada. I remember that huge green angel atop the church, greeting us with her open arms as we stepped off the boat, and how safe I felt. Every time the siren blasts a small piece of that feeling chips away.

The government says Montreal is a hot target because it's where the bomber planes are made before being sent to Britain, which I already knew from Benny. So we have to practice blackouts, just in case. The trial one happens on June 9. At sundown we turn off all the lights and pull our curtains tight, then sit in the parlour with nothing but a candle burning. At 10:20 a signal blasts for two whole minutes, followed by another one, ten minutes later. Finally, at 10:45 the all-clear sounds. It takes a few minutes before Louisa flicks on the light switch, like she's not sure what will happen. Everything is so quiet, until someone out on the street lets out a holler. It echoes off the walls but helps us breathe.

Annette knocks on our door a minute later. "Next time, let's do it together," she says. "It was creepy sitting there all alone in the dark. Now I know how Benny must feel up in his cockpit. I don't know how he does it."

When she says *Benny* I blush and wish it was still dark, to hide my face.

8.

Mr. Grass keeps the radio on for our last day of school—
Germany has invaded Russia. They've even given it a
name: "Operation Barbarossa." It sounds so lovely, like
a ballet or something. I picture tanks pirouetting and
spinning across the tundra.

"My ancestors were from Russia," Mr. Grass says,
sitting on his desk and spinning the big globe under his
hand. He stops it when Russia is facing us. "Here, in what
is called Siberia. You probably wouldn't have guessed
this, but my original family name was Grazinski. It was
shortened to Grass when my parents came to North
America during the Revolution."

I had no idea Mr. Grass was an immigrant, like me.
He has no accent at all. Maybe Mama and I should have
shortened our name to Pink.

9.

Louisa has become a "bomb girl" at the new Defence
Industries Limited factory in Verdun. She had to pass
a security check and is now in training, learning how
to handle dangerous chemicals like amatol and cordite,
that get packed into shells and turned into bombs. "I'll

have huge muscles in no time," she says as she flexes her biceps at dinner. "Those bombs are heavy and the hooks we lift them onto are pretty high up." She's not allowed to bring her uniform home, so she describes the white overalls and matching white kerchief that she knots on the top of her head. "It's real classy," she says. "Except we're not allowed to wear jewelry or nail polish and I have to change into special shoes that have no nails in them, so I won't set off a spark and blow the whole place up." At the end of her shift, she has to shower off any trace of chemical before coming home. She and the other women wear ID tags, just in case. "Like real soldiers," Louisa says.

I wish I was old enough to join her. I'd love to be making bombs that might land on Hitler's head. It seems more useful than going back to school when the whole world is falling apart.

10.

Annette wants me to go see *Ziegfeld Girl* with her. When she says that she waited to watch the movie with me, instead of going with Benny in between flights, something in me lights up, but I try not to let it show.

"It's a girl thing, you know. Benny just wouldn't get it," she says and I agree.

First, there's a ten-minute war newsreel that shows a French Canadian Forestry Corps working crosscut saws to cut down huge trees in a forest in Scotland. Then another unit rebuilds a church that caught fire in a small English village. Finally, men from a Highlands regiment in Montreal are practicing their bagpipes in Edinburgh Castle. Honestly, I can't believe that's what our men are doing over there. Is that how they hope to defeat Hitler? Maybe they just don't understand how nasty the Nazis are, not if they think they can beat them with lumber and bagpipes. I feel like jumping out of my seat and yelling at the screen. But then, finally, the real movie comes on and the musical sweeps me away. It's about three young women trying to make it as dancers in the Ziegfeld Follies. I can't help wishing me and Annette were them, singing and dancing our way to stardom. Annette has so much experience already, from her TNT Revue. In my mind, the third girl is Sabine.

"That Hedy Lamarr is gorgeous, don't you think?" Annette asks me later as we're walking home.

"Yeah, completely," I say.

"She reminds me of you, you know."

"No way, she's too beautiful."

"Hey, you're beautiful too," Annette says, stopping in front of a shop that sells tennis rackets and other sports stuff. She places her fingers under my chin and lifts my head. "You just don't know it yet. That takes time."

When she lets go I feel that spot sizzle, like it's on fire.

"And she's Jewish, just like you," Annette adds.

"Really? I had no idea. I didn't know you could be Jewish and become a big star."

"Sure, so there's hope for you, kid." Then she hooks her arm through mine and all the way home we sing "I'm Always Chasing Rainbows," trying our best to sound like Judy Garland. For that hour, I forget about Mama. I forget about Papa. I just focus on Annette's arm looped through mine, her voice singing in my ear.

When we reach our street, Benny's car is at the curb, waiting like a big metal lure. Annette squeals and runs toward it, taking my smile with her.

II.

Louisa seems happier than ever now that she's working. Instead of coming straight home after her shift, she and some other bomb girls hang out at the Prince of Wales Café. It's not like Louisa was the world's greatest cook, but it means I have to make my own dinner. It's too hot to cook most nights so I just eat cold cuts and bread. I'd go down to the deli to buy coleslaw or sauerkraut, but I feel like I'm betraying Mama just thinking about it. She never entered the deli once it had new owners, ones that replaced the Wetzlers. It's more of an English-style bakery now anyway, with fancy pink cakes sitting in the window. I doubt they'd still have the food I like.

Some nights I walk down to Woodland Park to see how big the hill of collected pots and pans has grown. Then I walk along the water to where the huge Victory sign stands. It's an ad for the Victory Loans we're all supposed to be buying. I know Uncle Max has bought several—he says it's all we can do from here, but the only valuable thing I own is the antique brooch Aunt Naomi gave me in Munich. Ripping open the seam of my coat and holding the pearled flower in my hand again gave me such joy when we first got settled here. Now, I don't want to let it go.

There are often recruitment tables set up at the park, and I know if I were older I could do more, like volunteer for nursing, but Uncle Max gets angry when I say that.

"What you can do, Edie, is stay in school and do well. That's how you can help: become something. McGill is there when you're ready and we'll help you."

"But don't forget the quotas," Aunt Naomi replied from the sofa. "It's not all as open as you like to pretend, Max."

"Quota schmota—that's why Edie has to use her brains, to change things like that. Bandages anyone can change, but people's minds, those aren't as easy."

I wish Uncle Max and Aunt Naomi weren't always talking about me like I'm the one who's going to change everything. I know they want me to be among the fifteen percent of Jews who are allowed to study law or medicine, but it's just not something that excites me. When I look at Uncle Max's hopeful face, I know I could never tell him that.

12.

One evening, when I'm alone at home, the doorbell rings and I open it to a woman with dark hair piled high on her head.

"Are you Hannah Pinker's daughter?" she asks.

My breath stalls. What if she's from the Mount Sinai

Sanatorium in Sainte-Agathe and she has bad news. Maybe she didn't want to deliver it to Uncle Max and Aunt Naomi on the phone, so she came to find me in person.

"Yes," I whisper.

The woman switches to German and says, "My name is Lea Roback and I'm here from the Garment Workers Union. We heard about your mother and we took up a collection. It's not much, but we hope it helps while your mother is not able to work." She hands me an envelope and smiles warmly.

"Thank you," I reply, the German heavy on my tongue, I haven't used it in so long.

"If you ever need anything I can be reached at that number on the envelope."

I feel my eyes tearing up. I want to invite this woman inside and ask her a million questions. She seems like she might know so much about things. I need someone other than Uncle Max and Aunt Naomi to tell me everything's going to be okay.

"I was over there too," Lea Roback says, as if she can read my mind. "But I left in '32, before things got really terrible. I can't imagine what you witnessed, dear girl."

I just let the tears come.

"The war effort is strong. Don't lose hope, Edie. That's your name, isn't it? Your mother talked about you all the time."

"Thank you," I say. "I won't."

"Good. You need to stay strong for three people, now. You, your mama and your papa," she says, squeezing my arm. "Goodbye Edie."

I watch her head up the street, dodging a group of boys who are pushing each other in milk crates strapped onto wheels.

13.

Mama needs surgery. The money Lea gave me is going to help pay for it, along with money Aunt Naomi was able to get from the Jewish Appeal. On Saturday Uncle Max tries to explain what the doctor told him about something called thoracoplasty, but the idea of collapsing Mama's lung on purpose just doesn't make sense to me. And they're going to remove some of her ribs to do so. Poor Mama! I'm not even allowed to see her to wish her luck. If only I could talk to Papa, to hear him tell me not to worry, that everything's going to be fine. The doctors will stitch her back together, weaving in and out of her fair skin as delicately as Papa making one of his silk suits.

Aunt Naomi says we should take a walk to clear our heads and think about other things. We wander down The Main to Sainte-Catherine, then turn toward Morgan's, where the fake king and queen stood on the balcony two years ago. Across, a crowd has gathered in Phillips Square, around the bronze statue of Edward VII, the current king's grandfather. As far as I can tell, the monarchy hasn't done much to stop the war, like Uncle Max said they would. But he won't allow me to disparage the British. He said they're fighting their hardest against the Germans, more than anyone else, and that if Hitler gets the United Kingdom, the world is sunk.

A group of men are shouting, waving their arms high in the air. I want to cross to see more closely but Uncle Max holds me back. "Haven't you learned, Edie? Crowds mean trouble."

A few men tumble out from the middle and my whole body shakes when I see what they're wearing— red arm bands with the black swastika. The symbol is a crooked hook that snags on my heart and rips it open. Before I know it, I'm running through traffic and across the streetcar tracks, charging toward the men. I gather all the spit I can in my mouth, forming it into the biggest ball I can muster. When one of the men, who's wearing a tiny moustache above his lips, is not more than two feet away, I open my mouth and hurl my spitball at him. It lands on his nose, as sure as a missile. His face turns toward me and our eyes lock. His are full of hatred. For a second I freeze, wondering what it would be like to be so hateful, but then I loosen up because I know. I feel it too. Every part of me despises this man I don't even know, who's wearing the symbol that shattered my life.

14.

When I get home, Louisa's not there. Neither is Annette. I can tell because if she's home there's always music upstairs, or the thumping of her feet as she dances around. But it's quiet now, completely quiet. Uncle Max and Aunt Naomi wanted me to stay with them overnight, but I didn't want to. They act like I'm still twelve and need protecting, but I don't. I don't know what I need. There's an ache inside me all the time and nothing makes it go away. All the people I felt closest to are gone—Mama and Papa, and even Sabine. And then there's Annette.

Being with her makes me feel so good, so free, but it's always just for an hour or two and her face never lights up when she sees me, like it does for Benny. And I can't tell Aunt Naomi and Uncle Max that. What would they think of me if they knew the way Annette makes me feel?

The summer before we came here, I visited Berlin with Mama. She and Uncle Max and Aunt Naomi went to a cabaret show one night, while I stayed at the hotel. They came back late and I pretended to be asleep while they sat around talking, giggling and squealing as they went over the act—the dances and the costumes and the music. Mama kept saying she never expected to see anything like that. Finally, Uncle Max said, "Hannah, Hannah, Hannah, you can be so naïve. Why should you be shocked? Girls with girls. Boys with boys. This is Berlin." Mama shushed them with one finger over her mouth, the other pointing at me. I kept my eyes closed, wanting to hear it all. They still smelled of cigarettes and excitement, as though they had carried a piece of the show in with them. They continued laughing for a long time, but would they be so lighthearted about something like that in real life?

15.

Going back to school is harder than ever before—I drag myself there, wanting to turn back with each step. No one would know. Louisa leaves for the factory before me. Annette never wakes up before noon and she wouldn't care if I quit—she never even finished high school. I'm not sure Mama would care, now that she's using every ounce of her energy to get better. All three surgeries were successful, but her tuberculosis hasn't diminished. It's persistent, more persistent than with other patients who've come and gone in the nine months she's been there. She's nothing more than a wisp now, and last time we went she couldn't even get up, so the nurse wheeled her bed over to the visiting area. In a way I was glad she couldn't sit up because I didn't want to see how collapsed her chest would look, with its missing ribs. It's only the thought of Papa and what he would say that pushes me forward toward school. I feel his hand at my back and his voice in my ear.

Up ahead, all the girls are standing around giggling, probably talking about the exciting things they did this summer. Dot and Betty are among them. I only saw them once this summer, sitting in a window booth at the

Prince of Wales Café in their Junior Red Cross uniforms, probably making plans to collect money or do other stuff for the war.

Our new homeroom teacher, Miss C., seems okay. She tells us to call her that because her real name has sixteen letters and is hard to say. "And even harder to spell," she says. She'll be our English teacher this year, so we'll see her first thing each morning and then later in the day too. I'm kind of glad because she seems nice and she wants us to perform some Shakespeare. When she hands out the assignment, to choose a speech of at least twelve lines from any Shakespeare play and memorize it, a flutter of both excitement and dread fills me.

"And remember," she says, "you can be anyone. You can be either sex too. You can be someone from another race or religion. Stretch yourselves. Or, choose a passage that says something you can relate to. There's something for everyone in Shakespeare."

She reminds me of what I loved about playacting with Sabine. We could be anyone or anywhere, even if we were just in that musty basement storage room. When we cranked open the little window and sang, we were performing for the world and not just the birds in the bushes.

16.

Miss C. doesn't blast the war news during class and I'm glad. She says that if anything major happens we'll know it soon enough and that people our age don't need to be inundated with bad news all day long. "School is the time for growth and creativity, not death and fear," she says. She's right. I catch what's going on in the evenings, listening to the radio with Louisa. Sometimes Annette pops down, always with some busywork in her hands, like nylons to repair or nail polish to reapply. Hitler's army is now swarming all through Russia. They were almost at Moscow, and now they've surrounded the city of Leningrad. In class, I look up at the vast yellow expanse that is Russia, stretching across the top of Asia, practically from one ocean to the other, and I can't believe there'd be enough German soldiers to capture it, but it sounds like that's what's happening. Uncle Max's worst predictions are coming true.

"I hope Brian's not in Russia," Louisa says. "It sounds awful, especially with winter around the corner."

"This isn't a sea battle, Louisa," I say.

"Well, still, you never know," she snaps. "Honestly, our factory can't pump those weapons out fast enough. You really should join us, Annette." It's not the first time

Louisa's tried to get Annette to become a bomb girl.

"We're all doing our bit in our own way, you know," Annette replies. "Sending the men off happy and boosting their morale isn't doing nothing. You should see the smiles on the men's faces when they watch the show. And Benny's doing more than his fair share. I hardly see him anymore. It seems like the minute he gets back they're sending him across with another plane."

I grab a flowered pillow and hold it to my mouth when she says that, so she won't see me smile.

17.

Louisa comes home all excited because a photographer was at the factory, taking pictures of the bomb girls for the *Montreal Star*. The story will be part of a series on women of the home front and what they're doing for the war. "We were actually allowed to take a ten-minute break to put makeup on, just for the shoot. We had to go wash it off again after they left, but it was so much fun. And they let us poke some of our hair out from under our caps. Imagine if Brian sees it, wherever he is."

A few weeks later, Louisa brings home a copy of the paper and flips it open to a ten-page spread.

The DIL factory in Verdun is just one of many places photographed and Louisa's face is a little smiling dot in the corner. She said they were just pretending to fill the shells with chemicals—it was all staged for the cameras. No kidding! I doubt she and the others smile like that when they're actually working.

"Isn't this something?" she asks.

I know Mama would want me to be kind to Louisa, so I don't tell her that if Brian and the other sailors do see the pictures, they won't be looking at her. They'll be looking at the inserts of gorgeous girls, smiling like Hollywood stars as they do various things, like packing bullets in big boxes. One girl is hugging a huge torpedo like it's about to twirl her around the dance floor.

"It's fantastic, Louisa," I say.

She cuts out her picture and tapes it to a kitchen cupboard, under the picture of Brian in his navy uniform. I wish I had a picture of Mama at the garment factory, bent over her machine sewing uniforms. That was work for the home front too.

18.

I'm sitting in science class when the principal's secretary

knocks on the door and asks for me. "Bring all your things, Edie," she calls out. I hate the feeling of everyone watching me as I shove my books into my schoolbag. My pencils roll off the little groove and land on the floor, the lead tips exploding loudly as bombs. Then it's all slow motion as I walk to the door, my hands sweating. As soon as I'm released from the staring eyes, my mind goes wild. Maybe they've found out I don't belong here and they're sending me back to Germany. We all had to take pictures for national ID cards, now that we're sixteen. Maybe that's when they discovered the error. Mama hasn't been able to do the paperwork, but Uncle Max is supposed to be on top of the things we need to do to get our citizenship papers. Maybe those horrid men in Phillips Square have turned enough people against us and they've decided Hitler is right—we are ruining their country. But the secretary wouldn't be smiling at me so warmly.

"Just have a seat dear. Mr. Wilson won't be long," she says. She pats my shoulder and disappears behind the swinging wooden gate. A minute later, Mr. Wilson's door opens and he waves me into his office. Uncle Max and Aunt Naomi are sitting in two big chairs opposite his desk.

"Edie," Aunt Naomi says, springing up. She takes my hand and pulls me to the chair beside hers. Uncle Max's eyes are red. Suspense is thick in the air, making it hard to breath.

"What's going on? Why are you here?"

"It's your—it's your Mama," Uncle Max says finally. "She … she …" He heaves up a huge sob and sticks his hanky under his nose.

"Oh Edie," says Aunt Naomi, standing behind me, her hands on my shoulders. "We had a call from the Sanatorium this morning. Your Mama had a very rough night and they think we should come right away."

"But what does that mean? Are you saying—"

"Your aunt and uncle have come to take you up to Sainte-Agathe, Edie. Best not to do too much speculation before you get there. We need to be strong in these situations, especially in times of war," says Mr. Wilson. "People will be dealing with all kinds of tragedies right now."

My head pops up and I glare at him. "Oh, I know, Mr. Wilson. I've already left my papa behind in a place that's trying to kill him. And Mama never would have caught TB back home, working with Papa in his shop and living in our warm apartment. So I know all about war and tragedy."

Mr. Wilson's face is bright red but I don't care. Uncle Max is standing too now and he and Aunt Naomi are moving me toward the door.

"Thank you, Mr. Wilson," Uncle Max says. "We'll let you know what happens."

The last time Uncle Max talked to Papa from Munich, he repeated the same phrase over and over, telling Papa not to worry. "Nothing will happen to them, Jacob, I promise." Uncle Max must feel the weight of Mama's illness as hard as I do. And Aunt Naomi too. Her face is crumbling. Mama is her baby sister, after all. I hook one arm through each of theirs and lead them out of the building.

19.

I don't remember the drive taking this long before. My stomach is starting to roil, like it did on the ship. This time, it's as much from fear of seeing Mama even sicker as from the twisting country roads. Finally, I see the mountains but it's like each one is the width of the Atlantic Ocean and I think we'll never get to where Mama is. As always, we pass the sign on the tree. All three of us go silent and keep our eyes straight ahead, as though we can make it vanish.

Mount Sinai Sanatorium is still impressive, with its three stone arches; it should hold the answers to any illness. The menorahs above the entrance and the huge Star of David in the foyer should be comforting, but when I see the expression on the doctor's face I know they weren't able to help Mama. The doctor greets us and takes us straight to his office and I know before he even opens his mouth that Mama has died. I can hardly follow what he's saying as he talks about the bacteria spreading to other organs. Her kidneys, her liver. Poor Mama! Her whole body was fighting the disease. It didn't have a chance. The fresh mountain air and the rest were supposed to be enough, but they weren't. And now everything that we did to get here seems like a waste. We could have stayed home with Papa. But when I look behind the doctor, out the window, I tell myself that Mama died in a beautiful place. She spent almost a year looking out at the pine-covered mountains. That has to be better than dying the way the BBC says so many of our people are dying back home. I hold myself together with that thought. But when the nurse brings Mama's bag into the room, I break down. I remember it packed and ready to go to Mount Sinai with her, so full of hope.

20.

After Mama's funeral, we sit shiva for seven days at Uncle Max and Aunt Naomi's tiny flat. We sit on little chairs, our bottoms almost touching the floor. Aunt Naomi explains that being closer to the earth is supposed to make us humble. People come in and out, bringing plates piled high with food. I've never met any of them, but Uncle Max and Aunt Naomi know them from the store or the neighbourhood, or the Bagg Street Shul nearby. Most of them never met Mama either, yet, when they take my hand and bow their heads, I feel their sorrow for my loss deep in my bones.

When I go to the bathroom, I lift the shawl that's covering the mirror and peek at my face. I think I should look different now, but I don't.

21.

Dot and Betty tell me how sorry they are about Mama, but they don't know what else to say. Their own mothers are alive and well and have started a wartime cooking club where they teach other mothers how to cook with less. Dot gives the class a presentation on a war cake that you make with no eggs or butter. The trick is to use tons of raisins. She gives us each a small piece to try but I only wrap mine in paper and stick it in my desk.

"I made copies of the recipe, if you want to bring them home to your mothers," says Dot. When she catches my eyes, she lowers hers, embarrassed. "Or, you can try making it yourself," she adds. I take one because I know she's trying to be nice.

Louisa's also trying her best to be nice but she doesn't quite know what to do. She and Annette came to the funeral and to Uncle Max's once while we were sitting shiva. I could see how hard it was for Annette to sit still and not talk. I remembered her describing a wake at Benny's house when his aunt died. They drank and sang and danced all night long, shaking the walls. "A proper Irish send-off," she called it. The shiva must have seemed so strange to her.

Louisa hasn't bothered me about moving into the parlour. I wasn't able to sleep in the back room, surrounded by Mama's things. Whenever I looked up at that unfinished dress all I wanted to do was rip the seams holding the various swatches together. I thought they were sewn, but when I looked more closely, they were only basted together with big ugly stitches.

22.

The roar of engines fills the grey November sky, drowning out the sound of our math teacher, who instantly stops scribbling formulas on the board. We look around at each other and shrug. Maybe we should jump under our desks. What if this is an actual air raid? Then white things start falling from the sky, floating down like strange birds. When they come closer, we see that they're sheets of paper, thousands of them. Suddenly, the back doors of the school open and kids are running into the yard to scoop up the leaflets. Our teacher motions to the door and our classroom empties too. I reach up and grab a sheet as it lands. On it is a picture of a woman in an overall, her hair tied up in the same type of kerchief Louisa has to wear. She's holding a bomb and underneath are the words, "I'm making bombs and buying bonds!" I look up at the sky but the planes have moved on. I wonder if one of the pilots was Benny.

23.

The German army is losing in Russia. The BBC announcer is so excited he's tripping over his words. When he throws out words like "potential retreat" and "likely defeat" I picture him dancing in his broadcasting booth. When he talks about Hitler being furious, I see the funny-looking Führer shaking with anger, throwing up his arms in all directions. When he describes the cold and frozen landscape the soldiers are fighting on, chills run up my spine. And when he talks about hunger and famine and emaciated frozen bodies it makes me feel like I shouldn't ever complain about my life again, even if I have lost Mama and Papa.

24.

The streets are noisier than usual one Sunday morning in December. People are hollering back and forth to each other like they do in summer, when everyone's sitting outside. When Louisa turns on the radio, we learn why. The Japanese have bombed an American naval base in Hawaii, a place called Pearl Harbor, which I'd never heard of before. Three hundred Japanese planes sunk eight naval ships and most likely killed thousands of people. The announcer says the war is closer than ever, but that's weird because Hawaii is farther away from here than Germany.

25.

The next day at school, the principal orders every teacher to bring their class to the auditorium to hear President Roosevelt's speech on the radio. In his scratchy voice, Roosevelt declares that yesterday, December 7, "will live in infamy." He talks about how the Japanese tricked the Americans into thinking all was well between them, but that they must have been planning the attack for a long time. He sounds like he's just realized that people are in "grave danger."

In English class, Miss C. looks like she wants to cry. "Oh, dear," she says, playing with the tip of her collar. "I don't see how we're supposed to focus on anything else today. What would Shakespeare have to say about President Roosevelt's speech? War was one of his big themes, you know?" She starts listing all the plays that have a war in them. The list is long and I let her words sink into the background as I stare out at the window and watch the snow fall. It's so white—it's like it doesn't know how much dirt there is in the world.

26.

The United States is officially at war with Germany.

Everything feels different now, bigger somehow. When I'm at Uncle Max and Aunt Naomi's for Chanukah, Uncle Max declares, "It's about time." Aunt Naomi can't stop smiling, like she's brimming with hope. The announcer on the radio says that this must surely mean the war will soon be over. I close my eyes and send a prayer to Papa as I light the menorah. I tell him to hang on. Wherever you are, just hang on. Roosevelt is sending over hundreds of thousands of men and planes and ships to rescue you.

27.

Benny won't be ferrying planes across the Atlantic anymore. He's joined the Royal Canadian Air Force and is going to be flying overseas instead. He broke the news to Annette last night, at the Picadilly, surrounded by a dozen other pilots. Annette's been crying in our parlour for an hour, telling us about it. In between sobs, she lets slip that he broke up with her too before saying goodbye. He said it would be best if they were both completely free, like the wings on his lapel, but I know Annette was expecting more. She was hoping Benny would ask her to marry him. So many men do before heading overseas that the city held a group wedding at city hall. I saw pictures in the *Star*. There were at least a hundred couples, all saying their vows and kissing at the same time, like a huge choreographed dance. I'm glad Annette and Benny weren't among them.

28.

Dot and Betty and two other girls are working on collecting items to put into Christmas baskets for children whose parents have no money to buy presents. They set up boxes, trimmed with tinsel, in the school foyer. Dot tells us that none of the toys we donate should have metal or rubber in them because she'd be obliged to turn those in for their materials. Wood is still safe, though. I think of the wonderful doll collection I left behind. I wonder if they'd be safe. They were mostly porcelain, with glass eyes. Papa made such wonderful dresses for them.

Dot is holding up a colouring book called "Your Daddy and Mine." On its cover, four men are marching off the page, each dressed in a different military outfit—a sailor, a pilot, a soldier, and an ordinary worker in overalls. "They only cost a quarter and our goal is to put one in every basket, so if you can spare any change at all, the JRC would appreciate it," she says. She passes the book around so we can see it more closely. When it comes to me I read the words under the picture: *Your Daddy and mine are fighting to make the world free, for you and me. Here are pictures of them in action for you to colour.*

What would a picture of Papa look like on the cover? Not now, but back when he was a German soldier in the First World War. I've seen pictures of him in his handsome uniform. It's impossible for me to believe that he was once on the side of the people who are now trying to kill him.

I drop a quarter in Dot's box and force myself to smile

1942

SABINE

I.

Winter is cold and we don't have as much coal for heating as we used to. Pictures of the *Kohlenklau* are everywhere. He's a short fat man, dressed all in black, with a sack of stolen coal tossed over his shoulder. He's supposed to scare us into using less coal, but the *Kohlenklau* just makes us laugh, with his long white moustache drooping down past his chin like animal whiskers.

We're only allowed one bath per week and we're supposed to share the water, so by the time Mama and I are done the water is cold. We can't ask Herr Pinker to step into a cold and dirty bath, so Mama boils water and he washes in a tin basin. On the radio, a daily announcement reminds us to "Save soap—preserve your linen," so we only do laundry every five weeks. My clothes are all grey and sweaty from working at the KLV. I hang them around the house at night to air them out, but it only helps a little. When we do wash them, we have to use grey powdered soap that smells like mud. Mama soaks our clothes overnight before boiling them in the kettle on our stove. Then she spends the day scrubbing them on the washboard. They almost turn to rags beneath her hands. We can use our ration stamps to replace some things, but Mama says we have to make these stamps last over a year. I started with 60 points, but two pairs of underwear used up 20, then 18 for a skirt and another 14 for a pullover. I have hardly any points left.

Herr Pinker says he wants to contribute, so he uses Mama's sewing supplies and mends our things, giving our stockings a bit more life, and letting down the hems of my skirts more professionally. Mama had a box of old curtains that he uses for trim, when there's no hem left. He knows how to add strips to the sides too, so my skirts don't pucker around my hips. Mama's clothes need to be taken in, she's gotten so thin, and sometimes I feel bad that hiding Herr Pinker has made her more nervous than she already was. Whenever we hear footsteps on the walkway Mama freezes. Twice, the Hitler Youth have come to collect metal and glass, but we've given all we have. We only have one pot—the rest got taken. It makes me sad to think of Papa's beautiful instruments, with their tortoise shell handles, melted down for ammunition, but I bet that's what's happened.

The boys don't always stop at the door; they barge right in to look around, like they live here. Once, Werner was with them. He hung behind the others and said he'd check the pantry. He came out with some empty tins that Mama had been saving.

"That's all you could find," one of his groupmates said. "What's in there anyway?" When he started to open the door, Werner braced his hand against the boy's chest, to block him.

"Hey, show some respect. See, it's an old war veteran." He pointed to Herr Pinker's Iron Cross that Mama had hung on the door handle. "The old man's not well. Leave him in peace." The door was slightly ajar and we could hear Herr Pinker breathing heavily.

"Even old war heroes have to do their bit, Werner. Step back! He probably has a stack of trophies or something he's hiding. I know the type."

I grabbed Mama's hand to stop her shaking as the boy marched into Herr Pinker's room. We could hear him walk around the tiny bed, then stop. I prayed Herr Pinker was pretending to sleep, with the blanket pulled up. If this kid, who must have taken Hans's place as the group leader, looked at Herr Pinker closely, would he be able to tell who he was, or what he was? We held our breath until the boy came out.

"Sorry, old man," he cried out. "Okay, let's move on. Hey, tell your opa he needs to stick a pin in Greece." Everything in me let go. So that's what he'd been looking at—Hans's map. *Thank you, Hans,* I muttered to the ceiling. Werner squeezed my hand quickly on the way out.

2.

The greyest part of my life right now is that Emma had to go home. Her duty year finished months ago, but Frau Prinz was too busy to notice, until now, when the papers came. It was so hard saying goodbye to her at the train station. We clung to each other until the last possible second, when a group of soldiers had to pull her on board and squeeze her inside, the train was so full. I worry about Emma, she is so bold. I think of her mother sitting in Ravensbrück prison and pray Emma will never join her there, that she'll learn to hold her tongue. When she said goodbye to Frau Prinz, instead of curtsying and thanking her, she said, "One day there will be a hell for people like you." Frau Prinz's face turned dark and she pulled back her hand, but she didn't strike. Emma's words had frozen her. By the time she melted, we were running down the road. If the KLV had a phone, I swear Frau Prinz would have called ahead to have her arrested at the station.

I hate being alone with Frau Prinz. Yesterday, she forced all the new girls to write to their fathers. She stood over them and watched, smacking the heads of anyone who wrote with their left hand, or who wrote anything negative. They couldn't even say they were homesick because that showed weakness. And if they said they didn't like the food, she sent them to bed with no supper. In the end, she dictated the letter for them, so that each girl sent the exact same message:

> *Dearest Papa,*
> *I hope this letter finds you well and strong in*
> *your fight against our Fatherland's enemies.*

*I am so proud of the work you are doing for
the Führer. I am well looked after here, in my
Kinderlandverschickung. It was so thoughtful
of the Führer to think of me and give me this
holiday in the fresh air of the country. I am
learning so many wonderful things that will
help me be a wonderful mother in the future
and I am staying strong and fit and healthy,
like the Führer wants me to be.*

Heil Hitler,
Your loving daughter

I imagine two fathers in the same tank reading the same letter. Would they laugh or cry?

3.

A letter comes from Hans and when Mama and I see it we look at each other and don't say a word. It must be awful for Mama to hope that her only son isn't coming home, especially since he's now eighteen and will soon be joining the *Wehrmacht*. My only hope is that he won't come here first. I imagine Hans will want to be where the action is, in Hamburg or Berlin. Those cities have already been bombed, although on the radio Hitler said it was nothing, just Great Britain trying to act tougher than they are. Only one unimportant building in each city was hit, compared to the damage the Luftwaffe is doing in London. Even Buckingham Palace was hit. I pictured the King and Queen hiding out in the palace basement, eating tinned peaches and cucumber sandwiches. Maybe Hans was doing his service as a flak helper in one of those Hamburg bombings, passing up the shells to the big anti-aircraft guns. If he does come home, he'll brag about it nonstop. What am I saying? If he does come home, Mama and I are in so much trouble, I can't even think about it.

Mama is reading the letter quickly and I know she's looking for one line only. When she's done, we collapse in each other's arms and Mama cries, "We're safe, for now. Hans is going straight into his *Reichsarbeitsdienst*, one year of service and training that will lead him into the army." Half the letter describes the spade that is the group's symbol. Hans says it shines like silver and they pass it around at roll call, like we used to do with Papa's instruments. He ends the letter with a request to Mama.

*My goal, as you know Mama, is to join the
SS. I'm sure you and Sabine have finished
working on the Ahnenpaß for our family. I
need to prove our Aryan blood back to 1800,
1750 if I hope to be an officer. I am sure that
will not prove difficult, only there are times I
am sure Sabine is related to the gypsies. Please
make sure it's all done and ready for me to use
when I need to, which I hope will be very soon.*

It was nice of Hans to throw in a joke, but he must
know it's the type of joke that could be taken seriously,
especially since his letter was read first. Much of it is
blacked out. And we haven't finished the *Ahnenpaß*; in
fact, we haven't touched it since he left almost two years
ago. But, if it keeps Hans away from home for longer, I'll
try to work on it when I can.

4.

The best thing in my life is Werner. When he's not
busy with school or his Hitler Youth group, he comes to
the KLV to help out. Frau Prinz likes him because he's
polite and does exactly what she tells him to, without

complaint. "You'll make an excellent soldier soon," she says. I hate when she says that because I know that his *Pflichtjahr* is coming up and he'll most likely get sent somewhere far from here, maybe even way up north like Hans. Wouldn't Hans love to have Werner to boss around again?

When Frau Prinz isn't around, Werner makes the girls laugh with magic tricks, pulling *pfennigs* out of their ears, or producing rabbits that he borrows from the hutches. It helps the new girls relax, especially when Werner places the rabbits in their laps to pet.

One day, Frau Prinz asks me and Werner to gather all the straw we can find, which isn't easy in the middle of March. She's teaching the girls how to make slippers out of old blankets and straw. The blankets are wool, but paper thin and worn with holes. The girls learn to cut around the holes and make the base, then sew up the sides. The straw slippers are plaited, round and round, like little rugs that will keep the soldiers' soles protected. Werner is our foot model. His feet are as big as a grown man's so the girls use them to check their sizing. He says the straw itches and the wool scratches but Frau Prinz says any good soldier is prepared to be uncomfortable if the cause is right. "That's something you'll soon learn," she adds, smiling.

When the girls have made one pair of each kind, Frau Prinz sends them off to cut pictures of Hitler out of *Neues Volk* to paste into their scrapbooks, alongside the cards the girls have already collected from their relatives' cigarette packs. Werner and I take the slippers to the local depot where all the goods being sent to the front are collected. We ride our bikes and stop halfway to sit by the river, where no one can see us. "We should throw the sack into the river," Werner says. "There are people all up and down the Danube who need warm feet." I picture a group of kids downstream, in another town or even country, finding the slippers and setting them on the bank to dry.

"Impossible," I say. "She'll be waiting for that receipt like her life depends on it, the old cow."

Werner pulls me close and kisses me. I close my eyes and imagine there is no war. Werner and I are just two sixteen-year-old kids, falling in love. We have nothing on our minds to worry us. We're just planning a bicycle trip for the weekend, with a picnic lunch in the basket. Or a stroll around town, past the *Marktplatz* that is piled high with food—no ration stamps needed.

"You know, it could all be worse," Werner says. "Way worse. Even if we were living just up the road, in Stuttgart. They've already been bombed. My aunt lives there and she saw it happen. Or up north. Or … well, you know, if we were like Herr Pinker. Have you heard the rumors about what they're doing? My mother heard some things at the market, from some women whose husbands came back from Poland. The stories they're telling are hard to believe."

"But Frau Prinz says none of it's true. She says our enemies started those rumors to make us look bad, because they're jealous of our success."

"And you believe her? Since when?"

"Since never!" I rest my head on his shoulder and watch the brown water float by. It's dirtier now than it was four years ago. The factory where my father used to work doesn't stop chugging and spewing out garbage, twenty-four hours a day. It's top secret now, what they're making. The roofs of the buildings have been covered in branches, to hide them from the sky.

5.

Hans filled in his *Ahnenpaß* back to 1820, through parish records, which were easy enough to find. When Opa was alive he could help with his side and he knew some about Oma's. Werner and I are walking through an old cemetery where the tombstones are so blackened and rotten they are hard to read. The priest suggested we come here since the newer cemetery in town only opened mid-1800. This one is hidden on the side of a hill, behind a cluster of trees. We're looking for Müller, Schmidt, Schäfer, Wagner, Becker, Bauer, Köhler, Huber—all good workers' names, the names of my great-great-great grandparents on Mama's side. That's my heritage: millers, smiths, shepherds, wagoners, bakers, builders, coalers, and one lone landowner. I imagine he was the rich landlord's son who fell in love with the baker's daughter and couldn't help himself. We're still Schmidts and it suits Papa because he's a metal smith, moulding that hard material into any shape he wants. Papa always said our region is known for its hardworking people and that its names reflect that.

A tiny tombstone sticking up like a rotten tooth draws my attention. I brush the dirt off the front and uncover the etching: Anna Schäfer, 1735–1755. Such a short life. A shepherd's wife, she probably died in childbirth, like so many women back then. But if she's our great great-

great-grandmother, Hans will have what he wants—
Aryan blood back to 1750. I hope that's far enough to
keep him away.

6.

Herr Pinker lies in his room, day after day, not doing
much of anything. We try to find things for him to read
but the only newspapers we have now are the *Völkischer
Beobachter*, *Der Angriff* or *Der Stürmer*, and they're full of
stuff that would only hurt him. Frau Prinz makes the girls
read them daily; they cut out the pictures of Hitler and
little Edda Goering, whose face is suddenly everywhere,
all curls and frills. She cuts out the daily cartoons and
pins them to the wall in the kitchen. They all have
some nasty Jewish man with teeth like a rat's, ripping
apart beautiful German girls or running off with bags of
money, their stark eyebrows across their forehead like a
pair of raven wings. I don't know why she thinks the girls
so far from home need to see such things. They already
cry at night and wet their beds.

I wish I could sneak some real books in for the girls,
but Hans took those away years ago to be burned, even my
treasured copy of *Heidi*, with the pretty coloured pictures

inside gold frames. My favourite was the one of Heidi and her grandfather high in the Alps with the sheep, little wooden cottages dotting the hillside. The only book in our house now is *Mein Kampf* and it seems wrong to ask Herr Pinker if he wants to read a book by Hitler.

We could bring him paper, but if he wrote to Edie, it would give us away, unless he lied about where he is. And even then, if we mailed it in this town, it would be traced. If we asked someone to mail it from another town, they'd ask why. Besides, he wouldn't know where to send the letter in the first place. He thinks Edie is at a relative's in Canada, in a city called Montreal, but he isn't even sure. And he has no specific address. Canada is a big country. I can see it stretching across the top of North America, from the Pacific to the Atlantic and up to the Arctic Ocean, in the map above Herr Pinker's head. Oh, wouldn't it be wonderful if we could take out all the pins and replace them with just one: Edie, safe and sound somewhere in Montreal. We'd use a pink one, like the colour of Canada on the map.

We help Herr Pinker up at night, after Frau Schilling has made her last round of the block. He holds a candle and walks around the house. Mama urges him up the stairs, to keep his leg muscles from turning to jelly. But for those twenty minutes we're all on edge, our ears peeled to the walkway. We're ready to whisk him back into his room if we have to. We're ready to swear on a stack of bibles, or a stack of *Mein Kampfs*, that he is Opa.

7.

Spring is finally here so we can let the girls outside to play *Völkerball* in the field. I'm glad Frau Prinz leaves me in charge while she does her paperwork. When she supervises she doesn't let the girls hide behind each other. She tells them they have to bravely face their opponents and not flinch when the ball hits them. And they can never cry, not even if a scarlet bruise sprouts on their skin. She tells the ones who are throwing the ball not to soften their pitches. "Your friend today might be your enemy tomorrow," she says, glaring right at me.

In the afternoon, an old man with a terrible limp comes to repair our water pump while the girls are napping. I'm in the kitchen washing dishes and I can hear him talking to Frau Prinz outside the window.

"But his own relative was there, Frau Prinz. He saw it happen. They made them dig the grave themselves, then they shot them, one row at a time. Some were still alive in the hole. You can't dispute what he saw with his own two eyes."

"I can dispute whatever I like. If it wasn't in the daily report, then I don't believe it. Those Russians are master liars. Your friend's nephew just fell for it."

"No, he wasn't told. He was there. He was one of the shooters. He says he probably shot 500 Jews himself. It lasted two days, in Kiev. He is not a man to tell tales, Frau Prinz."

"Well, just remember, we never know the whole story. They must have done something first, to provoke."

"What can poor people do to provoke? These were peasants, farmers, not lawyers and bankers. Anyway, I am just telling you what I was told. I'm not passing any judgment." They're quiet for a minute and I picture Frau Prinz scowling, pulling a piece of hair out of her perfect bun, a habit she has when she's trying to concentrate.

"Okay, so the pump should be better now. You were wasting so much water before. It was good of you to notice. Your operation seems very efficient, for so many people. You're doing a great job for the Reich. Good day to you, Frau Prinz. Enjoy the spring sunshine."

Frau Prinz is harder than ever on the girls at dinner. They have to sit straight-backed and use their utensils perfectly, and not let their elbows rest on the table, even for a second. A sip of sparkling water only at the end, not after every bite, like *schweinen*. If Werner were here, he'd find a way to snort like a pig and make the girls laugh.

8.

Biking past the town limit on my way to the KLV one morning, I see some Hitler Youth nailing a huge wooden sign to a tree. The background is brown and the letters are thick and white: *Hier ist und bleibt jüdenrein*. These boys think our town is now free of Jews and that it will stay that way forever. And they may be right, except for one. I have to acknowledge them as I pass. I have to smile or comment in the right way, or it will be noted. I do what's easiest and safest. I raise my hand and say, "Heil Hitler." They all say it back.

As I bike along, I think of the story the old man told Frau Prinz. It's so hard to figure out if those things are true. I know Emma would say they are, for sure. She seemed to know from an early age that this war and all the awful things were going to happen, because of her parents' work. And it's true that all the Jews in our little town—not that there were many—have vanished. But wouldn't most of them have left the country safely, like Edie's family?

I look out into the fields as I pedal and imagine a hole like the one the man described, filled with bodies. It's impossible. No such thing could ever happen here.

9.

When I get to the KLV, Frau Prinz is talking to a girl who looks about my age. Her head is hanging down, her hair in braids. "Ah, Sabine. This is Katya, our new helper. She's from Poland, so she doesn't know much about how we keep house and cook. Your new job is to teach her, make sure she does everything properly, the German way. Katya, do everything Sabine tells you. Now go, girls. You have hungry German children waiting."

I try to smile at Katya but she won't look up. She just keeps staring at my shoes. Her own shoes are wooden clogs and her flowered skirt is long, almost to the floor. On her blue blouse, a violet "P" is sewn onto a yellow patch. "What is that?" I ask, pointing to it.

"Me," she says. "I am Polish. We have to wear."

I remember the Jews at the train station with their yellow stars. This must be the same idea. "Okay," I say. "Come with me to collect the eggs, then we'll start cooking." I smile at her, but she still won't look up.

Katya follows me around all day like a shadow, doing everything I ask her to do, but she still won't lift her head. It's like she's been ordered to keep it hanging.

At the end of the day, Frau Prinz asks me how she did. Katya's eyes are closed and I can tell she's scared of what I'll say. "She did very well," I say. I don't tell Frau Prinz that she dropped the clean towels in the yard before hanging them to dry. Or that she cut too deeply into the potatoes, wasting half of them. Or that the sound of her wooden clogs on the hard floors woke the girls at naptime.

"You can have some rest time now, Katya, before helping with bedtime. Go on, to your room." Frau Prinz waves her away, like she's swatting a fly. Katya turns toward the barn, but Frau Prinz says nothing.

"Why is she going into the barn?" I ask.

"Because that's where she'll stay. She's not here on holiday, you know, Sabine. We can't have a Polish girl under the same roof as all these German girls the Reich has entrusted us with. The back of the barn is fine. Besides, if there's one thing Polish peasants are good at, it's milking goats. You can cross that chore off your list."

10.

Our BDM group is joining the Hitler Youth to turn the city park into a vegetable garden. The order came from really high up—the *Gauleiter* of our area. Frau Prinz says the garden will grow carrots, peas, beans, rutabagas, parsnips and kohlrabi, foods that will help keep the nation healthy through the winter. Rumors are that our soldiers are starving as well as freezing to death in Russia, but Frau Prinz would never say that.

"The countryside around here is all farms, so if we need more food we must be getting desperate," I say to myself, a bit too loudly.

"Is not here, is in the city," says Katya under her breath as we march to the town park, shovels and hoes slung over our shoulders. "I see it when I pass through Berlin and Dortmund and Frankfurt before they send me here. There is much bombs."

Frau Prinz yells at us to stop talking, but I wish I could ask Katya more. She's seen so much. Sometimes, living here, it's hard to tell a war is going on, except for the fact that there's a Nazi party office in our town square and because there are hardly any men left. Plus our ration stamps and all the things we've had to give up at home. But we're not hungry. And we haven't seen or heard any fighting. Sometimes a soldier will come back with injuries and that will remind us.

Werner maneuvers over to our side of the garden so that we're working side by side. The first thing we have to do is dig out the old garden. We tear up rows and rows of flowers and dump them into tin containers. I wish I could save some and bring them home to Mama. She used to love buying fresh flowers at the market. At this time of year the windows would be wide open and a bouquet would sit on our tabletop. The wasps would fly in and Mama would laugh at my fear and scoop them inside her fist to free them outside. It all seems so long ago that we lived that way. Now, she only opens the windows a tiny bit and keeps the drapes half-drawn. I've told her to stop doing that—it looks like she's hiding something. "We need to make the house look as wide open as possible, Mama." She nods, but every day when I come home it's closed up again. I'm afraid Frau Schilling is going to wonder.

Now we're digging the rows where the little plants or seeds will be sewn. Werner is the best digger in his group. "Hey, I know where they should send you when you join the *Wehrmacht* next year," his groupmate jokes. "To work in a graveyard." Werner's face goes hard. "Yeah, no shortage of work for a gravedigger these days," another one quips. "Especially for all the Jews." Werner is turning red and I wonder if he's thinking of the hole he dug in our cellar, to help conceal a Jew.

When we lower the new plants into the holes, Werner cradles them gently. I had no problem seeing Hans holding hand grenades or pistols, but not Werner. When no one's looking I lean over and kiss his cheek. Some of the girls see me and giggle. I raise my finger to my lips and point to Frau Prinz. She's monitoring us, along with our *Bürgermeister*, as though we're all part of some subversive group that might be planning an act of sabotage with the baby vegetables.

II.

Katya and I stretch the washed linens over the bushes to bleach. While they're drying, we make chamomile tea from the flowers the girls collect on their walks into the hills. We have to boil them, then strain them through a cloth. The first time Katya did it, she didn't sterilize the cloth first and Frau Prinz was so angry. She said maybe people didn't mind drinking germs in Poland, but in Germany people liked only clean things to go into their bodies. Then we had to start all over.

I also teach Katya how to make coffee out of roasted barley. For the kids we add molasses and turn it into a pretend Moka which they like. The kids also collect acorns by the basketful and Katya and I take them to neighbouring farms to trade for potatoes and beets. She makes us a cold beet soup called *borscht* that I like, but Frau Prinz refuses to serve it to the children. "Here, we put hot food in our children's bellies. Not cold food, like cattle." Katya's face falls at these words. I spoon the purple soup eagerly into my mouth while Katya's lips curl up into the smallest smile.

12.

In the fall, Mama finally receives another letter from Hans, but it doesn't say much except that he's doing well and working hard for Hitler. He gives us a field address in Dortmund to send the *Ahnenpaß*, and tells us to hope that it brings him luck. When I walk into town to post it, I see the rows of vegetables that have sprouted up, bushy and green, in the town garden. It's odd that things can still grow in the same country where so many other things are being destroyed.

13.

Werner and I go to the small cinema together. I lean close to him in the dark. Even though the smell of that horrible soap is on his shirt, the scent of his body is stronger. He puts his arm around me while the movie lights up the screen. For the next two hours, I'm lost inside *Die Große Liebe*. It's the most amazing story. Paul is a Luftwaffe pilot who falls in love with Hanna. Because of the war, they can never get together. While Paul's fighting in Africa, Hanna is singing in Paris. When they finally make it to Rome to be married, Paul leaves to help win the war at the front. He's torn between her and his duty to the Reich. I keep wishing he'd forget about the war and stay with Hanna. It's so romantic whenever they're together. But then he has to go to Russia, where our biggest battles are still raging. I like the way Hanna waits for him all the way through. I know I'd do the same for Werner. I can't get Zarah

Leander's song out of my head the whole way home. And, even though I try not to, I can't help imagining me and Edie belting out the lyrics to "I Know a Miracle Will Happen" at the top of our lungs. At my house, Werner kisses me on the walkway. If this were the movie, bomber pilots would be zooming overhead. As it is, the only thing that's falling is the pure white snow.

14.

Mama and I jump out of our skin one night when a group of men march up our walkway, their boots rattling our windows, and bang on the door. We close the door to Herr Pinker's room and try to settle our breath before opening. Three men in brown uniforms, with swastika bands around their arms, greet us. "Heil Hitler," they all say, raising their arms. "We are selling Christmas trees, the best German pine, for the Winter Relief. The Führer wants one in every German home this year. Ladies, are you alone here?"

Mama and I both nod, then I catch myself and say, "Except for my opa. He's very old and not well." The men walk in without removing their boots, but they do take off their brown caps and brace them under their arms. From where I'm standing, the red rims of the caps look like scars along the men's chests.

"And where is your opa?" the leader asks, scanning the rooms. "Can he walk?"

"He's asleep, in there," says Mama, her voice barely above a whisper. I wish she'd let me speak. Her voice betrays her nerves.

"We can get him up for you, if you wish," I say, "but he walks so poorly it will take time. He's had his medication for the night now."

"No, no need. Just show me," he says. I point to the pantry door, which still holds the Iron Cross and Hans's old poster about Hitler being our last hope. "A former soldier, I see. Wonderful!" Mama's knees are shaking across from me.

"Of course. I will tell him you're here." I open the door wide and bounce inside. "Opa, Opa. Are you awake? These men have come to say hello to you. They're selling Christmas trees for the Winter Relief. Isn't that great?" I lift Herr Pinker's head off the pillow and I can feel him playing along, making himself weaker than he is. He raises a hand to salute. He breathes out the words "Heil Hitler," as light as air.

"You would like to see these beautiful ladies purchase a tree, wouldn't you, old soldier? For the Reich." Herr Pinker nods and smiles. "Yes, I thought so. Okay men, bring them a big one, in honour of the Iron Cross. And, don't worry Opa—you can put a pin in big bad Russia soon enough. Early in the new year, I say." Herr Pinker manages a broad smile. "And a final solution for the Jews has already begun, so you can rest well, Opa, with no worries about the safety of these ladies." Herr Pinker smiles again and I think how it must take every ounce of will in his body to turn his cheeks soft.

"Heil Hitler, old man," the brownshirt says and Herr Pinker raises his hand and says it one more time, expelling his breath with great effort. He's not acting anymore—this meeting has weakened him.

The men drag a six-foot tree into our parlour, then lean it in the corner. Mama drops some coins into a red collection box that one of them shakes under her nose. They say *Dankeschön* and leave. The house should smell of pine, but it doesn't. It smells brown, somehow, like the colour suddenly has an odor, thick as mud.

15.

On Christmas day Mama turns on the radio and we hear thousands of soldiers singing "Silent Night" from Stalingrad, in Russia. They sound warm and happy and I imagine they just ate bowls of turkey soup. Or maybe purple *borscht?*

EDIE

I.

This is the coldest winter yet, so we only go into the back room to refill the coal bucket. I can't believe Mama and I slept here for three full winters. The biting wind seeps through the cracks, leaving a thin layer of ice on the exposed walls. Louisa says that as long as I turn the front room back into a proper parlour in the morning I can keep sleeping on the sofa—at least until Brian comes home.

If that happens, I might have no choice but to move to Uncle Max and Aunt Naomi's new flat, west of The Main.

"No more cold water flat for us, Edie," Aunt Naomi says. "See, turn the tap. What comes out? Hot water, just like at home. It'll be like old times soon."

But it's far from old times. She has no piano, no

china cabinet, no original artwork on the walls. And I have no Mama and Papa. But I don't say that. It's nice to see them happy.

"This little alcove here could hold a bed for you, Edie. Anytime, you know that."

"Thanks Aunt Naomi," I reply. Mama's older sister always had more than Mama—more height, more money, more shoes, more luck. But I can see Mama in her warm hazel eyes. Sometimes, when I look at them for too long, I have to turn away.

2.

Annette is now a cocktail waitress at the Esquire and she still dances with the TNT Revue. That means I don't see her much. She sleeps all day and leaves for work soon after I get home from school. Sometimes, if I hurry, I run up and catch her putting the finishing touches to her face. "Our boss says we have to pop, in more ways than one, if you know what I mean. That way, the boys will see us through the haze of smoke." Annette's shift includes serving drinks and dancing, in rotation. Her boss's motto is: "Send 'em off happy." She's not supposed to dance more than two times with the same soldier.

That way, they'll stop between numbers and order more drinks. But while she's doing those two dances, she has to make them feel like they're on top of the world and not about to go off into the inferno.

"I've gotten real good at half-listening and laughing," she tells me. "Watch." She pulls me up and tells me to pretend I'm the soldier. "Just say anything, go on." So I ramble boring stuff about what's happening at school while we twirl around her tiny room. Every few seconds Annette throws her head back and laughs and it works. She makes me feel like the most important person in the world.

I love the way she leaves her red lips on a tissue before leaving. When she's not looking, I slip one into my pocket.

3.

On February 22, the whole city goes dark for the practice blackout. Louisa, Annette and I sit in the parlour and hold hands. Nothing is moving outside—no motors, no horses, no kids whipping balls against the brick with hockey sticks, no ship's horn blasting on the river. It's one hundred percent still and dark. The moon's nothing more than a sliver and wouldn't even light our way to the bathroom. Annette is squeezing my hand tightly and I'm imagining that she and I are in London, taking shelter from the bombing, deep in the tunnels of the London tube where all the trains have stopped running. I read that when the whistling starts you can count to six before the bomb hits, but we'd be too deep to hear even that. Annette and I could sing songs in the dark to keep people's minds off their fear. And, if we did hear something scary, we'd have each other to lean into.

4.

The news reports are full of stories about people marching against conscription in Quebec. Ten thousand people gathered in a square in downtown Montreal, chanting: "*Non à la guerre*," but it didn't work. In April the majority of people across the country vote to release Prime Minister King from his promise not to conscript men. In Montreal, men throw garbage cans into government offices and burn war posters in open bins. Every bit of news breaks my heart. Why don't people here want to help defeat the Nazis and free my papa? I think how Papa would do anything to help other people. Every year, he made two white communion dresses covered in lace for poorer Catholic kids in our town. He said it would be awful if they went off to such an important ceremony feeling inferior. Their parents could pay him any way they wanted, even in food. Why can't everyone be that generous?

5.

Louisa and I are knitting socks for the navy with special waterproof yarn. "I love to think of Brian wearing one of my pairs," Louisa says. "I wish I could put an L on them somewhere, so he might know, but the patterns are so regulated." We also knit gloves for air force gunners, which are complicated because of the free index finger.

"I like to imagine whoever wears these killing Hitler," I say. "I wish I could knit some magic in them to make that happen."

The rough yarn is hard to work with and after a while our hands get sore, but we listen to Lux Theatre on the radio to take our minds off the pain. When William Powell and Hedy Lamarr star in *Love Crazy*, I hang on to every word. I love Hedy's voice—creamy, with just a hint of a German accent at the end of her words, so faint I wonder if anyone else would notice.

When we hear Annette's heels tap down the stairs, we turn to the window. Her coat is just a flash of red as she runs past the gallery. If she's on a date we can't tell. Her dates can't pick her up anymore because of gas rations. If Benny were still here, there's no way he'd have gotten a permit to drive his convertible around town. And if Mama were only going to the Mount Sinai now, we wouldn't have been able to visit her.

Nothing stops Annette though. Louisa always sighs and rolls her eyes. "That one!" she says. I sigh too, inside, but for a different reason.

6.

Dot and Betty have boyfriends now, two guys in Grade 12, who are almost old enough to join the army. I see them around school, doing their Junior Red Cross work, all four of them laughing like they're having a blast. I watch them string a huge banner across the hallway that says: "Contribute to the Mayor's Cigarette Fund." Dot's boyfriend is up on the ladder and Dot is passing up snippets of tape. When she thinks no one's looking, she sticks one to the zipper of his pants. I think she and Betty are going to die laughing.

The boyfriends also help Dot and Betty sell brownies and lemonade at recess to raise money for "ditty bags." They're a gift from the Red Cross for the soldiers overseas, with chocolate, sewing kits, and razor blades. They're also collecting for the POW drive, to send similar packages to the Canadian servicemen who've been captured as prisoners of war. Their sign shows a smiling soldier opening a box full of goodies—meat tins, cigarettes, and jam. I can't believe a Nazi guard would let a soldier keep that stuff. And, if they do, it makes me mad, in a way. The newspapers say the Jews weren't allowed to keep anything before being rounded up and sent away. Why should the Nazis treat enemy soldiers better than Jews?

7.

The largest mass attack on Canadian war vessels in the Atlantic Ocean took place today. We heard about it at school and now it's all over the evening news. Louisa is too hysterical to keep knitting, so she abandons her socks and paces around the parlour, filling the room with wispy grey smoke. It's going to seep into the yarn and make the men's gloves and socks smell bad, but they probably won't care.

"They were merchant ships, Louisa. Brian's not on one of those," I say.

"I hope you're right, kid. It's an awful feeling, not knowing."

"Yes Louisa, I know," I say, rolling my eyes behind her back. Louisa never remembers my papa, maybe because she never met him. Sometimes, I'm afraid he's becoming unreal to me too. I remember things he said to me, but not the exact sound of his voice, no matter how hard I try.

When the names of the sixteen ships are finally released the next day, the HMS *St. Croix* isn't one of them.

"It's all fine again," Louisa says over dinner. I don't bother to tell her it isn't.

8.

Keiko and Emiko slump down in their desks and turn bright red when the news reports that Prime Minister King has ordered all Japanese people living on the west coast to move inland to special camps. Heads swivel toward them as the reporter explains "the yellow peril" and why people's property and belongings are being seized. Keiko and Emiko are the quietest kids in our class—they rarely speak above a whisper. I can't imagine them being a threat to anyone. By the end of the day, they are sitting so close together, their dark heads are almost touching, like they want to merge into one person. If they go to the movies, they'll see the signs on the cinemas that say: "No Japs Allowed." But at least they'll have each other to walk away with.

9.

The *Montreal Star* has printed all the new clothing restrictions. I scan the list and think of Papa. He's a master with material and can whip up a beautiful dress or suit with next to nothing, but even he would struggle with these. Basically, clothing factories aren't allowed to produce any more "luxury or frivolous clothing." That means no more tuxedos, evening dresses or lounging pajamas. Papa wouldn't like the restrictions against extra pockets and cuffs and shoulder pads, either. Or the fact that men's suits can no longer have vests. Papa made such special ones, with little slits to protect pocket watches. Women's skirts can't be longer than thirty inches and dresses can't have wide collars or frills or lace. My mind casts back to the dresses Papa made for me and Sabine, with their wide collars and yellow trim around the bottom. We were the envy of every other girl in town. Today, that ribbon would be forbidden, just like our friendship.

10.

Miss C. reminds us that our Shakespeare recitals are due in a few days. Annette said she'd help me rehearse, but it's been hard to catch her, so I do it alone, pacing in the hallway under the tin pipes that carry the heat from the parlour stove. They crackle and creak above me and Louisa says it's because we haven't cleaned them properly since Brian left. I imagine them splitting open and drowning me in soot as I recite my lines.

On the day of the recital, the thought of Hedy Lamarr and her wisp of an accent gives me courage. I wish I'd made a costume, like some of the other kids have done. I imagine a character in a long medieval dress, with balloon sleeves. Mama could have helped me put something together, but I'm just in my tunic. I don't think I look like Miranda, shipwrecked on a desert island, but I pretend Papa is Prospero, watching over me. He's my only human link to the entire world. I've never seen another human being, but I have my papa at least and, for now, he's all I need.

I take a deep breath and begin:

> *One of my sex; no woman's face remember,*
> *Save, from my glass, mine own; nor have I seen*
> *More that I may call men than you, good friend,*
> *And my dear father: how features are abroad,*
> *I am skill-less of; but, by my modesty,*
> *The jewel in my dower, I would not wish*
> *Any companion in the world but you,*
> *Nor can imagination form a shape,*
> *Besides yourself, to like of. But I prattle*
> *Something too wildly and my father's precepts*
> *I therein do forget.*

Nobody makes a sound and it takes me a minute to realize that tears are running down my cheeks. Miss C. steps over and takes my hand.

"That was wonderful, Edie. So heartfelt. Why did you choose that particular speech?"

"It reminded me of my papa," I reply, barely above a whisper.

"We could tell it was moving for you," she says. "Couldn't we class?"

I don't look up. I can't bear to see my classmates' faces. I doubt they'd get it. How could they? After class, Dot comes up to me and says, "That was so great, Edie. It was like listening to a real actress on the stage. Is there still no news about your father?"

I shake my head.

She looks like she wants to say something else, but then Betty taps her shoulder.

"Mike and Rob are waiting. Let's go, Dot."

She smiles at me and turns, leaving me to my island.

II.

The Canadian government has set up a program to send students from the east to farms in the west, to help with the harvest, due to the shortage of men. "It'll mean a free train ride across the country and a chance to help feed the war effort. Remember, much of the food the Allies are eating is coming from us," Miss C says. By the end of the day, Dot and Betty and their boyfriends have signed up, along with twenty-eight other students from Verdun High. What if I was one of them? I imagine

Uncle Max's face if I told him I was going out west to gather corn or wheat, or whatever crop they'd need me for. He'd turn purple. Not that he'd mind me helping out, it's just not something he would have pictured me doing here. Besides, Aunt Naomi has talked him into giving me work at Brownstein's Department Store this summer, now that I'm sixteen. "You need to keep busy," she said. "And this will be good experience. Plus, we'll get to see you more, especially if you come stay with us. We're a ten-minute walk from the store. What do you say, Edie?" I couldn't say no. I wasn't looking forward to summer before, but now that I have something to do, it might not be so bad.

12.

Aunt Naomi hangs a red velvet curtain across the opening to my little alcove. In the morning, sun streams in the window and lights up the red, sending its glow back onto me as I lie on the mattress on the floor, listening to doves cooing on the tin roof across from me. It's my own private space and I love it. Uncle Max said they'd never come in without knocking and he pounded the wall beside the curtain to demonstrate. I hugged him. "Bless you, Uncle

Max," I said. "It's a palace." He squeezed me and I was taken back to that day in Munich when he picked me up and twirled me around the empty room, like we were in a Viennese ballroom. He tried lifting me like that again when I arrived here three days ago, tugging at my waist and heaving.

"Oi, how our little Edie has grown," he called over to Aunt Naomi, who was shaking her head on the sofa.

"Max, honestly, she's taller than you. Leave the poor girl alone."

It's true. I've sprouted up this past year and now have to look down at my aunt and uncle when I talk to them. But I'll never look down at them in my heart. They've made me feel so welcome. They even bought me my very own little radio to put next to my bed. I can listen to all the music I want now, even late at night because my aunt and uncle's bedroom is way down at the end of the long hallway.

13.

My job is in the accessories department, the first spot customers see when they spin through the revolving doors. Miss Moody, the department head, tells me it's my job to arrive half an hour before opening and make sure all the gloves, hats and scarves are impeccably displayed. "Think of it as modern art," she says. "You need to draw in the eye."

I have to wear a navy pencil skirt with a slit up the back that Annette would adore, and a white blouse with lace ruffles. It must have been designed before the rationing rules because the collars are so long they remind me of floppy bunny ears. Then on top I wear a navy vest with big pockets that hold keys to the cabinets and a notepad and pencil, in case I have to take down orders. My pumps have a two-inch heel that makes me even taller.

"You'll be handy for reaching the upper cabinets," says Miss Moody, her mouth as straight and thin as a pin.

We aren't allowed to wear jewelry because that's not our department; it's the one across from us, but when we get new scarves, we're allowed to wrap one in a fancy knot around our neck.

"You're a walking display," says Miss Moody. "Remember that. Chin high. And take it off when you eat. You won't sell any if they're full of crumbs."

I have to pull my hair back into a roll as well and wear light-coloured lipstick. "Nothing gaudy. This isn't a night club." When I stop to glance in one of the many mirrors that sit on our wooden counter, I can't believe it's me looking back.

14.

Uncle Max and his friend Samuel sit on the tiny balcony off the parlour, smoking and talking about the war. Sometimes I take a book outside and sit with them. I want to know what's happening in Germany, even if it's terrible. Somehow, I learn more from them than from the news on the radio.

"Fraulein, this might not be for your ears," Samuel turns to tell me, but Uncle Max says I can listen.

"Better to know. Knowledge is power," Uncle Max says. "If our people hadn't buried their heads in the sand in '33, who knows?"

"You're not blaming us, are you Max?" says Samuel. "Look at all the powerful people who turned their heads, even shook that man's hand. Look at the Berlin Olympics in '36. People all over the world said they were the best Olympics ever. Such magnificent stadiums, statues of gods and goddesses fifty feet tall. Who cares that he didn't shake Jesse Owens's hand? And there were Jews running for Germany. Window dressing, like at your store. Jews on display. You know all this, Max. And now, reports of mass killings. And death camps. And still no action on the ground, only by air. Honestly, it's hard not to believe that if it were Christians being killed ..."

"Hey, hey, that's not fair," Uncle Max responds. "The Blitz in London—those are mostly Christians. And in other countries too, even Africa."

Samuel switches to Yiddish, maybe because he thinks I won't understand, but I do. I'm surrounded by Yiddish in this neighbourhood. Families sit out on their stoops yelling at each other in Yiddish as their kids push each other to the corner and back in an old baby carriage. The older kids' legs hang over the edge and I can't believe the rusty carriage doesn't break. The mother's going to need it soon because she's pregnant again. No wonder Aunt Naomi has so much work to do at the Jewish Appeal. I can't imagine feeding a family that big on rations. They've now added butter and sugar and meat to the list. The cakes in the bakeries can't have icing and the restaurants can't serve meat on Tuesdays.

But when Samuel says that even kids have been seen in the Nazi work camps, I think that cake without icing isn't such a big deal.

15.

I miss Annette. I miss hearing her footsteps on the stairs as she flew down to take off for work. Somehow, I felt like she was flying down to me, even just for a few seconds. She always waved because she knew I'd be at the window, like a faithful cat. She encouraged me to take the job. "Never look a gift horse in the mouth," she said. And when I screwed up my eyebrows, she explained. "I have your aunt and uncle's phone number and I can call you from a phone box, or even from work sometime. We won't lose touch," she promised, hugging me. But it's been two weeks and I haven't heard a dickey bird. That's another expression I learned from Annette. Basically, it means nothing.

16.

Rebecca's the friendliest girl on my floor. She works in shoes. "Did you know there are 26 bones in the human foot?" she asks me one day as we're eating our lunch in a windowless back room that has tables and lockers. "One-quarter of the bones in the whole body. And 33 joints and 100 muscles, tendons and ligaments. I am simply in awe of the human foot. Let me examine yours, Edie."

I kick off my shoes and place my feet in her lap. "Are you sure?" I ask.

"Of course. I deal with feet all day. I only see the good in them. Your feet are beautiful. Look at these arches. Have you ever done ballet?"

"No," I say, smiling.

"Well, those feet were made for dancing. Maybe we can go sometime."

"I'm only sixteen," I say. "I can't get into clubs."

"What? With your height, no one will know. Trust me."

I remember all the dance steps Annette taught me, kicking around her little room. Maybe I could try them out for real.

17.

At break, I visit Rebecca in the shoe department and on her break, she comes to visit me. But only if Miss Moody isn't watching. We're not supposed to stand around talking to other staff. Rebecca loves my displays. I've gotten good at taking the half-mannequin that sits on our counter, wearing nothing but a white blouse, and dressing her up with a hat, scarf and gloves.

"You have a great eye for colour," says Rebecca,

whose thick red hair is pulled into a roll at the nape of her neck. I keep wondering how long it would be if she let it down. "I never would have thought of combining the navy and orange that way.

"So, Friday night there's a dance at the YMHA. Can you come?" She's leaning across the counter, so close I can see the gold flecks in her green eyes. "Say yes. It's going to be so much fun. There's a live band."

"I'll ask," I say, and Rebecca smiles.

"Tell your aunt the proceeds go to the Jewish Appeal, if that helps."

18.

Aunt Naomi is at least five inches shorter than me so the blue dress she is letting me wear to the dance barely covers my knees, but the top is elegant, with silk ribbons around the collar. I pin the antique brooch to my chest—it's the first time I'm actually wearing it, and Rebecca lends me some shoes from the sample box. "Don't tell anyone," she says. The heels click like tap shoes on the pavement as we stroll down Park Avenue, arm in arm, along the base of the mountain. Across the street, the big army tents of the Jeanne-Mance Camp sit in Fletcher's Field. It's weird to see an army so close to home. The YMHA hall on the corner of Mount Royal and Park is full of people by the time we get there. A big band is on stage, playing the swing music that Annette loves so much. Dozens of couples are dancing, the young men all in uniforms. Rebecca and I get fizzy lemonades from the bar.

"Is everyone here Jewish?" I ask.

"Probably most people. This place is open to everyone, but it's mostly our community that uses it."

Rebecca introduces me around and everyone is so friendly, asking where I'm from and how come they've never seen me before. Servicemen come over and ask girls to dance. I never realized how many Canadian soldiers are Jewish, but it makes sense. They'd be even more motivated to go over there and fight the Nazis. I imagine a band of Jewish soldiers breaking into a camp and finding Papa, then bringing him home.

I dance with a soldier who's a whole head shorter than me. It doesn't matter when we're spinning away from each other, but when we're back together it feels funny when his forehead touches my neck. He tells me he's leaving in a week for England.

"Good luck," I say, returning to the table. My feet are

pinching in the sample shoes that are a touch too small. I'm glad Rebecca's back. She was dancing on the other side of the hall. I caught glimpses of her as she was twirling and it seemed like she was looking for me too.

"Having fun?" she asks.

"Yes, I am. But I don't think I'm going to dance anymore. I'm happy watching."

"Me too," Rebecca answers. "Let's watch together." She pulls her chair right up beside me and we watch the action, swaying to the music in our own way.

19.

I love working at the store. Miss Moody tells me I would have loved it more a few years ago, before the war started. "People had spare money back then, especially the wealthier housewives from Outremont. But now, everyone's leftover cash is going into Victory Bonds. Plus, we just don't get the stock like we used to. Still ..." she sighs, her voice trailing away.

I talked her into setting up a second mannequin and now I dress two and make it look like they're out having a sophisticated night on the town. In my mind, one is me and the second one is Annette. Or now, sometimes,

Rebecca. At least it alternates between the two. Rebecca and I eat lunch together every day and sometimes we walk over to Carré Saint-Louis and throw crumbs to the pigeons. The Salvation Army Band is often there, playing marching tunes that, for some reason, make us laugh.

After work, if Rebecca doesn't have to rush home, we buy ice cream and lick it as slowly as we can while we stroll down Esplanade, under the massive trees. The houses here are so tall, with long staircases that reach all the way to heaven, or at least to top floor flats that have tin-roofed turrets, like little castles. Rebecca teaches me that maple leaves are super absorbent and make great napkins. Sometimes, I listen to myself laugh when I'm with Rebecca and I almost don't recognize the sound. What would Mama say if she could hear me? Would she be happy to know that I'm happier now? Or would she wonder, like I sometimes do, how I can be happy with her and Papa gone?

20.

For one whole week, we have to put away our showy displays and drape black cloth over the counter tops. Mr. Brownstein says no one should be heard laughing and our heads should be slightly bowed, in reverence to Dieppe. Yesterday, on August 19, Canadian forces tried reaching the Germans by landing on the shores of France, in a place called Dieppe, but it didn't work. Today, nine hundred families across Canada are in mourning. When we gather around the radio in the evening, we hear the announcer say that the word Dieppe will be as famous as Vimy Ridge. Many of the men killed were from the Fusiliers de Montréal and I wonder if they were men we saw in Fletcher's Field, or that Annette may have danced with at the Esquire, or even me and Rebecca at the YMHA. Fifteen hundred more men have been taken prisoner by the Germans. The announcer is trying hard to make it seem like the whole disaster was useful because it taught our army how German coastal defences operate. When he says the raid was a success, Uncle Max stands and throws his arms up in the air. "If this is success," he snaps, "what is failure?"

21.

The next day, pictures of the raid fill the newspapers and I can't get the images of dead soldiers strewn all over the beaches out of my head. I even see them when I'm making new displays to show off the fall scarves. And I think more than ever about Papa. He's down there, on the ground, surrounded by so much death. It would have been nice to think of thousands of eager men snaking their way toward him—over the beautiful valleys and rivers in France or Holland. "Hold on, Papa," I say as I pull rabbit-fur gloves over the mannequin's abnormally long fingers.

22.

I'm helping Rebecca take inventory in the stockroom on the weekend. Miss Moody warned me it would be dusty, and she was right, but we find a couple of men's overalls hanging on hooks and pull them over our skirts and blouses. We have to open boxes that are piled in a corner and take stock of what's inside. Our extra day's work will earn us two dollars each.

"What are you going to do with your money, Rebecca?" I ask.

"Straight to my mom."

"Really? You can't keep it?

"No way. My whole paycheque goes to my mom, except one dollar a week for my expenses. My dad doesn't make enough working at Berson's to support me and my four siblings. Mom can't work and I'm the oldest."

As we work, she tells me more of her family's story. Her parents came to Canada from Ukraine in 1915, just before the Russian revolution. They were expelled, along with thousands of other Jews.

"My parents nearly starved to death when they were younger. They spent the first five years of their married lives just finding enough food, until they came here. Now, my mom has a fear of starvation, for herself and her children. When the ration stamps came, I thought she'd pass out."

I tell Rebecca my story, including Mama and Papa. By the time I'm finished, she's holding my hand.

"My mom packed no-flour cake for us," she says. "Want a piece?" I nod and she pulls it out of her bag. "See—food. She's a miracle worker. She even makes her own candies out of beets."

With Rebecca across from me, sharing the raisin-soaked cake, it feels like sun has managed to penetrate the stone walls of the dingy stockroom.

23.

Rebecca comes over after work when she doesn't have to rush home to help her mother. "Your place is wonderful," she says. "Anywhere that isn't full of kids is heaven to me. I'm never having kids, are you?"

We're lying on my bed, listening to "Messages to the Home Front." One soldier goes on for ten minutes about training he did in England to learn how to roll barbed wire along the coast.

"I don't know. I've never really thought about it before," I reply.

"Really? You're lucky. It's all my mom talks to me about. When I have kids *this* and when I have kids *that*. I'm going to find a way out before that happens."

"How?"

"I don't know. I managed to finish high school two years ago and that was a fight. My mother wanted me to start working at fifteen but I put my foot down and graduated. I'm the first girl in my family to have a high school diploma, but I think I'm the only person who's proud of it."

"My family would be proud of you. School's all they talk to me about. My Uncle Max wants me to go to McGill."

"McGill! Oh Edie, you're so lucky."

We lie back and listen to a nurse in Newfoundland describing all the troops from different countries on her base. Another man talks about a hospital the Canadians built under the rock in Gibraltar. Then the news comes on and reports that thousands and thousands of Jews were rounded up in Paris and handed over to the Gestapo for deportation. It makes me wish even more that Allied soldiers would stop doing small stuff and head into Europe. They haven't even tried since Dieppe.

24.

On a beautiful Sunday afternoon Rebecca and I climb Mount Royal, winding our way up the gravel trail and watching the city shrink further away through the trees. The only way she could go was to bring her seven-year-old twin brothers. They're excited at first but then halfway up they start to whimper about how their legs hurt. "Pretend the squirrels are Jerries and you're on the hunt," she says. It works for a while as they make guns of their fingers and shoot fake bullets into the bushes. When they get fussy again, she tells them they won't get ice cream if they don't stop complaining.

At the big stone chalet, we buy four cones, then wander over to Beaver Lake where the boys amuse themselves breaking off bits of their cones and throwing them to the swans and ducks. Rebecca and I find a shady spot under a tree and lie back, close enough to listen for the twins.

"I like hanging out with you, Edie," she says, rolling toward me. Her hair is loose today, and it falls in long red curls over her shoulders. "I can share things with you and you don't judge me, like when I told you I never want to have kids."

"Thanks," I say. "I guess I just think people should live the way they want to."

"I wish you could keep working at the store, but I think you're doing the right thing by finishing school."

"Hey, maybe we can go to McGill together one day?"

"Not me. I could never afford it."

"Are you sure? Maybe there's scholarships, or something you could do."

"I don't think so, but if you go I'll be happy for you." Rebecca reaches out and runs her fingers down my face and I feel a tingle all the way down in my belly. The kids are squealing at the lake and the shade makes it seem like no one else in the world is alive except for us. The gold flecks in her eyes are sparkling and I want to stay like this forever. Then one of the twins jumps between us.

"We saw tadpoles," he chimes.

Rebecca sighs and sits up.

25.

The *Montreal Star* is lying on a table in the lunchroom. Thick black letters glare up at me. "Nazi slaughterhouse—Germans massacre a million Jews in extermination drive."

"I'm sure your papa is safe, Edie. Don't lose hope," says Rebecca, stroking my hand. I try to smile back, but can't.

Everyone's talking about it, all around the store, like a constant buzz. I'm not the only one there with relatives lost in the Nazi nightmare. It's like the dark grey clouds have come inside. Even the customers look gloomy.

26.

Louisa comes to visit on Labour Day, beaming because Brian's coming home on leave. She wants to know if I'm coming back to Verdun, as planned, once school starts. I can feel her hoping I'll say no.

"Well Louisa, if my aunt and uncle don't mind, I might stay here and finish up at Baron Byng." I don't want to say goodbye to Rebecca, I add in my mind.

"Oh, Edie. We'd love it," they say together, broad smiles stretching across their faces.

The four of us spend the afternoon strolling around,

stopping to buy sandwiches at Wilensky's. We eat them on a bench in the park, watching swans swim in the pond below the bridge. I ask Louisa how Annette's doing and she just shrugs and says, "You know Annette—still the same as ever." Then she and Aunt Naomi share a look that says they both think she's headed for trouble. If she is heading there, it's sure taking her a long time. Even Mama used to say that about her.

27.

Baron Byng is even bigger than Verdun High. The hallways and classrooms are full of new faces, but for some reason I don't feel like I stand out the way I did in Verdun. Maybe it's because there are other kids with accents and I'm definitely not the only Jewish person here. Or, maybe it's because I don't care as much. I only have Grade 12 to get through and I don't need new friends. I have Rebecca. When I sit at each new desk, I look for her initials scraped into the wood with the point of a compass, like she described. I only find it in one class, and I run my finger through the grooves of the capital R and K while the teacher talks. It makes me feel like she's here.

28.

The best news is that Uncle Max has fixed it so that I can keep working on Saturdays. They need more help on Saturday because lots of the girls aren't allowed to work on the Sabbath. Luckily, that doesn't include Rebecca, so we see each other at least one day of the week and, if she can get away from home, we go to the movies on Saturday nights. The war reels show British, Canadian and American planes bombing different parts of Europe, city after city, Hamburg and Bremen and Karlsruhe. And even outside of Germany—massive explosions on the German airfields of Holland, railyards in France and even the Italian city of Milan.

I sit in the dark and think about the holiday we took in Holland, with Papa. We rented bikes and cycled all over the country, along the dykes, stopping to picnic under windmills. Papa joked that his muscles were sore from so much flat land. "We need a hill," I can hear him say. "Look, I'm turning to jelly." Then he jiggled his calf muscles with his hand and Mama and I laughed so hard I almost choked. Now, those spots where we sat are probably full of burning holes. Rebecca takes my hand and tells me the reels are over and I realize she must have been watching me the whole time.

After the show, we link arms and stroll along Sainte-Catherine, stopping to look at the window displays in Eaton's and Morgan's. They all have war themes—women in fur coats with large photos of war planes behind them, as though the women are waiting for their pilots to land. One window contains an actual airplane wing, with a row of winter boots sitting on it. And another is done up like an air-raid shelter in London, with the round tunnel of the tube painted in the background. The mannequins are arranged sitting close together with their legs splayed out, showing off various styles of shoes.

"Aren't you glad we're here and not in Great Britain?" Rebecca asks me.

But when I look at the mannequins huddling so close together, I think it wouldn't be so bad to be in a shelter, if Rebecca were with me.

29.

German U-boats are slicing through the St. Lawrence, the same river I loved to sit beside at the foot of my old street in Verdun. One even torpedoed a ship, the SS *Caribou*, near Newfoundland. It's all too close for comfort.

30.

Rebecca's mother invites me over for Chanukah. Their table is chaotic, but fun. Neither of Rebecca's parents seems to be bothered by the constant bickering of the children, who are allowed to reach out across the table and take as much food as they want, without asking. Rebecca was right—her mother is a magician with food. In spite of all the rations, she's managed to make a large heap of delicious potato latkes. They're brown and crunchy on the outside and soft and salty on the inside. She made a big bowl of her own applesauce too, although it's not as sweet as it could be because of the sugar rations. For dessert we eat mandel bread. It's my first time and Rebecca's mama is surprised.

"Never?" she asks and I shake my head. The whole table turns quiet while I take my first bite. My teeth sink through the hard biscuit and the almond flavour explodes in my mouth.

"Normally they'd have raisins or currants, but ... we do what we can. There are many who don't have food at all, or maybe not enough." Rebecca's mother looks right at me and adds, "Like maybe your papa. Rebecca told me. We put him in our prayers this week."

I'm so grateful I think I'll cry, but then her father jumps in and says, "Dunk them if you want. Otherwise, you'll break your teeth." When he dunks his mandel bread, I notice the nicks on his hands. Rebecca told me his job is carving headstones for graves. I wonder if he cut Mama's stone. I know Uncle Max bought it at Berson's.

"See, safer now," he jokes, putting the cookie in his mouth. The kids all laugh and Rebecca's mother reaches over and slaps him across the shoulder with her napkin.

It's all warm and playful, like my family used to be. Rebecca smiles at me, like she knows what I'm thinking, and I close my eyes and say my own prayer for Papa.

1943

SABINE

I.

Everything in our town has changed. The streets are still. Kids don't skate on the river or slide down the hills. Women don't meet with baskets hooked over their arms, coming from the marketplace. And if they do, their baskets are mostly empty—maybe just a loaf of bread or a couple of eggs—and they never ask what's new, for fear of hearing bad news. Our neighbour received a visit from some army officials yesterday. I watched them hand over a brown paper package on her doorstep. She ripped it open and I could see the words "Fallen for Greater Germany" on the paper she threw to the ground. Inside lay the uniform of her eldest son, probably killed in Russia. I wondered if they would take back her Mother

Cross, now that she has only three children.

The bell is gone from atop the church steeple and so is the statue of the angel from our town square. The iron railings around the city park, where the seeds of our vegetables lie under the frozen ground, have also vanished. Even the signs forbidding Jews from sitting on benches or stepping into stores are gone. I guess they're no longer needed. Every square inch of wall space is taken over by posters designed to encourage us.

Today Germany, Tomorrow the World
One People, One Reich, One Führer
Victory or Bolshevik Chaos

I've looked at them so often, I no longer see them—they blend into the grey stone, or chipped wood, or black iron railings they're glued onto.

2.

Mama is so thin, she's always cold. Sometimes I come home to find her sitting in her winter coat and hat. Our coal rations have been cut in half, so we only light the stove for an hour in the morning, then again before we eat. Poor Herr Pinker. We can't give him more blankets because they were all taken, one by one, in the endless collections. I'm surprised we were allowed to keep our clothes. Still, I tell myself, he's warmer here than he would have been in his storage room, or wherever else he might have ended up. There are rumors about Jews being held in crowded camps with wooden barracks. I don't imagine they have fluffy blankets there either. When I'm working at the KLV, I pocket loose goose feathers and Mama restuffs our old eiderdowns with them, to fill them out. Herr Pinker never complains. If he's freezing, he doesn't let on. When Frau Prinz makes us rip up old hessian sacks and use the string to knit slippers, I sneak home a pair for him. He tells me they feel like sheepskin, even though I know they must scratch his soles as he's walking around in the dark.

3.

Katya must also be cold out in the barn. I thought Frau Prinz would let her inside once the temperature dipped below freezing. I hoped she'd think about Katya in a practical way, figuring she'd be more useful without frostbitten fingers. But the trains bring more and more Polish and Russian people every day, so maybe she figures she'll just replace Katya once she can't work anymore. Many of the farms around the KLV have help from the east. I caught Katya talking to a man in Polish the other day. It sounded fast and full of soft sounds. I'd never seen Katya animated like that. For once, her head wasn't bowed and her eyes, normally so far away, were completely fixed on the man. He looked like he was in his twenties and quite handsome, under all the dirt. I wondered if they were flirting like Werner and I do. But suddenly Katya started to cry and the man reached out a hand and placed it on her shoulder until she stopped. When he saw that his group had gotten pretty far up the road, he threw his cap back on and ran to catch up.

4.

Our soldiers in Russia must be coldest of all. I pray Papa isn't there, although Mama says he wouldn't be since he isn't fighting—he's helping to build things. "They wouldn't risk him being hurt," she says, but the way she says it sounds like she's trying to convince herself more than me. Now that there are lots of Russian men working around town, we've heard stories of people starving to death while trying to hack through the frozen ground to find food, and long lines of refugees moving like the walking dead across the frozen landscape. They even claim that the Germans soldiers are in retreat. The whispers pass from ear to ear and make it into the KLV, frightening the girls. One day, Frau Prinz makes everyone stop their work and pay attention. "If I hear one more person talk about how our men are losing the war in Russia, I will punish everyone. Do you hear me? Such talk is treason and I can report you for treason even if you're young. You are never too young to learn loyalty. And imagine if your papas could hear you, maligning their efforts. What would they say?"

But days later, on *Deutschlandsender*, Mama and I hear the report: "The army High Commissioner announces that the 6th Army has surrendered in Stalingrad." I imagine Frau Prinz spitting out her ersatz coffee as she listens. So much for that speech she made us all listen to three years ago, when Hitler promised that Russia would never rise again.

5.

Frau Prinz is in a foul mood and she's taking it out on the girls, as if they're somehow responsible for Russia's success. Like, if the girls were only neater or more obedient or stronger the outcome would have been different. She's marching everyone up the hillside, even though nothing is growing yet. In the woods, she makes them collect fallen pine and spruce needles that are so old and shriveled they can't possibly be used for tea. She makes them stand perfectly still every few minutes, as though she wants them to know how our soldiers felt when the cold seeped into their feet. If anyone sniffles, she makes them run back down the hill and up again. If they slip where it's icy, she slaps them.

I can only hang back and watch, but when we're back in the house and Frau Prinz finally leaves us alone, I try my best to make the girls feel better. Werner puts extra wood in the kitchen stove and we let the girls huddle around. Werner asks one girl to stand by the door to listen for Frau Prinz's footsteps. Then he fetches the rabbits and passes them around.

"This one is called a Flemish Giant. See her big ears that stand straight up and her white paws. And this one is a German Grey," he says.

One of the girls who never speaks much stands and says, "The German one is better. You can tell. Look how much bigger and stronger he is. He could kill the

Flemish one in a second if you let him." She glares at the other girls after her little speech, then at Werner and me, her lips set hard. Neither of us responds. Even a seven-year-old can be dangerous these days.

6.

Mama and I are huddled around our *Volksempfänger* radio, our coats across our laps for warmth, listening to Joseph Goebbels's speech from the Sports Palace in Berlin. People were saying he's going to talk about what happened in Russia and that everyone in Germany has to listen. His voice is loud and angry and when he says, "total war is the message of the hour," Mama burrows deeper into her coat. On and on he goes, with the crowd roaring and cheering in the background. "It's time to take off the silk gloves," he says and I look at Mama's cold hands. Her skin is cracked from that wicked soap and I wonder who in Germany still wears such gloves. He implores us "to only think of war," as if we can think of anything else. But the weirdest thing is that when he asks the crowd if they want total war, they scream and shout for two full minutes. An arctic breeze blows through the room when Goebbels tells all Germans to "rise up and release the storm."

7.

Katya has been here for a year now and, in that time, she has gotten rounder. Her young man is still working on the farms down the road. When his group of labourers walks by with their rakes and hoes, Katya finds an excuse to be outside near the fence. Even if he can't stop to talk to her, they nod or wave. They do it subtly, in case Frau Prinz is looking, but I see it. I wonder if Katya feels the same way about him as I do about Werner. Werner and I kiss whenever we can. Or he pulls me into the barn and presses me against the beams. Sometimes, I don't want him to stop and I can tell he doesn't either. The stall where the goats live would make a good place to lie down. Frau Prinz wouldn't see us, but she never leaves me alone for more than ten minutes. Katya's bed is in the corner—a heap of hay and whatever rags she could find piled there. Does she think of doing with her young man what I imagine with Werner? Frau Prinz says Slavic people are like animals, not like us. But, when I'm with Werner, I feel like an animal.

8.

Papa's money is slower and slower to come. Mama writes to him but we have no way of knowing if her letters actually reach him. Frau Prinz heard that the War Office is giving people a small wage to repair uniforms, so she has some of the older girls at the KLV doing it. I tell Mama about it and she agrees to give it a try. When Herr Pinker hears, he says he'd like to help. I remember Mama saying that his stitches were magical, so even and precise. Now, I sometimes come home to find the two of them sitting side by side on the sofa, a pile of jackets or pants between them. They sew wordlessly, but every now and then Mama will hold up a seam she's just sewn and Herr Pinker will nod and smile, or, in his soft voice, say, "A few cross stitches here would help." I wonder how he feels, handling the uniforms of people who've torn his family apart. It seems wrong, but the money helps. I picture him weaving curses and bad luck omens into the fabric.

Mama worries that his work is too perfect. "They're going to wonder," she says when he's back in his room.

"Don't worry, Mama. I've seen the depot at the station, when I deliver things from the KLV. There's mountains of uniforms. No one is stopping to scrutinize things that closely."

But I can tell she doesn't believe me.

9.

The Total War speech doesn't seem to be working. Rumors hit our town that small towns like ours with factories in the Ruhr are being bombed, dams are exploding, and the beautiful city of Hamburg is on fire. On the radio, the High Commander says it's just a minor setback. But how can it be minor when we hear that tens of thousands have died in the old Hanseatic city on the North Sea? Our own factory by the river suddenly makes me nervous. So many foreigners are working away in there, day and night, along with many women from town. The freight trains that load whatever it is they're making never seem to stop. What if the Americans and British are planning to bomb it too? We could never take Herr Pinker into an air raid shelter. It would be too risky. Sometimes, when I watch him sew, I wonder how much he knows about what's going on in the world. He rarely listens to the radio with us and we don't share the rumors with him. And he never asks. Maybe this is how he copes, shutting himself up in the old pantry, not letting anything reach him. Then he can just focus on Edie and her Mama. Every bad bit of news would cut into that concentration and stick a pin in his peace of mind.

10.

Werner is almost eighteen and we both know what that means. Any day now, he'll be called up to do his six months Reich Labour Service. They say every young man gets a spade and a bicycle in their workgroup. If there's one thing Werner is used to doing, it's digging, but I'd rather see him with a shovel than a weapon. He never even helps kill the rabbits. He feeds them and builds their hutches, but when it's time to eat one he always politely leaves. Frau Prinz does the killing and she always chooses a few girls to watch. She makes them stay right to the end, even when Katya hangs it from a beam in the barn and strips its fur. Some of the girls are okay with it, but others come back looking ill and refuse to eat their stew. "Children all around the Reich are hungry right now as we make this sacrifice for our Führer and you refuse to eat. What would he say if he were here in front of you, watching you refuse to stay strong?" I don't want to be the one to remind Frau Prinz that Hitler doesn't eat meat. She'd only yell at me.

11.

Werner is coming shopping with me today, since Mama gets too nervous in town and it's safer if she stays away.

We're desperate for food because the ration stamps came late this month. The young official who finally delivered them insisted on counting heads, but luckily he was content to stand at the door and peek into Herr Pinker's room while Mama showed him Opa's papers. I prayed he wouldn't notice how badly her hands were shaking.

The lineup outside the butcher's is long, but we don't care. The sun is shining and birds are singing on trees where green buds are sprouting. It could just be a normal spring day, and Werner and I could even be a young couple living in a normal world. Yesterday, I saw a poster on a wall that said, "Marry well, for race, health and party membership." I don't know about all that, but marrying Werner would be amazing.

"Someone's brought a donkey," a woman in line says. "Old man Huber's cutting it up now."

I'm trying to decide how I feel about eating donkey when a jeep pulls up and three brownshirts jump out. A few seconds later they're dragging a young woman out of the back. Her dress is torn and she's barefoot, but the most shocking thing is her bald head, shaped like a perfect egg. Two men take her arms and a third pushes her from behind.

"Everyone, stop what you're doing and gather round," one of them orders. "We want everyone to see. You there! Stop your shopping. Step out of line and come here, fast." When enough people have gathered, he hangs a sign around the woman's neck. Then he thrusts her forward. "Go! Show them, up close." The woman stumbles toward us. "Head up!" he yells at her and she raises it a few inches. Her face is puffy and streaked with dirt, and I can see that she's not much older than me. When I read the sign, every part of my body turns cold.

I have offered myself to a Jew.

"Again! Around. One more time."

The woman walks around the square again, each step so laboured, like her feet are lead, while people spit at her; others throw the few precious eggs they were able to buy. From the back of the crowd comes a bright purple turnip, smack onto her exposed head. She crumples, but the brownshirt kicks her back up. I want to leave so badly but I don't dare move.

"Throw something," says Werner.

"What?" I whisper. "Are you crazy?" Werner pulls a small cabbage out of my basket.

"Throw it! It could save your life." I've never seen

Werner look so fierce, so I step forward and pitch it.
It grazes her shoulder and the brownshirt nods in my
direction. He's close enough that I can read *"Gott Mit Uns"*
on his belt buckle.

Then, suddenly, they are gone. Off to the next
town, I suppose, and then the next, all the way to
Ravensbrück. I wonder if the girl has a mama at home
like I do, scared of her own shadow. Or if she was hiding
this Jew that she gave herself to. I'm shaking in every
part of my body, but I have to hide it. I have to hold my
head like normal past all these neighbours, who are
suddenly back in line like nothing happened. Like a
donkey's not being cut up for meat and a woman wasn't
just attacked in our town square. On a wall someone
has painted, *"Our walls might break, but not our hearts."*
But it's not true. My heart is breaking. Werner hurries
me home, my basket empty.

12.

On Monday, I keep seeing that young woman, the
sound of the cabbage hitting her shoulder playing over
and over in my mind. I think of a bucket of sauerkraut,
the way the rock on top presses down on the cabbage,

helping it to ferment. That rock is now in my head, pushing down on the image of the sign she wore around her neck—*I have offered myself to a Jew*. Katya and I rarely speak when we're working, but I need to get the words out, so I tell her about it. She doesn't look up from the goat she's milking, but she's listening at least.

"I felt so bad for her," I say when I'm done. Katya's still silent. When she looks up, it's not what I expected. She's smiling, like I've just told a joke.

She stops pulling on the goat's teats and turns to me. "This is best story you have to tell? This is nothing. You know nothing. My friend Anton, he tells me story of Warsaw. It is one girl you saw times thousands. All dead, killed inside their walls. Their ghetto. And you cry for one girl. I cry for my whole country." Katya glares at me with hard eyes, then continues milking. Stream after stream of hot milk hits the pail. I know she'll take it inside after and boil it. Then she'll hang it in a rag and let the whey drain. What's left she'll turn into cheese. Over and over she does this, day after day, probably like she did at home.

Maybe Katya's right. I know nothing.

13.

Werner gets papers ordering him to the Divisional District Labour Camp on the same day that Italy declares war on Germany. Frau Prinz once told us that our friends could turn into enemies and she was right. Italy was on our side, but now they're against us, like the rest of the world. Apparently, the Allies are currently climbing up the boot of Italy toward us, so the Reich needs more soldiers than ever. After his six months training, they'll probably send Werner to a Defence Strengthening Camp and then straight into the *Wehrmacht*. I can't bear to think of him gone, but there's nothing either of us can do to stop it. He leaves in three days.

14.

Werner and I hold hands all the way to the train station, but we don't speak. Every now and then, he squeezes my fingers extra tightly and that little gesture says it all. When we get there, we see a huge banner strung across the roof of our tiny station, held down by ropes. It says, *"We were born to die for Germany."* The Hitler Youth flag flies above it, red stripes at the top and bottom, white in the middle, an eagle with a swastika on its chest, holding a sword.

From here, the sword looks like a field hockey stick and the swastika like some team logo, which I suppose it sort of is. Werner squeezes again and I squeeze back.

A train on the westbound track has just pulled in and people are disembarking. A long string of darkly clad men begins trudging toward the factory. Next comes a group of children with a nurse—evacuees perhaps, from some bombed city in the north, or even from Stuttgart. Servicemen come last, many of them injured and walking with crutches. A couple are carried out on stretchers, our hometown boys whose names will be displayed at the *Rathaus*.

The eastbound train begins to appear around the corner, its brakes screeching, and I pull Werner to a quieter spot behind the station. "I have something for you," I say. "I want you to always keep it on you somewhere." I hand him half of the strip of yellow ribbon that Herr Pinker tied to the branch, the one that led me to him. The other half is tied to a string around my neck. "It saved someone once, so it's lucky."

Werner rolls the yellow fabric between his fingers, then slips it in his vest pocket. "Don't worry about me, Sabine. I'm coming back in six months. They're not going to recruit me, only by force. The war will be over soon. The Americans are coming. We'll have jazz music in the beer hall." Then we kiss and it's just like the farewell scene in *Die Große Liebe*, although this isn't a movie. It's way too real.

"Sabine, I have something for you too, but it won't fit in a pocket. Behind the KLV, in the tool shed, I left something there for you. You'll know what it is if you need it. But, in case you never do, it's better you don't know, so don't go looking."

I don't have time to ask him to explain. The train whistle blows. Crowds of people begin pushing into the rail cars, hoisting duffle bags through the windows. The train is so packed, I don't know how Werner will fit inside. We hold hands until the last possible second, until the force of the separation tears my knuckles. Werner is small inside the crowd, fading among all the brown and green, like he's been sucked into a swamp.

15.

Our BDM group has stopped doing collection drives because there's nothing left to collect. Everywhere we go, women tell us the same thing. "You can't get blood from a stone." All we can do is serve sandwiches and ersatz coffee to soldiers at the train station as they pass through. They're so tired they don't even flirt with us like they used to.

The slogan in the space where our BDM group meets still says, *"Children, Church, Kitchen"*—our three primary duties. I'm doing two out of three duties nonstop at the KLV, which is now so packed with little girls they sleep two or three to a bed. They're jittery and shy and don't know why they're here. Most of them have escaped the bombing in Dortmund, Düsseldorf, and Stuttgart. I can't imagine the things they've seen. The *Volkischer Beobachter* only shows pictures of our troops marching and smiling, or of Hitler with his faraway eyes, like he can see ahead to the end of the Thousand Year Reich he's promised. Frau Prinz tells the girls to thank the Führer for bringing them to safety and to forget about what they left behind. "This is what total war means," she says. "Staying strong and thinking only of the future." But Katya tells me she can hear many of them cry at night, even all the way from the barn. So much for what the BDM manual has to say about the "warmth of the homey hearth fire." If I didn't have Mama and Herr Pinker at home, I'd stay overnight and try to comfort the girls a little. I'd play Itsy Bitsy Spider on their backs, to replace their bigger worries with imaginary eight-legged ones. I'd love to hear them giggle as they nestle into their pillows.

16.

Katya's stomach is getting bigger and bigger and her face is puffier too. Everything, even her fingers, look swollen. Then, one day, I see her and Anton behind the barn. He lays his hand on her stomach and holds it there, until a smile starts to grow on his stubbly face and it all becomes clear. Inside Katya, a baby is growing—a Polish baby that Frau Prinz will not be welcoming with open arms. In fact, she'll probably report it to the authorities. Katya isn't a free citizen. What was she thinking, taking that kind of chance, now, in the middle of all this?

I wait for her inside the barn and when she comes in, I grab her arm. "Katya, are you crazy?" I screw my finger into my temple, in case she doesn't know the word. "Frau Prinz is going to be furious. She won't let you stay here. She'll send you away and I have no idea what Nazis do to pregnant Polish women and their babies. Do you?" Katya crumples to the ground and starts to cry so loudly I'm afraid Frau Prinz will hear her from the room where she's doing lessons on household etiquette with the girls.

"I know, I am stupid. You are right. But Anton is from my village and he is so nice. When he come at night, he make me less homesick. Me and him both. First time, I say no. Second time too. But after, I stop. I think it doesn't matter. Life is so hard. It cannot be harder. But, I am wrong." As she's talking, it strikes me how alone Katya is. The girls in the big house have each other at least. I glance at the pile of hay in the corner and suddenly I get it, how she'd welcome Anton into her arms at night, alone with nothing but goats for company. I sit beside her and put my arms around her. She soaks my entire shoulder with tears.

"Don't worry. We'll find something to do. It'll be okay," I say. But I'm not sure it will. "Give me your extra dress. I'll fix it for you." Katya fetches her dress that's hanging on a nail in the beam. I hide it under my arms and sneak it into the basket on my bike. It's all I can do for now. Frau Prinz is marching the girls outside to collect nettles for soup and dandelion leaves for salad.

17.

Papa sends another letter, shorter than the last. It tells us nothing we didn't already know. The one line that might have contained something new has thick black ink running through it. Mama carries the letter for days, crumpled like a hanky inside her fist.

18.

Werner writes too. His new bicycle has no tires, only rims, and makes his old one seem like a BMW. His new uniform is brown and on the armband is a picture of a spade. Poor Werner! He can't escape the digging. He can't say much about what he's doing, or where, but it involves new roads. *Best and smoothest roads in the Reich*, he writes, but the next line is blacked out. He ends the letter with *I love you, Sabine* and I'm so glad that wasn't censored. It's nice that we're still allowed to love each other.

19.

The cold wet weather of late November makes it hard to stay positive, and the enormity of hiding Herr Pinker hits me harder every day. His room is like a big black space in my mind. Before, I could share the burden with Emma and Werner, but now it's just me. If the war doesn't end soon, I'm afraid we'll be discovered. And now I have Katya's ever-growing stomach to worry about too. Herr Pinker added some panels to her dress to take it out and hide her stomach. With her apron on top it just looks like she's gained weight. Frau Prinz never really looks at her anyway. She just shouts orders in her direction. Anton has not been able to stop by for weeks and I can see the worry on Katya's face. She milks those goats with a fierce concentration, as though she's tugging all her worry into the pail.

If the war goes on another year, I'll turn eighteen and be sent off to do my Labour Service. Then Mama will have to manage Herr Pinker on her own, and do her own shopping. She'll have to stand in line and endure the endless gossip and speculation. I can see her starting to shake and everyone wanting to know what's wrong. She'll have to deliver the repaired uniforms to the depot near the station, and pop out some nights to be friendly to Frau Schiller so she doesn't step inside for a spot check.

Mama doesn't know that I take pieces of silverware with me to the KLV, and go trading after work with the farmers. She thinks the chicken and extra eggs just fall from the sky, but they don't. I'm not the only one in town doing it—we call it "hamstering," because it helps us hoard food that the rations can't supply. Katya loves it when I visit the farms because I can bring messages to Anton. She scribbles them on bits of paper, words that make no sense to me but bring a huge smile to Anton's lips, if I see him.

It occurs to me that if the Nazis found out everything I'm doing they'd want to recruit me as a spy.

20.

If we'd ever bothered to stick a pin in Kiev, we'd have to pull it out again. Part of me is glad because every loss means the war might end and Werner can stop digging new roads for the tanks and trucks and come back home to me. I try not to think about Hans and Papa.

21.

Christmas at the KLV is somber. Frau Prinz allows each girl to receive a small strip of chicken on top of their noodles, but there wasn't enough flour to make gingerbread or peppermint cookies or Christmas *stollen*. We'd have nothing to put in the *stollen* anyway, no raisins or nuts.

Instead of presents, the girls get a lecture about sacrifice and how all this is necessary so that they'll have a better future. There's no more piano at the KLV, so we can't sing carols, but Frau Prinz does allow the girls to listen to the special Christmas Wish Concert. Almost all the requests are sent out to men somewhere in Russia and I imagine the signals bouncing over the frozen tundra to men who aren't anywhere near a radio. We didn't even decorate the parlour with pine boughs, which would have been easy enough. The only festive thing is the tree in the corner, purchased from the SS for the Winter Relief, like ours at home, but it's so bare. Frau Prinz said the bareness is important, to remind the girls of sacrifice, as if they don't have enough reminders of that.

22.

Katya is never allowed to stay with us once dinner is served and she's finished cleaning the kitchen. I'm about to pedal home when I think of her, alone with nothing in her corner of the barn. I creak open the door and step inside. Katya has set up a candle on a beam, to light her space. She's sewing pieces of fabric together, with thread pulled from some old potato sacks.

"What do you want?" she asks, looking startled when she sees me.

"I wanted to give you this," I say, pulling a little pot of gooseberry jam out from under my coat. "It's from last summer, but Frau Prinz never lets the girls have any. She saves it for when she has important guests, like inspectors from the party."

Katya's face glows in the candlelight. She's quite pretty, with her wide face and almond-shaped eyes. She unscrews the top and dips her finger inside, then sticks her finger in her mouth. Her eyes close and it's like she's tasting the most delicious thing she's ever eaten. She holds the pot out to me and I dip my finger in too. And then the two of us continue to take turns, our fingers crossing like swords, savoring this moment like it might be the last good thing we ever eat.

EDIE

I.

In February, school is abuzz with news of the German army's retreat from Stalingrad. A kid named Bill scrunches a short pencil in his upper lip and sputters and yells in Yiddish, flailing his arms, showing how insanely angry he is at Field Marshal Paulus for the surrender. The students standing near him get showered with spit, but no one cares. We're all doubled over laughing, he sounds so much like Hitler.

When we've settled down, Mrs. Goldfarb assigns us a composition entitled, "Why I'm Lucky To Be In Canada." I write about being safe, even though German U-boats are cruising closer, and having enough food to eat, even with rations, and a warm place to sleep, even though it's not a proper bedroom. I write about being thankful that I can graduate from high school and keep Papa's dream for me alive. I write about missing Mama but being thankful for Aunt Naomi and Uncle Max. And I write about Rebecca and how having her as a friend has given me back my laughter.

As I'm writing, I think about how the last person I laughed with so freely was Sabine. I never thought I'd find someone who means as much to me. It's not that I've replaced her, but I didn't realize how much I missed having a friend until I met Rebecca. And, if I'm honest, this feels different—deeper, somehow—maybe because I'm older?

Dearest Sabine. I know she would understand and forgive me. I hope she has found a new friend back in Germany too, someone who makes her face light up.

2.

"It's the end of Hitler," Uncle Max says. "With Russia and the Allies on the same side, he cannot win, no matter how many new weapons his engineers design." He pours vodka into four little glasses and hands one to each of us, including me and Rebecca. "Skol," he cries. I've never had vodka before, and it burns like fire in my throat and makes my whole body shudder.

"These two," says Uncle Max, pouring himself another. "These two are what we need to stay strong for. Look at them, Naomi, such beauties. And the beautiful babies they'll make one day will keep our people going."

Rebecca and I look at each other and try to smile like we agree.

"All they need now are some young men," says Aunt Naomi.

"School first, then men," says Uncle Max. "Edie's going to McGill. We're going to make sure. But Rebecca? You must be turning someone's head already?"

Rebecca's mouth has fallen open. I feel my face flush, burning like the vodka has gone straight to my cheeks. The other day, I overheard Rebecca's mother tell her she should be thinking about finding a husband. "You're almost twenty," she said. "I married at seventeen." Rebecca's mom was standing at the stove, stirring a pot of laundry with a long wooden stick as she lectured. A heap of washed clothes sat in the sink, where Rebecca was rinsing them in cold water.

"That was the olden days, Mama," Rebecca said. "No one does that anymore. I have loads of time." Then she squeezed grey water out of a handful of socks, wringing them so tightly I wondered if she was squeezing her mother's words out of her head at the same time.

3.

When the snow melts, Rebecca's mother decides to plant a victory garden in their tiny back yard. The ground is hard as rock, but Mrs. Krasney is determined to get beans, cabbages, carrots, lettuce and tomatoes out of it.

"Back in Ukraine, before the revolution, we had such a big garden. Rows and rows of cauliflower and beets and radishes. We never bought a single vegetable at the market. In the fall, we'd spend days boiling and pickling in big jars for the winter. We carried the smell in our skin and hair for weeks and my fingers stayed purple until Christmas. We hated it then, but I'd do it here in a heartbeat if I had the space," says Mrs. Krasney. She stops digging and stares beyond the yard to the back lane, past the row of grey sheds with their peeling paint, to somewhere Rebecca and I can't see. When she returns to digging, she looks happy to be plunging her hands into the soil, churning over the earth.

The May sun warms our bodies. Robins sing in

the trees, puffing out their red breasts like opera stars. Everything is growing, everything is new. Even hope. Uncle Max heard that Jews living in the Warsaw ghetto smuggled weapons and tried to rebel against the Nazis. They didn't succeed, but he says it's a sign that the fight isn't over. "It means people are not totally defeated, Edie. They'll try it again, you'll see."

Rebecca and I drop seeds into the holes. I pray that by the time the green stalks shoot out of the ground there might be good news from Papa.

4.

For two weeks in June, I barely leave my little alcove, books piled all around me. I do nothing but study for my final exams. The acceptance letter from McGill, Faculty of Arts, came in the mail last week, but it's conditional on my obtaining an average of 75%, which isn't fair because it's only 60% for non-Jews. Uncle Max said to look on the bright side. "You'll already be smarter by the time you start. Look at it as a challenge, Edie. It won't always be this way." He and Aunt Naomi tiptoe around the apartment, quiet as spiders. Aunt Naomi leaves a plate of food outside the curtain and taps lightly on the wall to tell me to eat. I feel them holding their breath, willing me to take in the facts and figures and dates so that I get accepted to McGill. As if I need any more encouragement, Uncle Max tells me to think of my papa and how proud he'll be when he finds out his little girl is studying at one of the greatest universities in the world.

5.

Hundreds of folding chairs sit in rows in the gym and in four of them sit Uncle Max, Aunt Naomi, Rebecca and Louisa. I was surprised when Louisa accepted Aunt Naomi's invitation, but here she is, wearing her Red Cross uniform with its tight four-pocketed jacket. Our black gowns defy the clothing rations, with their yards and yards of material, but, judging by their state, they're probably ten years old. On our heads sit mortarboard hats with tassels that we're supposed to flip to the other side at the end of the ceremony. "That's when your new life will begin," said Miss Goldfarb.

You mean my next new life, I thought.

I'm near the back of the line, behind Harry Panofsky, who got into McGill too. He's beaming with pride and so he should be. Only ten percent of the students McGill accepts to study law are Jewish. He waves over at his parents, who are already crying. I wish Mama were here. I know she'd be crying too.

When the line starts to move, I think of that day five years ago, when I found the yellow star sitting on my desk. I thought I'd never go to school again, and now I'm minutes away from holding my diploma. I've decided I'm not going to hang it up though, until Papa comes.

6.

Back at the apartment, we drink tea with lemon in thin china cups that Aunt Naomi bought at Morgan's. They reminded her of the ones she had to leave behind and were a bit expensive, but Uncle Max encouraged her to buy a set of four, for today. Rebecca's mom sent over a plate of mandel bread and a bottle of Manischewitz wine that is so sweet it hurts my teeth.

"You look different," says Louisa. "Older."

"She's made us very proud," says Uncle Max. "Tomorrow, we're going to show Hannah the diploma, up on Mount Royal."

Aunt Naomi dabs her eyes and we all stare quietly at the floor.

"How's Annette, Louisa?" I ask, to change the mood.

"Don't talk to me about *that* girl," Louisa says, crossing her arms above the thick belt at her waist. "We all knew it, didn't we?"

"What did we know?" I ask.

"That she was heading for trouble." She looks down at her lap, her lips pursed hard. "She's ... I'm embarrassed to say it. She's with child."

"Annette is pregnant?" Aunt Naomi squeals.

"Yes, I'm sorry. I know I shouldn't say it in front of these two young ladies. She told me six weeks ago. She actually wanted to move in because she can't work anymore and her rent is months overdue, but I had to say no. What would Brian say?"

"So where is she now?" I ask.

"I imagine she's gone back to her family," Louisa says, sipping her tea. "But don't you worry about her. Girls like that make their way."

I can't imagine Annette living with her family, out in the boonies, all of her dancing stopped. The wine isn't so sweet anymore and the mandel bread sits heavy in my belly.

7.

Mama's plot hugs the lower slope of Mount Royal. Aunt Naomi and Uncle Max are waiting at the top of the path, to give me time alone. I kneel on the ground so Mama will hear me over the rumble of the streetcars that screech down Côte-des-Neiges road behind us.

"*Mama,*" I whisper, "*I've graduated. Look at my diploma.*" I unroll it and hold it up toward the tombstone. "*Can't you just picture Papa's face when he sees it? I can, I think. I'm trying hard, Mama, to remember all his expressions. It would have been easier if we could have brought some of the old photos with us, but I'm doing my best. And something else, Mama. I got into McGill. Isn't that amazing? My name was in the Jewish News. Uncle Max cut it out and stuck it on the wall in the kitchen. He shows it to everyone who comes over, even the iceman! It's almost embarrassing. But you would have done the same, Mama.*"

I wait a few minutes to let Mama take in all my news before continuing. "*And I have a new friend, Mama. You'd love her. She's kind and beautiful and we can talk about everything. I told her all about you, and about Papa. And when I talk about before, she holds my hand.*"

The stone I chose for Mama sits inside my left palm.

It's pink with a white line cutting it in half, a perfect reflection of Mama's separation from Papa. I place it on her tombstone which simply says *Hannah Pinker 1887–1941* above a Star of David.

8.

I've been back at my summer job at Brownstein's for a week now, thanks to Uncle Max, which means I see Rebecca every day. It's like I never left, and soon we're spending every spare minute together. One day, we're strolling around on our lunch break when we find a poster for the TNT Revue wrapped around a pole. It says they're performing in Woodland Park on Sunday as part of the homecoming celebrations for someone called George Beurling—"The Verdun Ace."

"Should we go?" asks Rebecca. "Your friend might be there." I told her all about Annette after Louisa left, and she said she'd love to meet her. I know the two of them would get along.

"Do you think so?" I ask, and Rebecca shrugs. Maybe Louisa got it all wrong and Annette's not back in the boonies. Maybe she is still in Verdun. "Sure, it's worth a try."

Woodland Park is packed with people waving little

Union Jacks and cheering. On a big stage sit the mayor and a man in a Canadian Air Force uniform who must be George Beurling. Behind them is a giant picture of Beurling sitting in the cockpit of his plane, goggles pushed up on his forehead, giving the thumbs-up signal. He's smiling ear to ear, so it was probably snapped after a successful mission. The real George Beurling looks a little embarrassed by all the cheering. When the mayor pulls him up to the microphone, he simply says, "This is no place for me. I'm a fighter pilot." Then he waves to the crowd and sits back down. The mayor pats his back as if he's comforting him then signals the band to start playing. A minute later, a dozen girls in red and white uniforms twirl onto the stage, waving blue pom-poms. I study the face of each of the girls, but I know it's hopeless. Annette would never get away with dancing now—the costumes are skin-tight. I scan the crowd and don't see her there either. It was stupid of me to hope. An unmarried pregnant woman wouldn't be looking for the spotlight, not even one as bold as Annette.

Rebecca and I stop at a recruitment table after the show. On it sits a poster of a woman in a navy uniform, standing in front of a row of men who are looking up at a plane in the sky. The words "She Serves That Men May Fly" run across the top and "Enlist Today in the RCAF" across the bottom. A woman leans forward and says, "It looks exciting, doesn't it?"

"Oh, it looks wonderful," replies Rebecca, her face lighting up. I remember when we went to see *Girl Crazy*. The war reel before the movie was called *Proudly She Marches* and it was about women doing important work in the army, air force and navy. I could feel Rebecca's excitement beside me in the dark.

"Looks like you'd both make great candidates," the woman continues.

"My mother would never let me," says Rebecca.

"If you're twenty-one you don't need permission," the woman replies. "Women can do all the same things as men except fly on actual bombing missions. We can get trained in meteorology or air traffic control or photo interpretation. It's because of women that men like George Beurling can do the work they do. We do all the other stuff."

"Thanks," Rebecca sighs, pocketing a pamphlet, and we walk off.

9.

Uncle Max is celebrating again. According to the news, 500,000 Allied soldiers, including a whole bunch of Canadian troops, landed successfully on the shores of Sicily yesterday—July 10. I don't know why everyone's so excited. Sicily isn't even on the mainland of Europe, plus it's thousands of miles away from Berlin. But at least it was a successful landing, not like the one at Dieppe.

"Here's to hoping they won't destroy too much," Uncle Max says, raising his glass. "Such a beautiful country."

"And the art," says Aunt Naomi. "All those masterpieces. Titian and Caravaggio and Michelangelo. I can't bear to think of their work being destroyed."

My aunt and uncle go quiet, looking down at their drinks, remembering. Maybe they're thinking of the beautiful paintings that used to cover their walls, or they could be remembering their honeymoon in Italy, where they spent two weeks visiting churches, villas, and museums to see the art.

10.

Aunt Naomi stays in her bedroom for eight days when she hears about the massive bombings taking place in

Hamburg. The reporter says that 40,000 people were killed in one week and the city is in ruins. Her mother, my Oma, was from that northern city and she and Mama used to visit it as children. Uncle Max reminds her that such bombings are necessary, to end the war and free whatever Jews might be left, but it makes no difference. She can't stop crying. We try everything to distract her, but nothing works.

II.

Mrs. Krasney invites me to dinner, to celebrate Rebecca's twentieth birthday. Once again, she performs miracles with food, especially now that meat is being severely rationed. Uncle Max says there's five cows and twenty chickens for every person in Canada, but most of the meat is being sent to Great Britain, on the massive convoy of ships, to feed the Allies. If it gives the soldiers energy to win Sicily and jump over to Italy, I say let them have it. These potato latkes are so delicious, I'll take them over sausages any day. We have carrots from the tiny victory garden Rebecca and I helped put in, and a cake that's sweetened with beets instead of sugar.

We raise a glass of wine to toast Rebecca. "*L'chaim*," says her father. "To life." Then he refills our glasses and says,

"And to the Canadian soldiers in Italy. They fought so hard in Sicily, they got Hermann Goering's Division to retreat."

Rebecca's twin brothers turn into soldiers and fly down the hall. They open the front door, letting a gush of hot air into the flat, and shoot their pretend guns into the sky.

12.

Uncle Max calls us to the radio and we listen to Winston Churchill address the country from the Citadel in Quebec City, where he and President Roosevelt are meeting to plan the rest of the war. My mind drifts in and out as he talks about France and "the torment and shame of German subjugation." When he says that Canadian and other commonwealth soldiers are now "fighting in wider and widening fields," I clap my hands. May that field grow wide enough to reach where Papa is, but let him also be safe from the nastier and nastier bombs that are falling.

13.

The Saturday before classes start, Rebecca and I walk along Sherbrooke Street and turn into the Roddick

Gates that lead to the McGill campus. My eyes are drawn to the Arts Building at the top of the wide promenade, its green dome reaching for the clouds. Just looking at it makes my knees shake. The man in the security hut looks up and I expect him to jump out and nab me.

"Rebecca," I say. "I'm not sure I can pull this off. I feel like I'm that sick girl on the ship again, tossing in the waves. It doesn't feel right, being here."

"But you belong. Your new card says so," Rebecca replies, looping her arm through mine.

Rebecca's right. I can walk into the Redpath Library and read any of the books sitting on the shelves against the round walls. I can fill my head with all the knowledge I desire—history, classics, politics, philosophy—just what Papa wanted for me. The man who gave the new student tour said they have books in many languages, even German.

We sit on a bench facing the sun, watching squirrels scramble in the grass around us. There's a light and happy atmosphere on campus. Groups of students are tossing balls around, and several picnics are taking place in the grassy fields. Everyone knows that the Allies, with Canadian troops leading the way, have finally landed successfully on the mainland of Italy. It's all the news has been talking about for twenty-four hours and the announcers are encouraging everyone to get out and celebrate. Cheers of "hip hip hooray" and choruses of "God Save the King" spring up all around us. Everywhere we turn, another couple is kissing to celebrate the good news.

I turn toward Rebecca. The only person I want to kiss is her.

14.

Aunt Naomi's face flickers with excitement for the first time in weeks when I show her the course outlines I collected on my first day at McGill. "Oh Edie," she exclaims. "Your Survey of European Literature course looks wonderful: *Anna Karenina, Bleak House, The Castle, Don Quixote, Middlemarch, Madame Bovary, To the Lighthouse*. And then all the way back to *Paradise Lost, The Decameron* and *Faust*. So many great books. It's exactly the sort of course I would have taken all those years ago, in Vienna."

"Do you regret stopping?"

"In a way, yes, but overall, no. I've had a wonderful life with Max. I can't imagine better. If I'd stayed at the university and finished up, what would I have done?

You know that all the Jewish professors were fired. That would have been me, perhaps on my own. Who knows ...? We'll never know how life would've turned out if we'd made different decisions."

"I'll pass each book on to you as I read it and it'll be just like you're back there," I say. Her eyes fill with tears and she hugs me.

15.

A few weeks in and I've found all my classes and am starting to feel like I belong, but I miss seeing Rebecca every day. Now, I only see her on weekends, if her mother doesn't need her. I take my time walking home, looking up at the grey stone buildings with their colourful windows, imagining what it would be like to live in one of them with Rebecca. Uncle Max and Aunt Naomi mean well, but they are all over me with questions about school. I can feel them waiting for my brilliant future to blossom—after all, it's why we came here. Aunt Naomi always has a treat, like a hot buttered bagel, waiting for me, like I'm still in Grade 9.

But today, the flat is empty when I come in, and completely quiet except for the drip of the kitchen tap.

There's a note on the kitchen table in Aunt Naomi's writing. "Brian's ship has been hit by a U-boat in the Atlantic, no survivors. I've gone to Verdun to be with Louisa." I pull out a chair and sit down, taking in the news. I think about how Brian never wanted us there, but didn't kick us out, either. I remember him giving me a quarter to go to Belmont Park, and the way he danced with me that first Christmas, twirling me around the little parlour with his big hands. Louisa must be in pieces. Her whole life centered on Brian, from their first meeting in the diner to the day he shipped out on the *St. Croix*. All her decisions were based on him, even though he was in the middle of the Atlantic, escorting supply ships to Britain. Even her decision not to let Annette move in was based on what he would say when he came home. Now, Louisa's the one who'll be lost at sea.

16.

Reading *Anna Karenina* in English is tough and it's taking me so long I can barely keep up with the assigned pages. When I confess this to my professor, he says, "Take out the German copy and read it in your mother tongue."

"Is that allowed?"

"Remember, Tolstoy was translated into German long before English. Tell me your story, Edie. How did you come here?"

So I tell him everything and his soft brown eyes never leave my face. He simply nods or shakes his head and, when I've finished, he says, "Your story is inspiring, Edie. Would you consider writing about it for our literary magazine, *The Forge*?"

"Really?"

"Of course. Why not?"

So I do and now my story is all there, in black and white—the yellow star, the brownshirts at the café, the church-top angel. I leave out Annette and Rebecca—they are part of another story. Uncle Max and Aunt Naomi beam with pride when I bring it home and I know Mama and Papa would be proud too.

17.

On the first night of Chanukah, Aunt Naomi lights the *shamash*, the big candle in the middle of the menorah, then uses it to light the smaller candle on the far right. We sit the menorah in the front window, where it will light up our street, now that dusk has fallen. Uncle Max says Mama and Papa can see the light, and, if not, they can feel it, in their hearts.

18.

Seven nights later, on the last night of Chanukah, we are all together—me, Aunt Naomi, Uncle Max, and Rebecca. Aunt Naomi doesn't have Mrs. Krasney's skill with food, but she puts together a beautiful meal of potato latkes and brisket, with bakery donuts for dessert. We raise a glass of wine and toast our small family.

"And to the Canadian soldiers who have done it once again," adds Uncle Max. "Making the Germans flee, in fear for their lives, in Ortona. What I wouldn't give to see the look of rage on a certain person's face when that news hit him."

Aunt Naomi surprises us by saying a short blessing for all the people being killed by the bombings in Germany, in places like Berlin and Düsseldorf. "Some of them may be good," she explains.

When the doorbell rings we all look at each other and shrug. None of us can imagine who would be dropping by on this special night. Uncle Max goes down the hall and returns a few minutes later. Standing behind him is Louisa and, a few feet behind her, Annette. And in Annette's arms is a bundle, wrapped in a pink and yellow knit blanket that looks just like the ones Louisa used to knit, before she started knitting war supplies.

I jump out of my seat and run to them. Annette holds her up her baby and says, "May I introduce you to Hannah?"

My eyes well with tears that I can't hold back. Hannah gurgles and sucks her tiny fist.

"I named her for your mama, Edie. She was always so kind to me." I wonder if that's a dig at Louisa, but Louisa is also smiling from ear to ear, looking down at Hannah.

"How ...?" I start to ask.

"Life is too short, Edie," Louisa cuts in. "We make mistakes, but we fix them. It took Brian's death to make me understand."

Hannah's gentle cooing and her smiles warm the room. We pass her around like a blessing, from knee to knee. I hold her to my nose and take in her sweet baby smell. And for a few minutes, I forget.

1944

SABINE

I.

Fewer and fewer new girls come to the KLV, and some of the girls that were supposed to go home two months ago are still here, like they've been forgotten. Then suddenly, someone from the district office comes in and grabs them, showering us with dirty looks, as if we've been trying to hoard the girls, like food. We learn that a five-year-old girl was taken home to the wrong city and was left at the station overnight until someone noticed her sitting alone in the corner. It's like the whole tightly sewn Nazi system is starting to fray at the seams, like one of my old skirts.

The girls who do arrive wear the expression of old ladies, their lips pursed so tight their faces wrinkle around them. It's like they've got cod liver oil stuck in their mouths. We don't even take them to play *Völkerball* when the weather warms up at the end of February. We don't have enough girls for teams and they probably wouldn't run anyway. They'd just stand there and take the hits, pursing their mouths even tighter.

Katya lurks in the background, lighting fires, chopping potatoes, milking goats. She has to spread her legs wide around the pail now, her belly bulging over the metal rim. Sometimes, I hear her hum softly, a tune that sounds like a lullaby. If only she could sing the baby to sleep for another year, I'm sure this war would be over. Leningrad was freed by the Red Army. No matter what Hitler or Goebbels say, that has to be bad for Germany.

2.

In early March, a letter comes from the District Office of the *Wehrmacht* informing us that *"Hans Schmidt has sustained an injury in his heroic fight for the Fatherland and is in the process of being transported home."* Mama and I collapse onto the sofa and stay there, frozen in time for so long that Herr Pinker wanders out to see if we're all right. Normally we're all eating supper by this time. We have to tell him, but neither of us has words, so Mama just hands him the letter. When he's finished reading it, he sits beside us and the three of us stare at the blacked-out window, as though we're waiting for some answer to magically appear on the dark curtain. Eventually, the heavy thumping of Frau Schilling's boots sound on the walkway and Herr Pinker scurries back to his room, like a mouse to his hole, chased there by a cat. Her heavy knocking rattles the door. At first, I think it's just my brain rattling inside my head, trying to take in the news, until Mama shakes my arm and sends me to the door.

"I will have to fine you ten Reichsmarks, Fraulein Schmidt, if you do not darken that window immediately. I am surprised by you. In four years, you haven't forgotten once," says Frau Schilling, pointing to my bedroom window on the second floor.

"I am so sorry, Frau Schilling. We got bad news about Hans and Mama is very upset. I was comforting her and forgot. I am so sorry. I'll run and do it now."

"I'm coming inside to speak to your mother," she responds, pushing me aside. Thank God Herr Pinker ran back to bed. Hopefully, he's deep under his covers by now, filling the room with his raspy breath.

Frau Schilling marches up to Mama and says, "Your

son was brave, Frau Schmidt. You're lucky he's coming home. Thanks to our enemies, many fine young men are not so lucky." She stares at Mama and I wonder if she'll fine her ten Reichsmarks for crying. She turns to go and I watch Mama's shoulders unfurl. At the door, Frau Schilling turns back and says, "His opa will be happy to see him home, I'm sure. They both served. That will be a comfort to Hans."

I cross my fingers behind my back, praying she won't ask to see him.

3.

Now, when my BDM group is working at the station, I study the faces of disembarking soldiers to see if Hans is among them. Each train dislodges the usual crowd, mostly men in muddy green and brown uniforms or groups of foreigners in tattered clothes who are marched off toward the factory. I haven't seen Hans for four years. Maybe he's a foot taller or broader. Maybe he'll be missing something, like a leg. Maybe something else has changed about him, something we can't see, something that will make him more understanding when he finds Herr Pinker in Opa's bed.

A soldier walks toward me and I recognize Erich, one of Hans's old friends. He holds a white cane in his hand and wears a patch over one eye, the kind he and Hans used to wear as kids, pretending to be pirates. His face is completely scarred with thin red lines, like he's been attacked by lions.

"Erich," I call out. "It's me, Sabine."

He turns his face toward me but his eye doesn't latch onto mine.

"Are you going home?" I ask. "I can walk with you."

"Thank you. That would be helpful," he says. I tell Maria a soldier needs my help and take Erich's arm. We walk slowly, without speaking, me leading him through the wet streets of our town, pulling him around piles of late snow.

Finally, at the door to his house, Erich turns to me. "The flak guns are perched pretty high up, as close as they can be to the American and British bomber planes. If a bomb's coming right down on you, there's nowhere to go. You have to keep shooting. That's why you're there. You can't go running into the tower for shelter, like everyone else. We got hit, that's all. I was luckier than my young helper."

And Hans, I think, although that remains to be seen.

The gate screeches like a flock of gulls when Erich opens it, announcing his return.

4.

Every day when I return from the KLV, I ask Mama if she's had any more news about Hans, but so far, nothing. I think of the poster Frau Prinz has tacked to the wall of the lavatory: *"That we live in this great age is a gift of fate; that we may fight with Adolf Hitler's Greater Germany is the greatest joy of our existence."* She put it up there so the girls would feel better about being away from home. She tells them that being away is their part of the fight and they must fulfill it with silent duty. Like Hans did, up high on his flak tower, spraying our enemies. I'm glad Werner is working down low. I don't know where he is or what he's doing, but at least he's not up in the sky, scraping the bellies of warplanes. If he's still digging, he might at least have a hole to jump into when the bombs fall.

5.

Katya has become frantic about Anton. When I trade with the farmers I look for him. I've taken all of Mama's silk gloves from the box in her cupboard. When the war is over, all the farmers' wives will be walking to market wearing Mama's gloves over their calloused hands. It angers me that they won't just share their eggs and chickens. Why do we have to beg? Aren't we all part of this great big new Germany? At each farm, I ask for Anton, just to put Katya's mind at rest. It would mean a lot to her just to know her baby's father is still alive. But, so far, nothing.

6.

Frau Prinz is thrilled to hear news of the new miracle weapon the *Wehrmacht* is developing. The High Commander can't give out any details over the airwaves but he says it will mean the end of the war and certain victory for Germany. Frau Prinz shares the news with the girls at breakfast, but they seem unimpressed as they chew their lumpy porridge.

7.

After our dinner of turnip soup, I stare in the direction of the pantry door. Poor Herr Pinker, he doesn't come out much anymore, except at night. I hear him pacing around the house in the dark, stopping often, as if he's contemplating his fate. Maybe he feels like Hans is already behind him, breathing down his neck and threatening to turn him in. Hans's old war map is still hanging above Herr Pinker's bed, the pins completely out of date. If Herr Pinker stares at the map at all, it would be to study the vast pink expanse of Canada, which must surely be the land of his dreams.

8.

Frau Prinz is in a foul mood. She's taking the girls on a march into the woods to look for mushrooms and pinecones. The girls have to march two by two and be completely in synch or she makes them back up and start again. It takes me all day to discover that her bad temper is because she found out that Marlene Dietrich sang for our enemies in Italy. It's on the evening radio. The speaker is as irate as Frau Prinz. I picture Marlene slung across a piano somewhere near Sicily, a fluffy boa around her neck, singing "We'll meet again." I'm hoping this news is some kind of omen for me and Werner, whose return is taking longer than expected.

9.

Marlene must have brought the Americans luck. The

United States army has taken Rome. Two days later, thousands of foreign troops land on the beaches of France. Frau Prinz makes everyone turn out the house for a complete spring cleaning, as though that will hold the Allied soldiers back. I stay late, to help Katya carry the heavy buckets of water. Frau Prinz tells me not to, but I pretend not to hear her. The girls have to beat their eiderdowns with sticks outside, to free the dust mites. Later, they cry themselves to sleep, deep in their beds where nobody tucks them in. As I'm biking home at dusk, I say Werner's name over and over, praying he'll come back. I picture a long chain of young men, digging a tunnel under the entire country, never coming up for air.

10.

We get another letter, this time from Hans himself. His writing is shaky, as if he was writing in a moving vehicle. *Don't worry about me. My injuries aren't as bad as they first thought. Change of plans. Not coming home yet. Still able to perform my duties. Will contact you soon, Hans.* Mama and I collapse on the sofa like we did after the first letter. I can't believe how relieved I feel, but I can tell by Mama's face that her feelings are mixed.

"He'll come home for real soon, Mama," I say. "But this is better. You know it is."

"Yes, I know." Mama sniffles into her hanky. "And your papa too. It's a strange world when a wife and mother has to keep wishing her family doesn't come home."

Not for the first time, I wonder if Mama regrets what we've done for Herr Pinker.

II.

When I get to the KLV, Katya is clinging to the frame of the barn, her hair loose instead of braided, and wet, like she's just washed it. She should be getting the fire in the kitchen going by now and warming milk on the stove. Suddenly, she folds in half and grabs her belly. "Is coming," she squeals. "I cannot stop it. Please, help me!" All this time I've avoided thinking about the actual birth. It's like I expected it to happen overnight, while I was asleep, and I'd just have to deal with hiding the baby in the morning. I'm not ready for this. How can I hide what's happening from Frau Prinz and a dozen young girls?

"Get back in your bed, fast. I have to find Frau Prinz and make sure she doesn't come looking for you," I say. I help Katya over to her corner just as I hear the door of the KLV bang open against the wall. Frau Prinz will not be happy about the delay. She likes the day to run like clockwork, every event in its perfect time slot. I run outside and find her halfway to the barn.

"Don't go in there, Frau Prinz. Katya has a terrible fever. I've never seen anyone so sick. She's shaking head to toe. If you catch it, who will run the KLV?" Frau Prinz straightens her spine and her eyes flash darkly.

"She must have a weak constitution to get so sick. None of us has ever been sick here. Or she doesn't keep her space free of germs. I know she often smells. And now we all have to suffer. What am I supposed to do?" She crosses her arm against her thin chest.

"I'm sure I can nurse her back to health if you let me spend the morning with her. I'll bring some hot water and clean her space too. Ask some of the older girls to do extra duties today. It will be good practice for them. I don't think we have any other choice." Frau Prinz spins on her heels and I follow her inside. I boil some water and pour it into a big tin bowl, then I grab some kitchen towels and hide a knife inside them. I can't think what else I'll need. I've never birthed a baby before.

12.

It's a miracle the girls and Frau Prinz don't hear Katya screaming. I find an old leather strap hanging from a nail and put it between her teeth to bite down on, which helps muffle the sound. I place a towel under her and hold her hand as she flushes with pain. Her whole face contorts and turns deep purple, then she collapses back onto her pillow of hay. Every now and then she calls for Anton, or she starts speaking to me in Polish, clasping my arms, asking for things I can't understand and probably couldn't give her anyway. I just want this baby born, fast. Frau Prinz will want me to help with lunch. Then something changes and Katya starts grunting. Her breath is fast and shallow, like she's blowing the seeds off a dandelion, only harder. I peek below and see a crest of black between her legs. It's the baby's head, growing bigger and bigger, followed by shoulders and then, in a huge gush, the rest of a baby boy. I grab the second towel and wrap him. I'm sure I'm supposed to do something else, like slap him to get him crying, but I don't want him to cry. So I just pass him over to Katya, who reclines back with him into the hay. I take the knife from my pocket and cut the cord that holds them together.

13.

I dump the bowl of bloodied water in the field behind the barn. Wild animals will probably come and eat the placenta at night. The rabbits stare at me from their hutch with their huge brown and red eyes, like they know what I've been up to. Frau Prinz and the girls are in the parlour doing lessons, probably reading from the state reader which is full of pictures of beautiful blond boys and girls obeying their parents and saying *Heil Hitler* all over the place. What would the state reader say about a girl like me? The story would have to end with some kind of terrible punishment, but I can't worry about that now. I have to find something that Katya can rip up for diapers. I sneak inside and search the linen closet for an old sheet, only to remember that they're all old. Nothing has been replaced in years. I'll just have to take a chance on one not being missed. I take it to the barn and cut it up into ten squares. How we'll wash them is another matter. I could kick myself for being such an ostrich, burying my head in the sand, bringing Katya gooseberry jam when what she needed were practical things, like a place to hide her baby while she's at the main house working.

Werner used to repair broken rabbit hutches in the old tool shed. Maybe there's enough of one left that I can turn into a sort of cradle, lined with hay. He used to leave the door open while working and I'd watch him from the yard. I remember what he told me the day he left—that he'd left something in there for me, in case I ever needed it. He couldn't have left something for Katya's baby—he never knew she was pregnant.

I look around the rough worktable, and see nothing but rusting tools that probably should have been handed over to a collection drive. The floor of the shed is dirt with old boards thrown on top. My toe catches the corner of one and I kick it aside. I can't believe what I see. Werner somehow managed to dig out a giant hole, large enough to hold a person. He must have meant it for Herr Pinker, if we needed to move him in a hurry. *"Bless you, Werner,"* I whisper, *"wherever you are."*

14.

Frau Prinz gets notice that the KLV is closing at the end of July and all the girls are being sent home, even though some haven't been here for six months yet. All the Reich's resources are being diverted toward the war. No money, food, clothing or coal can be wasted to keep children away from the harsh realities that their families are facing. I don't know what's worse—the sad faces of the girls when they arrived, or the frightened faces of the girls as they're marched back to the train station in their wooden shoes. Frau Prinz doesn't allow me to hug them. She stands over them and says, "Remember you are living in a great age. Prove yourselves to be worthy of our soldiers, no matter how young you are. Be as brave and loyal as they are." One little girl sneaks me a bouquet of blue snapdragons and yellow strawflowers as she passes by.

"Godspeed," I say, brushing her shoulder with my hand.

Katya's orders come too: foreign workers are being sent back because towns are flooding with refugees from eastern Germany. Frau Prinz has to deliver Katya to the war office in town the day after tomorrow, *"with all her belongings."* I don't know what belongings they think she has. She has one spare dress for herself and a pile of rags for her baby—nothing more. There's no way Katya and her baby could endure such a long ride on a crowded train anyway, even if we could find a way for her to hide Aleksy under her dress.

15.

I tell Mama I have something special to do at the KLV early in the morning and she doesn't ask any questions. Katya is in a panic when I arrive before sun-up, breaking the curfew.

"Don't be scared, Katya. I have a plan," I tell her. "Help me gather all your things."

"Where we are going?" she asks, clutching Aleksy.

"Not far. You have to trust me."

I put my finger over my mouth to indicate that she should stay quiet and we tiptoe across the yard to the tool shed. Katya watches me move the sheets of wood with my foot, uncovering the hole.

"Climb down, Katya."

Her eyes are as wide as *pfennigs* as she shakes her head.

"It's only for a few days, until the KLV closes," I say. "I'll tell Frau Prinz you ran off with a man. She'll believe that. She doesn't know about this place, so don't worry. Here, I'll hold Aleksy while you get in."

Katya eases herself into the hole, her eyes on her son the whole time, as if she thinks I'll run away with him at the last second. When I pass him down, she squeezes him against her chest. Then I pass her some bread and water and re-cover the hole, leaving a space for air. Luckily, Aleksy is a good baby who falls into a deep sleep between feedings. He won't give them away.

16.

When Frau Prinz shuts the door of the KLV for the last time two days later, defeat is written all over her face. Telling the officials she lost Katya was really hard for her. She was sure they were going to punish her, but so far nothing has happened. "Maybe one lost Polish girl isn't the biggest thing the Reich has to worry about right now," I say and she doesn't argue. She shakes my hand with a firm grip and says goodbye, but she doesn't thank me. I think she always sensed me holding something back, not giving her the admiration she thinks she deserved. And she knew that the girls liked me better. How could they not?

She stands in front of the KLV and raises her arm. "Heil Hitler," she says to me.

"Heil Hitler," I reply. I wait until she's out of sight before running to help Katya out of the tool shed and back into the barn.

17.

If Hans were here, he'd have to pull his pin out of Paris. I remember him sticking it there with Opa four years ago. They joked about the Nazi flag flying from the Eiffel Tower and beautiful French girls, with their polished fingernails, learning how to make sauerkraut. Then he'd have to do the same for Brussels. Our enemies have touched German soil with their feet for the first time, near the Netherlands. Days later Stuttgart is fire-bombed. That one hits us closest to home. I think of all the girls from the KLV who live there and pray they're okay. Somewhere, amidst all this news, we hear about that new miracle weapon, a super-powered rocket, hitting London. The *Deutchlandsender* announcer says it's the beginning of a turnaround and I'm glad Hans isn't here to see me roll my eyes.

18.

Army recruiters roam the streets, looking for young boys and old men to join the new *Deutscher Volkssturm*, the People's Army. It's an odd name, as if the other one was made up of animals. They'll probably take Erich back and give him something to do that doesn't require full eyesight. If Opa were still alive, they'd take him too, or Herr Pinker if they find out he's here, no matter that he now has trouble walking, his muscles have grown so weak, or that he's seventy-five. The people are calling it the Old Grandpa Army. No wonder Werner never came back. There wouldn't have been time. I'm sure he was sent straight from his Labour Service into the army.

Our neighbour's remaining son, who's fifteen, is pulled in. He recites his vow for me on the front steps: "I swear that I will be true and obedient to Adolf Hitler, the Führer and Commander-in-Chief of the *Wehrmacht*." Then he tells us his opa was there too, making the same pledge. "Me and Opa will be learning how to work a *Panzerfaust*. Opa looked scared, but I'm going to help him. We'll be hunting down Soviet tanks together," he says, laughing. I imagine his mother is shaking inside, thinking of losing a second child.

19.

Mama thinks I'm still working at the KLV, so it isn't hard to go there every morning and bring Katya food and water for the day. I think she's safe in the barn for now, but I know she can't stay there forever. The air is getting colder each night and our town is crawling with strangers and army officials, all of them looking tense. Frau Schilling knocked on our door last night to say the mayor wanted a head count, so she had to come inside and see everyone for herself. Mama and I stood in the hallway and when she asked whether Opa could come out too, I jumped in and said, "Frau Schilling, is there any way you could just count his head from the doorway? I can help him sit upright. It's so painful for him to walk, it will take twenty minutes to get him out here." She didn't look happy about it, but in the end she agreed, so she counted Herr Pinker's head from the doorway.

"That man needs a trim and a shave," she said. "He looks like an old Jew." Mama's face was turning blue, so I laughed and stepped forward.

"You're right, Frau Schilling. He does. We'll fix him up this afternoon. We're sorry. Right Mama?" Mama managed to nod. But if they're counting heads, they might also be checking buildings. Katya and Aleksy need somewhere else to hide.

20.

The letter I've been dreading comes—my orders to do my *Pflichtjahr*. I thought all my years of service at the KLV would count as my duty year to the Reich, but they don't. Too much help is needed in the north. They're placing me in a hospital somewhere between Berlin and Dresden. Mama collapses onto the sofa when I tell her. My worst fear will now come true—Mama having to deal with the town and Frau Schilling on her own. If she doesn't keep it together, Herr Pinker will be discovered and we'll all be killed. Mama even forgets to call him Opa sometimes.

I think about moving Herr Pinker into the hole in the shed at the KLV, but he'd never be able to walk that far, and then what? Rumors are going around that the Russians found some of those camps and that thousands and thousands of Jews were killed. If Herr Pinker were discovered at the abandoned KLV, they'd just shoot him in his hole, like a fox, without hesitation. I have no choice but to trust that Mama will hold herself together.

But Katya? What to do about Katya? She is a whole different problem. Mama doesn't even know about her. I can't ask a neighbour or anyone else in town to help me. I can't do anything that draws attention to us. Every plan I make has to involve no one other than myself and Mama. And I have to make it fast—I leave in one week.

21.

I've become so good at lying, the words roll off my tongue, as necessary as air. "Mama, I have good news. I got permission to get you some help when I go, so you won't be looking after a sick old man all on your own. She's a Polish girl named Katya. She's here alone with her baby and I've met her. She is clean and polite. She worked for us at the KLV, and Frau Prinz really liked her." I don't tell Mama that she was supposed to go home. The less she knows the better. If she really believes this to be true, she'll be better at sticking to the story. "I'm bringing her home tomorrow. She can have my old room until I return. Then we'll have to get rid of her anyway. Isn't that great?"

Mama looks unsure, but nods. Now, I'm glad she hasn't been the one to go into town for years. She's less up to date about what's happening and hasn't seen the lines of foreign workers snaking from the factory to the station, many of them sucking on sticks or blades of grass for food.

22.

Aleksy is wrapped in the extra blanket I've brought from home, to help shield him from the cold November air.

We wander through the forest and into the back of town, then stick to the quiet streets, avoiding the town square. Luckily, we don't pass anyone. I made Katya rip that P off her dress, just in case. I'll have to go back later and talk one of the farmers into taking the goat and rabbits, which shouldn't be hard. I can't believe Frau Prinz didn't make arrangements for the animals, but I'm glad she didn't because Katya has been drinking the goat's milk and eating rabbits.

Katya wasn't sure about this plan. "Maybe is better I stay here, wait for Anton," she said when I showed up before dawn. "He won't know where I am."

"Anton might already be far away from here," I responded. She looked like she was going to cry when I said that. "I'm sure he didn't want to leave, Katya, but he had no choice. When the war is over, you'll find each other, I know you will." I tried to sound convincing, but I'm not so sure.

As we're walking, I tell Katya about Frau Schilling and warn her about the exact times she should stay upstairs in my room, completely quiet. "And if Aleksy's crying, stick something in his mouth. She's the one person who can't find out about you."

Katya walks in silence. I hate to even think it, but she does smell bad, like Frau Prinz always said. But who wouldn't? She hasn't had a proper bath since she arrived at the KLV two years ago. I'll convince Mama to let her have my bath instead of me on Sunday. So what if I board the train dirty?

23.

For the rest of the week, the house settles into a new routine, with Katya doing the work Mama and I would normally do. Aleksy sleeps in a drawer in my old dresser and Katya sleeps beside him, on the floor. I catch "Opa" and Katya smiling at each other while she sweeps around his cot, but both know not to speak, even though I didn't tell one about the other. One morning, Herr Pinker pulls two small nightdresses, baby-sized, from under his pillow and hands them to Katya. She holds them up and her eyes fill with tears. The night before I leave, I walk into Herr Pinker's room and find him holding Aleksy. The baby's looking up at him with huge blue eyes and Herr Pinker looks the happiest I've seen him since Edie left. In the tiniest of voices, he sings him a song about a little boy who wanders into the forest.

Aleksy hangs onto every word, studying Herr Pinker's face and gurgling softly. I fix the image of Herr Pinker and Aleksy like this in my mind. It's what I'll cling to when I leave: the old and the new, both in danger, but exchanging breath, crossing that barrier of time.

24.

The train is full of broken people. No one looks at anyone else. As we pull into Stuttgart, where I'll transfer to Berlin, I gasp at the sight of so many bombed buildings. Small fires smoulder everywhere and children are climbing hills of rubble. I can't believe I'm being pulled further and further into the heart of this storm.

Almost a day later, as the train crawls toward Berlin, stopping for no reason for hours at a time, hunger claws at my stomach. I ate all the food I'd managed to pack ages ago. At some stations, girls in BDM uniforms pass sandwiches through the windows to soldiers. One offers me half and I take it, wishing he were Werner. Finally, we inch our way into Anhalter Station. The sun is just rising, lighting up the streets. I don't have the strength to gasp. My window must have turned into a movie screen, or else my fatigue is playing tricks on my mind. What I saw in Stuttgart is nothing compared to this. There are no streets, only heaps of smouldering grey, block after block, in the shapes of wild beasts with large humped backs, prehistoric and not of this world. I remember the High Commander on the radio saying that Berlin had been bombed but that the damage was minor. If this is minor, I don't ever want to see major. Katya was right, that day she told me I knew nothing.

Now, I wish that were still true. This knowing is terrible.

I push and shove my way off the train, with hundreds of other people who seem completely unfazed by the state of the city. I find the station office and locate the woman who is there to meet me. She is holding up a sign with the name of the field hospital I've been assigned to. Five other BDM girls and I, all from different towns, are scurried into a truck and begin the slow drive around the fallen buildings onto a country road that will take us there.

I say a silent prayer for Mama, Herr Pinker, Katya and Aleksy.

EDIE

I.

The Student War Council is holding a bunch of activities on campus today. One of them is a "Hang Hitler" demonstration to raise money for the Victory Loans Campaign. A young man slips a noose around the neck of a dummy of Hitler, then he loops the rope over the limb of a leafless tree and tethers its other end to a huge tray. When the stuffed dummy is secure, he shouts, "Okay, start adding your nickels!" I throw two onto the tray, wishing I could spare more. We cheer and clap as Hitler's body rises off the snowy ground, inch by inch.

The football field is dotted with small fires that groups of students have to put out with heavy hoses, gripping them in a line. Medical stations are set up near the goal posts and female students are taking turns disinfecting fake wounds on the men's arms and chests, then bandaging them, but that's not something I want to try. I'm more drawn to a tent on the patio outside the library, where students who are doing radio transmission training are demonstrating their equipment, which can supposedly pick up signals from underground stations far away. I wait for my turn to wear the headset, hoping I can catch some news about Jews in Germany. The Russians have taken parts of Poland back, but there's still talk of camps for Jews. I pray that Papa is far from Poland. But all I hear on the headphone is static, broken by an occasional crackling word that I can't understand.

2.

A girl named Tanya read my story in *The Forge* and slipped me a note through my European Lit professor. She said my experiences were unique and invited me to drop by the offices of *The McGill Daily* to meet her. It took a week to work up the nerve, but when I do she makes me feel so welcome. It turns out she's a second-year History major who wears men's shirts, ties, and a black fedora. Something about her reminds me of Marlene Dietrich.

She has the same long arched eyebrows and deep voice.

"We could use you on staff, Edie," she says. "What's your thing?"

"Thing?"

"Yeah, like, are you into politics? Some of us are trying to get women to register to vote in the next provincial election, now that we can. Duplessis never supported our suffrage, so we could lose everything we've gained if women don't get out there and show him we're interested." Tanya points to the wall behind her desk. "She's my inspiration, Rosie the Riveter." Rosie is wearing a blue shirt, her hair swept up in a red polka-dotted kerchief. She's flexing a bicep that's almost as big as Popeye's and saying, *"We can do it."* She reminds me of Louisa, who's still working at the bomb factory, only way prettier.

"I'm more interested in movies than politics," I confess, hoping this doesn't make me sound frivolous.

"Great, they're yours. Go see *Meet Me in St. Louis* and write up a review. We'll test you out with that. Remember, I want your personal take, filtered through your eyes, the eyes of a Jewish refugee."

It's the first time anyone's called me that. Maybe it should feel bad, but it doesn't. It feels kind of right.

3.

A B-24 bomber plane has crashed over Montreal, leveling many buildings in Saint-Henri, barely missing the big post office on Saint-Antoine. It was being flown from here to the RAF in Britain, the same route Benny used to take. I'm at Louisa's, visiting Annette and Hannah, when it comes on the news.

"Oh my God, Edie," exclaims Annette, running to the window. "That's right where the boarding house was that I stayed at before Louisa found me. Lots of unmarried women go there, until their babies are born. It was hell. The sisters made us feel like dirt, like we should constantly be punished, but at least it was somewhere to live. Now, all those poor young women will have no home."

I join her at the window, which faces east, but we don't see any smoke. We're too far away.

"They're lucky it's Tuesday, the day of Devotion to Our Lady of Perpetual Help," Annette says in a mockingly severe tone. "The sisters insisted on taking all the fallen women to mass, rain or shine. Otherwise, they might all be dead, along with their babies that haven't been born or adopted yet."

I shudder at the thought of losing Annette and Hannah. Hannah is trying to eat her toes, her cheeks all fat and rosy. I can't imagine life without either of them.

4.

Writing my first review is easier than I imagined. I read a few old ones in The McGill Daily to understand the format, and then I jumped in. Even watching the movie, ideas kept running through my head and I couldn't wait to start writing. I gave the actors, costumes, sets, and music a good review, but I couldn't praise the plot—it was so lame.

> *Esther's in love with John, the guy next door, and she's crushed when he misses the trolley she's on. All four sisters are crushed when their father announces they're moving to New York City for his new job, because they don't want to miss the World's Fair in St. Louis. In one of the pivotal scenes, Tootie, the youngest daughter, throws a fit and destroys some snowmen, with her father watching from the window. He is so heartbroken by the spectacle, he changes*

his mind about the move. The grand finale
is when the whole gang stands at the 1904
Fair and watches as lights illuminate the
grand pavilions, the two eldest girls happy,
with their fiancés on their arms.

I remember Tanya stressing that she wanted my take, as a refugee, and the thing that struck me most when watching it was how innocent the movie was—no violence, no trauma, none of the upheaval of wartime. Sitting in the dark of the theatre, I couldn't help wondering if this was deliberate.

Why would a studio make a movie like this
now, with the war in its fifth year and the
number of Allied casualties mounting daily?
Is it because there's so much darkness in
the world, and so many families have been
torn apart, that Hollywood is determined
to spread some light? Or is it because most
people in North America haven't seen the real
darkness of the war up close, apart from the
servicemen and women, of course?

Tanya also told me to make it personal—that means bringing in Papa. I thought of him all through the movie, from its opening scene to the last, the grand finale that the whole audience went wild for.

> *When the grand pavilions are lit up at the end, dazzling in such a way that even the audience gasped and squealed with delight, I thought of other buildings, like those camps we keep hearing whispers about. Will those buildings ever see the light of liberation and hope? If my own father, who is still in Germany and most probably suffering immensely under Hitler's regime, were here now, I'd follow him to New York or anywhere, even to the moon if such a thing were possible. I wouldn't care where he worked; I'd only care about his safety.*

The next day, Tanya reads the review in front of me, her face giving nothing away except the odd nod of her chin, her eyes hidden by her fedora. What if she regrets asking me to do this? But when she's done, she slaps the paper down on her desk and says, "Great job, Pinker. Really great. I love it and we'll want many more."

I am beaming. Me—the girl who didn't know a word of English on the ship across the Atlantic, now publishing movie reviews in The McGill Daily.

5.

Rebecca's mother is forcing her to start going back to the dances at the YMHA. "Spring is the season of romance," she says, "and other girls your age are finding husbands there. Mrs. Cohen across the street said her daughter's brought home four different young men for the Friday night meal."

Mrs. Krasney looks right at me when she says this, like she's accusing me of something. She's tending to tiny plants of dill and parsley that sit in pots on the kitchen sill. I watch her stroke the green shoots, as though she's coaxing them to grow, so that she can transfer them outside. It's like she's hoping to do the same to Rebecca, to transfer her to a new pot. I know it's not what Rebecca wants, but we go dancing to make her mother happy.

Within minutes, young men start coming over to

ask us to dance. "It's a girl's duty to dance with a future soldier, you know, for the war effort," one says, winking. He holds his hand out to Rebecca because she's the prettiest. I wish she'd say no, but she doesn't. Maybe she's taking her mother's pressure to heart and really is on the lookout for a husband.

From across the hall, another soldier locks eyes with me and starts weaving his way across the dance floor. I grab my bag and run down an empty corridor where everything is quiet, except for the tick of a large clock, surrounding me like a heartbeat. Eventually, I hear footsteps and step back into a doorway, in case it's that soldier.

"Oh my God, Edie. Why'd you take off like that?" asks Rebecca.

"Because. One of those guys was coming at me."

"You make him sound like a torpedo."

"Well, to me he would be."

"Don't you ever want to date a guy, Edie? Or kiss one?"

"No, I don't think I do." Until I said it out loud, I didn't know this was true. Now, the sound of our breathing is almost as loud as the clock, filling the dark space around us.

"Why not?"

"Because Rebecca. I only want to kiss one person."

"Who?"

"You know who," I say, shifting toward her. I can't see Rebecca's expression, but I reach out and touch her face, tracing her cheeks and chin, my fingertips light as butterflies. Then we pull each other close. We kiss once, then twice, then a third time for longer.

I'm back on the big boat, tossing in the waves, but this time I'm on deck and the sun is warm and the sea is magical. I see the bronze angel again, with her wide-open arms, only this time they're Rebecca's arms, giving me a soft place to land.

6.

Rebecca and I go see *To Have and Have Not* with Lauren Bacall and Humphrey Bogart. We hold hands in the dark of the theatre and lean close as we watch the main character, Harry Morgan, struggle to keep from getting pulled into the political world around him. The hotel owner wants him to use his boat to smuggle members of the French Resistance, but Harry only wants to deal with regular tourists on the Caribbean island of Martinique. It makes my heart heavy to watch him resist getting involved and that's what I'll focus on in my review—individual freedom versus greater duty. It makes my heart even heavier to watch him fall in love with the singer, "Slim." When he holds Lauren Bacall in his arms and kisses her, my arms ache to reach out and do the same with Rebecca. There's no way I'll be able to write about that.

7.

I can't get back my old job at Brownstein's this summer. Business is too slow. Even Rebecca's hours have been cut, so she's earning less money, which is making her mother push her even more to get married. Rebecca keeps using the war as an excuse, but I don't know how long that's going to last. The Allied forces have finally landed successfully on the coast of Normandy in France. The newspapers are calling it D-Day. The names of the beaches where the American, British and Canadians landed are so beautiful, I keep rambling them off in my head, like a poem: Utah, Omaha, Gold, Juno, Sword. Juno was ours. Fourteen thousand Canadian men, many of them in special tanks that can swim, and ten thousand sailors from one hundred and ten Canadian ships. *The*

Montreal Star said, "There will be no pause now until Nazidom is crushed." How I wish that could be true.

8.

I haven't visited Mama's grave since I graduated last year. The winter wind blew away my pink stone, but I have a new one in my palm. First, I tell Mama about school and how well I did.

"It was incredible, Mama, to walk into the Redpath Library and see all the books sitting in plain view, books that were burned by the Nazis. Some days, just touching them made me feel nervous. And I'm writing too, now. I published an article about coming to Canada in *The Forge* and I've written two movie reviews for *The McGill Daily*. All those hours dressing up and pretending to be Greta Garbo paid off, Mama," I say. "People tell me my reviews are so interesting I could do them for money one day."

Two fat robins land on Mama's tombstone as I'm whispering to her. "And one more thing, Mama," I say, lowering my voice. "I'm not sure you'd approve, but I've fallen in love, like you did with Papa ... only it's with a girl, Rebecca. I told you about her last time, Mama. Do you remember? Only then we were just friends. We're more than that now, but I don't know what word to use. I know I can't say girlfriend, but that's how it feels. I hope you approve. Will you send me a sign to tell me you do?"

I look at the robins, hoping they'll soar into the sky, sending a signal from Mama, but they only hop to the ground when I lay the stone on Mama's tombstone.

9.

As summer goes on, my little alcove at Uncle Max and Aunt Naomi's grows too small. It used to seem like paradise after my room at Louisa's, but not anymore. Without a proper wall, I can't really be private. When Rebecca comes over, we lie on the bed and listen to the radio with the curtain drawn, her head nestled in the hollow of my neck, the lemon scent of her hair filling me. Sometimes, something terrible will come over the airwaves, but the horror just makes us cling closer, like when we hear about the hundreds of women and children locked into a church that was set on fire in a small town in France. Rebecca cries, thinking of her four younger siblings. We both know it would be worse to hear things like this alone. I love the way she runs her hand down my side, and when we start kissing, I don't want to stop. But when we hear footsteps, we separate. It's like a V-2 rocket, the kind that is now destroying London, has blown us apart.

IO.

We're in the bedroom Rebecca shares with her two sisters, folding laundry that we brought in from the line that hangs over the back lane, when Rebecca's sister flings open the door and catches us holding hands, our faces only inches apart. Before we can stop her, she flies down the hallway and we hear her cry, "Mama, Mama, Rebecca and Edie were kissing." We hold our breath as we wait for her mom to come to us, but she doesn't. Later, after we've put away the clothes, we go back to the kitchen, and Rebecca casually tells her sister to stop telling lies. "Edie was just whispering a secret in my ear," she says. "Because you have big ears as well as big eyes." But her mom is quiet with us the rest of the afternoon and I can see the tension in her shoulders as she peels potatoes at the sink. When she sets the table, she lays out seven plates, and I know I'm not invited.

II.

Hannah is rolling around on her blanket. When I get down on the floor and roll with her, she explodes with laughter. I tickle her tummy with my nose and she tugs my hair in her tiny fists. I sing to her in German, songs Papa used to sing to me, about suns and moons and stars and a little boy who wanders deep into the woods and gets lost. She falls asleep in my arms, her tiny lips sucking the nipple of the bottle.

Katharine Hepburn is on the radio, delivering a speech from His Majesty's Theatre, encouraging Canadians to buy Victory Loans. I can't believe she's here, in Montreal. I saw *The Philadelphia Story* four years ago with Annette, and Hepburn sparkled in it—she was so lively and witty. I wish I could run downtown and see her, but I can't. I'm babysitting while Annette goes out on a date with someone named John. She met him while pushing Hannah in her carriage through Outremont Park when she visited me a few weeks ago. He was campaigning to get Fred Rose, the head of the Labour-Progressive Party, re-elected to Parliament. He didn't look at all her type, with thick black glasses and a serious face as he handed us a flyer, but he and Annette talked for a long time while I took Hannah off to see the swans. Since then, I've learned he has asthma and that's why he's not overseas. He told Annette he's fighting in his own way, making sure labour unions stay strong. I can't picture Annette going out with someone who's into politics and not nightclubs, but she seems happy. "John's opened my eyes," she told me after their first date. "There's so much more important stuff in the world than entertainment."

I know she's right, but I hope Annette never stops dancing.

12.

Rebecca's mother has set her up on a date with someone she knows from the synagogue—Matthew Goldstein. "For your twenty-first birthday," Mrs. Krasney told her, as if he was a gift.

The thought of Rebecca with someone else fills me with all kinds of sharp feelings that poke and jab. She says Matthew is tall and skinny and not at all handsome, and that she'll hate everything about the evening—but what if she doesn't? What if she discovers that she likes being out with a man? What if the quiet and shy Matthew transforms into the most exciting man in the world once the sound of the swing music hits him at the canteen? Maybe they'll spend the night dancing, pressed together, his hand on her waist, her head on his shoulder. And if he kisses her goodnight, they won't have to hide behind a tree first. Maybe that will make Rebecca like it better.

13.

The night of their date, I wander up and down the streets. I turn onto de Bullion and, halfway down, I notice that women in bathing suits and lacy robes are opening and closing wooden shutters and calling down to servicemen from third floor flats. Men are hooting and hollering back up to them, while others are running up the winding staircases, pushing each other out of the way. Some of the women are perched on their windowsills, blowing smoke from red lips into the night sky, like they're sending up signals.

In a square around the corner, a group of people are playing chess on some makeshift tables. I recognize the fedora right away. It's Tanya, hunched over a board, an unlit cigar propped in her lips.

"Hey, Edie," she says, tipping her hat. "Do you play?"

I shake my head. "Me neither. I stink at it. See you later fellas." She gets up and joins me. She's wearing a short-sleeved summer shirt tucked into a pair of baggy pants. "Heading anywhere special?"

"Just wandering."

"Want to come up? I live down the street."

We sit in Tanya's living room, which is sparsely furnished with mismatched pieces of old furniture. She puts the Saturday night concert on the radio and brings us each a Coke.

"Any news on your dad?" she asks, sitting in a rattan rocker that's badly in need of paint.

"Nothing," I reply.

"I guess there won't be any until after the war."

From anyone else that might seem cruel, but I know Tanya's just being matter of fact. And she's right. I won't know anything until the war is officially over. We talk about what's happening in Europe and the Pacific, which I don't know as much about.

Behind Tanya, on the bookshelf, sits a picture of her standing beside Thérèse Casgrain, the leader of the suffrage movement in Quebec, when she came to speak at McGill in the fall. Tanya's face lights up the frame, she looks so excited. Beside that is another picture of Tanya with her arm draped over the shoulder of a girl with long dark hair. Their heads are leaning toward each other in a way that seems familiar.

"Is that your sister?" I ask.

"No, Edie. She's ... well, she's a special friend." Tanya arches her eyebrows so high they vanish into her hairline. "I think you know what I mean."

My face flushes and my whole body grows rigid. It's like Tanya can see inside me, to where I'm holding Rebecca against my heart.

"I kind of wondered about that girl you take to the movies all the time. Is she also ... you know?"

Now Tanya's eyes are boring into mine. This is my chance to talk about Rebecca to someone other than Mama. Part of me wants to burst open with words, but another part shuts tight as a dam.

"Never mind, Edie. Sorry. It's none of my business. But, if she is, you don't have to hide that from me. I just want you to know. There's more of us around than you think."

I know what she's saying but the idea that I am part of an "us" is too strange, especially tonight, when Rebecca is out with Matthew. We sit quietly, sipping our Cokes, our feet tapping to the music, me wishing I could be as brave as Tanya.

14.

Rebecca's mom answers the door but won't let me in. She says Rebecca's going to be busy all day. I keep peeking over her shoulder, but there's no sign of life in the flat. In fact, it's eerily quiet, as if she's corralled everyone into a room and ordered them to keep quiet. I have an urge to shout down the long hallway. I picture my words reverberating off the flowered wallpaper and following the tin pipes along the ceiling to Rebecca.

"That's a shame," I say, forcing my biggest smile. "I was really curious about her date with Matthew. She promised to tell me all about it."

"That'll have to wait," says Mrs. Krasney, wringing a dish towel in her hands. I can tell by the way she looks at me that she doesn't believe a word I'm saying.

15.

Rebecca's been on three dates with Matthew, according to what she tells me when I find her at Brownstein's. "This is my last week here, Edie," she adds. "Both Mama and Matthew don't want me working anymore."

"And you're going to listen to them?"

Rebecca shrugs, her beautiful red hair bouncing on

her shoulders. "I don't see a way around it."

"I do, lots of ways." I think of Tanya and reach for Rebecca's hand, but she pulls back so fast she knocks a display of summer sandals off a glass shelf. Then she turns away from me.

"My mother doesn't want me hanging out with you anymore, Edie, and it might be for the best."

I don't know what to say. I'm as stiff and lifeless as the mannequins that surround us. Soon Rebecca is busy with a customer. She bends to slide this woman's foot into the steel measuring mould, and I know she won't look up. She's focusing hard on sliding the braces around the foot—with its one-quarter of the bones in the human body, 33 joints and 100 muscles, tendons and ligaments—until it fits snugly.

16.

The streets are full of cheering people shouting *"Vive la France!"* Tanya and I are cheering alongside them, waving our little French flags down rue Saint-Denis to Carré Saint-Louis, where a large crowd has gathered. The newly re-elected mayor, Camillien Houde, who spent the last four years in prison for encouraging people to defy the federal government's mandatory registration, is getting ready to give a speech. People are applauding him like he's a war hero, but he was the opposite. What he did encouraged the anti-conscription movement, the one that dissuades men from going over to fight the Nazis and help keep everyone, including Papa, safe from fascism.

The crowd is so lively here, I can only imagine the scene in Paris. People must be going mad, ripping down the swastika flags that hung from the Eiffel Tower and the Arc de Triomphe. The newspapers are full of pictures of American soldiers grabbing French girls and kissing them, swooping them so low the girls' heads are almost touching the pavement. Tanya and I are swept into the crowd singing "La Marseillaise." There is such a strong feeling of freedom in the air, I bet Tanya could kiss me as passionately as a soldier and no one would notice. Not that I want her to. There's only one person I still want to kiss and that's Rebecca. But she's not free anymore. August 25—the day Paris was liberated from the Nazis—is also the day Rebecca's mother announced her daughter's engagement to Matthew. I saw it in the Jewish News, along with the wedding date, October 14.

17.

No invitation comes to attend Rebecca's wedding and that is just fine. Uncle Max and Aunt Naomi are confused, but I tell them her mom just wants a small, family-only wedding. I can't exactly tell them the truth, can I? Besides, I couldn't stand to watch Rebecca and Matthew facing the rabbi, under the chuppah, or circling him seven times, binding themselves even more tightly together. In my mind, it's me who ends the ceremony by crushing their glasses under my feet. I crush them again and again, breaking them into a million pieces, until they look the way my heart feels.

18.

The Sunday before school starts, the Canadian army marches back into Dieppe, a little more than two years after their disastrous landing there. The papers say it's closure, the mission coming full circle. I try to think of going back to McGill that way, but without Rebecca I feel stranded.

19.

When I review *Arsenic and Old Lace*, I write about how no one would suspect that two little old aunties, who can trace their ancestors back to the *Mayflower*, could murder innocent men. Then I write about all the nice old people in our building back home who stopped talking to us and stopped bringing their work to Papa when Hitler said they should. One of them, we never knew who, spit on our door. And I write about *Kristallnacht*, when all our businesses and synagogues were destroyed—didn't nice little old ladies stop to look and smile complacently on their way to market the next day? Cary Grant keeps opening chests in the big old house and finding more and more bodies. With each one, he grows more and more amazed. But I have no doubt that, once the war is over, the whole world will be uncovering bodies for a very long time. And, like Cary Grant, people will stand with their mouths open, eyes wide, scratching their heads and wondering.

With a flick of her fedora, Tanya says my review is brilliant.

20.

I spend the day of the wedding housecleaning. Aunt Naomi and Uncle Max are out with friends and I'm happy. This way, I can keep busy without them asking me why I have a sudden urge to sweep and scrub and rearrange furniture. The one o'clock news announces that one of Hitler's right-hand men, Erwin Rommel, "The Desert Fox," has died. The Nazis are claiming he died in battle, but there's a rumor that Hitler forced him to kill himself. But even that good news only takes my mind off Rebecca's wedding for a minute, especially as four o'clock, the hour of the ceremony, draws near.

It's a cool October day and the street is full of people returning from mass at the church on the corner. The Catholic kids aren't allowed to run or scream on Sunday, so it's quiet, eerily quiet. The biggest noise is the voice in my head, wondering if Rebecca will escape at the last minute and show up at my door. She must look beautiful in her fancy dress, her red hair piled high. I've never seen Matthew, but in my mind I turn him dull and plain in a mud-brown suit, completely undeserving.

Suddenly, there's a knock at the door and I freeze, my heart racing. Could it really be her? I know she loves me. I know she can't bear the thought of marrying Matthew—she's doing it for her mom. That day in Woodlawn Park, when she rejected the woman who wanted to recruit her into the Women's Auxiliary, comes to me—the way Rebecca handed back the pamphlet with a sigh, handing back her dreams. This is the same. I close my eyes and breathe deeply to still my heavily beating heart, then run to the front door. When I open it, Mrs. Krasney is standing in front of me.

"Here, Edie," she says. "This is for you." She hands me a piece of paper. "Read it when I'm gone. I'm sorry, Edie." She turns and walks away, her fancy dress hanging below her jacket.

I take the letter into my alcove and shut the curtain. It must be an explanation, an apology even, from Rebecca. I take a deep breath and unfold it.

> *Dear Edie,*
>
> *I am ordering you to stay away from Rebecca. I don't know exactly what went on with you two, but Rebecca now has other plans for her life. If your mother were still alive, she'd be telling you the same thing. It is time to grow up and become an adult, to put away childish fantasies and games. We all have a place in this world and Rebecca's place is with Matthew, doing what should come naturally to all young women. Perhaps*

because you have lived without parents for so long you have lost track of what's important in life. I do not wish you any ill luck, Edie, but I certainly hope you find your way back to what's right and normal in this world. Rebecca knows right from wrong, even if you don't.

Best wishes,

Mrs. Krasney

My alcove loses all its air, the red curtain suffocating me.

1945

SABINE

I.

The dormitory is on the top floor of this grand old building that looks like a castle. Ten bunkbeds are pushed under the eaves for the twenty girls who've come from all over Germany to work in the improvised hospital. We wear our BDM uniforms with a crisp white apron on top, and a little white cap with a red cross on it. We follow the *Krankenschwestern* around and do whatever they ask as they look after the wounded men. Each room on the ground floor of the house is now a ward, holding two rows of iron beds. On my first tour, the sisters got angry if I lost focus by staring up at the grand chandeliers, or murals of men fighting battles on horses, or angels floating in clouds on the ceiling. "You're not here on holiday," one of them reminded me. "Soon, you'll see nothing but the wounded."

Six weeks later, I know what she means. On each bed, tucked under crisp white sheets, lies a wounded soldier, bandages wrapped around some part of his body—head, chest, arm or leg. Some have lost limbs, often more than one. It took me a while to be able to watch as the sisters changed the bandages, pulling the blood-soaked ones off with pincers. It's my job to hold the tin bowl, then carry the bandages to the washroom, where women who remind me of Katya stand over large boiling pots, sterilizing material, sweat rolling down their faces.

The wounded men are oddly quiet, like they don't have the energy to speak, but sometimes they'll reach out to touch me as I hold a glass of water to their lips. In each bed, I look for Werner. I don't know whether to be disappointed or relieved when he's not among the batches of men that arrive several times a day inside ambulances whose back doors are riddled with bullet holes, like they've been used for target practice. The head doctor reads the white tags attached to the men's arms, then gives orders for where they should be taken. The worst cases are sent around through a back door, to the main surgery. The ones who need minor patching up get carried up the wide front staircase and into a smaller surgery. Later, they're transferred to one of the recovery wards where we work. We aren't allowed to speak or respond to any of the men's questions. But no one told me not to smile, so I try to do that as I change linens or carry supplies to the sisters. I don't see how it can hurt.

2.

Some of the girls thought to bring photographs from home that they tack into the wooden beams above our beds, but I only have the pictures in my head. I write Mama one letter every week and pray that it finds her. I'm not allowed to say anything about what goes on here and I couldn't tell her where we are if I wanted to. There isn't a road sign in sight and this seems to be the only house for miles around. Wherever we are, it's close to where bombing is taking place—otherwise, the beds wouldn't fill up so quickly. We barely have time to strip the linen and cover the cots with fresh sheets before new men are rolled into them. When the soldiers' wounds have healed, they're taken away. When I ask the sister where they go, she says, "Back to the war, of course," tapping her forehead like I'm an imbecile. Only the men in the large hall, the ones with missing legs and arms, who are learning to walk or feed themselves, are spared. Even men with one missing eye or ear are sent back to fight. It's harder, in a way, to watch them leave than it is to watch them arrive. But I can't tell Mama that in my letter. I can't say anything negative. It will just be blacked out. Plus, it will make her think of Hans.

3.

One day, one of the sisters takes me into the main surgery. "I've watched you work. You have a gift for dealing with the sick," she says. She makes me scrub my hands and arms, then change into a fresh apron and put a mask over my face. She does the same, then leads me through the double doors into a brightly lit room. Three beds hold three men and each is surrounded by a team of people whose attention is focused downwards, their arms bloodied up to their elbows, their hands moving over the wounded men as if they're playing piano on their ribs.

The sister ushers me closer to the action. "Your job is to gather the used instruments and then take them to the pantry where you'll sterilize them and get them ready for the next operation. Watch me the first time."

She stands, holding a tin bowl behind the surgeons. Before long it is full of bloodied tools and she motions for me to follow her.

"This is a very important job we're trusting you with, Fraulein. If even one tiny germ is left on an instrument it could mean bacteria in the body and the end of a life. Imagine a soldier surviving the war but dying because you were careless?"

She rinses the bloodied instruments, then lifts the lid off the sterilization machine and lowers them into the steam with special tongs. As she does, I name them. "Razor, scalpel, lancet, trocar, saw." The names roll off my tongue, my voice boastful, and the sister's eyes widen. "I've seen all these before," I explain. "From my papa. He designs them."

She flashes the faintest smile and nods. "Good. I'll leave you then, since you are so experienced." She spins on her quiet rubber soles and leaves me alone in the tiny room that is full of sinks. As I squeeze the tongs around the instruments, I feel as though I'm touching a part of Papa.

4.

The casualties don't stop. Men are lined up on canvas stretchers all along the hallway, some so young they look like they should have teddy bears tucked under their arms. My fourteen-hour workdays are an endless stream of bloodied instruments, and that feeling of closeness to Papa dissipates after the first few days. There is no time for nostalgia and now I know why the sisters rarely speak or smile. It takes all their concentration to perform their duties. Nobody here has a past and we can't imagine a future. There is only now—helping to heal the wounded.

The shed out back that is used as a temporary morgue is so full, we're now storing the bodies in a big tent. It's freezing outside, so that is good, but what will we do in summer? The ravens and vultures will eat better than people here.

At night, we're careful about what we say. No one wants to admit it out loud, in case there's a snitch, but we know the war is lost. It has to be. The loss is etched on every face in every bed or stretcher we see. We hear rumors that the Americans are working their way through France and that the Russians have taken Poland. We hear they liberated a camp there and found thousands and thousands of starving prisoners, mostly Jews, and piles of bones, heaped into mountains. Ovens, even, where bodies were burned. "They're going to make us pay," one girl says and I wait for someone to challenge her unpatriotic behaviour, but no one does. We all know she's right.

5.

The deafening bombs fall non-stop for forty-eight hours. At night, an orange glow rims the horizon to the east of us. By morning, a steady stream of burned people is arriving and we learn that Dresden is on fire. Sometimes we can't tell if the patient is a man or a woman. We know the children because they're small, but we don't always know if they're boys or girls. We don't have enough bandages to help everyone. It would take a bandage long enough to wrap the earth to cover all the open flesh wounds and we have nothing at all to help with the burns, no salve or ointment. No supply truck has come all week.

For days, the lights in the surgery flicker and then finally shut off altogether. Without electricity, I can't sterilize the instruments. We build an old-fashioned fire outside and stick a cast iron kettle on it. But there's a cold wind and it's too hard to keep the flames going. At night, we hear the soldiers shouting about Russians coming to kill them. Many refuse to stay and we watch them hobble away into the forest holding their chests, bandages trailing behind them like ghostly tails.

A convoy of refugees passes by. Most are on foot, others in wagons drawn by mules, wicker baskets or bundles strapped across their backs. Some push wheelbarrows laden with dishes and blankets, toy bears and babies. The *Krankenschwestern* give them water but we have nothing else. It must break the nurses' hearts to watch the children pass by, clinging to their mothers' hands, many without shoes, as they flee on the snowy ground. "We should go with them," says Angelica, one of the BDM girls. "We could walk home. It's safer than staying here." I know she's right but can we really just leave? Don't we have to have orders or permission from someone?

6.

An air-raid siren peels into the night, pulling us from our short sleep. We throw on our boots and coats and run to the cellar. The wounded who can walk come with us but many have to stay where they are. I can't bear the thought of the injured men alone in their cots, but there's nothing I can do. Bombs whistle and explode all around us, shaking the walls, showering us with dirt and dust. The BDM girls huddle together in the musty cellar, with only a candle for light, and pass around a cigarette. "They'd never bomb a Red Cross sign," one of the doctors says. "But they must be close." All my thoughts turn to Mama. I pray she isn't going through any of this.

Then the whole world explodes and it's like plaster is falling straight into my heart.

7.

The bombing has stopped, or else I am now deaf. Angelica and I clutch each other so tightly, I think the welts in our arms will never disappear. We wait and wait, but the all-clear never sounds. Little shafts of light poke through tiny holes in the two windows, telling us it must be morning. Finally, a few people start up the wooden stairs. The white aprons of the sisters and the white coats of the doctors are covered in a film of grey. I hear heaving and shoving and finally the door opens and a male voice calls out. We form a chain, similar to the chains we formed back in the early days of the BDM, when we ran round and round the campfire, singing cheerful songs. Slowly, we emerge into the destroyed hospital. The front of the house is gone, sliced off like a piece of bread, exposing us to the outside where sheets of heavy rain are falling. We pick our way over stones and beams and eventually lose each other's hands. Twisted frames of what were once cots block our progress. I close my eyes and step over the bodies, covering my face with my dirty apron to filter the dust and smoke. Chunks of plaster cherubs and spears of chandelier glass slide away under my feet. Someone is yelling at us to get out as fast as we can because the whole house might fall. I can hear people trying to free others who are stuck under debris, but I keep going, following that voice to safety.

8.

Within an hour, the wounded men who could be saved are lying in the wet grass. The BDM girls help the sisters do what we can, but without supplies we can't do much. No one has drinking water. No help arrives. The refugees from the east continue to stream past, a steady train of rags. They glance our way but don't seem fazed by the bombed hospital. When we've done all we can, we lean back against some trees and listen to the hospital creak and groan. Small fires dot the upper floors. We wait and wait for someone to tell us what we should do, but no one does. The doctors seem as confused as we are. Angelica whispers in my ear, "I'm going to join them." She points to the flow of people heading west. Suddenly, a desire for home flares up in me, as vibrant as the fire shooting out of the attic where we slept. I take Angelica's hand.

9.

We wind through forests and come out on country roads that are pockmarked by shells. Some farmers give us water and bread, others wave us on, shaking their shovels. We help mothers carry the children who weigh down their fronts, while bundles weigh down their backs. We're lucky to have shoes and coats— many don't. We wear our coats back-to-front to shelter the babies. At night, we slip inside the woods to sleep, finding dry ground under the tree cover, huddling together for warmth. Sometimes we come across small groups of people speaking Slavic languages, maybe Czech or Polish, but no one challenges their right to be here. Once, a foreign woman hands a German mother a hardboiled egg and points to her two children. The gesture makes me cry.

We travel through a huge forest for several days, eating snow and pieces of stale bread passed down the line. Our train grows smaller as people break off to search for relatives who might take them in. Sometimes an army vehicle passes us on the road and we hold our breath, expecting the soldiers to turn us back or harm us for fleeing. Angelica and I turn our BDM coats inside out, to hide the insignia. Weeks later, we reach Würzburg and cross the bridge over the Main River into the broken city where Angelica's aunt lives. "She'll let you stay, I'm sure," she says, "if ..." But I don't want to stop. I'm like a homing pigeon, set southwest. We hug goodbye and promise to find each other again one day. The idea of *one day* is impossible to grasp, flimsier than air.

10.

They hang from a tree and we stumble upon them so suddenly we don't have time to cover the children's eyes. Two young soldiers, stripped naked, signs around their necks: *Traitors to the Fatherland*. They swing gently, pushed by the breeze. Our group is small now and one of the mothers wants to cut them down. "They could be my boys," she says. But the others stop her. "If they find out, you'll be hanging next to them. And then what about your daughter?" They point to the little girl whose arms are wrapped around her mama.

So, we leave the young men there, but I feel them for days, swaying in my mind.

II.

Days later we reach Stuttgart. It's like every other place we've passed—bombed beyond recognition, but then we pass a café where tables and chairs sit amidst the rubble and people are actually sipping ersatz coffee, enjoying the spring sunshine. The one-armed waiter wears a white shirt and bow tie. It's like a scene from a movie. Flowers actually sit in a box in the window, looking too bright amidst all the grey. Near the train station, a makeshift hospital has been set up in a tent, a large red cross inside a white circle painted on its sides. We're a small group now, just me and two mothers, each with one child, who are hoping to reach Freiburg in the Black Forest. When we pass the tent, a *Krankenschwester* steps out and calls over to me. "You there, you look capable. We need all hands. Come!" She must have seen my BDM coat.

The tent looks like the hospital near Dresden, but without the iron cots. The men are on raised canvas platforms, squashed closer together. "Here," says the sister, handing me a bowl of water and a roll of bandage. "You must know what to do. Start anywhere and do what you can." I squeeze between the beds, roll up the sleeves of my dirty shirt, and start cleaning and bandaging wounds. I pause between cots to tie a knot in the waist of my skirt, which keeps slipping down, I've become so thin.

After a while I don't see the faces of the men anymore—just the wounds. It's like the whole earth has a terrible case of measles, one that will never clear up, with unusually large spots. Sometimes I think I see metal deep down inside the holes and wonder if I should identify them to the sisters, but they must know. The slogan *"Strength Through Joy"* pops into my head. Way back at the beginning, when Hitler was turning Germany around, his plan was to help people experience joy and happiness in the countryside or at the beach or at music concerts. A whole happy nation, suntanned and humming. And now that slogan turns inside out in my mind: *Weakness*

Through Misery. That's all I see around me.

I don't want to be here and these sisters can't make me stay. No one can make anyone do anything anymore—aren't all these men proof that there's no more order? I bandage the last wound and grab my coat. Evening is a good time to leave. Walking at night is safer. I'm just about to slip out of the tent when a face over in the far corner catches my eye, taking away my breath.

12.

Hans's eyes are closed and his chest is wrapped from his waist to his collar bone. He looks like the pictures of mummies in my old history book, the one we used before Hitler. But the thin eyebrows and the cleft chin are his. I look at his hands, which used to be strong from all the boxing. Now, a paper-thin layer of skin covers them, making his knuckles bulge. It seems impossible that I used to be scared of him, especially when he raised his voice. He looks like he couldn't wrestle a sparrow. I kneel and entwine his fingers in mine and whisper his name, but he doesn't stir. His mind is far away like so many of the men's.

"Don't wake him up, Fraulein," a stern-faced sister says, standing over me. "He's one of the lucky ones. He's had surgery. He's sedated. Let him be." I know I can't leave my brother, in spite of everything, so I make a nest of blankets in the corner nearest him and slide my coat over me. I'll check on him in the morning. If he's better, I'll take him with me. What might be waiting for us at home can't matter now.

13.

I only work near Hans. The sisters have given up trying to get me to help anywhere else. I've changed his bandages twice now and I've seen the holes all over his chest, sides and back. It's miraculous that he's alive. The stitches circle his heart and apparently one lung was collapsed, then reinflated. The nurses tell me he was in a truck that was attacked by the Americans in France, but managed to keep rolling, then eventually ran out of petrol near here. I run my fingers over the wounds that are knitting back together and tell him stories with each one. Stories of mischief, involving Max and Maurice, a book Papa used to read us when we were kids. I tell him how they put gunpowder in the professor's pipe, or released the sacks of beetles in their Uncle Fritz's bed. I tell him about Mama and how much she would want

him back home. I'm careful too though, in case I let slip
something that could get me in trouble. I remember the
poster: *"Dear God, make me dumb, that I may not to Dachau
come."* I wonder if there's still a Dachau. We heard talk of
it as we were walking and meeting up with others. It's
another camp like the one in Poland, where so many
people were killed. But who knows what's happening
anywhere? It's best not to ask. There's no radio here,
and by now I know the reports on *Deutschlandsender*
are unreliable anyway. Best to just work and stay quiet,
except when I can whisper in Hans's ear.

14.

On the third day, my brother's eyes open. I move my face
above his, willing him to recognize me. His lips open and
the word *wasser* escapes faintly. I run to grab a cup and
hold the water to his cracked lips. He takes the smallest
sip and closes his eyes again. My heart sinks but I stay
there, holding his hands, until a sister yells at me to
keep working. New men are arriving as the old ones are
taken away. I have to get Hans out of here. He's already
been injured and returned to duty once; it could happen
again. Rumor has it the Americans and the French are

getting closer every day. If Hans is not sent off to fight again, he might be captured. I don't know which would be worse.

15.

That night, Hans begins to stir. It's pitch dark in the tent, except for some gas lamps near the entrance, but I can feel Hans's eyes staring at me. "Sabine, is that really you?" I take his hand and squeeze. "Yes, it's me. Oh Hans, I can't believe I found you." He squeezes back and I'm so happy to know he has some strength left. It's the first time I've held my brother's hand since we were little.

"I want to get you out of here. Can you move your legs?" He bends at the knee and moves his feet.

"But I'm sore in the chest. I won't be able to move fast. It's better you go without me."

"What's coming is going to be terrible. You need to get home, for Mama's sake." I imagine her face opening up like a flower at the sight of her two children, returned together.

"But I don't know if I can. And I might have to go back."

"There is no more back, Hans, believe me." I brace for an argument from my broken brother, but none comes.

"I'm not going without you. Day after tomorrow. In the morning, I'll find us some food to take, and in the meantime I'll feed you as much broth as I can, to build you up. If we're lucky there'll be a piece of turnip in it. And we'll get you to stand every few hours to regain your legs, no arguments!"

He turns his head toward mine. "Am I dreaming? I must be dreaming. Pinch me, Sabine." Instead, I lean over and kiss his forehead.

16.

We leave two nights later. It's not hard to sneak past the sister who's snoring in her chair by the tent's opening, her head flopping back against the canvas. Hans has been in bed for a long time, so he's shaky and has to lean against me. We stop a lot and, little by little, make it a few blocks down. Eventually, Hans can stay upright for more than ten minutes without pausing. We don't need to get far tonight, just out of the city and into the woods. If it takes all night to hobble there, we'll do it. I gave him my coat to wear since we left the top of his *Wehrmacht* uniform behind—it's better that way. He can't wear anything that identifies him. I took his *Ahnenpaß* from his pocket when he was sleeping and burned it.

Eventually, the buildings thin out and country cottages appear, smoke rising from the chimneys. We enter the first batch of trees we see and stop for the night. Two hours walking is all Hans can do. "My legs are like *spätzle*," he says. We share a stale roll and sip from the canteen I stole. If he's in pain, he hides it well. I help him lie flat, to rest his chest muscles. The stars shine brightly under a half-moon, twinkling when they peek out between passing clouds. It strikes me that nothing in the natural order of the universe has changed. The moon still grows and wanes, the stars still flicker. None of this madness has touched the sky, except for the jet fuel and smoke.

17.

We keep to the woods that run beside the road, rising over hills and dipping into valleys. Hans gets stronger as we go, but still walks slowly. Every now and then we come across a circle of stones around a pile of ashes. We dig in the debris to look for food, maybe the skins of a potato or chicken bone, but all we ever find are scraps of old uniforms. The woods must be crawling with soldiers trying to get home before the big invasion. I remember the two young bodies dangling from the tree and I know we have to be careful. The war isn't officially over and Hans is a deserter.

18.

Hans is shivering beside me. I touch his forehead and recoil—it's hotter than burning coal. Infection! I've seen enough of it to know. But I have nothing. No antibiotics, no disinfectant, not even any water left in the canteen. Was I wrong to take Hans away from the medical tent? But no—I never could have left without him. I try to raise his head but it flops back down, heavier than a stone. I picture infinitesimal pieces of bacteria from the wounds running through his veins and attacking his heart. I throw my arms over him to try to still him but that doesn't work.

The sky lightens as the sun rises—Mother Nature carrying on while my brother stops breathing. Spotted mushrooms sprout behind me, bright red with white spots, perfectly shaped. They draw my eyes and keep me grounded, like a signpost. I can't cry. My body is too dry. My ears pick up the sounds of war in the distance, the whistling, the whirring, the booming. I want to plant myself here, beside Hans, and take root in the forest. But

I can't. I have to go on, for Mama. I pull his shirt over his face so he has some privacy at least. Then I reach into the pockets of his pants, in case there's something personal I should save, something to give Mama, but there's nothing.

Somehow, I rise and place my right foot in front of my left—again and again, moving forward, my entire body numb. Four days pass and then, finally, I am on a rise looking down on my hometown. Smoke is spewing from the factory, floating over the river, and blocking much of the town. So much for the foliage disguise on the roof.

Nothing can hide us now.

19.

Our house looks the same, yet entirely different, like a house I only remember from a dream. I don't know if I'm ready for what's inside, but can it be worse than what I just left behind? Even though it's dusk, the blackout curtains aren't drawn, and light spills out of the parlour into the garden where spring crocuses are poking up through the earth. I picture Frau Schilling on her knees, frantically pulling out the flowers, muttering, *"Too bright, too bright."*

I have to knock because everything I once owned is lost, including my key. Footsteps sound on the other side and I take a deep breath. Please let Mama be alive. If only one person in this house made it to now, please let it be her. I shut my eyes as the hinges creak and when I open them there is Papa, standing tall as ever, but with an old face. For a second, I think he's Opa and maybe I've dreamed the last few years. Maybe Opa never died. Maybe Herr Pinker was never living in our pantry, the scent of parsnip and turnip sinking into his skin. But then Papa calls my name and I fall into his arms.

20.

The next few days are a fog as I drift in and out of sleep in my old bed. Sometimes I'm back at the hospital near Dresden and my skin is peeling off in red strips, like grilled meat. Then I'm in the forest, trying to feed Hans a batch of red poisonous mushrooms. The baby under my coat turns into a squealing pig. Sometimes, Mama is beside me, holding a cool cloth to my head. Then Herr Pinker is dancing and singing a Yiddish song, his arms above his head. A baby cries and Mama picks it up and rocks it. Hans sticks pins in my stomach and shoulder.

The whole world spins and Frau Schilling yells at us to make it stop.

Then, suddenly, all is calm. My stomach rumbles and Mama spoons soup into my mouth. Papa stands behind her. "I knew you'd come home, Sabine," he says.

"It's true, Sabine. Papa and I talked about you every day, about how strong you are," adds Mama. A thousand questions storm through my mind. If Papa's home, does he know what we did? Is Herr Pinker still here or has Papa sent him away? My mind floods with an image of Hans, dead in the woods. I have to tell them. I open my mouth, but the words won't come.

"When did you get home, Papa?" I ask instead, my voice raspy. He sits on my bed and takes my hands.

"Just last week. I came home to help salvage what's left of the factory in town. Things are not lost, you know." *But they are, Papa, they are.* I want to tell him what I've seen but he must have seen it too. And Mama is shaking her head, telling me not to argue. Papa still believes, in spite of everything. Maybe I'm dreaming. Maybe I'll wake up again and we'll all be in that camp called Dachau.

But then it hits me. Here's my papa, whom I haven't seen for five years. I thought I'd never see him again. I don't care that he still believes. I sit up, my head spinning, and throw my arms around his thin shoulders.

21.

When Papa leaves for work the next day, I ask Mama to explain.

"He just showed up. We had no warning. Then he opened the pantry door and saw Herr Pinker lying on his cot and he just stood there for a few minutes. It was so strange. I was waiting for him to turn around and yell, but he didn't say a word. He didn't even ask about Opa, not that day and not since then. I don't know what he thought, or thinks. So, I just played along, like nothing unusual is in there. And all week it continued, this charade. Papa never mentions him. It's like the room is empty. Oh, Sabine, thank God you're home. I was worried sick. I didn't know what to do."

"And Katya, Mama. Where is Katya?"

Mama shakes her head. "A man named Anton knocked on our door late one night and took her and Aleksy away. I tried to stop her, but what could I do? He told me they'd be safe." Mama puts her head in her hands and starts to cry.

"It's okay, Mama. It's not your fault. You did your best. I saw many refugee families living in the forest and they seemed to be staying alive. The war is over, Mama, no matter what Papa says."

"Anton left something for you," Mama says. She pulls an object from the top shelf of my wardrobe and hands it over. It's a wooden carving of two rabbits, a mama and a little bunny, tucked between his mama's paws. The wood is shiny and smooth, the grains circling the rabbits' ears perfectly. It's beautiful. "He said it's to thank you for helping Katya."

I know I should tell Mama about Hans, but I can't do it to her, not yet. I fall asleep and dream of Katya and Anton lying in the forest, little Aleksy stretched out between them, a protective canopy of leaves above them.

I tear myself awake before the dream is ruined.

22.

Papa goes off to his old factory every morning, then returns around dinnertime, his uniform dusty and reeking of oil. We eat quietly, sipping the thin broth and noodles. The empty fourth chair sits at the table, reminding us that Hans is not here. From time to time, I catch Mama looking at it, her eyes watering. The words to tell her and Papa what happened, to tell them what I did, what I tried to do, rise in me, but they get stuck and I wash them down with my soup. When Papa retires to the parlour to listen to updates on the radio, Mama or I sneak into Herr Pinker's room with his dinner. If Papa knows, he doesn't comment. When Herr Pinker first saw me, he grabbed my hand and squeezed and muttered my name. I could see how relieved he was to have me back. On our long trek through the forest, some kids made slingshots and hunted rabbits. One kid would hold a smouldering branch to the hole to smoke it out and the other would shoot it between the eyes with a big stone. Trapped. Nowhere to hide. Herr Pinker is like that rabbit, unsure when the fatal blow is going to come now that Papa's home.

23.

We're gathered around the radio, Papa in his uniform, eagle pins above his pockets, along with several badges and medals. Mama in a dress that's been patched all over, probably by Herr Pinker. The High Commander tells us that the Russians are closing in on Berlin, but *"our soldiers are holding them off, fighting the Bolshevik threat with their last breath.*" Then a high-pitched whistle cuts into the broadcast, interrupting it for a special announcement. We sit, stunned, as the reporter announces that yesterday, on April 30, Adolf Hitler died. *"He has fallen at his command post in the Reich Chancellery fighting to the last breath against Bolshevism and for Germany."* A few seconds later, Admiral Doenitz is introduced. He calls on us to mourn our Führer, *"who died the death of a hero in the capital of the Reich."* Nobody speaks. Papa shifts a few times, as if he's about to get up but doesn't know where to go.

24.

Later, someone is making noise in the middle of the night. It can't be Herr Pinker—he wouldn't dare. I tiptoe downstairs to find Papa pacing back and forth in the parlour. He's breathing heavily, his sighs following his footsteps in perfect rhythm. Maybe he's upset about Hitler's death—after all, he has spent the last six years working to fulfill that man's dream. I'm trying to decide if I should go to him and ask him what's wrong, when his voice calls out, "Why did you do it, Sabine?"

"Do what?" I ask cautiously, sitting on the sofa. Is it possible that Papa, with all his connections, already knows about Hans? My heart is racing.

"Don't be smart, Sabine. You know what. Him, in there." Even in the dark I can see Papa's arm rise and point to Herr Pinker's room.

"So, you do know who's in there?" Papa stops pacing and plants himself like an ominous tree beside me.

"Of course I know. What do you think I am—an imbecile? I knew the second I walked into the house. Even the smell was different." My body stiffens. "Do you not think I'd know the difference between a Jew and my own father?"

"Opa died, Papa. We didn't kill him."

"*That* would have killed him, knowing you put a Jew in the bed where he once slept. I don't even want to ask what you did with Opa, since you have so little respect for him. Replacing him with filth."

I have a flash of Papa at the dinner table, showing off his fine craftsmanship, telling me and Hans that you could never take too much time to make something perfect. One nick in the steel, one screw at the wrong angle, or too much glue and the whole instrument was ruined. He was the master in his field.

"Do you know what they would have done to you and

Mama if they'd found out? Or to me? Or Hans? I can't believe you'd take such a risk. It was foolish. Pointless. And now, I have to go along or else, or else ..."

I shift back, trying to find some space where Papa's anger isn't hanging over me. "But Hitler's dead, Papa. The war is over, so it doesn't matter now."

Papa bends toward me and the room darkens even more. "It is not over. Don't say that. All the work we did. My factory in Berlin was churning out ten thousand weapons per day. No one has more. It's just a setback."

"No, Papa. It's the end. I've seen things too. I watched hundreds of men die, thanks to somebody's wonderful weapons. Their death was pointless." Papa lurches and slaps my face, stinging my cheek. I'm stunned for a few seconds, but then I jump up and run to my room, leaving Papa and his quaking anger.

25.

Within days, the French army occupies our town, red, white and blue flags flying from every truck that rumbles through. The soldiers that stand in the open backs scan the streets as they pass, wide smiles on their faces, eager to jump down. It's how our soldiers must have looked when they slid into Paris, their swastikas reddening the sky.

Papa runs to the radio and turns it on, but there's nothing but a quiet hum across the wires. It sounds like all of Germany holding its breath. A few minutes later Papa barges into Herr Pinker's room and throws his army jacket on the cot. For a second, I think he wants Herr Pinker to dress up like a soldier. Maybe Papa will turn him out and watch the French attack him. But then Papa says, "We saved you. Now, you help save us. All those badges must come off."

Papa comes out carrying a fistful of medals and pins, including two brass eagles and his iron cross. He grabs Mama's biggest wooden spoon and marches outside. From the window, we watch him dig a hole under the hedge. Then he dumps all the metal inside, covers the hole with the dirt, and stamps it down with his feet. I wonder if every home in Germany has so many strange things buried in its soil.

Papa burns the badges in the sink, filling the house with the smell of burnt fabric and fear. It's only later that night that it hits me that Papa said we—as if he was an ally in our plan to save Herr Pinker. Something about that bothers me more than when he slapped my face.

26.

A voice booms through a loudspeaker, summoning us to the town square. Papa wears his everyday clothes, looking awkward, like he's forgotten how to walk in plain slacks and shirts that aren't decorated with braids and bars. A crowd has already gathered, mostly women, children, and old men. The younger men who've made it home are in bad shape, thin and limping.

Eventually, our mayor shows up, his Nazi armband gone, along with the Nazi Commander who was always with him, whispering in his ear and telling him what to say. A Frenchman stands between them on a wooden platform, wearing a blue uniform with a fleur-de-lys badge on the pocket. A fourth man, with a big barrel chest, stands behind him. The Frenchman nods and the heavy man steps forward. "Listen up, listen up," he says, his voice loud and booming. "The war is over. The Nazis have surrendered, twice, once two days ago in Reims, France, and again yesterday, on May 8th, in Berlin. Field Marshal Wilhelm Keitel signed the German instrument of Surrender, along with representatives of the Allied Expeditionary Force and the Soviet High Command. Your town will now be under the command of this man,

Commander Jean-Philippe Desautels. Please await further instructions from your new Commander."

The four men leave and we all stand there stiff as wood. I imagine the celebrations going on in other parts of Europe, and even the world. There will be singing and dancing and music and cheering. Instead, we're all standing here like idiots waiting for someone to tell us what to do next.

27.

I march straight into Herr Pinker's room to give him the news. He puts his head in his hands and says, "Thank God," but doesn't cry. I sit on the edge of his cot and neither of us speaks. Our breathing fills the small pantry.

"What does this mean for me?" Herr Pinker finally asks, raising himself off his pillow.

I look at him, more closely than I have in years, and wonder if Edie would even recognize her father. His eyes are sunk far back in his skull and surrounded by so many folds of skin it must be hard to see.

"I'm not sure right now, but I'll find out. I promise," I reply, squeezing his thin hand. I wish I had a better answer for him but I don't know what this means. Can he just jump out of bed now and run around the block, announcing to the world that he's still alive—perhaps the only living Jew in our town? On my way out, I rip Opa's old poster from the door—Hitler was never our hope. I don't care if Papa notices.

28.

Papa stops pretending to go to the factory. He just paces around the house sighing, like he's lost something. The schools reopen and kids march hand in hand to class, like nothing has happened. We stop hanging blackout curtains over the windows and sit in the parlour, feeling totally exposed by the glare of the streetlamps. The radio still doesn't work. All our news comes from Commander Desautels, through the town crier, who summons us with a bell. But rumors break through as people shift and trains start running again. We hear more and more about the death camps—at least that's what they're calling them. Millions murdered. Jews and Gypsies, Communists and homosexuals. Papa says the stories are all British lies, but I wonder if Emma's mother made it out of Ravensbrück alive. News of the camps must be everywhere. Edie and her mother must be frantic over in Canada. If only I could find a way to tell them that Herr Pinker is okay. At night, Mama and Papa argue about what to do with him—Mama says we should just tell whoever's in charge—he can't stay in the room forever—but Papa says not yet, like he doesn't trust that it's safe for us. "When the time is right," he keeps saying.

29.

"No more bicycle trips alone for you, Sabine. It's not safe," Papa says, avoiding my eyes. Papa was away for so long, he has no idea how much we need the extra food I get from trading with the farmers. Our ration stamps are not enough; they never have been. Last time I biked past the KLV, where the French Army trucks are lined up in the yard, I was able to get some meat and extra eggs traded for Mama's china teacups. How does Papa think he's able to have chicken in his soup?

"I'm going, Papa. I'll be fine," I say.

It's true we've heard stories about French soldiers roaming the streets at night, looking for women. Some families are hiding their daughters in cellars, to keep them safe, but that would never be an option for me, not with Opa buried down there.

30.

One evening during dinner, Commander Desautels knocks on our door and marches into the kitchen. We immediately jump to attention, including Herr Pinker. Mama insisted he start joining us to eat, even though Papa won't speak to him or look at him. The first few nights, Papa took his plate to the parlour and refused to join us. Then he exploded and said it was his house and he wasn't going to let a dirty Jew chase him away. Mama and I had to coax Herr Pinker to return to the table after that.

"What is your full name, sir?" Commander Desautels asks Papa.

"Hermann Joseph Schmidt," replies Papa.

"And occupation in the war?" asks the Commander. "And don't lie. We can find out easily enough. One thing you Nazis did well was keep records."

Suddenly, Papa starts pointing to Herr Pinker. "You see, Commander, it would be wrong to persecute me or my family. This man is a Jew. We've been giving him shelter all this time. Would a family of Nazis do that?"

The Commander looks at Herr Pinker, whose eyes are on the floor, his skin as white as flour. How can he know who to trust? I don't even know. Here's Papa, acting like he knew all along that we'd hidden Herr Pinker. And that he approved, when clearly he doesn't. It strikes me that I don't know Papa anymore. Maybe it wasn't hard for him to go from making instruments that saved lives to ones that destroyed them. Even Mama is looking at him like he's a stranger. She reaches out and steadies Herr Pinker with her arm.

"General Schmidt," continues the commander. "Is this not you, standing outside the Fabrik 123 in Berlin?" He holds up a photo—the same one that Papa sent us. Papa is standing tall and proud outside the gates to a factory. He has more medals on his breast and hat than the other two men, both of whom stand a bit behind him. "And we have more pictures of the factory, of what went on inside. Foreign workers, slave labour, deplorable conditions. Do you want me to show your family? We have photos of prisoners lying dead on your floors, others barely able to stand. All here ... " He starts to pull photographs out of his folder, but Papa raises his hand.

"But I had nothing to do with that. I just controlled the designs, not the workers," Papa says. The commander lifts a photograph and turns it toward us. "Don't ... " starts Papa.

"No, Papa. I want to see them," I say. "I want to see all of them. No more hiding." I pull the folder from the Commander's hands. On it, in thick red letters, are the words *"Hermann Schmidt, General der Pioniere Berlin Fabrik 123."* I open it and flip through the photographs. They are horrible. The workers are so thin, they're barely wider than the levers they're pulling. The machinery looms over them, dwarfing them with gigantic metal claws. They wear grey overalls with smudged badges. Somewhere a badge factory must have been running twenty-four hours a day, seven days a week for the past seven years. Papa didn't care about these workers any more than he cares about Herr Pinker. Herr Pinker is only a tool to save his own skin.

"Is this true?" the Commander asks Herr Pinker. "Are you a Jew?" Herr Pinker begins to stammer and we all hold our breath. It would be so easy for him to say yes, then point out that Papa had nothing to do with it. It would be his way of taking revenge on a man, a Nazi, who's done terrible things, things that helped kill many of his own people. But he says nothing. He looks like he's about to collapse from standing, or fear.

"He's ..." Mama starts to speak, but Papa jumps in.

"We didn't believe in Hitler's plan. That's why we took him in." With every word, I hate Papa more. "We've been waiting until it's safe to reveal him," Papa adds, "to turn him over to the proper authorities, to make sure he's safe. Haven't we, *Mutti*?"

Papa fixes Mama with a hard stare. I can feel her starting to shrink, but when Papa reaches across the table to lay his hand on Herr Pinker's shoulder, Mama pulls him close. For four years Mama has worked hard to keep Edie's father alive, even when the sound of a pin dropping could make her shake with fear. That protective instinct is now making her keep Papa away.

"It's not true, Commander," I say, returning his folder. "This is my opa, my papa's papa. Look, you can see his Iron Cross on the wall and the war map above his bed. I don't know why Papa would say he's a Jew." Papa's face grows so dark, it's like rain will start pouring out of it. He starts to speak, but Mama cuts in.

"It's true, Commander. I don't know why my husband would say this. He's confused."

"I thought so. You'll come with us," he says, and I'm not sure who he's speaking to, until he clamps his hand around Papa's arm and pulls him. Something tugs in my heart and a lump grows in my throat as I watch Papa go off without putting up a fight. I remember bringing him his lunch at work all those years, the way he'd turn his cheek to me and say, *"Always kiss your papa goodbye."* But then I flash back to the death and destruction I saw when I was working at the hospital and then later, on my journey home. Even Hans, lying dead in the woods. I know it's all connected somehow. Nothing Papa has done could be right.

31.

When they've gone, Mama collapses into her chair and I run to her. "What have we done, Sabine?"

"We had to do it, Mama. You know it wasn't right what Papa was doing. We rescued Herr Pinker, not him. And we know why we did it, don't we Mama?" Mama nods weakly. "Not to cover up for Papa. They would have taken him sooner or later. They had the proof. This is going to be happening all over Germany for a long time to come. We couldn't fight it."

Mama turns to Herr Pinker and takes his hand. "We are so sorry, Herr Pinker," she says. "We'll make it right, don't worry."

Herr Pinker is shaking his head, like he doesn't know what to do or say. He was seconds away from being discovered by people who could have helped him and we ruined it. I hope he understands why we did it. But when he looks up at me, his eyes so full of sorrow, I know that why doesn't matter to him. All that matters is that he's still here and Edie and her Mama are thousands of miles away.

32.

I lean my bike against the barn and cross the yard which is now pitted with deep tire tracks. I knock and tell the soldier who answers the door to the old KLV that I want to speak to Commander Desautels. The inside looks the same, except for the cigarette smoke and empty wine bottles that sit on every tabletop. The soldier leads me upstairs to Frau Prinz's old room. I hardly ever came in here—it was forbidden, except in emergencies. The sweet perfume that she somehow managed to wear all through the war still lingers, turning my stomach. Commander Desautels is sitting at her old desk, which is way too small for him. The little drawer where Frau Prinz kept her brushes and hairpins is open, letting off more of her scent.

"Fraulein Schmidt," he says, smiling. "What can I do for you? Please, sit." He points to Frau Prinz's old bed and I shake my head.

"I came to tell you that part of what my father said yesterday was true—that man is not my opa. His name is Herr Pinker and he is a Jew. Mama and I took him in at the end of 1941, when it was clear all the Jews were being removed from the town. But Papa knew nothing about it and, if he had known, I think Herr Pinker wouldn't be alive today."

"*Et bien*, you are very brave, both to have done this and now to come and tell me. Why did you do it, Fraulein?"

"I did it for Edie, my best friend. He's her father. She'd have done the same for me." A flock of starlings lifts off the roof, tumbling and spinning like a circus act across the sky.

"I'm going to call the Red Cross about this Herr Pinker and they'll take care of it. If his family is alive, they'll find them."

"They're somewhere in Canada, or at least that's what he thinks, in Montreal maybe. If they made it there."

"You know that you and your mother would have been killed if he'd been found?"

I nod. "We knew. But he'd have been killed if we didn't help him."

Commander Desautels stands and shakes my hand and tells the soldier to show me out. Through an open door, I see the bed where Werner first kissed me and my heart cracks in half.

33.

A Red Cross jeep pulls up and a woman in a grey jacket comes to the door. She introduces herself as Frau Walker, from the International Red Cross in Stuttgart. I lead her to where Herr Pinker is sitting at the kitchen table with Mama. He's wearing some of Opa's old clothes—trousers, a shirt and jacket—that he altered for this occasion. The air is heavy with unspoken words and Mama looks like she's about to cry.

The woman, speaking German with an English accent, calls his name and he replies, "Yes, that is me." Mama asks her to sit and I sit too. Herr Pinker has been sleeping upstairs in Hans's old room for weeks now, since Papa left, and, although he no longer needs to hide, he hasn't left the house and barely walks around before nightfall. Today though, there's excitement in his eyes, shining through the fear the way candlelight flickers through a dark room. Frau Walker asks him a lot of questions about the past four years and each time he answers, his voice becomes less raspy, finally loosening up.

"And you've been well looked after, in general?" she asks.

Here, Herr Pinker looks from me to mama. "I have," he says, nodding. The nod is deep, expressing a million things he could never say with words. They spend the next few minutes going over what Herr Pinker knows about where his family is. All he can tell her is what he told me all those years ago. "Somewhere in Quebec, possibly Montreal, to Hannah and Naomi's cousins." He doesn't even have a last name, only a first, Louisa. And even then, he's not sure they made it.

"No matter," Frau Walker replies. "This will help. Now, in the meantime, can Herr Pinker remain with you?"

"Oh yes, of course," says Mama.

"These things take time. There's no guarantee and no timeframe. It could be weeks, it could be months, but you should be prepared that it could even take years."

Herr Pinker's shoulders slump. We all know he might not have years.

"Perhaps Herr Pinker and I could have a moment alone," Frau Walker says. "He can walk me to the car if he likes. It's a beautiful day outside."

At the mention of "outside," Herr Pinker's head snaps back and he rises slowly. He hesitates at the door—this will be his first step out of the house in four years. Mama and I come up behind him and we each take a hand. We lead him down the stairs and along the walkway to the jeep—the same path Frau Schilling used to patrol.

"There, we will leave you now," Mama says. She looks at him as she would a child heading off to school for the first time, like Herr Pinker should be carrying a *Schultüte*.

"Don't worry, Frau Schmidt, I'll be fine," Herr Pinker says, releasing Mama's hand.

"Thank you both," says Frau Walker. She shakes Mama's hand, then mine. Her palms are sweaty. Maybe she is nervous too. And now she wants to talk to Herr Pinker alone, in case he was afraid to tell her the truth in front of us.

Herr Pinker shuffles back a few minutes later, winded from the effort. Mama and I help him to bed and sit back down in the living room. The ticking of the clock on the mantlepiece is so loud, it's like a drumbeat in our ears, a drumbeat echoing back through time to all the incredible things that have happened, but also one that beats ahead into the future, to all the unknown things that are still to come. Lately, I've been thinking about what I want to do with my life. The seed of the idea was planted in Dresden, or maybe earlier, watching Papa show off his instruments and describe their function. I want to study medicine, cardiology to be precise. I want to learn to heal the human heart. Many hearts will need mending in the years to come, starting with Mama's.

I turn back to her and take a deep breath. I can't put it off any longer—it's time to tell her about Hans.

EDIE

I.

A few weeks into the winter term, we're discussing *Jane Eyre* in my English Literature class. I love the story of the plain governess who captures the heart of the aristocrat, Rochester, against all odds. Our professor asks for our interpretation of Rochester's wife, the madwoman in the attic. A young man raises his hand and says, "She was probably a lesbian," and everyone laughs.

"Why do you say that?" asks our professor, perched on the edge of his desk. I try to focus on the red argyle pattern of his socks.

"Because, it's obvious, lesbians are insane. Why else would a woman not want to be with a man? That's how I see Bertha Mason. Her family forced her to marry

Rochester to cover it up and it drove her insane. Only Grace Poole can calm her down. It doesn't take much to imagine how." He grins widely and looks around the room, soaking up the snickers. Some of the girls actually blush. I turn the room into a movie screen and pretend I'm just here to watch, which calms me down a bit. But I feel battered, somehow, by his comments. The last time I felt this way I was twelve and the teacher was ordering me to return the gold medal I'd won for being best at gymnastics. She made me hand it over in front of the whole class, just because I was Jewish. And everyone laughed and the laughter was so loud, it hurt my ears.

Before I know it, I'm standing. All eyes turn toward me.

"For your information, lesbians are not mentally ill. It has nothing to do with sanity. It's simply about who they love. And lesbians have been around forever. Homer wrote about them, so did Shakespeare and Zola and Virginia Woolf. I thought university was supposed to broaden people's minds, not narrow them."

"Ah, there you go," the young man says, grabbing his jacket lapels. "Woolf was a lesbian too. See …. insane. That's why she put stones in her pockets and walked into a river."

"And Shelley? He drowned himself too. Was he also a lesbian?"

This time the class laughs with me.

2.

On January 27, the news is all about the Red Army liberating one of the Nazi concentration camps in Poland, a place called Auschwitz. They say thousands of Jews have been found alive but living in appalling conditions. And they found gas chambers where they suspect thousands of people were being killed daily. Even more may have died when the Nazis forced anyone who could walk to march away from the camp when it was clear the Russians were near. Pictures start appearing in the papers in the next few days but I can't bear to look. They're too horrific. Each emaciated face I see somehow bends and twists into Papa's.

3.

Uncle Max cries at Passover over the firebombing of Dresden. "So much beauty destroyed," he says. "It's hard to feel happy when I think of all the treasures in the Green Vault—the amber and ivory and those fabulous gilded ostrich eggs."

Poor Uncle Max! Art is everything to him. If anyone heard him, they'd think he cared more about paintings than people, but Aunt Naomi and I know that's not true. It's just that the destruction of beauty hits him hard. He once said that art is how we measure how civilized we've become. The more art is destroyed, the more Uncle Max loses his faith in humanity.

"Don't think about it, Max," replies my aunt, stirring her matzo ball soup. "Focus on the positive. The Allies have crossed the Rhine and are now in Germany."

"Hold on, Papa," I say, raising my glass of wine. "The Allies are parting the blood-soaked lands and coming to liberate you, wherever you are." I imagine Papa listening to the thump of thousands of pairs of boots marching toward him.

4.

British and Canadian troops have liberated another camp, near Bergen. The *Montreal Star* carries more horrific pictures for days: heaps of naked bodies filling deep holes, or men in striped pajamas beside a wire fence, staring blankly at the camera, their eyes bulging out of hollow cheeks. The only one I can stand to look at shows a group of women, also in striped pajamas, coming out of a hut, carrying stacks of bread that look like bricks. At least many of the women are smiling.

Every evening, the radio is full of stories from overseas. We listen to a soldier with a shaky voice. "What I've seen will never leave me," he says. "The sight of so much death and horror is something I simply cannot express. Shakespeare himself would not have been able to mould words around the sights, the smells, the sounds of the slowly dying. The worst was an emaciated mother clinging to her dead baby. The baby was nothing but bones, but she was crying for milk. She even knelt down to the dead and begged for milk. And me with a photo of my new baby girl in my pocket ... " He stops here and all that comes through is the crackling of the wireless.

None of us knows what to say when he's finished. The reporter continues giving figures—15,000 dead bodies, 50,000 prisoners. It's impossible to make sense of those numbers. And it's impossible not to let my mind wander to Papa. They say the younger prisoners, in better shape, were kept for work, but Papa's in his seventies. What could he do, apart from sew? If he was in one of those camps, I have to pray the Nazis needed lots of stitches.

5.

Hitler is dead! Everyone at McGill is talking about it and everyone has a different theory about how he died. Some people are saying he had a cerebral hemorrhage and others say his own right-hand man, Heinrich Himmler, killed him. I say who cares? The important thing is that he's dead.

To celebrate, the entire McGill campus is decorated with effigies of the dictator hanging from tree limbs. Signs are pinned to the chests, bearing stats about Allied victories. One reads "February 3, 1945, 1,000 B-17 Bombers demolish Berlin Railway." Another says, "February 13 & 14 Dresden Destroyed." And one down near the Roddick Gates says, "Dortmund bombed by 1108 Aircraft—Eviscerated." Some simply have aerial shots of cities demolished by bombs, or ones of the liberated camps. At the end of the day, all the effigies are gathered on the football field and lit inside large metal drums. I stand way back on the edge of the field and watch the flames lick higher and higher. Before long, the black smoke that surrounds the spectacle is picked up by the wind and blown toward me. That's when I leave.

"Hey, wait up." I turn to see a girl who's in my English

class. She's wearing an elegant camel-coloured coat that makes me even more self-conscious about my threadbare blue one.

"I'll walk with you," she says. "Quite the show, eh?"

"I don't know why, but the effigy burning doesn't comfort me, even though I'm thrilled that Hitler's dead. It should, but it only disturbs me," I tell her.

"Me too. I lost a brother and an uncle in the war. They were both pilots. Their planes were hit so they would've died in flames. I couldn't bear to watch a second longer. My name's Jenny, by the way."

"I'm really sorry, Jenny. I'm Edie." When Jenny shakes my hand, she looks intently into my eyes, and I can't help thinking how familiar she looks.

"Thanks, Edie. I went down to join the RCAF after my brother's death, but they're not taking any new recruits. They said we're too close to the end."

I think of Rebecca and how disappointed she would have been if she were free to try.

"That was brave," I reply. "Given what happened to your brother and uncle."

"Desperate more like. I felt I really needed to try to take revenge, in any way I could. Still, here I am. I'll have to do it another way. My brother wanted to be a doctor, so that's what I'm trying to do, for him, and for myself. It's been hard work so far, but I'm doing pretty well. The literature class is just an elective for me, but it's a nice break from biology and chemistry."

We continue toward the Arts building. At the top, she turns to me and says, "I thought you were brave too, to stand up to that idiot, the one with his dumb analysis of *Jane Eyre*."

"Oh that. I'd kind of forgotten about it," I lie.

"Well, I haven't. You put him in his place. You wouldn't believe what I have to put up with sometimes in my classes. I mean, it's been less than three decades since they even started letting girls study medicine at McGill. I've wanted to stand up and fight back many times."

"Gosh, I didn't realize," I say. "I thought I'd just made a fool of myself."

"Not in my eyes you didn't. Well, I'm off this way. Take care, Edie. Nice talking to you." She waves and trots off, veering left. I stand for a while and watch her go, trying to figure out why she seemed so familiar. I turn through the side gates onto University Street and head toward Fletcher's Field. Minutes later, I'm walking past the base of Mount Royal, looking up at the Goddess of Liberty, with her wide-open wings, when it hits me— Sabine. She had the same round blue eyes and dainty nose. And her cowlick was just like Sabine's, leading to the long wave of hair across her forehead. And even though I haven't seen Sabine for eight years, I know she must look something like Jenny now.

6.

I'm alone one afternoon when the rabbi from the Bagg Street Shul knocks on our door. For a terrible second, I imagine that Uncle Max and Aunt Naomi have found out about me, maybe through Rebecca's mother, and they've sent the rabbi here to scold me.

"Hello, Edie Pinker," he says. "Do you remember me?"

"Yes, Rabbi Cohen."

"May I come in for a minute?"

"Of course." I open the door wider and he steps into the porch.

"This is far enough. I'm not here for long." Rabbi Cohen holds up a white envelope with my name scribbled across the front. "It came to me from a priest, Father O'Connor. He does work in the POW camps and

I meet him there from time to time when I'm visiting one of ours. It's hard to believe but some German Jews are actually imprisoned as foreign enemies from Great Britain. Anyway, I digress ... Father O'Connor has been visiting a POW from your hometown who seems to know you and wants you to have this letter. So here Miss Pinker, I hand deliver it to you on behalf of the young man."

Rabbi Cohen bows slightly as he hands me the envelope, revealing the yarmulke perched on his skull. Then he reaches out and places his hand on my shoulder, squeezing gently. "I hope it brings you good news. Goodbye, Edie."

When he's gone I just stand there, staring at the letter. In the corner is an official-looking stamp that says POW Camp 40A, Farnham, Quebec. And under that, in handwriting, Werner Gärtner. The name means nothing to me.

I sit on the torn couch and, with shaking hands, open the envelope and pull out a piece of paper. When I unfold it a strip of yellow ribbon falls into my palm. It takes a minute but then it hits me—the trim from the matching dresses Papa made for me and Sabine. The ribbon is no more than six inches long, but it feels so much longer. As I caress it with my thumb, I feel myself careening back through time, to a place that's warm and familiar, but cold and ringed with danger all at once.

I take a deep breath and read the letter.

> *Dear Edie,*
>
> *My name is Werner Gärtner and I have been a German prisoner of war at the camp in Farnham for six months now. You might find this unbelievable, but I was very happy when I found out I was coming to Canada. I knew it would allow me to send you a message that my dear friend, and yours, Sabine Schmidt, would want me to send. It is about your papa. I feel it is safe to tell you this here, as Father O'Connor, who has been so kind and helpful when I explained the situation, assures me that nothing I write will be intercepted and thereby pose a threat to your father's life, or to Sabine's. He helped with the translation, to satisfy the censors here, so he is well aware of what I am about to tell you.*
>
> *When I left for my training, in 1943,*

*your papa was safe with Sabine. Once I left
I was unable to have any more contact with
her and, of course, I could not have asked
her anything in a letter as all our letters
were scrutinized. I never expected to be gone
so long, as my duty assignment was only
for half a year, but at the end I was taken
to basic training and then initiated into the
Wehrmacht immediately. I fought in Italy,
then North Africa, and eventually was
captured and brought here. I feel it is a piece
of divine intervention that I was brought to
Quebec. Now, I am able to share this news.
I am sorry I can't tell you more about what
is happening now. I too am anxious to know
that both your father and Sabine and her
mother are safe. My concern for them is most
likely equal to that of yours for your father.
True, Sabine is not family, but if things had
been different, I believe we may have been
married one day. Now, who knows what I
will return to, when and if I do return. There
is, as you know, so much uncertainty. I don't*

even know if my own parents and sister are still alive. I have had no word.

If you hear any news, perhaps you could tell Father O'Connor, who works out of the Notre-Dame-de-Bonsecours Chapel. He visits once a week. If I have news, I will do the same.

I know we never met, but I feel I know you because of all the stories Sabine shared about your years of friendship and your mutual love of movies. Through many hard times those memories lit up Sabine's face like nothing else could.

Let's pray, even though I'm not very religious, that the war will be over soon and old relationships can resume, although it is hard to image that anything that existed before the war can ever just continue on in the same way.

With best wishes,
Werner

My body feels as heavy as lead and as light as cotton all at once as waves of relief wash out of me. Papa's not dead! I squeeze the piece of ribbon in my first. It's the key to Papa, his message to me. His sign. If I try hard, I can see the rolls of ribbon that used to line the back shelf of his shop. I'd run the loose ends through my fingers and Papa would tell me to stop. He didn't want me to get them sticky from my candy-fingers. I especially loved the roll of golden yellow. When he made the dresses and asked which trim I wanted, I pointed to it immediately. He knew I'd never forget.

7.

When Uncle Max and Aunt Naomi come home an hour later, I run to greet them at the door and shove the letter into their hands. Tears start running down their cheeks as they read it, and they suck in their breath at the exact same second, holding it for so long I start to worry. When they've finished reading, they both exhale, but neither of them speaks. They simply reach for each other's hands across the sofa, then over for mine, so that we are all linked, like a human chain, around the small table. Uncle Max lowers his head and closes his eyes and I know he's saying a prayer to whatever powers in the world can exert influence on the other side of the ocean.

Aunt Naomi and I do the same. No matter what I've lost—Mama, my home, Rebecca—maybe Papa is alive and waiting for me. There would be no better gift than that.

"We must go straight to Hannah and tell her," says Aunt Naomi. Uncle Max agrees and even offers to splurge on a taxi, to get us to the cemetery faster.

"You go first," says Aunt Naomi when we arrive. "We'll wait." I wend my way between the rows of tombstones. The crabapple trees are in full bloom and the blossoms are an explosion of pink against the blue sky. I kneel beside Mama's grave. I had planned to tell her about Papa, but instead I tell her about Rebecca. The whole story falls out of me. It's like the tombstones around us turn into large stone ears, taking in my story. I pause to listen for ghosts laughing at me, but all is quiet. I bend closer to Mama and say, "I don't think you would have been as disappointed in me as Mrs. Krasney was in Rebecca, Mama. I don't think you could ever be so cruel."

Then I start to tell her the best news—about Papa— but my aunt and uncle's figures, waiting by the gate, catch my eye. Where would I be without them? I can't share this news with Mama alone. They have to be with me, one on either side, my pillars of strength, so I call them over. We all hold hands and I tell Mama about the wonderful letter, full of hope and promise. I show her the strip of yellow ribbon, which I have tied to a string around my neck.

"Remember, Mama?" I ask. A gust of wind swirls some petals around our feet.

"Yes," says Aunt Naomi, "I think she does."

8.

I know what I'm going to do. Mama told me I had to. I heard her voice whisper through the graveyard while I was standing between my aunt and uncle, my arms hooked through theirs, feeling their support. Mama told me not to be afraid.

Aunt Naomi is filling our bowls with soup and Uncle Max is flipping through one of his books. He wants to show me a painting. "You'll love it, Edie. Today reminded me of it. Ah, here it is." He turns the huge book around and holds up a painting of a garden in spring. The sky is a canopy of blossoming trees, much like the one we walked through today on Mount Royal.

"It was painted by Max Liebermann at his Wannsee villa garden in Berlin. That's his granddaughter and her governess off to the side, all in white. They reminded me of you and Hannah somehow, when you first came to us in Munich. It was summer and you were wearing a white dress and walking up our street, holding your mama's hand, under the fully bloomed trees. You were no more than five and you said the leaves had disappeared the skies. Such a way with words, even then."

Uncle Max looks to the wall, where he taped up all my *McGill Daily* movie reviews. He even wrote a sign above them: "Pinker's Pictures." It's not bad—maybe I'll use it one day if I ever make it into the *Montreal Star*. My latest review, on *Gaslight*, was my best. It was full of praise for Ingrid Bergman. When I read about her, I found out she too used to play dress-up for hours in her father's studio and had to go live with her aunt after he died. I felt an instant connection.

"Oh, Max. Why do you take these trips down memory lane?" asks Aunt Naomi. "They always make you cry."

"No, I love it, Uncle Max. It's beautiful. I love all the art you share with me." I take a deep breath. "And now, I need to share something with the two of you."

"Something else? My dear, you shared enough today already, don't you think?" asks Uncle Max.

"No—there's more. Just listen. It's about Rebecca."

I tell them everything—how Rebecca was way more than just a friend, how I loved her, and how I thought she loved me. Then I tell them about Mrs. Krasney's horrible letter and how it made me feel. By the time I finish, I'm the one in tears.

"And if you two also feel there's something wrong with me and you want me to change I don't know what I'll do, because I don't think I can."

We are all quiet for a minute or two, then Aunt Naomi speaks. "Well, Edie, it's possible to have really strong feelings for a friend. It happened to me once or twice when I was younger too, at university in Vienna."

"No, Aunt Naomi, this wasn't like that. I know the difference. I felt the same way about Rebecca that you do about Uncle Max—no different."

"But if you meet the right man, like when I met Max ..."

"I've met lots of young men, at all those dances and at school, but I never feel that way. If I ever feel that way again, I know it will be for a woman." Jenny's face, with her beautiful blue eyes, pops into my head when I say that. I never thought I could feel that way about blue eyes—the eyes of all those perfect German children that were on all those Nazi party posters around town. None of us in the back row at school had those eyes.

"But we came all the way here so doors would be open for you, so you could be free," Aunt Naomi continues. She's wringing her hands now, above her bowl, and the steam from the soup is making them sweat.

"But Aunt Naomi, how can I be free if I can't be me? Isn't that also why we came here?"

Uncle Max has been quiet, staring at his bowl. Suddenly, he lifts his head. "She's right, Naomi. She's absolutely right. We came here so we didn't have to hide, like poor Jacob. So we could be free and live the way we want, without fear. Edie," he says, pausing to reach over and grasp my hand, "we will always love you. But times will be hard. Homosexuality is illegal. That could be dangerous, Edie. You have to be prepared."

"When have times not been hard, Uncle Max?" I ask.

"When, indeed," he replies. "When, indeed."

"It'll just be little harder, since I'm a lesbian." The word's three syllables trip off my tongue and fall into my soup. I can almost hear the splash. "Let's eat while it's hot."

My aunt and uncle nod and lift their spoons. I know they're taking the news in with every bite. I feel their heaviness. But I picture Tanya's face when I tell her I've finally used the word out loud. She may even tip her Fedora in my direction. The thought makes me smile wider than I have in ages.

9.

The road down Place Jacques Cartier toward Rue Saint-Paul is made of cobblestone, just like the streets of my old town. Sabine and I used to hop from stone to stone, not stepping on the cracks, which would break our mamas' backs. I see the little church up ahead, and, as I get closer, I realize it's the one that holds the statue of the angel that I saw from the ship, almost seven years ago. She sits atop a dark brown tower at the back of the church, facing the Saint Lawrence River.

A sign in the porch says "Bureau," so I follow it and ask a nun who's sitting at a desk for Father O'Connor. She gestures for me to wait a minute and disappears through a back door. A few minutes later a short priest with a round jolly face appears.

"Yes, how may I help you?" he asks, smiling.

"I'm Edie Pinker. I received a letter from—"

"Oh, of course, I remember, I remember," he jumps

in, taking my hand and pulling me toward him.

"I hope it's okay for me to come here."

"And why wouldn't it be?"

"Well, you know. I'm not Christian. I'm a Jew."

"Well, my dear, so was he," says Father O'Connor, pointing to a large crucifix that hangs on the wall. A loin-clothed Jesus is nailed to it, spots of blood on his hands and feet.

"Now, what can I do for you?" he asks.

"I was wondering if there's any way I could go with you to Farnham today," I say. "I've decided I want to meet Werner in person, to ask him some questions."

"I see," replies Father O'Connor, stroking his hairless chin. "I'll have to make some calls. Can you wait? You are welcome to sit in the church. You will find it very peaceful."

I study the stained-glass windows, which are full of images of mothers and children. Hanging from the ceiling beside each one is a tiny wooden boat. This church was probably the first thing sailors saw when coming to New France hundreds of years ago. Even Marguerite Bourgeoys, who helped found the church, came over from France in the 1600s. We learned about her at school. Papa would have loved her, because she made sure all the girls in her parish, Catholic or not, were able to attend school.

Father O'Connor returns a few minutes later with an even wider smile on his face.

"You can come," he says, "but I must remain with you at all times. Security, you understand. He is still a prisoner. The war is not quite over yet, although we can only pray that is imminent. Are you ready?"

"Yes," I say. And when I say it, I realize it's true.

10.

The drive takes us over the green-gabled Jacques Cartier Bridge and out of the city onto a two-lane highway in the countryside. The land is mostly flat, with a few hills here and there. We pass picturesque rivers and small lakes and hundreds of barns with tin-covered roofs reflecting the sun.

"It's hard to imagine there's a prisoner-of-war camp in such pretty land," I say.

"I know. But it's hard to imagine much of what's happening in the world today, isn't it?" replies Father O'Connor.

"Yes, that's true, sir, I mean, Father." I feel funny calling another man Father but that's what he said to call him.

"There's more than one POW camp out this way—there are at least five. I've visited all of them over the years, but now I mostly deal with Farnham. The others are a bit far for an old man like me."

Father O'Connor's head barely reaches above the steering wheel. I wonder how he can see the road. I feel like a giant sitting beside him. The top of my head practically hits the roof when we ride over one of the many bumps.

Finally, we reach the camp. It's recognizable immediately, because of the high barbed-wire fence that surrounds it, and the two guards with rifles standing at the gate. They wave Father O'Connor through with a friendly smile. Two more guards are standing in a high tower, binoculars and rifles slung across their chests. Father O'Connor parks outside a brick building that says "Office," and we go inside. The officer in charge gives me a visitor sign to hang around my neck. He's neither friendly nor rude, just official, but when he looks at me his brow is creased and I can tell he has no idea why someone like me would want to speak to a German prisoner of war.

"You can meet him in the common room for an hour only. After that, the room will be flooded by men coming back from the farms."

Father O'Connor and I walk the dirt path, passing a dozen wooden barracks. Up ahead, a wide river is gushing past, the same blue-brown colour as the Danube. And it's banked with willows, just like the ones Sabine and I used to read under.

We enter a hut where a young man in a dull grey shirt is sitting at a long wooden table. On one end sits a stack of chess boards, magazines, cards, and even a few ping-pong paddles. He stands when he sees us. We have to speak English—no German allowed, so I wonder how we'll manage.

"Hello Edie," he says, nodding. I stare at him and realize he does look familiar, from school, even though we were never in the same class. But he's so much taller now. His head is shaved and his grey-green eyes are friendly.

"Werner," I say, pronouncing it the German way, like it starts with a V.

"So, you are Edie? I told Sabine I remember you, but now I am not so sure."

"Yes, it's me. Where did you learn English?" Werner's English is slow but good.

"Here, in camp, we have little school. Some prisoner from Great Britain, they teach us." He must mean the Jewish prisoners that Rabbi Cohen told me about. What would Hitler have said if he knew that his soldiers were taking lessons from Jews in another country?

Werner's hands are tapping the table. His fingers are long and bony and his nails are rimmed with dirt.

"Do they treat you well here? I mean, *behandle dich gut?*"

Father O'Connor clears his throat loudly and shakes his head.

"Yes, yes. Very good. Good food, better than German army and we play, how do you say … *fußball.*"

"Soccer?" I say and Werner nods. "And what about work?"

"Yes, but I am happy. I love to work on farm, with plants, like corn and potatoes and even with cows. It is my … *traum?*"

"Dream."

I keep hoping Werner will look up and into my eyes, but he speaks with his head down, like it's hard to look at me.

"And my papa?" I ask finally.

Werner takes a deep breath and holds it. Then he stands and paces the length of the bench behind the table, exposing the back of his shirt for the first time. A large bright red circle is sewn onto it. It reminds me of a clown's costume—then I think of those armed guards up in their wooden tower. Of course—the circle would give them a clear target to aim at.

He sits back down and finally looks at me. He begins, drawing his thin shoulders forward.

"Three years ago, when her opa dies, Sabine has the idea to change with your father. She convince me it will work. They look little bit the same—white hair, long ..." Here, Werner makes the sign of a beard by stroking his chin. "Grey eyes and very skinny. I am sorry, but your father very thin. He is hiding in basement of your building. The *Juden*, Jews in our town all disappearing. Sabine say she must do something."

Dear Sabine! I suddenly feel her presence here, as though she'd squeezed in beside me like she used to on the benches in the town square where we'd sit and talk about our dreams—before that became *verboten*.

"But what did she do?"

"I dig and we put Opa away in the *Keller* and your papa he become Opa, in the little room, a *Schrank*, in Sabine house."

"The pantry?" We both look at Father O'Connor but he seems to be okay with the odd German word.

Werner nods and I think how Sabine's opa used to scare me with his crinkled eyes that scrunched up even more whenever he looked at me. He used to inhale so deeply around me, like he could smell something fishy coming off my body. And now Papa is him. I bet Papa is doing a great acting job.

"And is he still there and safe?" I ask.

"When I leave in 1943, your father is safe. Only problem is Frau Schilling, the *Blockwart*. She searches homes but your papa lie in bed and he is like Opa, like a sick old man."

Poor Papa, having to pretend to be that hateful man. Then it hits me that Werner just confessed to burying Sabine's opa in a cellar. What would her parents have to say to that? To everything?

"But Sabine's parents, and Hans!" I'd forgotten Hans. He'd rather kill his own mother than live with a Jew. That I know for sure.

"Hans is gone to fighting since many years. And

Sabine father to Berlin, for working. I don't know about now. *Es tut mir leid*. I am sorry."

Werner hangs his head and I feel the waves of sorrow coming off him. Who knows what else he has to feel sorry about? Maybe he fought Canadian soldiers in Italy, or even killed some in North Africa.

When he looks up again his eyes are teary. I look at the dirt in his fingernails and I imagine it's the dirt from Sabine's cellar, where her opa is now buried. I picture Werner throwing his weight into the shovel and digging and I am overcome. I put my head in my hands and cry. For Papa, for Sabine, for Werner, and even a bit for her opa—for everyone who gave something up so that Papa might live.

Then I reach out and put my wet hands on Werner's. They are hands that once touched Sabine with love— I'm sure of that. I can feel it in his skin. He loved her like I loved Rebecca.

"I hope you have Sabine again when you return, just like I will have my papa again one day."

"We can pray for that," says Father O'Connor. I think he means in general, but then his head lowers and he clasps his hands. Werner does the same across from me.

I don't know if it's okay for a Jew to pray with Christians, but I do it anyway. The words are comforting as Father O'Connor calls on a bigger father, the one that lives in heaven. When he talks about daily bread, I see Sabine carrying some sliced bread, buttered and covered in jam, to Papa in the pantry.

"And now, our hour is up," says Father O'Connor.

"Goodbye Werner," I say, standing. "And thank you. Thank you so much for everything."

"*Bitteschön*, Edie." He stands too and I think how much older he looks than twenty-one. He's seen and done too much for someone so young and the lines on his face, furrowed like the corn rows we saw in the fields, show it.

We're walking back up the dusty path to the car when trucks start pulling in through the gate. A load of men sits in the back of each one, all in the same grey uniforms with red circles on their backs. From a distance, it looks like the truck has chicken pox. As they draw closer, the men wave to Father O'Connor and he waves back. A few whistle at me. The whistling catches on and soon three trucks full of men are whistling like a flock of gulls. They're doing it with such gusto, like I'm the first woman they've seen in months.

"I'm sorry, my dear," says Father O'Connor, opening my car door. "The men are not on their best behaviour. But you are very pretty." His eyes crinkle up when he smiles.

And I smile too, because it's suddenly funny. If only they knew.

II.

Winston Churchill's strong voice floods our tiny living room with three magical words—Germany has surrendered. The surrender was signed at 2:41 in the morning, in General Eisenhower's headquarters in Reims, France. The Germans have agreed to give up all their land, sea and air forces in Europe to both the Allied forces and Russia. It will take effect at one minute after midnight tonight, so officially on May 8. Churchill goes on to say we should all be allowed a brief period of rejoicing on Victory for Europe day, but that we shouldn't forget that the war with Japan is far from over and we must fight for justice and retribution on that front. He ends with "long live the cause of freedom and God save the King."

Aunt Naomi, Uncle Max, and I remain silent long after Churchill has stopped talking. We should be jumping and screaming, or even dancing, but we're too stunned to move. It's the moment we've been anticipating for eight years and, now that it's happened, we can't take it in.

Uncle Max sits down again. The three of us breath in unison. I feel the relief in each gush of air.

"Jacob," Uncle Max says finally, whispering to Papa. "It's over."

My mind plays a reel of all the horrible pictures I've seen from the camps in the past few months. None of the faces were Papa's. I know it. I close my eyes and see him on the cot in Sabine's kitchen pantry. I wonder if they know about the surrender yet. And, if they do, have they told him?

Can Papa finally turn back into himself?

12.

Tanya are I are swept along Sainte-Catherine Street by a sea of cheering people waving Union Jacks. Girls are perched high on boys' shoulders, waving their arms and screaming, while a conga line snakes past. People are hanging out of office windows, throwing down streamers, while church bells peal into the air. Abandoned taxis sit at the side of the road and groups of people are jumping on their roofs.

Another couple is dancing on top of an ambulance. Above us a plane flies through the sky, trailing a sign that says, *"Victory for the Allies in Europe,"* and every few minutes another blast booms from a ship in the harbor. Sailors are passing around a jug of rum and someone on a motorcycle is trying to ride through the crowd. When he gets closer, I see he's wearing a Hitler mask with a big X across the face. People are throwing cans at him and one old woman is beating him with a cane. Signs hang from store windows, saying "Closed for Victory Day." Up head, a newspaper kiosk has been set on fire.

I pull on Tanya's arm and we veer off at Mackay and head toward McGill. Exams have been postponed for two days, so students can celebrate, and a large crowd has gathered outside the Roddick Gates. Many people are climbing to the top of the gates, then pulling others up to join them. Inside, the whole campus is alive with music and dancing. Every few steps Tanya and I are swept into another whirlpool and twirled around. Within minutes, I lose her. I look for her fedora but she's nowhere in sight.

Up ahead, I catch sight of a familiar pair of blue eyes and sandy hair. Jenny is smiling and waving at me across the middle of a party where two girls are juggling, one sitting on the other's shoulders. I wend my way over to her and she throws her arms around me.

"Oh Edie! Isn't it marvelous?" she screams.

"It is!" I shout back.

"I'm going to celebrate twice as hard, for my brother. If he were here, he'd be up that tree." She points to a tall maple beside us.

"You know what?" I say. "That's a great idea. Let's do it!"

"Really? Are you sure?"

"Yes. Yes I am. If we can't be silly and take a risk today, when can we?"

I grab Jenny's hand and we run to the tree. Its lowest limb is easy to reach so I pull myself up, then help Jenny, who's a few inches shorter. We keep climbing, limb by limb, higher and higher. The music of the various celebrations blends together like one loud noise, but the constant beat keeps us going, until we're pretty high up and perched on a strong thick branch.

"Oh, I never thought I'd be able to do this, Edie. You're so brave."

"You have to be brave in this world, Jenny. Don't you think?"

She looks at me and the blue of her eyes matches the sky.

"Yes, I do."

"Then let's sit here and be brave together for a while," I reply.

Down on the ground, small fires are blazing all over the campus. Several footballs, the word "Victory" painted in white, are being thrown from person to person up and down the fields. No one is standing still.

I inch closer to Jenny, open my mouth and holler, "Woo hoo!" Jenny joins me and we shout it together.

It sounds so much better with two.

EPILOGUE: 1948

A sandy-haired woman holds the arm of an old man as he hobbles down the gangplank. The yellow ribbon pinned to the lapel of her coat flaps in the river breeze, and she steadies it with her free hand. The action anchors her while she scans the crowd below.

On the pier, a tall woman stands beside her blonde companion. They look at each other constantly—smiling, pointing, shrugging. The blonde woman holds a bouquet, as bright as hope, against her chest.

Suddenly, the tall woman raises an arm, then waves, unfurling a yellow ribbon that catches the wind. Dark curls bounce on her shoulders as she runs toward the ship.

The crowd melts away when she and the two travellers lock eyes, the moment punctuated by the

484 The Ribbon Leaf | Lori Weber

screeching of gulls that circle overhead. The old man falls into her arms and she lays her head on the soft pillow of his white hair, breathing him in, filling herself with the impossibility of his presence.

Now, the two young women embrace. All of time stands still as they reach past the years and miles and hurts that have separated them. They are young again, reading *Heidi* under the willow tree, parading around the marketplace in their matching dresses, ripping through the box of castaway clothes and singing hit songs from movies, their voices escaping the basement window and lifting past the bushes.

Standing in the sun's spotlight, they feel it again— the soaring sensation that friendship can bring.

The woman with the bouquet has come to greet them. She is lovely and the way she smiles at Edie makes Sabine look westward, where a young man stands in a golden field. The letter asking her to join him is tucked in her purse, unanswered. Her mama is back on the other side of the ocean, and so is her spot at the Heidelberg university.

Her old friend takes her hand and the heaviness of her decision vanishes.

This is enough, more than enough, for now.

ACKNOWLEDGEMENTS

Thank you to Ron and Cassandra Curtis, as always, for being my biggest supporters and for reading, with much patience, my early drafts—you never fail to make me think I can do it. Gratitude to Sharona Granovsky for reading the novel for its Jewish content and putting my mind at ease. Hugs to my dear friend Lori for opening her home in Newfoundland and giving me such an inspiring setting in which to write an early draft. The Canada Council for the Arts provided financial support, which enabled me to travel to Berlin for research, and I am so appreciative. A huge shout out to my editor, Beverley Brenna, for believing in the book and showing such enthusiasm in wanting to publish it. In this difficult period of Covid, you cannot imagine what a gift this has been.

Thanks to the entire team at Red Deer Press for all the hard work in bringing the book to completion. And thanks to all my family and friends who never fail to ask about my writing and show genuine interest—you keep me going! Last but not least, thanks to my mom, Maureen, for being the biggest bibliophile I know, and passing on her deep love of reading.

INTERVIEW WITH LORI WEBER

This book deals with important and serious subject matter related to a particular time in history. What made you want to tell this story?

My father spent his childhood in Nazi Germany and I grew up hearing stories of how his life was affected by the war. Many of his dreams were aborted, such as riding in the Tour de France; he grew up hungry and afraid that his father, a vocal anti-Nazi, would be punished. I visited his hometown twice as a child and was struck by how present signs of the war still were, and never forgot certain images and feelings from those experiences. I began to wonder about other children in his small town and how the war had affected them; had it shaped their emotions and worldview, as it had my father's? I wondered, in particular, what happened to children who were suddenly not allowed to be friends because one was Jewish—how would they make sense of that at a young age? I also wanted to show the everyday lives of people during wartime, which is why I decided to set the story in a southern German town that was quite far from the action, at least until the end of the war. At the same time, I wanted to explore the history of my hometown, Montreal, during the war years. The vibrant Jewish community in Montreal has a rich and interesting history and I was keen to explore it. My mother was a very young child in Montreal during the war and she had an uncle who was killed. So that side of the war interested me as well. Basically, I always knew that I would tackle WWII one day and try, in my own way, to understand its effects on my father, who remained reluctant to talk about his experiences his whole life. He died when I was partway through writing the book, and I believe that what I learned brought us closer together.

The historical details in this story are compelling. What considerations does a writer of historical fiction

have when creating a novel such as this one? How did historical research support your process?

As the story grew in my mind, so did my interest in the history of WWII, which had always been strong. I read extensively for two things: facts and details about major events in the war, and also everyday details about household life during this period. I read fiction, nonfiction and memoirs. I took extensive notes in a large notebook, then made a list of the larger historical facts I wanted to weave in for each year, and also of the interesting smaller details, like rules for the use of soap! The balancing act was including these facts and details while making sure the characters and story were developing in an interesting way. In other words, history could not get in the way of story. In the end, there were some details I simply had to leave out—they felt too forced and didn't fit into the story in an organic way. I also spent six weeks in Berlin doing research and walking the streets where so many historical events were planned and executed. When my father was still alive, I picked his brains frequently and he reluctantly shared what he could—he did not like to talk about those years. I went through the same process for researching historical details about the war on the home front, here in Montreal, and learned a lot about my city in the process. The archives and material at the Montreal Holocaust Museum here were very valuable. I have a bibliography of books and films that I used for my research that is almost as long as the one for my Master's thesis—clearly I love doing research.

This story unfolds from two different perspectives as best friends Sabine and Edie experience their lives on opposite sides of the world. What benefits and challenges arose from choosing two narrator voices? Did this choice appear in early drafts of the book, or did you approach this story in quite another way to start with?

I knew right from the start that I wanted these two perspectives: one girl is German, the other a German Jew who leaves for Canada. That meant I could explore two home fronts—one in a small southern German town, another in Montreal. I didn't strive to make the two trajectories parallel, but there were times when similar things happened on either side of the ocean, or when the same event could be explored from the different points of view. It was important that the two girls were given equal relevance, so that neither story is the main storyline; maintaining this sense of equality was challenging.

I love writing from various points of view and this is something I have done in other novels, so it came quite naturally. I enjoy the process of switching personas and entering a different mindset as I work. I wrote the book year by year, not person by person. That meant I held both girls in my head and heart as I progressed through the lengthy first draft. Another challenge was length. The initial draft was 30,000 words longer and this meant I needed to do a series of edits and lose material that I was quite fond of.

The book actually started out in verse form. I remember the first line: "There is nothing interesting in my hometown." I proceeded with the verse format for a quite a while before realizing it was not working and I had to start afresh in prose. I enjoy this process of trial and error as I don't outline before I start a book; I do, however, have a vague idea of where I want to go. I think starting in verse form was helpful in allowing me to hear each girl's voice. I grew very fond of both of them as I wrote. I didn't know how their individual stories would end, but I did know that I wanted their bond to remain strong.

Uncle Max emerges as a character that many readers will love and appreciate. Is he based on a real person? What were your thoughts as you developed this character and his role in this story?

I love uncle Max. He was a complete surprise to me. I had no idea who he would be when I started writing, or even that he would exist at all. And then, suddenly, Edie and her mother were off to Munich, and there he was, displaying deep emotion. In an early scene, where he dances with Edie in his empty living room, he danced into my heart and I knew he would be a loving character. He became more and more avuncular as the book grew, standing in for Edie's Papa in his absence. I love how he is gentle and unafraid to show soft emotions and often cries. His love for art is a big part of his character; he is drawn to beauty and that is why he is such a positive character and why destruction of any sort affects him deeply. His support for Edie is unfailing. I love it when he cuts out her film reviews and tacks them up on the wall. My thought was just to continue making him as loveable as he started out to be, and for him to be there as a steady positive force in Edie's life. She needs that and I think the reader needs that too. The book is already

In some of your previous books, the title changed during the course of the project. In your journey to write *The Ribbon Leaf,* its title was chosen right away and stayed the course. How did you think of this title, and why do you like it for the cover of your book?

The yellow ribbon is the thing that connects the two girls, even though they are separated without any warning at the age of twelve. It is also how Sabine is alerted by Herr Pinker to his precarious situation in the basement of his building. It becomes important when Werner includes a piece in his letter to Edie, to prove that he is connected to Sabine. And then the two young women wave their ribbons on the pier at the end when they are reunited. Therefore, the ribbon is an important symbol of their love and bond with each other. From an early stage in the writing, I could see the yellow ribbon tied around the branch of the bush, blowing like a leaf and the title came to me. A good title, in my opinion, should contain meaning and suggest an image: I think mine does both. I never for a second considered another one and am very happy that my editor loved it too.

heavy with villains. Examples of love, especially from a man, were important to balance the hatred of the Nazis and the war, and to balance the ugliness of Sabine's father. Uncle Max ended up being one of my favourite characters that I've ever created.

You are the author of a number of books, and in many of them, you write about young people facing extreme challenges. Why does this theme appeal to you?
It appeals to me because that is life—the facing of tough challenges. It's all part of the coming-of-age process. Some of the challenges may seem small on the surface, like the fear of playing piano in public, or anger at having to move. Others are larger, like facing near-death by the Nazis, or dealing with parents' divorce, or even cancer. But the sum total of all of these challenges, big and small, is what makes a person who they are. We can't prevent the challenges, but witnessing how different people face them and tackle them is infinitely interesting. That is what a book explores best: conflict and counteraction. I enjoy taking a young character through this process. I think I have learned something about myself through each of my protagonists' journey.

What advice do you have for young writers?

Read! Read for pleasure, to be taken away into different lives and worlds, but then read to learn your craft. Reread a book that really grabbed your interest several times to try to understand how the author managed to pull you in and keep your attention. How did they handle plot and character? Keep a notebook where you write daily, recording things that caught your eye or made you feel a certain way. Capture your emotions. Record the sights, sounds, and smells of your universe. Bits and pieces of your daily observations can turn into catalysts for future novels. Take writing workshops where you can, and be brave enough to share your work and get feedback. Fall in love with words. Then read some more!